Grey Daze

WALKING GREY: Book 3

by

Rachel DeFriez

Rachel DeFriez

Two Cents Publishing

First Two Cents Publishing edition June 2020

ISBN- 978-0-9893459-2-7

Grey Daze

For Curt,
Here's to sailing off the grid

Chapter 1

About a month ago, we left Houston writhing in the jaws of an all-out zombie invasion. It feels like I abandoned my home in its time of need, but my home abandoned me. No one wants to camp out with the grey girl for the apocalypse. Maybe it's because they know I would gladly light up a fire, rip out their kidneys and wolf them down, like franks and beans, without the beans—or the campfire for that matter. I don't blame them. It keeps me up at night knowing my idea of fast food is a kid on a scooter.

Our aircraft carrier docks at the island of *If* in the early hours of the morning. The dying hum of the engines wakes me. I open my eyes, startle, and then exhale a sigh of relief—Amber still has all her vital parts. My brain didn't deteriorate in the night and uncage the savage animal I keep locked inside. I wake up to the same nightmare every morning, the fear that the Z-Virus hijacked my brain in the night. Surrounded by French marines, at sea where the virals can't reach us, protected by Lieutenant Ryan Samson, this boat should be a haven in the storm of the apocalypse. But what I fear is not on the outside; it's on the inside. I don't know how long I'll be able to control it.

On this floating paradise, I'm the biggest threat to my little sister. I used to be the force keeping her alive—well, me and Greyson, *but he's gone...* No, I absolutely cannot go there. My whole chest collapses in on itself and the screaming inside overwhelms my brain every time I think of him. I have to keep a clear head—for Amber. Here, on this boat, I almost believe she'd be safer without me. Then again, is anyone safe without love, or is love the thing that makes us feel safe? If it is, I should feel safe with Ryan, but I don't. I haven't felt safe since the bombs on the Knight compound shrouded Grey in a cloud of smoke.

Every time that image replays in my mind, I shiver and grit my teeth against the sob of rage it raises. Alone in our cabin, I let two fat tears dribble down my cheeks before I wipe them away and pull myself together. To face what's coming today, I can't be a pathetic puddle of emotional soup.

My little sister snores in our bunk, curled into a ball and plastered to my chest. She only woke up drenched in sweat and screaming twice last night. Progress. Her fragile fist clings to the leather handle of a knife—a Glauca G-1—her PTSD therapist. Along with a custom blade, the knife features a plastic handcuff cutter and window breaker, the perfect apocalypse teddy bear. Multi-tool of French badasses, it's a gift from Ryan, or maybe one of his marine buddies. She's got the entire platoon of camo-clad nannies wrapped around that coquettish little pinkie of hers.

Amber's au-pair flavor of the week is Clément. Why wouldn't he be? He's a giant among French men—a 6' 4," ripped killing machine with a snuggly bearhug, a shoulder perch heads above the crowd, and an unlimited supply of Skittles in his pocket. Why wouldn't she feel safe with him covering her weak side?

After only weeks of onboard basic training, Amber is tiny but lethal. Ryan's squad gets a kick out of teaching her new tricks. Her baby hands can assemble a FAMAS assault rifle faster than some of the privates. I don't cringe at the sight of a six-year-old toting military-grade weapons anymore. We're past that. She's alive and NOT infected; everything else is irrelevant. Amber is hope in skin. And to survive these days, hope needs to know its way around a variety of weapons.

My stomach grumbles. I'm starving for human organs, but I'll happily settle for some bloody cow liver. On this ship, the menu choices for greys like me are more *à la carte* than *prix-fixe à la zombie.*

Slipping a pair of camouflage pants over my marine issue briefs, I grab an elastic and restrain my hair in an unruly, loose knot on the top of my head. In the corridor, leather boots slap against the metal floors. Here they come.

Inhaling, I brace myself. Meeting the new boyfriend's dad is always about as fun as approaching the judgment bar of God. I can't see how meeting Ryan's dad, general of the surviving French military, can end in anything short of being cast down into Danté's Fourth Circle of Hell.

There's no way General Samson is going to welcome an infected American teenager into the *Chateau d'If*, especially not one that has her teeth sunk into his son's heart— figuratively, and possibly—eventually—literally. The chateau is the only sterile zone in southern France. Kind of ironic since, for centuries, plague-ridden ships were quarantined here to stop the infection from reaching the mainland.

Ryan assures me his dad is a reasonable guy. But Ryan hasn't seen reasonable people take to bat bashing the heads of their own infected sons and daughters. Can't really blame them. How can they be sure their grey teen won't wake up one morning, decide to cheat on her self-inflicted "vegetarian" diet of animal organs, and sneak a snack of spicy, hot brains straight off the skull of the nearest trusting, overly confident loved one? Ryan's dad is going to want to save his son from himself. No question.

To the tune of heated French in the hall outside my door, my fingers race through the twists and turns of lacing up my combat boots. Roughly translated from French Military to American, the argument goes something like this:

"Do you have shit for brains, Lieutenant Samson? What were you thinking, bringing an infected predator like that onto this ship?"

"You don't understand, Dad—"

"General!"

"You don't understand, General—Sir!"

"There's nothing to understand. She's a threat."

"Didn't you hear a word Dr. Pêsqué said? Dr. Vadlamani is a grey, like Evelyn, but Dr. Pêsqué is still bringing him to the lab. Nicolas Vadlamani's research is invaluable. Who cares if he's infected? He's close to a cure."

"We've already shipped Pêsqué and his infected pet specimen off to a secured lab in Paris. Gérard can risk his own butt up north. The *Chateau d'If* is a sanitary zone. No exceptions." I can't see it, but I hear the response of weapons jostling and assume they've been ordered with the jerk of a thumb to target my door. A dull thump against the portal intervenes. "Stand down, Lieutenant," General Samson growls.

Slipping a camo shirt over my tank, I bend over to kiss Amber's forehead. A stray sob convulses my chest, but I stuff it back where it came from. God, this hurts, like ripping out half of my insides. But I have to do this even if it kills me inside. I can't be with Amber until I'm not a threat. How is it possible that the right thing to do feels so wrong? She stirs and whines and the knife jerks in her fist. I won't wake her, but if things go the way I think they're going to, I might not see my little sister for a while. They've already voted Nicolas Vadlamani and his research off the ship. It's a sure bet I'm next.

General Samson won't bother to run the idea by his son first; he'll have my brains plastered to the wall the minute he gets me in an isolated room. Not that I blame him. I am a risk. I know it better than he does. If it weren't for the fact that I know Nicolas has made a breakthrough on the cure, I'd be the first to suggest my elimination—for Amber's sake. But since there's a chance out there, I'm going to survive to take it—for Amber's sake.

If I have to leave my baby sister somewhere, this is the place. She has Ryan and half a dozen special ops officers to babysit her. She'll be safer with them on this island than with me on the mainland. Months before all hell broke loose in Houston, the virus waltzed through airport security in Marseille. The city already has a full menu—alphas, greys, simple ZV infected virals, and plain, old-fashioned zombies.

"Look, dad." Ryan's voice has gone quiet—son to father. I can only hear him because my hand grips the wheel that opens the portal. Amplified senses of a predator, just one of the many perks of being a grey. "Evelyn is not a threat. If anything, she's an asset. She can take down a target and run decoy better than any man on my team." That's what is so irresistible about Ryan—I mean besides the French accent, smoldering eyes, and coffee cream cheesecake voice. He still sees me beneath the grey—the Homecoming Queen, the AP student, the track star. "For God's sake, she was ground zero for the virus and she's never taken a bite out of anyone." That's not 100% accurate, but it wasn't the virus that drove me to it. It was justice. "She was a vegetarian before the outbreak. We only know that's what causes the grey mutation because SHE figured it out. No one knows more about the virals—"

For all his military training and skill, Ryan is a romantic at heart. He hasn't loved me long enough to see me for what I really am, for what his dad knows I am—a threat, an infected specimen. His hormones are messing with his vision.

"That's because she IS a viral. The greys are unpredictable. She's infected. Period. Too risky."

The handle groans when I turn it. Safeties unlock and automatic guns shift in a chorus of metallic clicking as I step into the corridor. Pushing past the shield of Ryan's body, my boots stomp against the metal floor. Ryan grabs my arm to pull me back.

Shaking my head, I unlatch his fingers and dust off my rusty AP French—it's in my best interest to appear non-threatening, as minimally foreign as possible. *"Il a raison, Ryan. Je suis un risque."*

The general is a shorter man than Ryan, and fairer—I didn't expect that. A look of loss warps the skin around his eyes. Ryan's are wider, brimming with audacity.

"Alors, Général," I nod down the corridor, *"on y va?"* Calmly, I push through the gauntlet of the general's guard.

He didn't bring just one or two men. He knows what a grey can do. I don't recognize any of the dozen or so soldiers, but I recognize the look behind their eyes. I've seen it on brutes packing blood-stained bats on the streets of my hometown in Salt Lake's suburbs. These soldiers don't see grey. They take in my pale skin, the purple tint of my lips, the spider veins in my eyes, and they only see the monster that devoured their loved ones. Hoping none of them get twitchy, I stroll past the biting end of their automatic rifles. Ryan hustles to follow. He still believes they'll spare me for his sake. Adorable.

We reach the open portal to the stairs. Ryan ushers me past. Our eyes meet as I duck through, one leg on his side, one leg in the metal stairwell. He knows what I'm going to do. He doesn't approve. His lips compress into a straight line.

"Amber?" I whisper, my hand on his cheek, my lips brushing the skin of his ear.

He nods, his eyes tight.

I shove him away. The door slams shut on his face as he stumbles backward into the corridor. I spin the handle before clanging up the stairs three at a time.

I'm on the deck before boots and shouts stampede past Ryan into the stairwell. Locking the portal behind me, I run for the starboard side and vault myself over. It's the Mediterranean, but it's February. The chill saturates my camo. Thank God the virus doesn't just enhance my predator skills. It dampens my pain receptors and lowers my body temp so I'm immune to cold. It's the drag of my wet fatigues and boots that worries me. Fifty strokes out, I've become Edmond Dantès, swimming towards the Marseille coast.

No one wastes bullets on me.

Chapter 2

A lazy wave vomits me onto the shore like undigested jetsam from the gut of the sea. My boots squelch. My hair hangs limp and salt-crusted around my face. And yet, *O my God, I'm in France!* Who doesn't dream about a summer on the French Riviera? To die for food, avant-garde fashion, boys with really cool accents—what else does a girl need? Well, maybe a waiter who brings hors d'oeuvres on a plate rather than snatching them from your gut.

A metal sign, pock-marked with bullet holes, announces that I'm the newest guest at *Le Centre des Permissionnaires de la Légion Étrangère de la Malmousque*. Seriously? Of all the places on the *Côte d'Azur*, I wash up on the beach of a Foreign Legion vacation resort? *Merde!* That's bad. The survivors will be armed. One look at my grey skin and purple-streaked eyes and any uninfected legionnaire will have me between crosshairs before I can define my viral orientation. I'm not sure which is worse, hunted by soldiers or zombies. Here I am again, alone, the grey fighting both sides from the middle. Squaring my shoulders and taking a deep breath to fill the void in my chest, I pick a destination that forces me forward.

My boots slosh on the concrete stairs that wind up to a large boardwalk. Daylight bounces off the sun-bleached cement and burns my lips and salt-sore eyes. At the top of the stairs, sunny, yellow umbrellas twirl in the ocean breeze. Facedown in his bowl, a bloodied, dismantled corpse enjoys his putrefied *bouillabaisse*. Shedding my soaked camo shirt, boots, and socks, I pry off his deck shoes. My right big toe is a little snug, but overall, not a bad fit.

Keeping a 360° watch, I wander around to get my bearings. The place is empty. The virus has only been in Marseille for a couple months, but Ryan got reports on the crossing that the alpha strain evolved immediately, exponentially increasing the number of living dead. I have more experience dodging SNCHRs—ZV Institute Snatchers—and uninfected vigilante ZV bashers than zombies. These zombies are the fast kind. Scouting out the exits is a first priority.

A small path disappears down the side of the building. A train of paving stones leads out to a parking lot and a street. Abandoned cars with open doors stand idle, but otherwise, traffic is dead. Black smoke rises up from skyscrapers visible along the horizon beyond.

The moldy scent of the viral dead hangs heavy on the salty air. The instincts that resurrect with the zombies are the pack hunting ones. They hide; they coordinate; they ambush—and if they're following an alpha, it's masterminding their maneuvers. The first time I ran into the walking dead mutation, I didn't see them coming. That's how I lost Greyson…*he's gone, he's gone, he's gone.* God, I can't even think his name without wilting a little inside. I crave Greyson like I crave human organs, reluctantly and ravenously. But I get by on something less destructive, don't I? I have to because….*he's gone.*

When I wander back, a curtain on the top floor shifts. I crouch instinctively behind a table. An adrenaline rush kick-starts my viral upgrades. My hand drops to my hip but doesn't find my gun, a PAMAS G1, a gift from Ryan. Obviously, I wasn't going to walk out into the corridor of General Samson's ship and face down a dozen of his personal guard with a gun plastered to my side. Of course, my knife is holstered beneath my pant leg, but a blade doesn't do me much good against a sniper's bullet and, against the zombies, I prefer something a little less up close and personal.

When my head peeks out from the cover of the table, shots from the window riddle the eerie hush. Bullets shatter the umbrella pole behind me when I hit the deck. Mortally wounded, it crashes down on top of me. Hoisted over my head, the deceased umbrella covers my sprint to the lobby. A cacophony of shots pulverizes the cement behind me. A body—

or should I say part of one—blocks and props the double doors open. The torso's been hollowed out and used to finger-paint the lounge floor. The sack of bones and gore looks like security.

Abandoning my umbrella shield just outside the automatic sliding doors, I step through the broken window beside them and crouch behind an enormous plant. The guard's limbs flop loosely and the body rolls when I shove it with my foot. Pay dirt: a sidearm in the fist. Poor guy must have been gang devoured. His bullets wouldn't have slowed the pack of living-dead hunters. *Where are all the bodies of the half-eaten?* They should be piled up here by the door. This mess has alpha written all over it. Only zombies would get up and walk away.

Quickly, I pry open the guard's fingers, pocket the gun, and scrounge up a few extra rounds of ammo from the utility belt. Moans stutter from the other side of the room, freezing me in my tracks. I'm not alone in the lobby.

Beyond the lobby, directly opposite the patio, large double doors, surrounded by shattered floor to ceiling windows, lead to a parking lot with a horseshoe-shaped drive beyond. A big, black truck waits just outside the doors. Greyson was the master car thief. I'll need keys because—*he's gone…gone.*

Shaking off the loss that stalks me, I focus on the present urgency. It's not surviving that drives me as much as making sure I can get back to Amber. I trust Ryan with my life, but keeping Amber safe isn't his only purpose the way it is mine.

The sharp shooter's crosshairs and the moaner at the end of the hall trap me between them. Whether or not I can sprint across the lobby to the exit before the owner of that guttural whine virals up and goes predator on me depends on what kind of ZV it is.

Slowly, I peek around the plant. A shot screams through the hollow door and pottery explodes in my face. Low and flat, I army crawl across blood-stained white tile to a sunny sofa, in the "no man's land" between my two stalkers. Sweat and seawater drip down my neck into my cleavage as I work out which of the two threats I have the best chance of escaping.

The pattern of the bloodstains puzzles me. Not a crawling smear of flight from a blood bath, too many handprints, lines too precise, almost geometrical. But it all makes gruesome sense when I finally raise my eyes above the sofa. The white wall opposite me displays Rothkoesque geometric swaths of color on canvas. Coordinated plants punctuate the gaps between the paintings.

A flash of red disappears around the corner. There is someone here. Not the sniper shooting at me from one of the upper floors, a much more psychotic specimen of ZV—an artist. The work in progress in front of my eyes rolls the acid in my stomach.

Traces of blood on the white tile floor imitate the paintings hanging above, a bloody impression of the art. At the end of the wall, the source of the moaning growl sprouts from a ceramic planter that reflects the orange, yellow, and red geometric patterns of the paintings.

Foot planted in the soil of the enormous pot, a girl bobs her head and jerks in restraints. Smaller, but not much older than I, her arms and remaining leg splay to resemble the limbs of a tree. Blood-smattered screws secure her fractured appendages to wooden stakes. The bloodstains lack the purple hue that coats the open cavern of her carved abdomen. She was still human when the nails pierced the muscle and bone of her arms and legs. Her organs, carved into cubes and spheres, dangle from morsels of intestine to decorate her limbs. Her mindless grasping against the restraints creates an impression of wind rustling the leaves of a solitary tree.

I've never actually felt pity for one of the rabid dead. But, lodged in her neck, there's still a stun dart, the kind they use on animals, the kind they used on me when I tried to liberate Bridger from the Institute. The artist, presumably the flash of red that disappeared down the hallway, hunts down subjects—prefers them alive. Turning my face away, I vomit a green splotch of stomach acid onto the tiles.

Behind me, a service entrance to the kitchen beckons. With the back of my hand, I wipe the tainted spit from my mouth and crawl towards it.

I blame the virus-induced feeding frenzy, but I completely lose my shit, stand up and jog for the swinging door. Glass crunches beneath my feet. Everyone in the building knows I'm here now, and I don't even care. But, seriously, where are all the bodies? These zombies are the fast kind. Resurrected to hunt. Marseille should be littered with corpses.

A giant metal counter dominates the kitchen. The stainless-steel cupboards lining the walls above and below the sink stand open and pillaged. Not my cup of tea. My target is the row of refrigerators across the opposite wall. That's where the meat is.

Smeared blood tracks lead away from the units. Plopped in front of the door of the last of the three, a large duffle bag overflows with someone else's scavenging. Either they're coming back for their haul, or they were surprised before they could drag it out. I shuffle through the boxes and bags: tomatoes, pasta, beans, squash, cucumbers, mushrooms, some baguettes, cheese, boxes of tea bags—nothing that interests me. The gatherers are still human. No threat—unless they're armed.

Cold air from the first refrigerator unit chills my damp camo pants. I'm really more interested in the freezer, but the scavengers left the thawed meat here. Tearing open a cellophane package, I rip a chunk from a thick steak with my teeth. The virus wants organs, but the raw meat settles the riot in my gut. Gnawing at the slab, I skip the second unit and open the third. Jackpot. It's a freezer. All the less popular parts line the bottom shelves. Not the prime human pieces, the leftovers: liver, stomach, intestines, brains, everything the Egyptians used to pull out of the body of a mummy—except the lungs; can't ever find those.

I toss a couple brown bags onto the counter to thaw and then can't resist tossing aside the steak and tearing into a bag of liver. The frozen soufflé crunches in my mouth. The mashed morsels thaw on my tongue. Juices melt into my saliva, relaxing my whole body as the virus gets a shot of its opioid. Animal guts are the generic brand, but they deliver the buzz.

And then the frenzy sets in. The beast in my brain rears up, snarling and desperate for a kill. My lungs heave, adrenaline rips through my veins, anger rises from my chest. Gritting my teeth, I slam my fists against the metal counter and roar. My fingernails dig deep enough into my palms to draw blood. God! I hate what I am.

My knees buckle. A sob strangles in my throat. I haven't been this alone since before Greyson pulled me out of the chamber of horrors that was the ZV Institute and gave me back my little sister. God! Why did I walk away from him? Why did he let me? Couldn't he see through the pain? I'm a ZV infected adolescent! I don't think straight. My aunt and uncle were slaughtered because I led a pack of ravenous greys right to them. Excuse me if I was a little upset, for God's sake!

And there's the sticking point. God. Greyson and his god damn, god complex. He just refuses to see that the virus hasn't made us into superhuman, immortal angels; it's made us into demons. Although, as far as that goes, I can't really see any difference between the two. It's just a matter of whose side you're on. Frustration, viral hormones, despair, they all rise up in my throat and spew from my mouth in a screeching howl.

Rudely interrupting my pity party, frantic thumping resonates from inside the refrigerator behind me. I stare at the door like I've got x-ray vision or something. I have no idea who—or what—is in there.

Chapter 3

Glass crackles and crushes against the tiles on the other side of the swinging door. I don't have much time. A shiver slithers up my spine at the thought that the deranged artist who sculpted the masterpiece in the lounge lingers, scavenging for more ZV medium. My ears tingle at a high-pitched note that rips the silence. What the hell is that? A dog whistle? I wait to hear it again, my hand suspended in front of the freezer door handle. Nothing. One mystery at a time. The prisoner raps again.

This is tricky. For all I know, the survivors that filled the duffle stuffed a full-on, ravenous zombie in the fridge. Then again, I don't think the living dead would knock. Might be a grey or a confused ZV that got trapped trying to escape the hunters. Worse, it could be an uninfected survivor stuffed in the fridge for food storage. I've seen worse. My hand slips down to the ankle of my clammy camos and withdraws the knife. I have no way of knowing if whoever is in there is armed. At a Foreign Legion resort, the odds are good.

No vibration on the handle. The refrigerator was turned off. That requires some planning. The thumping raps again. Poising the blade, I pull the handle up and out. The door clicks open. Air rushes past my face and into the vacuum. The sticky, sweet smell of orange-glazed salmon seeps out.

A gagged and bound kid stares back at me with enormous brown eyes, rounded in surprised horror. She wasn't expecting me, but I wasn't expecting her either. She's wearing chain mail and a helmet, like medieval armor. It might just be the salty sea air, but the uninfected have more of a fishy smell here on the coast.

She obviously knows what I am because her first instinct is to fight. Kicking the door wide, she drops her head and barrels into my gut. The blow knocks my breath away and sends us both crashing into the stainless-steel counter behind. This girl is no wilting French lily. Flipping her off me, I pin her neck to the tiles with my forearm. "*Arrête! Je ne vais pas te faire mal!*" I realize I probably AM hurting her and ease up. "*Écoute! Je suis infectée, mais je ne suis pas dangereuse. Je suis végétarienne.*"

The irrational logic that I'm not dangerous because I'm vegetarian slows her down and buys me a few seconds to alter the stereotypes of her first impression. "*Je vais t'aider.*" When my knife rises to her chin level, she flinches and squeals, but then realizes I'm going to cut the gag. "*Je ne mange pas de chair humaine.*" My knife slips through the kitchen cloth. "*Parles-tu anglais?*"

My accent gives me away. As soon as the cloth falls from her mouth, she works her jaw and then responds, "*Américaine?* Yes, I speak a leettle English." She does. All her i's sound like e's and she keeps the syllables wrapped in the back of her throat instead of spitting them at me.

"Who stuffed you in here?" Before I cut the binds on her wrist, I clasp a hand to her shoulder and lean around to look her in the eye. "You understand, I'm not like the others? I was vegetarian before I was infected. I live on animal guts, now. I can fight the urge to eat human organs."

She nods and I slit her free, half expecting her to bolt or charge me again. Instead, she rubs her wrists and removes her helmet. An obsessively tight ponytail bobs loose. It's not just her big brown eyes that remind me of Amber. She extends a hand. "Laure."

I take it. "Evelyn." I guess we're teaming up, the grey and the D&D nerd.

Every ounce of logic rebels at giving up my solitude. My goal is to find a way back to Amber. I can't afford a distraction, but, I don't know, maybe my *raison d'être* has been to protect my little sister for so long that this little girl, so fragile and yet so fierce, triggers all the maternal instincts of the beast inside of me like a mother wolf adopting an abandoned human baby. Or maybe, I'm just looking for redemption from the sin of abandoning my sister to save my own sorry skin. Either way, the touch of her untainted human skin on mine welds a bond.

Our conversation becomes an awkward skipping dance of French and English. "One like you—*un gris*—pushed me in the *frigo*. He has the eyes and the skin. But he not nice." Freed, she heads for the duffel bag, cinches it up, and tosses it over her mail-clad shoulder. "He is hunting. We must to leave. He going to come back."

"Don't worry. If he's popping human organs, the virus has its own poetic justice. Where are we going?"

Laure's mouth opens to respond, but instead, she yells, "*David! Non!*" The knife has already flown from the hand of the chainmail-clad kid in the open doorway. It's spinning for the sweet spot between my eyes. Laure dives to shove me aside. "*Attention!*" She's too late.

My viral reflexes slow everything down and jerk me to the side fast enough that the blade only nicks my ear as it whistles past. Blade metal penetrates fridge metal with a shrieking thud. Laure collides with me milliseconds later and the two of us tumble over. The duffel bag thuds to the floor. Tomatoes squelch and tin cans clatter across the tiles.

Eyes wild, the kid has already decided what I am. It's a race between the two of us for the knife. Shoving the girl off me, I yank the handle free and turn the pointy end on him before he can get past the counter. Fury fumes in my brain. I have to remind myself he can't possibly know that greys don't heal—not unless we happen to have a little sample of Nicolas Vadlamani's miracle cream in our pocket, which I don't.

The virus howls and stomps a war dance in my veins. *I don't eat people; I don't eat people.*

"*Calme-toi, David. Elle est avec nous. C'est un gris—comme Joseph.*" Laure is much smaller and obviously younger than David. His eyes scrunch up suspiciously at the knife poised above his head, ready to strike a killing blow. To him, it doesn't much look like I'm with them. David must be the one she was expecting to let her out of the fridge. No wonder Laure didn't bolt or attack when I cut her ropes. They already have a grey in their—group? Someone named Joseph.

"Y'all are vegetarians?" Lowering the tip of the knife tentatively, I keep my eye on David. He looks twitchy and keeps checking the door. A wave of my hand takes in the period clothes they're both wearing. "What are you?"

Laure has to look down to notice what I'm asking about. "Ah, this. *Oui,* we come here from *Paris* for a tournament. We are part of the *Société pour l'Anachronisme Créatif.* My brother and I throws knives. He also compete with the—euh—*tir à l'arc.* How you say *la flêche et l'arc*?" She gathers up her spilled spoils as she explains. David's unsure but Laure's calm steadies him. In a holding pattern, he watches us both.

A glimpse at the quiver on David's back and I fill in the words for her. "Archery. Bow and Arrow."

"*Ah, oui, c'est ça.* Ar-che-ry. But we are not vegetarian, no. Only Joseph, before the bite. He is allergic to meat and my mother has the—euh—*maladie coeliaque,* so we must search for food."

Shit! *Coeliaque.* Celiac disease. That's what Nicolas's brother Sam had before he evolved into the alpha demon that started the apocalypse in Houston. David and Laure's mom is an alpha waiting to happen. Someone has to tell them what's going on.

"After the bite, Joseph, he have the grey skin, and the eyes and the lips with the purple. But he is not sick. And he is not dead. He is strong and he can choose—like you." She tucks the last can in the bag, closes it, with a knot this time, and stands up, shouldering the strap. "And you, why come you here?"

"I came on the boat that just docked at the *Château d'If.* I'm with the science team." That's not exactly true, but close enough. Nicolas Vadlamani and I have been working together since before Greyson broke me out of the ZV Institute. "We were ground zero for the Zoser Virus in Salt Lake. The sick, the ones that can still think but can't fight the urges to feed on human organs, they're just infected ZVs; the walking dead, they're a mutation. Greys, like me—like Joseph—who were vegetarian before we got infected, the virus turns us into predators, hoping we'll consume the organs of other humans.

Our meat-free organs don't spawn the chemical soup the virus thrives in. Tell your friend Joseph—"

"He is not our friend. He is our brother."

"Family vacation gone wild? How's your dad taking it?" I only ask her because mine turned me over to the Institute to protect my siblings. It's not like I resisted—at first. I wanted to protect them from me, too. They all died anyway, though—except Amber. Greyson pulled her out of the feeding frenzy…*but he's gone and I left her. I have to get back. God, I have to! Whatever it takes.* My eyes cinch with the effort of blocking out the people I love. The members of that club keep dwindling. As long as Amber's on a safe island surrounded by military personnel, I have time to work out a plan, make my way back to her, and get us the hell away from everyone. But is that safe? What if the virus gives up on me, goes into self-destruct mode, and devours my brain? Is that what's best for Amber? Alone with a brain-dead psychopathic predator?

I just don't know. There's not enough research. At least, I can educate the locals here. They're even more clueless than I am. What I really want to do is get to Nicolas in Paris. Knowledge and salvation lie only a three-hour TGV ride away.

"*Laure, dépêche-toi.*" David's face blanches as glass crunches in the lounge again, but not in a straight line this time—consecutively, from multiple directions. The putrid smell of black blood wafts in from the cracks under the door. The high-pitched trill pricks my ears again.

The knife whispers across the stainless-steel counter when I slide it to David. I'm not sure how effective it is in a fight. It's nothing like the military-grade weapon I got from Ryan. It's made for aerodynamics, the hilt and blade a continuous stretch of metal—more like a hand-thrown arrow than anything. But he nods his thanks, and I mouth the question, "*Gris?*" I don't think David's English is as good as his sister's. I assume we're about to face off with the grey that was shooting at me from the upper window and locked Laure in the fridge. He shakes his head. The word he utters is barely perceptible, "*boches.*" That's worse.

Boches. Appropriate. It's not the first time mindless monsters have invaded Marseille, set up defense positions, and devoured the inhabitants. Nazi bunkers dot the limestone cliffs all along the coast. The French called the German invaders "cabbage heads." That's what the *boches* are, aren't they? The brain-dead who've lost all their humanity and mindlessly feed off society to satisfy their endless appetites.

The gun in one hand and my knife in the other, I ease around the counter towards the swinging door. "Tell Joseph to stick to animal guts. Once he starts down the human organ path, it's a slippery slope to brain decay—and there's a cure on the way if he can hold out." That's why I need to get to Nicolas. I want to volunteer to be part of the human trials.

Through a quarter-inch crack in the door, I survey a slice of the lounge. My stomach clenches at the sight of the artwork. I can't see the *boches*, but I can smell them. If I can smell them, they can smell me. Padded footsteps. I ease the door open a little wider. Before, there was just a bloody 3D mural. Now there are bodies strewn across the floor.

Chapter 4

The *boches* are playing dead. They aren't feral walking dead, either—they're a pack. My bones shiver. The scent is slightly different from what was hanging on the air before. The alpha artist smelled, I don't know, sweeter. A moldy overtone permeates the stench now. Judging from the rust color on the bloodstains of the artwork and the faintness of the fruity scent, I think the artist did its handiwork and vacated the premise. We're dealing with a different breed now. A slight sigh of relief whispers through my brain. I'm not sure why, but I guess if I'm going to be a zombie, I don't want to be on display. I give my new allies the straight shit. "There's an alpha out there."

"Alpha? What is 'alpha'?" Laure steps forward to see, but David grabs her shoulder. He's a head taller and lanky. His hands and feet seem too big for the rest of his body. One palm engulfs his little sister's shoulder. Under all that chain mail, she's actually pretty small—well, she fit on the lower shelf of the refrigerator. David holds her back reflexively, the way I instinctively grab for Amber. In this scenario, he's the father figure, and I'm the stinky, infected, mangy cat his little sister dragged home. My heart warms up to him, even though I know he'd be happy if he could call animal control and have me dragged away on one of those poles with the choke collar on the end. He's seen the atrocity in the lounge. I don't blame him for wanting to keep that image from tattooing itself onto the skin of Laure's nightmares.

I forget that these Frenchies don't know anything about the Zoser virus. It didn't incubate slowly like it did in Salt Lake, with just a smattering of infected teen couples and more than a year before the Knight cult created the first alpha by feeding body parts to a ZV with Celiac disease. If nothing else, I have to educate these survivors—even if the truth cuts deep.

"Look, we don't have time for a grand explanation. A bite from a *gris* just infects the victim with the virus. But Celiac disease creates an alpha if the infected carrier consumes human meat. It's the alpha's bite that makes a *boche*." At the mention of Celiac disease, both their eyes go wide. "Yeah, I know. But you'll have to deal with that later. Right now, our big problem is that an alpha mind-controls its living-dead minions and this one is setting up an ambush in the lobby. There are about a dozen *boches* playing dead on the floor, waiting for us."

David and Laure exchange glances. She explains to him in French. From the side of her duffle, Laure extracts a couple combat axes, hands one to her brother, and then pulls the knife from the leather holster at her side.

The chain mail protects the organs of my two knights, but they're still a couple of clueless teens with an immortality complex. They're zombie kibble if they step into that lounge; I don't care how good they are with those knives and axes. I've already had a playdate with a pack—that's how I lost Greyson—*oh god, don't go there…not now—*

The solution is obvious and completely unacceptable. I need to keep my eye on getting back to Amber. There's no way I'll find Nicolas and get myself cured if I get distracted and die trying to save a couple of kids I don't even know.

There's a reason why the *gris* that shoved Laure in the fridge hasn't come back yet. He's as scared of this pack of *boches* as I am. Maybe he's not with the alpha. Maybe he was warning me off, not shooting at me. It's a little late, but I finally get the message.

They're both waiting, eyes wide, for me to come up with a plan. God, they're just babies. Did Laure really have to look so much like Amber? Shit, those big eyes of hers trigger all the maternal instincts that protecting my little sister ignited.

No. I can't do it. It's too risky. I owe it to Amber to just get the hell out of here and survive.

I crack the door open again, judging my chances of racing for the front door. One more glimpse of the psycho artwork on the wall and I just can't picture myself running off and leaving these two to their fate. It's too cruel. I'd never be able to sleep again.

Shit! The game just got trickier. Not only do I have to get them out of here in one piece, I have to survive in the process. "Look, my scent is a mix of infected, healthy, and putrefied blood—with a hint of vaguely rotting flesh. It activates the flight or fight instincts, mostly the fight ones, of the living dead. I'm going to run decoy."

"Decoy? What is 'decoy'?"

"One sniff of my grey blood and those *boches* will climb all over each other to rip me in pieces. We're competing for the same food supply. I've seen them charge right past a juicy, uninfected, organ sack to get a shot at rupturing my jugular. Sort of an Asimov's pyramid thing: eliminating the threat comes before snacking."

"*Leurre?* You will be lure?" Laure is already shaking her head and looking to David to stop me.

I nod. Now I don't have any choice. She's too loyal and courageous to just leave behind—even if David will stab me in the back the first chance he gets. "I'll head for the patio. There's a path that leads around the building to the parking out front. You two aren't on foot, right? Please tell me you're not riding horses."

"We have vehicle." David's the only one that looks old enough to be drive, but nobody is checking licenses in the apocalypse.

"*C'est ton camion devant l'entré?*" I dust off my rusty French to try and ease the tension between me and the brother.

He nods. The truck I spotted outside is theirs.

"Perfect. Once I'm out this door, those *boches* will be on me like bees on barbeque. Y'all can slip out the front and I'll hop in the back on the fly."

My French must be decent because David grins and nods, obviously pleased with the plan. He can't see grey. His eyes are shifty, and ten to one he's been trying to figure out the best way to ditch my grey ass. Well, I've just handed him one. If he's driving, I'm on my own.

Laure hesitates, eyes tense and lips pursed. She can see grey. I'm guessing she's adopted me already because she's close to Joseph. She still sees the brother beyond the infection. She knows we greys walk a thin line between human and monster. We're a risk, but the hinge on which this war of colors turns.

"And if you are bited?" Laure presses. "You are immune—because you are already infected?"

I should just lie, but life is too short, and Laure needs to trust me. More importantly, I can't spread disinformation about the virus. I shake my head. "If an alpha or one of its minions bites me, I go *boche*—just like everyone else."

"*Non! Non, alors.*" She shakes her head and her brother shoves her shoulder. He's all in. If the *boches* take me down, he doesn't have to.

"Listen, to bring in the organ soup it craves, the virus enhances a grey's human predator skills. It's not feeding off me. I'm in charge and I'm fast. The *boches* are scary, vicious, and disgusting, but they're dead and decaying. I've got an uninfected little sister to watch out for and there's a cure on the way. If I didn't think I could leave these cabbage heads in the dust, I wouldn't have volunteered." I sound so much more confident than I am. I'm a novice against the predator dead.

Laure shakes her head while I talk, but when I finish, inhales deeply and nods.

"Give me a couple seconds to clear the room before you slip out." The flat of my palm pushes against the swinging door and I take a deep breath, steeling my nerves. Adrenaline carries the virus out to play in my blood.

Laure grabs my shoulder. "*Merci, Evelyn. Merci!*" She kisses me on both cheeks.

There's something very human about hearing your own name and the touch of flesh on flesh. I nod and slip through the crack into the battlefield.

My new deck shoes quietly navigate the litter of glass shards until I glance up to check the status of the dead. My toe crunches the corner of a particularly jagged piece. I freeze, knife and gun poised, but I've already tiptoed past enough corpses playing dead to cut off any retreat to the kitchen. Grinding glass and guttural moans tell me it's time to run. As I sprint to the patio door, the dead resurrect like sleeping hyenas that have just caught the scent of a lion. Their territorial instincts rage against my perfume. They claw and trample over each other to destroy the competition. I hurdle the security guard blocking the door. The horde stumbles over him and the yellow umbrella blocking the window. I don't waste the head start.

Laure and David don't have to wait long before the distraction is total. If they didn't believe me when I said the *boches* would ignore everything else until they'd made *ratatouille* of my guts, they do now. As I tear past the windows of the lounge, from the corner of my eye, I glimpse the two of them slipping through the kitchen door and breaking for the front exit.

Leaning tightly to the left, I lose a few of the closest *boches* turning the corner. A bald soldier in fatigues, skin flapping at his neck, pushes hard on my heels up the side path. Only a few paces behind, a short brunette, with half a nose, a military buzz, and silver hoop earrings, scrambles after him.

An engine rumbles to life in the parking lot beyond the fence. Behind me, the sprinting dead gurgle and screech. Gravel crunches beneath our feet.

The gate's not going to open by itself, and I obviously don't have time to fiddle with the latch. My only chance is the recycling bin. If I can vault to the lid, it's only another short leap to the top of the fence. Hurdles were my thing in high school. I'm six feet out, ready for the leap, when I shift gears in midstride because the gate swings open by itself.

Four more strides and I'm through the gap. The chainlink slams back on the face of the bald *boche*. The brunette plows into him, snapping and clawing. Her face bulges through the clanging links as the running dead pile up behind them.

The black truck screeches away, fishtailing out of the parking lot. There goes my ride.

Chapter 5

The gurgling on the other side of the fence rises to a feral screech. The dead hurl themselves against the barricade, shivering the wires.

The bald soldier's blood-smeared face scrapes through the crack between the post and the gate. The dead skin peels away from both sides of his nose. There's no possible way he can fit through the gap, but that doesn't stop him from trying—screaming and gurgling like a demon at birth. Beneath the latch, halfway down the post, his blood-crusted fingers squirm, grasping and straining to reach us.

Sucking in a breath, I round on the grey who opened the gate for me. The pistol I scavenged off the security guard targets the sweet spot between his eyes. I have no idea what kind of sick game he's playing. He's got an automatic rifle slung over his shoulder. From beneath raked lashes, he glances up at me with eyes like phantom moons and lips meant to reveal the mysteries of the cosmos. The grey of the virus coats his bronzed Mediterranean skin.

Ignoring the spitting end of my gun, my savior takes a drag off a half-burned joint pinched between his grey fingers. He inhales deeply and holds it. The winter sun reflects off his slicked curls. Nodding in the direction of the truck, he exhales. "Your friends didn't wait."

"Can you blame them?" I certainly don't blame David. If it meant keeping Amber safe, I'd have ditched me too. Oh, yeah, I already did that. "You scared them off." I'm pretty sure this is the guy that was shooting at me on the patio, but he just saved my ass, so it's hard to tell if he leans dark or light grey. If anyone can see grey, I can—except maybe when it comes to myself. These days, though, the lines between moral colors are all smudged.

The decaying brunette, sandwiched next to a blond, has worked her smaller fist through the links. A portly retiree, with a full head of grey hair, an enormous nose, and an obscene, blood-crusted hole in his face, has latched onto the fence above her head. The wire metal diamonds squeeze her face into quilted blocks of flesh as he climbs up her back.

"Me? I'm harmless." The grey offers me a drag on the joint. I decline, shoving the gun in the back of my camos. He shrugs and takes another puff. "Your loss. Cannabis controls the hunger." Ha! Ironic—if it's true. The grey's English is flawless—not American, real English, laced with the hint of a French accent and something more Middle Eastern.

"Harmless? Hardly. You stuffed that little girl in the refrigerator for later."

He shrugs. "Keeping her safe from the *boches*, wasn't I?" He nods towards the clamoring horde. "Didn't think the other kid would make it back. He was supposed to be the sacrificial lunch. I was going to let the girl out and send her on her way, but then you showed up, and all hell broke loose."

"I have that effect." Is he the artist? The thought strangles me. I could be standing here chatting with a psycho, mass murderer. I assumed the artist was an alpha, but it could totally be a grey. My foot slides back. "Send her on her way, or sculpt her into one of your gruesome masterpieces?"

"What?" He's totally perplexed.

"The artwork in the lobby?"

"Ah. *L'Impressioniste*. Ghastly savage. Terrorizing any of the uninfected that didn't evacuate. It's not pretty when she gets a hold of one of us. She doesn't bite. The victim lives through the whole thing, trapped in her canvas."

"So, this 'Impressionist' is an alpha?"

"Alpha?"

"The mutation of the virus that creates the zombies—*les boches*."

25

"Yes. We've been hunting the reds—alphas—trying to eliminate them. I thought you were with it. Figured I'd made a mistake when I saw you run decoy for the girl and her brother."

The snarling behind the fence crescendos and the gate bulges, bending under the weight of a half-dozen dead retirees and vacationing legionnaires. They climb over the bald guy and the brunette like they're scaling the corporate ladder. The two fins of the latch rattle around the post and then wedge tight against the collapsing metal. The brunette shoves her arm through the link, past the elbow, shredding the skin into a gooey mess. Her close-cut claws stretch and grasp.

We greys exchange looks and step back.

Definitely need to get the hell out of here, but where? The top of my list should be getting north to Nicolas. If anyone can get me back on the boat with Amber, it'll be him. "You have a car?" My mother taught me not to take rides from strangers, but then my mother taught me a lot of things that stopped making sense when "hard to get" and "fast food" took on whole new meanings.

Behind us, a couple Renaults and a Citroën litter the parking lot beyond the flower bed. He nods towards an electric blue Peugeot sports car parked in front of a cargo van at the far end of the building. The drive forms the bottom of the long U-shaped drive where my "friends" used to be. "Where do you want to go?"

I'm no connoisseur, but I'm guessing a car like that can challenge a TGV's time on the Marseille-Paris run—especially out on abandoned, zombie-plagued roads. "North. I have a friend doing research in Paris. He's close to a cure. You in?"

A pale, decaying hand with purple nails slaps onto the top railing of the fence. The gate creaks forward. The grey tips his head at the pack. "I'm not like them—" he nods as he thinks it over, "—maybe I need some space from Eugène—Yeah, I'm in." He extends a long-fingered, well-manicured hand. "Kasim."

I grasp the hand. "Evelyn." I guess this means we're a team. The flimsy fence won't hold much longer. I shove the gun in the back of my pants and my new wingman leads the way to his sports car. I keep the knife handy because, well, I'm not exactly sure what game we're playing.

Kasim is not what I imagined when Laure told me he locked her in the fridge. I was expecting someone more along the lines of Miguel from Houston—hungry, angry, and embracing the predator inside to wreak social vengeance. Although he's pushing a pretty good pace, under the circumstances, this guy seems pretty chill. He's wearing European fitted jeans and a white linen tunic shirt. It's clean, not what I'd expect from a hired butcher. "Let me guess, you were vegetarian before you got infected."

"Yes, well, my *compagne* was, so I was by default. How did you know?"

"Was?"

"Didn't survive." Hitching the gun strap on his shoulder, he looks away, eyes cinching, like some of the pain is still seeping through the numbing cloud of smoke. It can't have been all that long ago.

The tortured lines along his eyes conjure up my own shredded ghosts—my parents and brothers, the last breath of my uncle, the flames that stole my aunt from me. Every specter dissolves into Greyson, running as the planes dropped their payloads. The cloud erupts and then—*he's gone, gone…*The virus, still rampaging through the adrenaline of the chase, feeds on the soup of sadness, digests it into anger, and vomits it into my bloodstream. I want to kill someone.

I grab the joint from Kasim's fingers, take a drag, hold it, and choke. "You're grey—*cough*—fast and strong—*cough*—because you were vegetarian." A lung full of clean air lets me speak again. "The virus wants you to be a predator, hunt down human guts." I hand the diminishing stub back to him.

Behind us, the fence moans and squeals. The gap between the post and gate widens enough for the bald *boche* to shove his shoulder through. His pack surges against the fence and he forces his head into the breach, howling. Kasim and I push to a power walk. The front of the resort spans at least the length of a football field. Kasim's car is parked at the far end, and the front entrance is in the middle.

He offers me the last drag of the joint. I take it. Guns, now medical marijuana. My mom would freak—if she weren't dead. Adapt or die—survival of the species. Nothing is absolute anymore. If I can control the ravenous urges, I can tame the monster inside and be with Amber again. Worth it.

The fence groans and swells, a festering pimple ready to pop. The gap wedged around the bald guy's square head loosens. Kasim digs in his pocket—amazing anything fits in there. A keyless fob dangles from his elegant fingers and he hitches the gun strap on his shoulder.

As we close the last ten yards to the entrance, the marijuana tickles my blood. The microbes in my brain smile, loosen up, and crawl off for a nap. *God! Is this what human felt like?* I've got the munchies, but for a salad with some field greens and a little *fromage de chèvre* on the side.

Even though the glass of the entrance doors is all broken out, they slide open when Kasim's foot hits the mat a stride ahead of mine.

"*Sale putain!*" Spitting obscenities, a projectile kid shoots through the door and t-bones my new play date. On impact, the sunglasses perched on top of the kid's unruly, black hair clatter onto the asphalt with Kasim's keys. The two ZVs tumble into the drive in a whirlwind of leather and a racket of metal.

Chapter 6

Fear—such a human trait. Bad timing to lose my drug virginity to the butt end of a joint. At the moment, I'd be happy to embrace the monster inside, but I've lulled her off to sleep. The human in me doesn't stand a chance against an alpha—the grey barely did.

The human projectile that skewered Kasim must be the alpha he was tracking—scrawnier than I imagined for one of the badass ZVs responsible for the fall of Marseille. His long leather trench coat and black jeans scream comic book geek. The look in his eyes hovers on the wrong side of sane. Familiar. Sam, Nicolas's younger brother, the only other alpha I've seen, had it.

Scrawny as he is, the alpha manhandles Kasim, rolls him flat on his back, and then shoves a forearm into his neck. The breath rattles in the grey's constricted throat.

"Always popular with the ladies, *non, Kasim*? Does she know you go both ways?" The alpha speaks French. Why wouldn't he? We're in France.

Kasim's gun is inconveniently stuck between his back and the asphalt. Taking off across the parking lot and letting him fend for himself crosses my mind, but we just shook hands, and that would be too low for words. His glance flits to mine, and he stops me from going for my gun with a gesture behind the alpha's back. These alphas are volatile sons of bitches, the Zoser virus at its finest. Kasim needs to keep the alpha calm so his unfortunate relationship choices don't come back to bite him. I settle for a tight grip on my knife.

"You weren't going to abandon me for a bit of a blonde, were you, *ma biche*? Not after all I've done for you. I saw you slipping supplies into the boat."

"You know I wouldn't leave without you, Eugène. We're family. Your doubts pain me. I told you, we need more like me. We need recruits."

Eugène finally acknowledges my presence with a sneer and a dismissive puff of his lips. "Don't shit me, Kasim. I know you."

"And I know you. You are the son of the new dawn. The light sent into the darkness to lead the blind. There are no others before you. By your mouth, the dead rise." The praise of his disciple melts the vicious grit on Eugène's face into an unholy serenity and half a smile. His eyes glaze over and his arm relaxes. Kasim's voice grows richer, harmonizing into a chant of supplication. "Lead us not into temptation, but deliver us from evil, for thine is the new kingdom on earth." Eugène nods in rhythm with the words, his face a silhouette of proud serenity. My own frantic breaths melt into the hypnotic calm. The alpha sits taller, chest inflated. Kasim slowly rises to his elbows beneath.

What is it about these alpha's that they sink their teeth so readily into delusions of a divine calling? Is it the power over life and death? Or is it a deep-seated human need to be more than just a smear on the windshield of our universe? Me, I'm not so much interested in finding my purpose for being as in just being here for Amber—I should have been there for Greyson...*but now, he's gone, he's gone*...

The rumble of an engine at the top of the street mingles with the desperate groaning of chainlink. The metal fence posts bend, giving birth to the hollering demon spawn pushing through the widening orifice between the fence and the gate.

Eugène rises to his feet, carried upward on wings of worship.

"Brother, forgive me for I have sinned," Kasim pleads, sliding into a servile crouch.

The alpha's eyes meet mine. A thin smile creeps across his face and some mysterious, evil purpose narrows his eyes as he holds my gaze. "In mercy, I forgive you, brother." The engine roars closer. "But mercy cannot rob justice." Kasim stands cautiously, alert. His eyes flit left and take in the black truck barreling towards us.

"Where there is sin, there must be sacrifice." Eugène swings his arm back and snatches Kasim's wrist before he can back away. "Don't fear. You have been spared the suffering for your infidelity. The Lord has sent us a ram in the thicket." The alpha holds out his hand, palm up, fingers wiggling like I'm some kind of alley cat he's trying to coax into sniffing them, so he can grab me by the scruff. "*Viens ici, Minette.*"

I stand my ground, but the knife feels heavy and awkward in my hand like suddenly my bones are rubber and my flesh is foam. I stifle the fear welling in my chest and refuse to back away, hoping Kasim has the balls, and the decency, to back me up against Eugène. Who am I kidding? He and Eugène go back. I'm a stranger.

The alpha springs. The tails of his coat fly back. My knife crashes to his chest, but he collars my wrist, freezing the blade in its arc. His fingers strangle the blood from my hand. When we hit the ground, my shoulders take most of the impact. Cement scrapes the skin off, and my knife skitters away. Bending my knees, I shove my feet into his chest.

Eugène lurches back, gasping for breath as I scramble to my feet. His grip tightens around my wrist and pulls me off balance. He yanks me to his chest. With my right wrist caught in his vice grip, I have only my left arm to keep his fangs off my exposed skin. His putrid breath raises the hair on my neck. "Is it true what they say about American girls?" My arm shakes with the strain of holding him back. God, he's strong.

"What? That we'll eat your heart out and come back for your guts?" My teeth clench, mocking my bravado. One arm braced against his bite and the other trapped in his grip, I have no free hand to get to my gun. Something has to give. *Where the hell is Kasim?* As usual, I'm my own knight in shining armor.

Behind us, the gate rattles a death knell and collapses. The wires creak under the trampling footsteps of the horde released. The groans of the *boches* rise to a frenzied squeal. They run, knocking each other over and stomping on the maimed.

My knee jabs at Eugène's balls but goes awry and tags his gut. He grunts, and I try to shove him off. With his free hand, he punches my stomach. For a second, the world becomes a vacuum. My gut collapses in shock and then expands in a throb of pain. Doubling over, I lose my shield against Eugène's deathly bite.

With a volley of automatic rifle shots, Kasim finally gets in the game, mowing down the oncoming tide of running dead. My fingers fumble the gun free from my waistband. Eugène whips his foot around my legs and pulls them out from under me. The single shot from my gun punctuates the spluttering fire of Kasim's. Glass from an upper story window shatters as I fall. The gun clatters into the drive when I hit the pavement.

With one foot on my chest, Eugène nails my back to the ground, smirking at my pitiful, all too human charade of fighting back. Through the frantic rant of the automatic rifle, the gurgle of stampeding *boches*, and the squelch of bullets in putrid flesh, the black truck screeches to a stop just beyond the front entrance. Eugène doesn't even spare it a look. He's too busy gloating—until a knife flies from the bed and drills into his shoulder.

Chapter 7

Alphas are like greys. The virus numbs the pain but doesn't eliminate it. Eugène bawls out his agony, gripping the knife handle. The second his focus shifts, I'm up off the sidewalk and out from under the crush of his foot.

"Move, Evelyn, go!" Kasim retreats towards the truck in the drive behind us. Bullets spit from his rifle. The *boches* just keep coming, stomping and tripping over the post-human debris.

Her arm still extended from the knife throw, Laure reaches for me from the back of the truck. "Get in, Evelyn!" David yanks her back from the oncoming tide behind Kasim. Scooping up my knife, I vault into the bed.

I don't even know who the hell is driving and I don't care. Eugène stumbles around the entrance, bellowing and tugging at the knife in his shoulder. The blade rips free, dripping purple alpha blood.

The machine gun rattle dies with a click. "I'm out!" Kasim rushes the tailgate. One of the *boches* grabs his ankle as he climbs up. Another half dozen reach around him for a handful of shin. He can't kick them off. He smoked a whole joint. Without bullets, he's just another sack of organs.

"Go, go!" I yell. The marijuana fades in my veins. The humanity faints with it and the virus stirs. Leaning over the tailgate, I stab through the head of the bulbous-nosed legionnaire with the hole in his face. His glazed-over eyes roll back and he falls into the mob. The truck rumbles and lurches forward. Freed, Kasim scrambles into the bed and turns to bash purple heads with the butt of his empty gun.

From the front near the cab window, Laure screams. Vengeance livid on his face, Eugène brushes off her frantic blows. Locking her wrist in his vice grip, he pulls her out of the bed.

Snarling mouths, and grasping hands block David's path to his sister. His axe slices through the sleek, black cranium of a one-armed legionnaire sergeant. The blade penetrates deep, splattering blood across my pants.

"*Merde!*" The kid tugs at the axe, his foot leveraged on the tire hump. It's stuck tight in the skull. If I don't stop to help him before I run for Laure, there are two white-aproned, hair-netted kitchen employees hanging on the sides, waiting to serve him up *al fresco*.

Laure screams, thrashing her legs and beating her fists on Eugène's back as he races past the driver's window.

Anchoring my foot next to David's, I heave on the axe handle. The blade wrenches free. The truck jerks to a stop again, presumably inviting one of us to jump out and help Laure. We tumble back into the bed. The sergeant slumps onto the drive taking the cooks with him.

Circumventing the crowd crawling up the sides, I vault to the cab roof, and my feet blaze a trail of dents down the front hood. Laure is now limp, slumped over Eugène's shoulder as he races towards Kasim's electric blue sports car at the end of the drive. *God, please don't let her be bitten. She would have been safer in the freezer. This is all my fault—again!*

Eugène drops her into the passenger seat and slams the door. About five car lengths stand between me and ripping the passenger door open. No chance at all that Eugène bothered to buckle Laure in. I vault the curb.

As my feet hit the sidewalk, the cargo van parked behind the Peugeot vomits a bloody pack of ravenous corpses onto the walk.

Three more strides, and my hand grips the handle, swinging the door open. My fingers brush chain mail before the Peugeot roars to life and squeals away. The fastest of the *boches* from the van digs her claws into my arm and yanks me back. As we tumble, her breath sprays my neck with spittle and I stab David's knife through her eye. In a smear of black spandex and sneakers, the ex-woman falls limp, half her scalp flopping to one side.

Dragging myself off the asphalt, I sprint after the sports car, running from the dead gaining on my heels as much as towards the girl I'm trying to save.

None of the shamblers can match my sprint, but the leftovers from the gate are closing in from the other direction. The Peugeot is only yards from the hood of the oncoming truck. Standing in the back of the bed, David pounds on the cab roof, "STOP!"

Whoever is driving the Ford is insane—or just insanely shrewd. The engine roars on a high-speed, head-on collision course with the sports car. Neither driver swerves. The Peugeot doesn't stand a chance against the half-ton truck.

My front foot catches up to the back tire of the Peugeot. Eugène finally loses his nerve. His car swerves left, away from me and 5,000 lbs. of certain mangled death. Swerving, the truck blows by me as I dive out of its path.

The sports car's undercarriage clunks against cement as it jumps the curb and tilts onto two wheels on the grass strip that separates the two arms of the U-shaped drive. I half expect Laure to fly out of the seat, but the jarring slams the door shut. The car squeals towards the cross street, ripping tire tracks down the lawn.

When the truck stops skidding, Kasim lowers his hand. "Get in!" Latching on to his forearm, I swing myself into the bed. A bald soldier, a tenacious son of a bitch, grabs my ankle. The driver speeds after the Peugeot barreling up the grass bed. David lops off the legionnaire's hand at the wrist. The rest of his body tumbles into the drive, his fingers still gripping my leg.

The driver pursues the sports car on a thin line through twisting roads. In the chicken match, the truck had the advantage. Playing cat and mouse through the tangled streets of Marseille, the half-ton Ford is a beached sea lion in pursuit of a cheetah.

Pink, orange, and yellow stucco walls fly by as we twist along narrow streets. We race down residential roads with sidewalks no wider than a hotdog and I'm sure the truck will scrape and stick between the walls on both sides.

Man-high stucco walls hide the front yards. Glass shards protruding from the tops of the walls mock second story flower boxes bubbling with inviting winter blooms.

The tires squeal as we burn left. Kasim, David and I slide across the truck. David's chain mail rattles against the metal bed. He crawls back up and peers over the side. "*Merde*! He's losing them." We swing right and slide again.

It was inevitable. Down an alley masquerading as a street, two parked cars narrow the road to two-thirds its width. All fine and good for a slim European sports car. Disastrous for a monster American truck. The driver jerks to a stop.

"*Mais, qu'est-ce qu'il fait?*" David doesn't get the driver any more than I do.

"*Calme-toi.*" Kasim pats him on the shoulder. "*Je sais où ils vont.*" He nods towards the inland horizon. In the distance, a hill rises into the azure blue sky. At the summit, a large church gazes down on the Marseille port. Notre Dame de la Garde. I've only seen it in textbook pictures. From the top of its tallest tower, the Virgin Mary guards her city. Kind of makes me wish I were Catholic. Laure's going to need some prayers.

Pulling myself off the floor, I hop out of the bed to have a word or two with our chauffeur about his driving. The viral cocktail has burned through the marijuana haze and boils in my blood. I storm around to the other side of the truck.

The cab door swings open. A bare grey foot drops onto the running board. Another grey? Maybe this is Joseph, Laure's infected older brother—that would explain the desperate, reckless driving. A close-cropped, ragged blond head leans out, stopping me in my indignant tracks.

The breath freezes in my lungs. I stumble back. One hand grabs the side of the truck for balance while the other flies to my mouth. "Oh, my god!"

"*That's what she said*," the driver grins, "but you can still call me Greyson."

Chapter 8

The Resurrection. That dream has been warped and twisted into so many nightmares that I've forgotten the childhood awe Easter inspired in my Sunday school days. I can still see the picture hanging over the pulpit. The ethereal man in white glows among the clouds. The angelic hosts on a field of crystal blue sing praises to the miracle.

Is that what this is? A miracle? It's not possible that Greyson is standing in front of me. "I watched you die." The words come out breathy—too much blood pumping, my lungs racing to keep up. "I saw the explosion—watched the smoke billow into the sky." *He's gone...gone.*

But he's not gone. I'm seeing him with my own eyes—the thick smatter of dirty blond, the amber eyes, sexy, even tinted in purple, the square jaw. Everything down to the cheeky grin. I left him because he couldn't resist playing god. Maybe I was wrong. Maybe he IS god. Is that what the apocalypse is? The rebirth of the sublime and the resurrection of the damned? Heaven and hell fighting their final battle for earth?

"I told you, Ev. We are the future. The future never dies."

The animal magnetism between us draws me straight into his arms. Tears well up from the cracking of the dam that I built around the abyss I used to call my heart. I throw my arms around his neck and wrap my legs around his hips. I need this boy like I need water. My lips find the fountain of his and quench the thirst that has parched my chest for weeks. When the dam breaks, I drown in the flood. Gasping for breath, I pull away from the satin of his lips and stare into the eyes I thought were locked up forever in the mausoleum of my memories. I already lost my heart to him, so what am I losing now?

"How the hell did you get here? How did you survive?"

"*Excusez-moi de vous déranger, mais ma soeur...*" The irony in David's voice bites. He doesn't have to finish his sentence.

Loosening my death grip around Greyson's neck, I drop my feet solidly back to the ground to provide an ad-lib translation. "He's apologizing for interrupting 'our moment' to remind us that his sister is speeding through town with a homicidal psychopath." It's not the time for gushy reunions, but even though my feet are back on the ground, my hand searches for Greyson's. I need the touch, the physical proof that he's real, the reconnection of the electrochemical circuit that runs between us and completes me.

When my fingers brush his, he draws his hand away, pushing the hair back out of his eyes—a habit he had before the ZV Institute shaved his head to dissect his brain. Now he's just raking his fingers through the thick, short lawn pushing across his scalp, compliments of Nicolas's miracle cream. He might as well have slapped my face.

So that's what really died in the explosion—the obsession he's had with me since second grade.

I hardly blame him. I'm emotionally unstable. The Zoser virus messes with your hormones. Or maybe it's not me. Maybe it's that Knight girl, the cult leader that fed his god complex, created the first alpha, and gave birth to the apocalypse in Houston. I search his eyes for the indifference of someone who belongs to another. But he won't look at me.

My heart sort of dies. He's here, but *he's gone*...The misery warps to anger, and the urge to rip my fangs into raw meat has me clenching my fists and gritting my teeth to keep from going after the exposed flesh on David's neck. He's got this delicious butter-fried trout smell running off him. I'd gladly take a drag from one of Kasim's joints, but the butt is long gone. Besides, I'm going to need the animal inside if we're tracking the beast to his lair.

"He's taking her to *Notre Dame de la Garde*." Kasim hops out of the truck to join the resurrection party. How appropriate that we're going to a church to celebrate. The color has drained from my festive mood leaving nothing but grey ash. It's like finding out Jesus lives, but you're not invited to the feast. "Eugène and his 'parishioners' worship at the *basilique*. He'll want a ceremonial sacrifice." David blanches. I know how he feels. I only lost Amber once, but the need to get her back consumed the purpose of my every cell. "Eugène lives for pomp and circumstance." Kasim nods at Greyson as if they've already met.

"You want to navigate, buddy? I don't know the turf." Greyson is driving, obviously—even if the truck is David's.

"There's a more direct route on main roads, if you're not trying to lose a tail. Don't worry. We'll close the gap." Kasim heads for the passenger seat. How appropriate. That leaves me in the back with David. I vault the side while David scoots around to climb up the tailgate. My back against the cab window, I cross my arms over my legs and bury my head. After weeks of being dead, Greyson is less than six inches from my head but separated from me by a glass wall.

It's totally logical that Kasim would take shotgun. He's the only local. David's on vacation, and this is my first time on the continent. But give me a break! I thought Greyson was dead. Dead! Dead puts all the petty peeves to bed, wipes dirty lenses clean.

God help me! I can see it so clearly now. Grey was right all along: we *are* soulmates. I've been only half a person for weeks. I kicked him to the curb in Houston because I couldn't see his brand of grey, and the worst of it is, Ashley Knight was waiting there, open-armed, convinced he was literally god's gift to the world and...*and he's gone...*

The truck squeals back and flips around. Greyson doesn't need anyone's permission to push the pedal to the floor. David and I lurch.

"Tu le connais, ce mec?" David wants to know if we can trust Greyson. It's not exactly what he said, but it's what he meant. With no one but him in the back for company, French suddenly becomes real. It used to be just a game I was good at.

In comparison to the worry on David's face, my relationship issues shrink. Relegating them to the realm of "for later," I stuff the ball of bitter regret in my throat down to marinate in my chest. David needs hope and I have it—in sketchy French. "If anyone can get your sister back, it's Greyson." I tell him how Greyson saved my ass over and over, that he rescued me from the ZV Institute slaughterhouse, that he sacrificed himself to save me and Amber from the SNCHRS, and that we'd be long dead without him.

I don't tell him Grey led the zombie gang that murdered my family, or that he bit a cop to stop him from giving us away, or that he had the chance to stop Miguel before he led the murderous raid on my aunt's neighborhood, but let him go because he was a fellow grey. Instead, I finish with Greyson shooting the last zombie off Nicolas's leg so our chopper could escape—even though it meant we were abandoning him to the bombs.

David inhales, nods his head reassured.

We've hit a major boulevard now as we wind up towards *La Garde*. From the old port, the city rises steeply up to the peak of the basilica. The view from the hill showcases leftover Nazi remnants. White bunkers dominate the port in the surrounding cliffs.

We swerve around a corner and the *Chateau d'If* comes into view in the sea below. "My little sister is there." Amber was always the padding between mine and Greyson's rough edges. Without her, the prickly traits that bind us also tear gashes in our thin, infected skin.

"We were told no civilians on the island. It was strictly a military clean zone."

I point at the carrier. "We came in on that ship."

"You are military, then?" For the first time, he takes in my camo issue and looks encouraged. I hate to disappoint him.

"We have military friends. They're looking out for my sister. There's no place there for people like me."

"You must miss her."

"She's safer there. She's a little *coquine* and has the whole platoon wrapped around her finger." The dried leaves in the truck bed suddenly become fascinating. I'm not fooling David. Of course, I think that Amber is safer with me. When push comes to shove, I'll die to keep her uninfected. Who else would do that? Ryan? He might. I hope it doesn't come to that.

David falls silent for a moment. We pass an American tank that was damaged by a German grenade and left in the middle of the street as a memorial to the men who liberated Marseille. We won't be liberating with tanks this time. It'll be with syringes—Nicolas willing.

"I'm really sorry about Laure, David. I think if I'd left her in the fridge where Kasim hid her, she'd still be there."

"It's not your fault. It's mine. She is my responsibility. I should have died before I let that monster take her. Instead, I just abandoned her to him." David's head falls into his hands.

If he only knew how acutely I feel his pain. For a second, I forget I'm a repulsive grey and pat his knee. He could be my little brother. He and Cory are about the same age—or Cory would have been if I hadn't let him down too. "You wouldn't be any use to her dead, would you? At least, you're coming for her and not lying half-eaten in the parking lot. She knows you're coming for her. Hope is everything."

Please, God, let Amber know I'm coming for her. That thought, that prayer, gives birth to this completely illogical, and yet compelling, notion that if I help David save his sister, someone out there will help me save mine. Maybe that's what god has become to me—poetic justice.

"I was supposed to be protecting her. Instead, I led those *boches* right to her because I didn't want to fight them alone. Joseph usually watches out for Laure. He would have been like you. He'd have run decoy to keep them away from her." David's head drops between his legs. His fingers lock over the back of his neck. We share a bitter drink called "regret."

The virus has molded me into a creature of instinct, and David stirs up my atavistic need to protect the pack. I hardly know him, but in this moment, he's become the family I lost. "I promise, David. I'll help you get her back home."

"I can't go back without her. I was supposed to keep her safe."

Red clay roof tiles checker the landscape below. The sea twinkles and winks in the bright summer sun. "The *boches* are out there. It's just a fact of life now. Nobody is safe. Even Joseph got bitten, right?"

"Yes, and my mother."

Now that little piece of info he should worry about. Her gluten intolerance makes her an alpha in embryo. "Your mother is sick, right? Super weak?"

"Yes. That is the odd thing. Joseph grows stronger. He eats meat now—not people, you know—but he is fast and powerful. His skin is grey, like yours," he nods back at Grey and Kasim, "and theirs. He can smell the *boches* before anyone else in the camp. My father has given him the night shift on lookout because his night vision is so acute. Still, he's tethered—on a very long chain. My mother is grey like him, but she is weak and very ill. We do not understand."

We reach the bottom of the hill that winds up to *Notre Dame de la Garde*. "It's because your mom is gluten intolerant. The virus reacts differently. Whatever happens, don't feed your mother human meat. Greys who were vegetarian can control the urges. Your father should trust Joseph. The greys are the ones who can stand up to the *boches* and the alphas that spawn them. Without us, the alphas are invincible."

"It's not so much my father as Joseph himself. He's afraid of the cravings—he doesn't want to hurt Laure."

Doesn't that sound familiar. "Talk to Kasim. Weed controls the urges. It works, but there's a trade-off. It calms the other animal instincts as well, which made it a bit inconvenient for taking on an alpha and his pack of *boches* at just the wrong moment. Joseph will have to choose. Does he want to use the virus to protect his family or douse it to be human again?"

The truck pulls to a stop in the shadow of the old fortress at the crypt level of the basilica. The ruins of the limestone walls block the view of the truck from the windows of the church. From a spur of the ancient fort, still dangling from the relatively new flesh of the *Basilique de la Garde*, I can see the old Nazi bunkers that dot the limestone cliffs of the Marseille coast. The new invaders don't need bunkers—or forts. They're already dead. I still can't figure out why all of the apocalypse crazies congregate in churches.

"Let's go, David. Right now, we have only one goal. We're getting Laure out of here."

The two of us hop over the side. Greyson and Kasim join us from the cab. Greyson is still barefoot. I wonder what happened to his shoes. The last time I saw him, he was sporting a pretty pricy pair of Nikes that he lifted from a clothing store in New Mexico. He shades his eyes with his hand to scout the layout and then nods, all self-assurance. "Here's the plan—"

Chapter 9

The *Basilique de Notre Dame de la Garde* towers above the lower parking. Below the church, a drawbridge crosses directly into the foyer of the crypt. A statue of a pope and a bishop stand guard at the entrance.

The congregation gathered in the crypt chapel isn't there for the sermon. Today, they're more interested in the sacrament. Their guttural groans chant an unholy prayer, pleading with the alpha priest to grant them a wafer-thin slice of Laure. A bunch of decaying sacks of flesh, their idea of a baptism is a fresh organ dunked in blood, hold the holy water—more than a sprinkle, please.

Through the open glass doors, the aroma of musty bones and decaying flesh taints the stagnant air of the entry. I can't be sure if the smell comes from the stones, the parishioners, or me. I crouch, unseen, but more importantly unsmelled, in the cover of a model of the basilica. Behind me, a shadowy stone stairwell leads to the floor above. In front of me, through the glass wall, I can see the opposite end of the crypt chapel.

His back to the ungodly congregation, Eugène mumbles Latin over a struggling sacrifice bound on the altar. Raising my head to see better, I catch Laure's eye when he raises a cross over her body. A glimmer of hope ignites there. Now I feel even more guilty. I wouldn't say it to David, but the chances of us breaking her, unscathed, out of this Sunday school for the damned are slim. Eugène has removed the chainmail that protected her. She's only got a light tunic and some tights on underneath. More likely than not, we'll all end up as converts today. We're outnumbered ten to one. I raise my finger to my lips and sink slowly back into the shadows of the model.

Behind the altar, the Virgin Mary, her son in one arm and a bouquet of wilted roses in the other, smiles benevolently down upon the sacrifice. Laure's organs will keep Eugène alive, her blood and flesh will satisfy the hunger of the *boche* mob. Bread and circus, the ruling strategy of tyrants. Dressed in white robes, Eugène turns and offers a prayer.

Every time Laure quivers or squeals, my heart clenches a little. She came back for me—probably Greyson's idea, not hers—but it's my fault she's not stowed safely in the freezer where Kasim stuck her. With Amber safe on an island military compound, I guess I've adopted for my own David's need to rescue his little sister. I feel like a PETA warrior releasing live lobsters.

A robed monk meanders up and down the aisles swinging a thurible. Clouds of incense billow from tiny holes in the ball at the end of the chain. The fumes settle over the worshipers like soothing words of salvation. The monk's pale hand gives her away. She's a ZV. Kasim told us she'd be here.

Catherine was Eugène's girlfriend before he was infected. Of course, they had no way of knowing she could catch the virus just from being around him. Only Nicolas knew that the hormone soup of love incubates and spreads the Zoser virus as effectively as a bite. That's why they thought it was an STD in the beginning.

Catherine cowers before Eugène but needs the free room and board he offers. While ZV adults die rapidly, the teens remain sentient but succumb to the hunger. Catherine has been dipping her hand into the human cookie jar for a while now, which means she's well advanced in the decaying process. The same thing happened to my friend Chase before he blew up the Institute. Feeding the virus what it wants kills a ZV and shuts down a grey's superpowers.

The Frankincense fumes mask Catherine's scent as well as mine. The *boches* will tear apart a simple infected ZV as well as a grey. Only the alphas control them. The incense is laced with marijuana. It has to be, or the dead would rise up out of their pews, sniff Catherine and me out, and annihilate us.

Floating up the stairway, the relaxing strains of lavender settle on my nervous system. An airy fog creeps into my brain, and my head wobbles like the magnetic poles of the planet have reversed. Catherine reaches the back bench. She's wearing a gas mask under her hood.

At the front of the chapel, near the altar, the smoke has thinned. A pock-scarred parishioner roars and jumps out of his seat. One eye dangles by tendons and veins over his cheek and half his right arm flops loosely at the elbow. Without the calming agent of the incense, the bakery fresh smell of organs is more than he can take. He tramples and stumbles across the legs of his fellow disciples to reach Laure. Her eyes dart to my shadow on the stairs. Her bare feet pummel the marble altar as she hefts her bound body away from the charging *boche*. A shriek gurgles through her gag.

I could make my move now, but I'm counting on the alpha to control his pack. Kasim and Greyson still need to raid Eugène's armory. Grey needs a gun and Kasim needs ammo. We all voted for David to wait in the truck and drive getaway. A rare concession from Grey, one that only staring down the obstinate faces of three grey ZV predators could convince David to accept.

Eugène doesn't disappoint. His purple eyes narrow as he directs the heads of his obedient horde to swivel. With one, icy, communal stare, the congregation condemns the heretic who dared move without the consent of their priest. The alpha stretches his index finger towards the sinner. Obeying his telepathic command, the dead mimic his motion.

All is still for a moment.

My muscles tense. The virus bubbles in the adrenalin in my veins. I can smell the hunt. Eugène waves his arms in an upward arc, a priest cueing his choir. With a single note, the dissection begins. A tall, thin man moans and grunts. In the place of his left sleeve, a jagged hole gapes from his perfectly tailored blue suit. He grasps the flopping eyeball with his remaining arm and plucks it. A slurping snap of tendons and veins splatters black sludge on the apostate's cheek. The dead businessman holds up his trophy as an offering to the pontiff. Eugène nods his approbation and the dismantling frenzy begins. Fingernails become claws and teeth become fangs, ripping and tearing at the heretic brother. Backing warily away, Catherine ducks into an alcove.

This is my chance. I haven't a clue where the hell Kasim and Grey are. They were supposed to deal with Eugène while I grabbed Laure. Grey's plans are usually more like outlines and I'm not going to sacrifice Laure's life to Murphy's law.

The tricky part is that the door opens squarely in the center of the altar's direct line of sight. My eyes fixed on Eugène, I wait until he's completely enthralled in the public execution and then crawl across the mosaics to the cover of the pews. Body parts literally erupt from the growling mass of refuse humanity. Only two feet from the pews, another alcove dents the aisle. I dive in before the riot dies down. A statue of Jesus crucified lies on an altar. He had his own problems with a different breed of *boche* and alpha. If I have my way though, Laure won't be the next sacrificial lamb.

The riotous dead emit a rancid odor that cues my viral instincts to fight or run for cover. Dominating the reflex isn't easy, but in my mind, that's Amber up there on the altar and I'm not leaving without her. I promised David, and I have an idea.

My back against the wall, I slide to Catherine's alcove. Roman columns jut into the aisle at the opening of each of the alcoves and hide me from Eugène's line of sight. The guttural din quiets, the dismantling dies down. Some of the restless *boches* around the outside of the crowd begin to wander aimlessly towards the back where I'm plastered to the wall behind the column.

Fortunately, Catherine's thurible floods her alcove with the weed concoction. The vent of outside air from the open door pushes the fumes towards the altar. They float among the *boches* that venture close to my hiding spot, infecting them with their numbing sermon.

Lulled by the incense, the last of the vagrant dead gives up the hunt and wanders back to the pack. From his perch at the altar, Eugène gathers in his flock. With a wave, he wills them to sit. His face exudes a narcissistic arrogance that reminds me of Grey when he first discovered he could influence the ZVs he'd bitten. But Grey never had that hypocritical aura of benevolence that smears Eugène's face. At least he knew what he was doing was unconscionable.

Chapter 10

Taking a deep breath of fresh air, I scramble into the cover of Catherine's alcove. I need that gas mask before my breath runs out and the marijuana works its magic on my microbe buddies. Terrified, she scoots into the shadowed corner between the altar and the wall. As far as she knows, I'm an aberrant *boche* immune to the calming power of weed. My knife leads the charge, but Catherine cowers away. She doesn't even try to defend herself. When I rip off the gas mask and invert the straps to the front so I can slip it on the way Ryan showed me, I can see why.

She's emaciated. Abrasions riddle the poor girl's face. Her nose is clearly broken. The spasmodic jerks she responds with tell me the brain decay has begun. When she clasps her hands around the sides of her neck and begins rocking back and forth, I see she's lost the top half of her two middle fingers. Clean cut. I've seen this kind of ZV bashing before. It churns my guts to think about.

Shoving my nose into the cup, I pull the straps over my head and cinch them to create a tight seal. Thank god I'm already used to tight spaces—underground polygamy hides, ship cabins.

The marijuana fuming from the thurible has flooded the alcove and calms Catherine's jitters. She settles back and hardly resists when I drag the habit and hood over her head. Pulling the knife from the holster on my leg, I slip on the robes and conceal the blade in the sleeve.

"*Reste ici! Je reviens pour toi.*" I don't know if she's relieved or more frightened that I'm coming back for her. Now that she's inhaled enough weed, she really doesn't care either way. Maybe that's how she copes with the abuse.

Grabbing the thurible, I reemerge into the chapel aisle and, slouching submissively, approach the front pews. My heart races. A couple *boches* on their own are ferocious and tenacious but manageable. A whole pack of them crammed into a tight space, blindly following the twisted whims of an alpha, that's where the situation starts to get dicey. The incense camouflages my scent as I pass the congregation on the left aisle. Catherine's mistake was that she moved too quickly and didn't leave a thick enough film. Taking my time, I saturate each area before moving on.

It seems odd that my scent would trigger the hunting instincts of the dead since I'm pretty sure they're not breathing. But smell is a predator tool, and the virus targets those. I'm not enough of a scientist to know how the hell that works. That's a question for Nicolas and Dr. Pêsqué. Right now, I'm just a little freaked that the members of Eugène's motley congregation keep targeting me with their purple eyes as I make my way up to the front.

A gold chalice, encrusted with jewels, and a really large gleaming silver knife adorn the end of the altar. Behind it, beneath the statue of the Virgin and child, Eugène rambles on, barking out some sort of perverse gospel. "And the blessed shall partake of the bread of life and drink the wine from the pure vessels…" Hopefully, I'm scared enough that the monk's habit and gas mask will camouflage my identity from Eugène even though I'm taller and much meatier than his ZV slave.

He's way too excited with his homily from hell to spare me a glance as I stumble past. The smoke rises up to him, and I know he's breathing. *Please, God, let weed subdue the virus in the alphas as well.* Looking him in the eye for signs of a buzz would give me away. All I can do is hope in this chapel of the damned. *Where the hell is Grey?* The vague rumble of engines in the parking lot above us trickles through the entry and down the aisles. I have a hard time believing David lost his nerve and bailed on us again. Visitors?

Tears dribble down Laure's cheeks as she sobs. She must think the *boche* melee scared me away. Fighting the urge to rush up the steps and grab her out from under Eugène's spittle challenges every ounce of self-discipline I have. But the heads of the *boches* on the other side of the room swivel and fidget inattentively like three-year-olds at Sunday services. They smell me. I can't make my move until I've calmed the organ-lust the mob violence has awakened in their black blood.

On my second round, I speed up the process a bit. Eugène has picked up the knife. I could really use some backup now. Grey and Kasim were supposed to charge in, fully armed, and pick off Eugène before he could do any damage while I snatched Laure from the altar.

At the railing that separates the crowd from the priest, I take a deep breath and brace for the assault.

Gunshots! Finally!

But they're on the upper level. They rattle the pristine silence of the crypt. Eugène stumbles in his pontificating. The entry behind us gapes empty. *Where the hell are Greyson and Kasim?* I'm going to have to do this by myself.

An anxious urgency tightens Eugène's face. Picking up the silver dagger, he poises it directly over Laure's chest. With this cumbersome monk's outfit on, I don't have time to get over the wood railing that separates the mob from the priest and stop him before he stabs her through the heart. I whip the thurible across the railing. The ball flies straight at the altar. The chain catches on Eugène's wrist and swings the pot of incense around his arm. The surprise barely has time to widen his eyes before I tug on the chain and yank him across the altar. The silver knife clatters to the floor, but the real weapon here is still in play—Eugène's teeth. Gathering up my robes with my free hand, I use the chain as leverage to heave my weight over the rail. The robes restrict my movements, but the pull on the thurible keeps Eugène from bending back and condemning Laure to zombie hell with his kiss of death.

"*Sale putain!*" he rages. The incense must have relaxed his viral instincts as well. While he condemns me with sexual obscenities, my knife slips through the thin cords that bind Laure's feet. Once they're free, I pull on the thurible chain to drag the priest off her chest. When he tumbles over the front of the altar, Laure scrambles off. Furious, Eugène tugs at the incense cage, unwinding as fast as he can.

"Viens, vite!" I yell for Laure to follow me. The only exits lie back through the aisles of *boches*. The smell of the weed and lavender lingers, but the fumes have faded. The parishioners, alerted to my scent, are starting to twitch. The one-armed mob leader stands and sniffs the air. Swiveling back to Laure, I slice through the bands around her wrists. She needs her hands or she's toast. The silver dagger lies on the floor near the rail. Laure and Eugène spot it at the same time.

"Non, Laure. File! Sauve-toi!" She ignores my commands to get the hell out and dives for the weapon. Facing a ravenous mob of *boches* with nothing but fingernails and teeth isn't ideal. Eugène beats her to the blade, but in his rage, he didn't bother to finish unwinding the chain. One last yank pulls his hand away. Laure snatches the knife and heads for the pews.

"Salope! Je te mangerai le coeur!" His free hand grips the chain and jerks me to him. Stumbling, I let go. Whatever calming influence the fumes once had is now dissipated. Snarling, the infuriated priest literally catches air when he flies at me. My reeling feet slip out from beneath me, and he slams my back onto the altar.

Pinning my shoulders to the marble, Eugène lunges at my neck. Mouth open, teeth gaping, breath reeking of decayed flesh. I'm not letting this comic con punk take me down. Not after so many have tried and failed. *Where, in god's name, is Greyson?*

My fist drives the knife in my sleeve straight for Eugène's brain, but he's too fast. It skewers his neck, just above the clavicle and sticks. All I have left are my legs, but the monk's robes are too restrictive and Eugène's legs are wedged between mine. Snarling at the blade protruding from his neck, the priest strains against my arms, the only weapon I have left. My fingers circle his throat and squeeze as I force him away, but he's strong.

I can't see Laure, but the sounds of a skirmish echo from the back of the chapel, so maybe she's close to the exit. She's lost her chain mail, but she's good with that knife. She stands a chance if she gets up to the top of the stairs and hops in the back of the truck. She and David can drive away. *"Va, Laure! Va! Je te suis."*

I tell her I'm right behind her seconds before my elbows give. Eugène's face falls closer to mine. I'm looking straight into the eyes of hell after death. In the back of my mind, I always suspected I'd die saving Amber. I guess this is close enough.

Eugène's hot breath steams my neck. I tuck in my chin. Shit! I gave myself too much credit. Amber and I survived because of Greyson. Without him, I'm just another casualty. If I'm lucky, which I'm not—I was the 1% that caught the Zoser virus—the alpha will be so furious he won't be able to stop himself from ripping my guts out—death, the final kind. Oh, God. This is it.

My entire body shivers with the strain of keeping the alpha's teeth off my neck. The solid, wet bone of his tooth touches skin. Boots trample in the stone stairway. My dying hope gets a jump start. Laure squeals. Shots pelt the altar. That has to be last-minute Grey, showing up for his big entrance! The gunfire distracts Eugène from the kill. His body jerks two or three times before he twists around incensed. No one needs to tell me to grab the moment of distraction and heave myself off the altar. A spray of bullets slows the exodus of *boches* on Laure's heels. Under cover of the heavy fire that distracts and infuriates Eugène, I hurdle the railing. Farther up the aisle, Laure dives for the cover of the pews. I follow suit. The last thing I need is a bunch of permanent holes in my skin. Bullets level the crowd—all except for Eugène—and splinter the ancient wooden pews.

"David!" Laure's scream startles me enough to raise my eye level past the pews to the stairwell. David isn't supposed to be anywhere near this nest of nightmares. Blood trickling from a gaping hole in his thigh just below his chain mail shirt, he stumbles through the door. Double shit! It's not Grey and Kasim fending off the *boches,* it's a militia of greys, and they've taken David hostage.

Chapter 11

These greys aren't just a neighborhood gang. They've raided the GIPN and the RAID and are all decked out like the French version of an American SWAT team—black helmets, black suits, utility belts, weapons all over the place. The only reason I can tell they're grey is that the visors on their helmets are up. Their grey noses and purple-streaked eyes show through the ski masks they wear underneath. Smart. If they're hunting, they don't want to hinder their sense of smell.

The last gang of greys I met in Texas was collecting the uninfected for food storage. It's not the time, but I can't help wondering how I always land anyone who dares to get close to me in the worst of the ZV shitstorm.

Eugène ignores the volley of bullets splattering the infected brains of his flock across the wooden pews and charges the pseudo GIPN team as they spill into the chapel. His white robes fly behind him as he hurdles the railing, screaming.

The commander of the group, the smallest with a ring through her nose, shouts back to the child catcher holding David, "*Joëlle*!" Under Eugène's attack, she orders the petit soldier to secure her package. Joëlle retreats and shoves David down behind an altar in an alcove on the opposite side of the chapel, holding him captive by the scruff of his neck.

Laure jumps up, knife in hand, ready to take on the entire grey assault team by herself in her underwear. Before she can throw her blade, I tackle her from behind. Her face slams into the mosaic floor, and I come down on top of her. The silver knife clatters away. Beneath me, she thrashes, throwing elbows at my gut, sure she's been attacked by *boches*.

"*Viens, Laure! Il y a une sortie!*" Hopping off her back but keeping low, I drag her towards the entryway.

She resists. "*Non, non! David! Je dois l'aider.*"

"This isn't the time. They're not going to kill him—not right away. If we get out, we can help him. If they take us too, we're all dead meat." I can't help myself. Call it force of habit. I'm all about saving the little girl. Everyone else is secondary.

Uncertainty strains her face for a few seconds before I crawl away towards the back of the chapel. The gang of greys advances on the *boches* and Eugène in a pack. They know the risks and what they're up against. They're playing it safe, clearing the room from the opposite aisle. David's chaperone keeps him on a short leash behind the protection of the advancing gang. Laure crawls behind me towards the entry foyer. Screams piercing the firestorm tell me an overconfident grey took on Eugène and went down bloody.

Across the pews, I spot the alcove where Catherine hunkers down. The fumes have worn off, and she peeks timidly around the altar. A tinge of guilt racks me. I stop to motion to her. She'd have to make a run across the aisle and through the pews to get to us. Bullets explode the limestone all around her. The right hand of St. Thérèse crumbles.

Catherine shakes her head, refusing my offer. The compact squad leader slides across the outside wall, shouting orders and sweeping up from behind. She turns into the alcove before Catherine can retreat to her hiding spot. The smell of fear radiates across the pews. Quivering, Catherine begs the girl for help. The gang leader looks her up and down and sneers at Catherine's obvious neuro-decay. Without even an apology, she raises her gun and shoots Catherine in the eye.

Laure cringes and I freeze. I've seen worse. The GIPN team's death stroll takes them past our aisle. The benches are pretty thin and the space between them wide enough to spot us, but the gang targets the standing *boches*. They're the deadly ones. Eugène actually does us a favor keeping the GIPN greys too busy to scan the floor for escaping refugees.

We have to get to the exit before the gang reaches the front of the chapel and starts down our side of the aisle. Tugging on Laure's tunic, I double the pace. The last few rows of pews are clear. We make a break for the entry. Through the glass walls, I watch the grey gang converge on Eugène. Even surrounded, riddled with bullets, blood streaming from the knife wound in his neck, he attacks ferociously with teeth and nails, avenging his fallen flock. A line of bullet holes rips the scalp off his head. He finally stops, reels backward, and falls on the heap of his damned children.

A few walking *boches* at the front of the chapel keep the grey gang occupied while Laure and I crawl along the walls towards the exit and the drawbridge to the parking lot. The black combat boot of a guard left outside to patrol the exit breaks the beam of light streaming in from the open door. Pulling up, I shove Laure back behind a table.

"*Merde!*" Searching the entry, my eye falls on the dark, narrow stairway that leads up to the basilica above. If we wait for the guard to pass on his rounds, we can try our luck escaping from upstairs. Who knows how many of them are here? There can't be that many vegetarians in France. They eat their meat raw, for god's sake. This is the land of *Boeuf Bourguignon* and *Coq au Vin*.

I swear again. Can't be sure if it's in French or English. The two are mixing freely at this point. Instead of walking by on his rounds, the guard turns into the doorway, hollering at the gang leader. "*Margot!*"

Hauling Laure by the arm, I dive into a dark corner near the statue of the crucified Christ in the tomb. My heart beats loud enough to give us away. The demon rioting in my blood makes me want to pounce and attack the unsuspecting prey, but going hand to hand with a well-armed, armored guard is not going to get Laure out of here. Besides, it's the *bouillabaisse* sweat coming off Laure that the virus really wants, not this grey.

An automatic rifle dangling from his arm, the guard breezes right through the entry and into the chapel. He yells over the last popping remnants of gunfire. *Il n'y a plus personne en haut. Vite! On s'en va! Tu as éliminé l'alpha? J'ai mis les deux gris dans la navette.*" Grabbing Laure's hand, I sprint towards the stairwell at the other end of the entry. The air strangles in my throat as I run, and I want to scream. The guard just told Margot that he stuffed the other two greys in the van. They already have David, and the sinking feeling in my gut tells me the two greys are Kasim and Greyson. Why else wouldn't they have shown up? A cold hand grips my heart. I saw what Margot did to Catherine. Maybe if Kasim and Grey aren't already dead, it's because this gang is only wiping out simple ZVs, *boches*, and alphas.

The stairway spills into the red and white marbled majesty of the basilica. For a second, the gold trimmings, the awe-inspiring mosaic domes, and the sumptuous luxury take my breath away. I've never been to a church outside of Utah. I attended a Christmas concert once at the Cathedral of the Madeleine in downtown Salt Lake. The stained glass and brightly colored frescoes distracted me from the music. But this, this is truly a palace of the gods.

Must be commonplace to Laure, she doesn't even blink before heading towards the massive wooden exit doors. I hustle to catch up and stop her before she pulls them open. We don't know how many greys are out there. "Wait here. They've already cleared this chapel. I'll check it out and come get you if it's safe."

"*Et David?*"

"First, I'm getting you the hell out of here. Once you're safe, we can figure out how to get David back."

Her face scrunches, and she's about to revolt, so I cut her off. "*Ne t'inquiète pas*. I think they have Greyson and Kasim, too. We'll be coming back for them as well as David." Laure nods and finds a dark corner to hide in.

The door creaks. Shadows shroud the narthex. Creeping across the mosaics, I crack the outer door just enough for a blinding stream of light to cut through and shave a yellow scar across the floor. A broad limestone porch overlooks the port, the red-roofed city, and the sea. The *Chateau d'If* lies in the direct line of sight of the entrance. The heartstrings that connect me to Amber twang. They urge me to abandon this insanity, make my way back to the island, grab Amber, and find us a safe refuge to wait out the apocalypse. I'm a grey. I can protect her better than anyone else—except from myself. That's what it always comes back to. I don't know how the virus will progress.

I'd feel safer if I had a stash of marijuana. Maybe that's as good a reason as any to go back for Kasim.

As if I needed a reason. He's with Greyson…

Even if Grey is through with me, I owe him.

The empty patio reflects the sun. In order to see the parking at the crypt level, I have to slink to the railing near the flight of stone steps. A van, that was a *Novotel* shuttle in another life, waits with the rear cargo doors thrown open. I expected it, but still gasp when I see Kasim and Grey, barefoot still, both out cold in the back. Voices echo up. The guy in GIPN gear standing guard nods to Joëlle as she shoves David into one of the back seats.

Another GIPN grey drives up to the back of the van in our truck. There goes my ride—again. I'm calculating the odds— not good—of sneaking down, surprising the driver, and stealing the truck from under his nose with only my knife when I hear a muffled scream from inside the basilica and race back. Laure!

The heavy smell of chemicals seeps through the crack in the closed door. The second I throw it open, I meet the source and the open end of a black bag. Thrashing blindly at my assailant, I realize I'm blacking out.

Chapter 12

The pounding in my head wakes me. Stone walls spin before nausea overwhelms me. I spew the few bites of liver from my morning binge onto the cement floor. But was it this morning that I found Laure in the freezer? I have no idea how long I've been out.

Wiping my mouth with the back of my hand, I try to sit up and figure out where I am. No windows. No doors. Laure crashes back into my consciousness and, close on her heels, the heavily armed grey gang. Nausea convulses my stomach again and I dry heave. The only thing worse for Laure than being eaten alive by rabid humans is being locked up as food storage.

My heart constricts. Amber's brown eyes and tight ponytail twist and meld in light-headed delusions with Laure's. The steel I pumped into my veins so I could walk—swim—away from my little sister melts a little, and the self-loathing and doubt I feel for not protecting her seep in, merging with my fears for Laure. Somehow, I feel if I can keep Laure safe, karma will kick in and the universe—or Ryan—will protect Amber.

Seconds pass before my roommates awake, moaning and retching on the opposite side of the room. The world is still spinning when I try to focus on the heaps across the floor. Grey and Kasim. Kasim is still out cold, maybe because he smoked a whole lot more weed than I did. Grey struggles to sit up. There are three green camping cots in the bare room and a community piss pot. They didn't bother to lay us on the beds, they just dumped us on the floor. The only other feature in the room is a camera in the corner on the ceiling. They're watching us.

With a groan and a deep sigh, Grey gives up on standing and leans his back against the wall, tucking up his knees and dropping his head between them. The residual headache from the chemical in the bags they put over our heads throbs and burns. Making a play for getting to my feet, I brace my hand on the cold wall. The world somersaults and ripples. Nausea erupts again. Nothing but bile spews out this time. I fall back onto the cot and stare at the ceiling.

The silence ticks away. Alone in a room with Grey, shut off from the predators, the smell of him stirs up a spiraling vortex of memories. Before he jumped out of the cab of David's truck, I'd have chopped off my own arm and fed it to a horde of *boches* if it meant another ten minutes alone with him to tell him I was sorry, to tell him I can't live without him—literally. All the bitter dregs of words left unsaid, words that have been swilling around on my tongue for weeks at sea, and the first thing out of my dry mouth is an accusation. "What happened to you guys back there?" The second they're out, the words choke my insides and strangle the rush of emotional confessions bombarding my brain. *God! I'm such a bitch.*

Greyson knows it, too, but he doesn't let it slide with that sexy half-smile he usually breaks out to indulge my rants. Instead, he snorts quietly and shakes his head. "They surprised us at the back of the basilica where Eugène keeps his arsenal. Too much marble in between us and the parking lot to hear them drive up. Didn't catch a whiff of the drugs in the bags until we'd already given up our guns." He shrugs. "They didn't seem hostile, so we didn't resist.

"Not hostile? They were wearing body armor and killing anything that moved."

"Not us."

"Classic, Grey. This is Miguel all over again. You let him go because he was 'one of us,' and then he brought his little gang out and murdered my whole family." Grey's convinced that we greys need to stick together. He refuses to see the difference between us and the greys that join up with the black bashers or those that go pale, white cannibal. Not all of us stay in the middle.

The gulf between us drowns my wringing guts. Floating around in the murk, the soft, uninfected part of me pleads, *he's not gone, he's not gone, you can just hold him, feel his pulse through the grey skin*...but the accusations pile up and clog my throat.

The magnetism of Grey and me together pulls on invisible strings. I want nothing more than to stumble over and cuddle up under his arm, feel the oneness. But he pulled his hand away. The smile is gone. I couldn't bear it if he pushed me away again.

He doesn't bother to raise his head when he asks, "Where's Amber?"

My little sister is the neutral ground where we both agree. "*Chateau d'If.*"

Now his head comes up. "You left her?"

That question, in that tone of disillusioned astonishment, has been bouncing around my brain since the moment my feet left the deck of the aircraft carrier. The guilt boiling in my chest overflows and spews out in indignant, hollow justifications.

"She's surrounded by water in a clean zone with Ryan's entire Navy commando squadron to guard her. Unless the *boches* learn to swim or sail, she's safe. She's not Adventure Cat. You're not seriously suggesting I should have pulled her out of that sanctuary and brought her here in the middle of the bloodbath?" I wish I could buy my own bullshit.

Grey doesn't speak for a minute. He's like me. He doesn't trust that anyone else will do what it takes to keep Amber uninfected. Kasim's breaths wheeze for a second in the silence. "You and this Ryan guy, you're a thing then?"

Were we a thing? He's in love with me. I didn't ever think about it. I'm grey, he's uninfected. I saw the moment when I would have to jump ship coming from the day we pulled out of the Gulf. All my little girl butterflies twitter thinking about how hot Ryan is, but only Grey has ever awakened the woman inside me. I shrug.

He nods, puts his head down, and then raises it a thought later. "How come you jumped ship?"

"His dad, the general, thought I was a bad influence." How does Grey even know about Ryan? I didn't meet the lieutenant until I stormed out of my uncle's BMW with my nephew in tow and Grey drove back to Ashley Knight and her ZV worshipping cult. "Where's the Knight girl?"

"Dead. Shrapnel. Piece of stained glass through the eye."

Let's be real here. If I can't look inside myself and see the white coexisting with the black, how can I see the grey in anyone else? The evolutionary matchmaking bitch inside of me smiles. The human side bites her lip. "I'm sorry."

"Don't be. She ratcheted the ZV epidemic up into a full-blown zombie apocalypse. She was insane—and infected." A rare hint of remorse—or maybe mourning—tinges his confession. "A two-week vegetarian doesn't make a grey. She'd have decayed anyway, just a lot more slowly." And there's the calloused realism that gets under my skin. Problem is, I can't tell if that's why I love him or why I hate him. Sometimes, with Grey, I can't really tell the difference.

Kasim moans and stirs, but he's not anywhere near regaining consciousness. Grey reels slightly when he slides his back up the wall. Once steady, he leans over and heaves Kasim up in his arms. The muscles bulge under his t-shirt, and I miss the comfort of those grey arms around my waist. Wobbling still, he deposits Kasim onto the far cot then takes the one near mine.

We sit knee to knee on the edge of our cots. Both of us clutch the metal edges, stiff arms raising our shoulders. We stare at the floor. A wave of silence washes over us, stripping away the barnacles of loss, the soggy strands of discord, the sands of the past. There's nothing left but the rawness of me and Greyson. When I look up, his eyes are there, waiting for me. "Where have you been, Grey? How did you even get here?" I lean over and drop a hand on his thigh so I can see in his eyes, so he can see what's really in my mind—see it over what comes out of my mouth. "What happened to your shoes?"

He doesn't even bother to answer. Leaning across the gap between our cots, he furrows his fingers into my hair, pulls my lips to his, and kisses me like I'm dry land after years at sea. And I kiss him back, like he's been dead for weeks, and now he's alive.

Metal hinges creak at the door. We both jump to our feet, ready to gang up on our visitor. No such luck. A flap near the floor opens up, and a tray of food slides in. Three plates offer a variety of meat delicacies. The most scrumptious, home-cooked stew aroma wafts off the human giblets.

Both Grey and I smell a trap, but we don't know what it is. If the food were poisoned our viral superpowers would be able to tell. The human guts are the choice pieces. The smell riots my blood. The tiny cannibal that scurries around in my brain would drop down on all fours in a second and scarf it right off the plate. Fork? No, thanks. I could use a drag off a joint right about now. The thought of who might have donated this feast of kings churns my stomach.

On the other hand, I'm no saint, and I haven't eaten a real meal in over a day. The remnants of our scavenged breakfasts fume in two heaps on the floor. Greyson and I snatch the cow liver off the plate and rip away. The angry urchins in my blood scramble to lick up the crumbs and then, sated, crawl off, grumbling, for a nap. Eating cow organs has the same effect as settling for the corner diner when you had your taste buds set on Chez Henri. At least, it doesn't take much to calm the hunger tantrum.

Clenching my jaw against the tantalizing smell of the human meat, I shove the tray back against the trap door. Greyson and I shrug and lie back on our cots. His hand crosses the gap and clasps mine.

"So, you going to tell me how you got here? The last I saw of you, you were saving Nicolas's ass sharpshooting zombies. The bomb dropped—and then nothing but smoke."

"It's a long story."

"Ha! We're not going anywhere soon."

Seconds later, the latch on the door clicks, and a couple faux GIPN greys step into the room, targeting our faces with automatic rifles. Without a raving mad alpha at my back, I can see why Greyson opted to just go along. There's nothing we can do. If they were uninfected, we could risk the bullets and bolt, but these two, a girl and a guy, are both greys. By the looks of them, they're still vegetarians—no telltale decomposition from dipping into the human flesh cookie jar.

"*Allons-y!*" I recognize the voice. The girl, vibrant red hair and a ring in her nose, led the grey assault team at the basilica. She shoves my shoulder with the tip of her gun. I move to the door. Greyson follows. The second guy, close-shaven black hair and eight diamonds up his left ear, drops the muzzle of his rifle between us.

Now, Grey decides to put up a fight. "You're not taking her anywhere without me, dude." He shoves the gun away. The Frenchie has no idea what he's saying, but he reads the aggression and gets in Greyson's face.

"Grey, forget it. I can handle myself."

"Yes, you can, baby, but they're not taking you anywhere without me." The guy shoves Grey back into the room, and the girl collars me to keep me from intervening in the scuffle.

"Grey, let it go!" The words rasp out through the chokehold on my throat as she drags me into the hall. This is not worth the damage these two grey goons can do. "I've been on a boat with a platoon of French ZV bashers for weeks all by myself—"

"Like hell, you have." He lands a fist in the guy's jaw. He reels. His partner shoves me to the ground and jams the butt of her gun into Greyson's gut. He doubles over, and she hauls her partner through the door and slams it in Grey's face.

"Son of a bitch! God damn it!" Greyson's body slams against the inside of the door as the lock clicks. The girl kicks me onto my feet and marches me down the hallway.

Chapter 13

Cement and rock. We're in a cellar. A metal conduit, obviously much newer than the rock wall, barely illuminates the hall and highlights the black mold smeared along the stones. The musty smell is almost as strong as the scent of grey. Whatever this place is, it's been around for a while.

The girl pokes her rifle into my back to push me along. Behind me, the guy complains that he thinks Grey broke his jaw. She tells him to stop whining and go see the doctor. A doctor? They're more organized than I thought they were.

At the end of the hall, we pass through a doorway that dumps us into a very modern, three-story sunroom. Light floods through immense walls of tinted windows. The grounds have been excavated to make the rear entrance to this area above ground. The structure shares the fourth wall with what appears to be a chateau. The place has obviously been restored—the stones of the exterior wall inside the windowed hall look fresh. In here, the stubborn scent of mildew flees before the reek of greys—dying flesh, faintly putrid. *Essence de grey* is the new lemon fresh. The main hall used to be the entrance and front desk for whatever museum this was. It's now more like "ops" for the GIPN squads. At least twenty greys are in some stage of mobilization.

"Gilles!" My guard yells at two of the soldiers I recognize from the raid on the basilica. "The count wants the reconnaissance report on that *non infectés* camp ASAP." She tosses a throwing knife, blade and handle one sleek aerodynamic design, onto the red counter marked ACCEUIL in front of them. It's David's. "Stéphane, get your team down to the power station. The count wants everything on the grid redirected here. Get another team over to the solar field. We need security over there."

The guide that Greyson punched breaks off down a hall littered with posters for *Jean de Florette* and *Manon des Sources*, probably to go find the doctor. If we're in some kind of commune for greys, nothing makes me suspect we're in any immediate danger—other than the violent kidnapping and the fact that I watched my guide shoot Catherine in the head. But if they wanted us dead, Grey gave my chaperones sufficient motivation to shoot our brains out on the spot. I suspect, based on the food sampler plate they slipped into our cell, that they weed out the simple ZVs and the weak greys, the ones with no self-control, who dip into the human honey pot and start down the slippery road to decay. So if they don't want us dead, what do they want?

It's too presumptive to start a conversation in English. To give the impression I'm not a complete moron, I break out some respectable French. "What is this place?" I'd like to get a sense of the deal here, but what I'm really wondering is where they've stashed Laure and David.

"*Le Château de la Buzine.*" My guide isn't the chatty type. She's got a few earrings running up her earlobe. The butch cut really brings out her big, brown eyes and the complexion that is so light grey, it's almost lavender. With a jerk of her head, she motions me to keep going. She looks tiny, but she's like me—her looks are deceiving.

"No. I mean, there's a bunch of greys here. What do y'all do here?"

"We do whatever *le Comte de Gris* asks."

She stops in front of an entry to double doors marked CINEMA in bold, red letters. The low mumble of movie dialogue and gunshots seeps through the cracks. She nudges me to go in first. Running isn't really an option here, even though my guide is small and has to be a fairly new grey. She can't have had nearly the street training I have, not to mention the formal combat training on Ryan's ship. But the room is literally an arsenal, and the dozen greys milling about all have access to automatic weapons. Even if I did grab her gun, maybe take her hostage, I'd have to come back for Laure and David, and I have no idea where to look. Going along and asking questions seems the prudent choice. I push through the doors into a shadowy black theater lined with rows of red seats. The ray of light from the projector illuminates a thin layer of marijuana floating on the air. The scent is starting to feel homey.

In the fourth row from the screen sits a solitary spectator. My escort and I walk up the aisle in the flashing light of the movie that I recognize as the ending of *Inglorious Basterds*. As the Jewish girl laughs in silhouette behind them, flames rip through the screen and shroud the theater where I'm standing in a fiendish burnt-orange fog.

The guard stops respectfully and waits until the spectator waggles a finger, giving her permission to interrupt the film.

"*M. le Comte, c'est l'Américaine.*"

Lazily, he turns to appraise "the American." The film highlights one side of his face in its red tinge, and the other side melts into the shadows.

His voice has a hypnotic coffee and toffee flavor, a perfect pairing to enhance the scrumptious effect of spoken French. "They were right, you know."

"Excuse me?" I look around at the screen. There are only two choices: the Nazis or the resistance wiping them out with extreme prejudice. "Who?"

"The Nazis."

Oh, God! The room retracts around me, and I can't breathe for a second. If the world wasn't already upside down, it is now. We're already in an apocalypse, we don't need genocide to top it off.

The count motions for me to take a seat and then shoos away the armed guard. He exudes an egocentric confidence that I won't even think of running off. The metal hinges creak, and the cushion exhales under my weight. The screen explodes in gunshots as the Americans mow down Nazis behind locked doors in the chaos of a burning theater. Languidly raising his hand, he snaps his fingers. The projection dies in response. The low lights come up, and silence falls.

He's very French. Not dark Mediterranean French, like Ryan, but the rarer, northern blond. He has a straight nose, angular face, and piercing eyes that might have been blue, but the virus has melded them into steel grey. He wears his hair long to his shoulders. It looks tousled, but I know better—I share that obsession. Since we greys don't grow hair, the virus has frozen a blond stubble along his chin and above his well-curved lavender lips. If I had a heart, it might have fluttered. But we all know that part of me shriveled up and died a couple weeks ago.

Raising his fingers to his lips, he takes a slow, sensual drag off a joint. He could sell weed to minors. Still contemplating the screen, languid in the dimness, he offers me a drag.

I decline.

He exhales. Inhales. "Racism—the Master Race."

My eyebrows pop up on their own. Leaning as far away as the chair will allow, I cross my arms.

The motion draws his attention. He turns and favors me with a patronizing curl of his lips. "You don't agree?"

The last thing I wanted from this interview was a philosophical debate about racism, but I just can't help myself. The part of my brain that revolts against social injustice is just as hot-wired to my mouth as the virus is to my predator instincts. "That's absurd. No race is inherently 'better' than another. Even if there are differences, who decides what's 'better'?" Philosophie is all Latin, so the words are the same in French and English. All I have to do is French them up a bit. I can get by. "Cultural bias deludes the unenlightened into thinking one race is superior to the other. Racial superiority is nothing but Nazi propaganda and the opiate of white deplorables."

I've caught his attention. I'm not the dumb blonde I appear to be. His eyes brighten. "Yes, of course. The uninfected are weak no matter the color of their skin or turn of their religion. The differences are insignificant." His seat creaks lightly as he leans towards me. "But the idea that the more evolved should rule those who are inferior, this is Nature's way. Just think of the food chain. And is there not a hierarchal order in every herd? Even with their minuscule differences, the human species has followed this law of nature—capitalism favors the most astute, the wise, and the ambitious. The one percent always rise, just as the feudal system favored the strong in the beginning and gave way to the aristocracy."

Frankly, I prefer Eugène's brand of straight-up, wild-eyed, crazy to the count's calm, calculated sophistry. At least, somewhere, deep inside, Eugène knew the virus had driven him mad. The logical lunatics are the most dangerous—and influential. It doesn't help that the tripe comes packaged so scrumptiously. "Just because that's nature's way doesn't mean we have to follow. Mother Nature is a breath-taking, brutal bitch. We've loved her and been at war with her since the dawn of man. With her, it's win or die. Haven't you watched *Planet Earth*?"

"But we all die and she wins, sooner or later. Why fight her?"

A snort is all the reply I can muster on the fly. It doesn't help that my French expertise doesn't quite extend into eloquently defending social justice. I can see where he's going. The world is no longer divided along racial lines. We're now divided along viral lines—the uninfected, the ZVs, the greys, the alphas, and the living dead. He's going to try and convince me that the greys should exploit the others. That's where this line of thinking ultimately leads. Anyone who took World History knows this.

Finally, I find some words. "Because we're civilized. We have a social conscience. We redistribute the resources and the wealth. Your own country is socialist. The French revolution threw down the aristocrats—and the church while they were at it—because you believe in equality: *Liberté, Fraternité, Egalité*. Sound familiar?"

He wags his joint lazily instead of shaking his head before taking another drag. "But we were wrong, and now nature has corrected the imbalance."

The fumes seep into my brain. The humanity in me stirs. "What? You mean the Zoser virus? You think the outbreak is nature trying to restore order?"

He shrugs as if the answer were self-evident. "What a mess we've made of the planet in our rage to outwit Mother Nature—

overpopulation wrings her dry. Our waste poisons the air, the land, and the sea. She'll die if she does nothing. Perhaps she has created us, the greys, to be her agents. The masses need a strong hand of guidance. The virus chooses who lives and dies—and who will rule." He offers me the butt of the joint.

I don't need it. Either second-hand fumes lull my viral reflexes, or my year of self-imposed immunity does. Normally, the indignation I'm feeling would rile me up into a frenzy. I'm pretty calm—considering. "If Mother Nature's plan was to thin the herd, she totally overshot her mark. The infected that spawn the living dead, alphas—" I stutter for a second, not sure if he knows this term or even if he knows why some greys have the lethal bite, "—they were the beginning of the end. They'll overrun the planet. None of us will survive."

His smile would tame piranha in a blood bath. "Precisely! Clever girl. This is where you and I agree."

I shiver shamelessly at the brazen compliment. Don't judge me. I spent twelve years in the public school system being conditioned to respond to positive reinforcement. And then, he's *that* tasty.

"Have you heard the proverb, *What you fight, you strengthen*? Predators play a crucial role in Mother Nature's plan. She fashioned us greys to rule, but we mustn't become soft. This was the downfall of the aristocracy. We must battle the predators and protect our loyal vassals, the uninfected." His eyes pan away into a fantasy world he's fashioned in his mind. "Imagine the tranquility of such a new world order."

Oh, I can imagine it, all right. This can only end in a world where my little sister becomes the slave of an ego-popped grey. But I bite my tongue. My goal in coming in here was to get information about Laure and David and to find out what this place is. The answer to my second question is all too clear. Somehow this conversation needs to work its way around to the first. At least, he's talking about protecting the uninfected. That bodes well for my D&D protégés.

He takes my silence as concession. It's to my advantage to let him think I'm on board. Now, I understand why Grey cozied up so quickly to Ashley Knight. It's a survival instinct. Grey and I, we are, above all things, creatures of instinct. I knew he wanted me and not her. Being jealous was just an excuse to blow off the anger and grief when my aunt and uncle died. He's always wanted me.

Until now.

Chapter 14

The door to the theater opens up, and a stream of daylight cuts through my conversation with the count. The butch red-head that escorted me here slips into the room again.

The count props a foot up on the chair in front of us. He wears a long leather jacket that matches the boots. Brown designer, not black government-issue like everyone else. "Tell me, Evelyn, have you heard of *Man and Superman*?"

The A student in me creeps to the surface and chides me for my ignorance. Before I can blush though, I blanch. How does he know my name? What else does he know about me, and who told him?

He misreads my silence again as embarrassment at my ignorance and nods, not patronizingly, just as if it's natural that someone my age wouldn't have run across that particular piece of literature yet. "The English playwright George Bernard Shaw suggested that nature gave to the female the sole purpose of pursuing a male whose genes would combine advantageously with hers and produce a superior progeny. Tell me what you think. I find your opinions—exhilarating."

Man and Superman. Maybe that explains Greyson's unbreakable tug on my heart. His genes fill in all the gaps in my DNA. We argue so much, I'd say we were incompatible, but might as well say my lungs are incompatible with air. I can't breathe without him.

The woman's boots pad down the carpeted aisle. The count raises an eyebrow, his eyes smoky, his smile suggestive, waiting for my response.

Either my mind is flooded with the murky waters of Greyson or the marijuana fog is slowing me down, but it takes me a second before it dawns on me where he might be going with this. Is he really contemplating hooking up with me? These cults always come around to the charismatic leader explaining why he should have sex with all the women. Believe me. I know. I'm from Utah.

"I can't really say. I'm not familiar enough with the text."

Saved by the soldier. She walks across the aisle behind us and leans over to whisper in the count's ear. "*Ah, Kasim!*" He seems quite pleased with the news and hands her the nearly expired butt of his joint. "*Merci, Margot. Amène-le ici.*" She nods, but before she can turn on her heel and fetch Kasim, the count leans his head back and motions to me. "Evelyn, may I present my *ministre de l'armée* General Margot Gagnon."

She nods politely and extends a hand. I glance at the count before taking it. His general is obviously smitten with him. I'm a woman, I can smell the attraction. He doesn't seem to notice the grimace and the slight tightening around her eyes. She camouflages her suspicion of me beneath a stiff smile.

"*Enchantée,*" I say. Margot nods curtly and double times out of the theater—off to do the count's bidding. I guess she wasn't exaggerating when she said that what they do around here is whatever the count wants.

My conversations with Kasim file through my mind. He knows my name and that I was heading north to Nicolas and his cure, but I don't really see when he could have passed the count that info. "So, you know Kasim? I thought he was with Eugène."

"He was. Most alphas find it advantageous to employ a grey or two. It's really quite remarkable how quickly the social system established itself. Converting greys to our way of life, though, is quite simple. Already, we've been able to eliminate the majority of the large packs of *boches* and destroy their alphas. Only one or two herds remain, now that Kasim has helped us rid the city of Eugène's influence. His was the largest following.

"Kasim is working with you? Why would your team knock him out with me and Grey?"

He grins. "Ah, yes, well—Kasim was not altogether on board with the elimination of Eugène. It seems they were quite close before—" He waves his hand in small circles to encompass the whole of the zombie apocalypse. "Of course, the virus changed everything." He pats my hand confidentially. "You understand, don't you? It had to be done. The alphas would destroy the planet."

Chills straighten my spine because I don't understand. I do understand that the only way to win this war is for the greys to eliminate the alphas. What I don't understand is the blatant betrayal of trust. Yes, there's no hope for *boches*. They're already dead. They need to be put out of their miserable existence. But the alphas—they're crazy, they need to be stopped, but they don't need to be exterminated. Nicolas would never have shot his little brother if there was any other way to stop him from devouring me. Alphas are not that different from greys. We're all infected, and we can all be cured. Something tells me though, that the count isn't interested in a cure. He's in love with his new world order. This is right-wing fascism in its infancy. "So Kasim just happened to be at the resort where I washed up because he was tracking alphas?"

"Yes. One of the last few known alphas is particularly," his mouth purses, "unsavory. It seems Kasim stumbled upon two at the same time. Of course, we couldn't allow that type of an alliance to go forward, so Margot decided to send a whole team. But, we were quite interested as well to learn about the two little fish that washed up from the *Chateau d'If*."

He knows I came from the clean zone. I wonder if that's his interest in chatting with me. He's looking for some insider intel on the opposing team. But what really makes me think is the fact that I didn't wash up alone. "Two?"

For the first time, I've surprised the count. His eyebrows betray him, and he leans back to look at me, intrigued. "You didn't know? The surveillance tapes gave us the impression that you and the other American were—together."

He's obviously referring to that kiss and the way Grey and I bicker like an old married couple. Why would he think that Greyson came from the *Chateau d'If*? God! I really am slow. Before Margot hauled me away, he said I hadn't been on the boat all alone. I thought he was talking about Ryan. "Yeah, we assumed you were watching us." Another symptom of the fascism virus—no more privacy.

"Just a small test. We have to know, of course. Not all greys are created equally. Those that have sullied themselves with the flesh of the uninfected, they are unreliable, ungovernable if you will. They lack the self-discipline necessary to join us in our social revolution."

Finally, we've meandered around to the questions I'm interested in. "If you're not eating the uninfected, why are you rounding them up? Where did the human caviar on that plate you tempted us with come from?"

He's truly offended. "Evelyn, we are not barbarians. You can imagine, I'm sure, the ease with which my team salvages small bits of the recently deceased when we make our raids on the *boche* herds. We don't want to destroy our civilization, only return it to the natural order. The strong must rule and protect the weak for their own benefit. Of course, we round them up. How else will they survive?"

"So, they're fine, Laure and David?" He doesn't know who I'm talking about. "The two kids they brought in with me? Can I see them?"

"Ah, yes. The brother and sister dressed in medieval battle attire. They made quite a sensation here. Quite entertaining, very—spunky." Our eyes meet. His smolder, and his head tilts in an appraising stare. "I see now what Kasim admired in you." With one finger, he corrals a tress of my sea-salted, wind-blown hair and slides it gently across my cheek and behind my ear. My grey skin, only half alive, lacks sensation, but he knows just exactly how much pressure will send a tingle shivering from my earlobe to my chest. "You have an admirable concern for the *non infectés*. And you are astonishingly adept at defending them." His finger slides down the strand of hair and lets it drop at my shoulder.

Call it intuition, but I don't want this grey to know I have an uninfected little sister. I also don't want him to know Nicolas is working on a cure. That would be like telling the oil magnates the electric car is coming. My breath hitches. Kasim. I told him I wanted to go to Paris. He knows about the cure. The question is, did he pass that little piece of info along. He didn't really have time to chat with the count between the time I told him and now. "Pretty sure anyone would do the same."

The count throws his head back and laughs. "*Mais non, chérie*! Many would simply have eaten the prime morsels and left the corpses for the *boches*. But the fact that you think so, and that you passed our little test, this is why I have an offer for you. *"* He snakes an arm around my shoulders. Inside, I bristle. Outside, I smile and relax against the involuntary flinch. The count needs to believe I'm with him if I want access to Laure and David. "Not many leaders of the New Order have a sufficient—what shall we say—appreciation for the *non infectés* for me to entrust one of them with their security and well-being."

"You mean they treat them like sub-humans and slaves. And, in this grey supremacist society that you've created, that surprises you?"

The door behind us opens, and a beam of light cuts the shadows. Kasim strolls into the room, followed by Margot. Her badass gun hangs idly on her shoulder. Kasim is one of theirs.

"Ah, Kasim! We all congratulate you." The count motions Kasim to sit next to me. The cushion brushes my leg, and I use the opportunity to adjust and squirm out from underneath the count's arm. But not before Margot incinerates me with a glance. Poor girl. She's got it bad. She turns her head, and I notice that her left eye is newly swollen, on its way to black and purple. Grey doesn't like being left in the dark. Wonder what *he* looks like.

The count leans across me to shake Kasim's hand. "So sorry, *mon ami,* for your loss. You understand. Couldn't be helped. So unfortunate. I know you cared for your alpha friend, like a little brother." The count's condolences drip with insincerity. What chills me most, though, is the glance at me he calculates when he mentions "little brother." Does he know about Amber?

Kasim's calloused shrug fools the count, but not me. I'm good at reading people, and the count doesn't even bother to skim Kasim's face. He just assumes everyone agrees with him. "You're just in time." Margot turns to leave, but he stops her, "No stay, Général." He grabs her hand. The look that flies from her eyes at his touch would melt steel, but his heart must be made of something harder. For the first time, he actually sees her and notices the swelling around her eye. "*Mais, chérie, qu'est-ce qui s'est passé?*"

Embarrassment plays across her face as she explains. "The other prisoner is 'difficult.' He insisted I bring him to *her*." I believe she's hoping to undermine the count's obvious interest in me. What she's really done, is put Grey in danger, made him a rival predator for the same prey.

The count crosses his arms and taps a finger on his chin. "This will not do. Not at all. You are aware, no doubt, Evelyn, that we do not heal. Nature's immutable rule: she creates nothing without flaws."

"Not even the super race."

"This is true. Not even the super race." He brushes a finger lightly across my first face gash of the apocalypse, courtesy of my scuffle with Eugène. "We must be vigilant. Kasim—" he pauses and turns to explain, "Kasim is my prime minister, Evelyn. I value his advice." Kasim nods, but there's something veiled in his eye that the count doesn't notice. He might not be the fanatically blinded servant that Margot is. "Kasim, you met this prisoner. What would you suggest we do with him?"

Kasim doesn't even blink before he responds. "Highly valuable asset with impressive combat skills. Tactics and Assault Team."

Margot snorts. "Over my dead body."

"Don't let him hear that," Kasim drawls.

"You see, Evelyn—may I call you Ève? It seems somehow more appropriate in our new world."

My gut turns at the insinuation that he intends to use me to spawn his viral super race, but I smile obligingly.

"Effective government depends upon healthy dialogue. What are your objections, Margot? Kasim has presented a very compelling argument for his point of view."

"He's volatile and emotional. He acts without thinking. We won't be able to rely on him."

"And you, Ève, you know him quite well. What would you suggest we do with him?"

What to do with Greyson? That is the question that plagues me 24/7. Only now, it seems I'm no longer in the driver's seat of that car. How appropriate. Greyson did always prefer to drive—and our roads have diverged. The best thing for me to do right now is to figure out what the count wants to hear. My gut tells me he doesn't want to hear me lobby to get Grey and me assigned together.

"I'm afraid I have to agree with Margot. Greyson and I had a falling out because he's stubborn and unpredictable." And that's why I'm hooked on him. "Greyson is a loose cannon waiting to blow. Give him a gun and ammo at your own risk. He does what he wants, and he doesn't always think of the consequences."

"A quick-thinking soldier with initiative and courage, then. I understand he, too, has proved himself quite the hero of the *non infectés*—especially the children."

I'm not sure that's what I said. Even worse, I wonder how the count could possibly know so much about Greyson. Again, the fear that the count might know about Amber snakes down my spine. My head shifts just enough to interrogate Kasim with a squint. He responds with a shrug. Did I tell Kasim about Amber? I don't think Amber came into our conversation about Nicolas and the cure.

"I believe I agree with Kasim's assessment. Let's outfit him, Général."

Margot sneers and turns on her heel, resentful, but always loyal.

"But wait! I have a small announcement I would like you to hear as well, *chérie*." He squeezes her hand and then releases it with that creamy smile of his. Margot's unrequited love is not unintentional. He nurtures it. "I'm about to make our new American ally an offer she can't refuse." He means that literally—in a threatening sort of way. "Kasim, *premier ministre,* et Margot, *ministre de l'armée*, may I present our new ministre des non infectés—"

I've just been offered a position in the count's new government: minister of the uninfected.

Apparently, it's not an honor.

Kasim looks mortified, like the count has just insulted me. Margot's face contorts to hide the grin.

But the count isn't finished, "—*et des affaires étrangères.* The double entendre of the word "affaires" in English and French makes my skin crawl.

Kasim's left eyebrow arches a fraction of an inch. Margot's whole face tightens up.

"*Calme-toi, Margot.*" He hands her his joint. "*Tu ne fumes pas assez, chérie, tu sais?*"

She takes the roach, but doesn't smoke it. She's the ashtray.

Nodding, as if he's just come to a decision, the count stands. The seat cushion, released, folds back in with a quiet creek and a puff of stuffed cushions knocking.

"I have a diplomatic mission in mind for you and Kasim and, of course, our two new American allies."

Chapter 15

When I exit the cinema with Kasim, I'm no longer a prisoner under guard, I'm now a minister of the New Order. Funny, I feel a little more trapped than I did in the basement. Instead of ushering me back to the cot with Greyson, Kasim leads me out the underground stairway to the front grounds. To our right, stands a blush-red building, probably servants' quarters or the carriage house. But it's been refurbished. They could be using it for anything.

Kasim walks me up the steps of the chateau to the ornate double doors.

"No more servants' entrance for us?"

He shrugs. "The count reigns over about 100 greys. The general dormitories are in that building." He points to the carriage house and throws the door open for me. "Ministers of the realm and chief officers sleep here. Many of the greys live in the small neighborhoods surrounding the *Parc de la Buzine*." The chateau entry takes my breath away. I've seen pictures of Versailles and some of the chateaux of the Loire, but this is my first, in the flesh, tour of a restored chateau in all its Empire glory. Gold accents glitter off the moldings and furniture. Olympic gods hover in pastel blues and greens on the walls and ceilings. To my right and left, open doorways allow a glimpse into sumptuously furnished sitting rooms and maybe a dark, wood-paneled library.

My steps slow so that my eyes can take it all in. The attraction of living in a place like this floats in silky spider tendrils about my skin, sticking in places. This life is what the count is proposing for the greys. So tempting—the wealth, the power, the charm of aristocracy. But who pays? Heaven and hell must have a symbiotic relationship. For one faithful man to go to heaven, seven virgins have to go to hell. Who would do the work that makes this life possible? Uninfected children? Amber?

Briefly my thoughts fiddle with the idea that Amber might be better off grey like me. She'd be strong, fast, lethal even. She could be one of the elite. But even as I think it, the human side of me revolts, repulsed at the image of the count's society. Not all greys will resist the urges. Not all greys will be benevolent masters. There will be atrocities, massacres and abuses of innocents. And where will that lead? To this new, evolutionary government executing the ZVs and the weak among the grey, the way Margot shot Catherine with a sneer and not a second thought?

And the *non infectés*? The uninfected. Oppression demands violence. It can only end in war, slavery, or the extermination of humans as they are. The images sober me up, and the seconds of drunken lust for the life of leisure and elegance on the curbed back of humanity dissolve. The virus is no evolutionary jump forward. It's an illness like the plague. The survival of the human species depends on our ability to fight it.

Kasim notes my openmouthed awe before the reality that created this illusion melts it from my face. He ushers me about the rooms, each one furnished more luxuriously than the last, but never to the point of gaudiness. Everything here is amazingly tasteful. "It didn't take long for the rich to evacuate the infected zone. The count takes what he wants in the confines of his realm."

"I noticed." We both know I'm not just talking about the elegant furnishings. I'm talking about Eugène. Kasim's shoulders stiffen and his eyes tighten. As much of a little prick as I thought the kid was, I think he meant something to Kasim. "I'm sorry about your friend."

Kasim glances around before allowing himself a brief, whispered moment of mourning and consolation. "He was more than a friend. He was my little brother." To cover the grief that flashes across his face, he lights up another joint.

"I'm so sorry—I didn't realize—" Understandably because Kasim is obviously Middle Eastern, and Eugène definitely was not. "When you called him 'brother,' it sounded, you know, like a religious thing."

"My mother was French. She married into a very wealthy oil family in Qatar. When she divorced my father, she brought me to France with her where she married Eugène's father."

He points down a hallway. "That leads to the back entrance and the front parking. We use the cars mostly for patrolling the neighborhood borders, but you can take them when you need."

Good to know, but I don't want to lose the thread of his pain. He can't just hold it in like that. What I want to say can only make his loss more tragic, but my blood is boiling with indignation, and I can't reign in the words because he has to know the extent of the crime that the count has committed in betraying his trust. "Eugène didn't have to die, Kasim. Nicolas was so close to the cure before he left."

He shakes his head, obviously grateful that someone even noticed, but not as immune to the count's propaganda as I hoped—at least he doesn't want to give the impression that he is. "We're not looking for a cure, Evelyn. The world is changing, and great change requires great sacrifice. In the New Order of Grey, there is no room for alphas." He hands me the reefer like it's the cure for all social injustice.

I push his hand away. "No! I don't want to relax and just accept what's going on."

He opens the door to a lovely, wood-paneled library—a haven for sitting and immersing in words, a place to forget the apocalypse. The volumes, floor to ceiling, call to me. The door clicks behind us.

Kasim joins me in front of the shelves and offers me the joint again. "Take it, Evelyn. You don't know—"

"I do know. I've been fighting the urges for longer than you have. I don't want to get weak or lose my edge in a fight. I can handle it." My bravado is mostly wishful thinking. I know damn well I wake up every morning next to Amber with a gasp and a sigh of relief that the virus didn't take over in the night. I've seen so many kids my age, their hands and faces smeared with blood, sobbing in the road over the mutilated bodies of their loved ones. We don't know enough about the greys and the virus to be sure that won't be me one day.

Kasim grabs my arm. The violence of it shocks me. "Take it."

"No!"

"Look!" He uses the cigarette to make his point. "I told you my *compagne* didn't survive. You want to know why? Because I had to kill her! That's why. I had to strangle the woman I loved with my bare hands because we were foolish enough to believe we could master the virus. I murdered her—and for what?"

For a second, I can't breathe. He's lived my worst nightmare. "God, Kasim, I'm so sorry."

Shaking his head, he falls into the chair behind him. This might be the first time he's told anyone about this. He's pale, even for a grey. He covers his face with his hands, like retelling the memories resurrected them, and now they haunt him. After a minute of silence, he inhales deeply from the joint and then blows the smoke away, but the pain doesn't float off with it. "We thought we were strong, too. Everyone else gave in, but not us, we resisted the urges. We assumed we were special because we weren't bitten, we just caught the virus."

I sit in the chair next to his and drop my hand on his knee. "That's what happened to me and my boyfriend. It's because you were in love. The chemicals of love incubate the Z-Virus. Horrifying, isn't it? Bridger and I both became ZVs, wandering the streets, shunned by our families. The hunger took him and he deteriorated fast. But we greys, Kasim, we're not like that. We can choose. We're stronger, we can—"

"No. We can't. It happened in the middle of the night. Mirabelle was restless and growling in her sleep. I thought it was a nightmare. She calmed down for a bit, and I dozed off— until I heard Eugène screaming down the hall."

"Oh, Kasim—"

"She wasn't even herself. She'd bitten him before I could stop her. She was going to kill him. I swear, she was. I had no choice—It was like she was dreaming and couldn't wake up. The virus wormed into her subconscious—"

"We're all different, you—"

"You just can't understand until you live it. What Eugène became, all the people he murdered, that's on me because I was arrogant enough to think we were stronger than the urges."

The door opens up and a few greys, two girls and a really tall guy, saunter in. "Hey, Kasim! Well done with the raid. We didn't lose a single grey."

Wiping his brow, Kasim stands with a plastered smile that erases the sorrow hanging in the air. "Thank you, Joëlle."

I take the cigarette from his fingers and inhale. He flashes me a brief smile of gratitude.

It's hard to be sure, but I think I recognize Joëlle from the raid on *Notre Dame de la Garde*. She was the child catcher holding David. She kisses Kasim on both cheeks. In her yoga pants and little brunette pixie cut, it's hard to imagine her in assault gear. I actually kind of like her. She's exactly what I think of when someone says "French girl." Maybe because I've watched a ton of Audrey Tautou movies. "That alpha of yours was sure a mean bastard."

"Yes, they can be quite aggressive." Kasim blanches at the slur on his brother, but the emotion gets swallowed up in the rounds of kissing. He turns to me and makes the introductions, so I'm back in French mode.

The taller of the two girls, Chantal, wears a sneer that looks permanently molded into her face as if she's determined to measure everything and everyone and find them lacking. She's another Northerner, maybe a sort of Scandinavian hybrid. Her style tends more towards the military, except for the deep, red lipstick she wears. Maybe the film I just watched with the count is stuck in my head, but she reminds me of the actress that played Shosanna. Her blond hair cascades in long tresses around her face.

"*Ah, l'Américaine.* We've already heard quite a bit about you. Kasim is quite impressed with your skills." She smirks. One eyebrow arches as she glances at Kasim. She shakes my hand, holds it in a grip that's meant to intimidate. "I hope you'll join us for training tomorrow morning." What she really means is that she can't wait to get the chance to kick my butt.

"Chantal is our tactical officer. She used to be RAID." Now I know where they got the outfits. Kasim nods at the boyfriend. "Gabriel is our weapons chief."

Gabriel IS a weapon. I'm not sure even Clément matches his mass. He towers head and shoulders above me. His tank top and shorts in the middle of winter display his bulk. One of his arms pretty neatly equals my thigh. A nasty purplish gash snarls from his left shoulder, but the cut is precise and not very deep like it was intentional. His inner core is obviously rock hard, not soft and chewy like Clément's. He wears a baseball cap backward over a tangle of brunette curls. His eyes, small stones marbled in purple streaks, assess and then dismiss me. The mouth, set in the stubble of an extended goatee, relaxes in a frown. He sees the world in threat and non-threat. If he weren't grey himself, he'd be a basher. I can practically see the baseball bat in his hand. And the count thinks people like Chantal and Gabriel will make the ideal benevolent overlords? My ass!

Both Chantal and Gabriel have taken one look at the blond American with sexy hair, well, not so much now—I need a shower and a blow-dry in a bad way—and underestimated me. They aren't the first. Very few people understand the training of dodging bashers and fending for myself for over a year—not to mention life on the road with Grey or a short training tour on Lieutenant Samson's helicopter carrier. So much the better. I've learned to capitalize on faulty assumptions.

Kasim makes the formal announcement. "Evelyn is our new minister of the uninfected—"

From the looks that skitter across their faces, he might as well have announced I'm the new queen of sewage. Chantal grimaces, clearly disgusted by the idea. "Somebody's got to do it." It's happened already; the *non infectés* have become untouchables.

"—and foreign affairs," Kasim finishes, ignoring her.

"Of course, she is. She's the only foreigner." Gabriel doesn't even try to hide the smirk when the double entendre penetrates his thick skull at a slight delay. "And she seems well equipped to handle the count's international *affairs*." Apparently, the count's proclivities are common knowledge.

Kasim very diplomatically changes the subject. No wonder he's prime minister. "Actually, Evelyn is not the only foreigner. Her—" he glances at me, searching for the right word to define my relationship with Grey—good luck with that! "—fellow American Greyson will also be joining us on the combat team."

Chantal and Gabriel frown, but Joëlle grins suspiciously. "The crew-cut blond from the raid on the basilica? Oh, I liked him." She meets general disapproving frowns from her associates, who are philosophically opposed to outsiders. I'm embarrassed to admit, I start to rethink my original affinity for her warm, bubbly personality and begin to wonder if she's the sort of girl Greyson would find attractive. God! I have serious baggage.

Under siege, Joëlle walks back her original outburst, "Well, he was funny, you know—and practical."

No argument there. Grey is nothing if not practical.

"I guess we'll see what kind of an asset he'll be to the team at training tomorrow." Gabriel pats Kasim on the back. The friendly admiration in the gesture surprises me. Is it Kasim's willingness to sacrifice his own brother that Gabriel admires, or is there something more to Kasim that I haven't seen yet? The trio skips up the steps, warbling about their exploits in the basilica skirmish.

Kasim chuckles indulgently, shakes his head, and shrugs the way I used to when Josh and Jeremy embarrassed me in front of my friends. The way I do now when Amber is too cute to scold. And then it hits me, the tug of family, of solidarity, of having a place where I fit in, where I'm not a pariah. It almost makes me want to ignore all my ethical misgivings and blend in—almost.

My step follows Kasim's up the grand winding staircase. "The count resides on the first floor. The ministers have rooms on the second and third floors." We've reached the landing at the top where two enormous carved white doors dominate the view of the staircase and the entry. Obviously, the count's apartments.

The landing hallway leads to a smaller side staircase that we take to the top floors. From beneath one of the doors we pass, I can hear the mocking laugh of Chantal and Gabriel. Is it egocentric to think they must be laughing at me? I need to get a grip.

The odor of grey is heavy up here. At least I'm used to it. In the New World Order, this will be normal. A calming green *fleur-de-lis* pattern carpet muffles our footsteps. "I'm sorry, but our new government has grown quickly. The only spaces available are the rooms up here. They're quite comfortable, but double occupancy with rather standard furnishings. I hope you won't mind sharing with your, uh, friend, Greyson? The only other American—you know—more comfortable for both of you."

Comfortable? Hah! Mind? At the Knight compound, they put us up in male and female dorms on opposite ends of the square. I'd have jumped at the chance to share with Grey. Now it's going to be awkward. What can I do? I have to keep my mind on the main goal: find out where they've stashed Laure and David and get them back to their family.

Kasim throws the door open on a room that looks like something out of a bed and breakfast brochure. What Kasim calls standard, I call the Ritz Carlton—then again, I spent the last year living in a basement polygamist hide. Light floods into the space from open windows that look out over the back gardens. Sheer white curtains billow in the breeze.

"The bathrooms here are communal. But it's just down the hall. You should find everything you need to settle in and clean up for dinner. The dining room is on the main level. There's a bathrobe in the closet. If you leave your clothes outside the door, Rémy, our minister of the interior, will find you something suitable for dinner and training tomorrow. He's quite good at handling all the day to day concierge details."

How did this place get so organized so fast? It's almost as if the count knew what was coming and had already put a plan in motion.

When Kasim steps out with a promise to see me at dinner, everything else takes a backseat to the prospect of a shower. Wrapping up in a plush white bathrobe that could only have come from a very high-end hotel, I drop my clothes at the door to wait for the fairy wardrobe service and pad off to the *salle de bains*. The nozzle on the end of a hose and the washcloth that's actually more of a terry oven mitt strike me as a bit odd at first, but after a couple minutes, I get the appeal. Practical. In true American form, my shower runs on way too long, but God! It's heaven.

This Rémy character lives up to his reputation. Everything a girl could possibly want adorns the marble counters. From the brushes in sanitizing solution, I select the softest and start the daunting, tedious task of brushing out my hair without pulling out a strand. The mirror reflects the casualties from my scuffles with Eugène and the *boches*. Besides the small, purplish gash across my cheekbone, close to my ear, another laceration blemishes my throat. What I wouldn't give for a little of Nicolas's magic potion right now. At least, there's a new toothbrush with my name on it.

When I get back to my room, a little stack of neatly folded clothes waits for me outside in the place of the filthy camos I dumped there. I scoop it up and open the door.

Greyson, barefoot, hands in his pockets, turns to face me.

Chapter 16

The wall of windows behind Greyson drenches his black silhouette in an aura of blinding, golden sunlight. A sweep of his hand highlights the luxury accommodations—marble mantle on the fireplace, Second Empire furniture, the kind my mother wouldn't let me sit on—if I still had a mother. Only one bed, but it's a peach—four-poster, with a flowing, white embroidered comforter that matches the billowing, sheer curtains hanging on the walls and tied up around the posts. "Nice upgrade. You must have earned platinum points with management."

My eyes roll. "It's not like that."

He crosses his arms—not sure if its belligerently or if he's protecting his heart from the gorgon that broke it. "The hell it's not. Soldier girl hauls you off to parley with the count and suddenly we're getting the VIP treatment. What did he want from you?"

"Probably access to my contacts on the ship in the clean zone—and to be the benevolent overlord of the sub-humans in his grey supremacist society."

Grey crosses his arms and turns his back to me, staring out at the garden. Beyond the backyard forest, square plots checker the landscape framed in the windows up to the horizon. "Super race, huh? That's a step down from angels and gods."

"My charm isn't quite as convincing as yours." I lay the little black dress out on the bed. It's been ages since I wore a dress and heels, but I can't quite embrace the novelty because the ties between Grey and me have shrunk and torn.

"I doubt that."

"I have a sharp tongue; it cuts deep."

He doesn't contradict me. "So now what?"

"So now, you drop your clothes in the hallway and take a shower. Dinner attire will show up magically outside the door when you're done—maybe they have shoes your size." I dangle the strappy kitten heels that came with my little black dress. Very French. Rémy has impeccable taste.

Greyson opens his mouth, but I let my eyes wander to the ceiling, to the chandelier, anywhere there might be a bug or a camera. "This place is a safe haven for the uninfected. They'll take good care of our friends Laure and David." Greyson catches my drift.

"Yes, ma'am." He pulls off his shirt and saunters to the door undoing his fly. God! No, seriously, he was meant to be one. He doesn't even look at me as his bare shoulder brushes past mine. I can't stop myself. My fingers hunger for the touch of his flesh the way the virus craves human organs. My hand latches onto his wrist. He stops, just behind me—the intellectual sentimentalist back to back with the cunning pragmatist. The attraction of opposites binds us.

My eyes close because if he walks away from me again, I think my heart will implode. I turn my head over my shoulder. Our eyes meet. He's seen this look before, usually behind my tears when he's slipping away from me. The silent words in my eyes are a promise that I have trouble keeping.

He turns away, eyes closed, and shakes his head, slowly detaching my hand. With each finger he unlatches, a corner of the iceberg that is my heart cracks, slides, and crumbles into my ocean of grief.

A tear slips down my cheek. My pinkie comes loose. But he doesn't let it go. Instead, he turns and tugs me around to face him. I can't look in his eyes for very long. The debate going on behind them forces mine to the floor. He brushes a finger across the gash on my cheek and my eyes flutter up again. His hand fumbles in the pocket of his combat cargos and brings up a vial that I recognize. Squeezing a small drop on his thumb, he smears it across the open cut on my face. A second drop he caresses across my neck and smooths the residue onto the cement burns on my shoulder. My breath catches. Even half-dead, my skin still surges at Grey's touch.

"Nicky boy gave me two. I saved one for you." He rubs his chin, glancing appreciatively at the little oval mirror near the door. "The stubble beard and crop cut are growing on me. Look rugged." He ruffles his hair and then takes my chin between two fingers and swivels my head from side to side. "You're in pretty good shape, considering." His face changes. The Grey I only see when I need him, won't survive without him, surfaces. "A face like this needs to be preserved through the war—like the Mona Lisa. I didn't think the good doctor would last long enough to make you another batch." He holds the bottle out for me to take. He's really offering me a grail from the fountain of eternal youth. Any grey would kill—literally—to get their hands on this stuff. He passes it to me like it's a stick of gum at a funeral.

Of course, I close my fist around it. But I also throw my arms around his neck and plaster my lips to his. His mouth on mine devours my insides. There's nothing left except this craving for more. I'm only wearing the fuzzy white bathrobe, and his hands slip through the folds and wrap me up in his embrace. His arms around my waist and his palms on my back steady me like I've been floating aimlessly on the tide, and someone just dropped me an anchor. Two turns of a feral waltz and my back bumps against the wall.

Grey closes his eyes and steels himself. He unlatches his arms and raises them in surrender, taking a step back. He doesn't trust himself. What grey does? This kind of rampant passion excites more than the hormones, it revs up the virus. His chest heaves under smoldering eyes. Is this what I want?

Hell, yes! I've been regretting this lost moment ever since he disappeared in a cloud of smoke and ash. We could both die tomorrow—or worse. Grasping my robe by the collar, I push it off my shoulders. Freed, it puddles to the ground around my feet.

Grey doesn't move for seconds. His eyes absorb the curves of my breasts and my hips. With his hands, he worships my form, like I'm the marble statue of a Greek goddess. His fingertips graze my nipples as he drops to his knees in front of me, hands sliding down to my waist. Palms on the small of my back, his lips brush past my navel. My head falls back in the sheer ecstasy of the sensation. The tip of his tongue leaves a moist trail up my torso as he stands to kiss my breasts. Wanting builds in my chest, and I drape my arms around him, locking him in a kiss deep enough to latch our souls together. His fingers fumble to undo his half-open fly.

And then an obnoxious rapping at the door rifles through the moment.

"Fuck!" I gasp.

"Too late for that." Greyson backs off, sucking up the rush.

"No!" I hiss, scrambling to pull the bathrobe back around me. "There's probably cameras and microphones."

"So, the count likes to watch."

"Minister Cross!" The voice is Margot's. "His Excellency the count would like you and your American compatriot to join us in the dining room in ten minutes. Please be punctual."

"Minister?" He drops his camo pants in front of the door and swings it open wide. "Who'd you have to sleep with to get that title?" I still don't have enough breath for a perky response. Margot can't help but stare, which is what he wanted, but he doesn't really care. Greyson's last words are for me. "Ten minutes, huh? Good thing I don't need a blow-dry."

Margot watches him stroll down the hall, mouth open. The tip of her tongue touches her upper lip. The color Grey's fist painted around her eye won't heal, but it suits the diamond piercings and red butch cut she wears.

I pat her shoulder. "He's all yours, Minister." I need to make sure the count thinks I'm on board. I suspect his own narcissism assumes we'll jump at the chance to star in his production of *The New World Order*. Greyson's already started to play his role. Typecasting.

Chapter 17

Dinner for greys. The dining room sparkles with gold-tipped china and crystal stemware. Pretty sure the utensils are real silver—old too. The wealth of the infected zone is an open safe for the count's picking. A huge wall of windows looks out on a veranda and garden behind the chateau. From the *rez-de-chaussée*, the forest blurs the horizon.

The count sits at the head of the table in a well-tailored suit with Kasim on his right and Margot on his left. The general is stunning in a black cocktail dress that plunges almost to her navel and flaunts all the well-toned curves that her RAID suit strategically conceals. The room looks more like a black and white version of a Cannes Festival Halloween feast than the feeding frenzy of rabid predators. Evidently, Rémy only raids the high-end shops.

Greyson cleans up well in ten minutes. He doesn't speak any French, so the count has everyone shift to move *l'Américain* from the seat to Joëlle's right, at the end of the table, next to me halfway down, so I can translate. Joëlle is visibly put out, but the arrangement lets me get away with quiet side conversations in English while the dinner guests recount the day's raid on the basilica. The table holds about 20 of the count's ministers and chiefs.

It's hard to sit next to Grey after what just happened and focus on the pressing target, but I suck up the residual passion and fill him in. I need him—I always need him. "We have to blend in, gather insider information, whatever it takes to find Laure and David." I nod down the table. Joëlle mistakes the gesture for an introduction, smiles coquettishly, and winks at

Greyson. "Find a target and work your magic. Joëlle is already smitten." I nod up the table. "Margot's in love with the count, but your casual display earlier didn't fail to impress. Long shot, but high-value target—close to the top."

"Really? That's what you want? Cozy up to the lunatics running the circus? Last time I did that, you got your panties all in a wad."

"Look, I'm sorry. But this is different. We're not just holing up here for a bit. There is no government out there waiting to haul us into their chop shops."

"Not that different from where I'm sitting."

Margot eyes us suspiciously. I put on my most gracious debutant smile and gesture towards Gabriel and Chantal like I'm making the introductions.

"The count sees himself as the leader of the New Order." My voice chitters away the deadly serious note of my words.

The guy to my left, chunky glasses and a whopper of a nose, is clueless. And I'm not just talking fashion sense here. He smiles, points to himself and enunciates, "Stéphane, Sté-phane. No speak English. Engineer. *Électricité, énergie solaire.*"

"*Enchantée. Je m'appelle Evelyn. Je te présente Greyson. Il ne parle pas Français.*"

"*Dommage.*" Sighing, he turns and picks a conversation with the girl on his left who speaks his language but is much more interested in chatting with the Ivoirian sitting on her other side—minister of agriculture.

"The count has deluded himself into thinking the virus is trying to cleanse the earth and restore its natural order—super race protecting and governing the weak. They don't herd the uninfected for food storage, they round them up as subjects and serfs to serve their utopia of the deluded."

A tonality of silver on crystal brings all our attention to the count. I translate softly for Greyson.

"Before dinner is served, I would like to congratulate Margot, our minister of the army, on the outstanding success of today's maneuvers." Glasses clink around the table. "Of course, we must not overlook the critical contributions of our chief tactical officer and chief of weapons." Margot raises a glass to Chantal and Gabriel. "All objectives were achieved. We have now eliminated the most prolific of the alphas." The members of the group nod and congratulate each other as the butler's door swings open. Kasim keeps a thin smile and tight control over his features as his colleagues celebrate his half brother's death.

Dressed from head to toe in white, a few uninfected slip into the room laden with shining silver platters of delicately displayed animal guts. Not one of them is older than fifteen. The count's next words, and the smothered giggles that follow, are lost on me when I lock eyes with one of the serving girls.

"—Ève Cross, our newly appointed minister of foreign affairs and the uninfected."

Laure carries a plate of giblets and takes her place in the small line behind the count's chair as the guests erupt in a round of applause. Greyson kicks me under the table, and I close my mouth. The count's last words finally register a response—a smile and a lift of my glass to His Excellency.

The line of house servants behind the count begins making their way around the table distributing paper-thin slices of cow guts with elegant silver forks. I nudge Greyson and follow Laure with my eyes.

Another uninfected girl—her nametag identifies her as Martine—leans over my shoulder and pours me some type of blood wine. The mixture of alcohol and salt twitches my nose. Gentle beads of sweat smear the girl's forehead. Her hand shakes, and the decanter clinks melodiously against the glass. She has a nice *herbes de Provence* aroma that gets the juices rumbling in my stomach. If she weren't so scrawny, she'd make a lovely picnic. As it is, she's more of an *hors d'oeuvre*. No wonder her hands tremble. Any lamb serving the lions a salad would be a quaking mess.

Greyson tries the wine and shrugs. Martine moves on. I tip the glass to my lips. Never really was a party girl. Smells like hairspray, but the tang of iron and salt tempts me. A drop stains my tongue, and my whole face grimaces. Grey laughs.

Laure reaches my shoulder. I have to say I'm starving. It's been an eventful day, and I had an early start. The couple of bites I grabbed from the hotel kitchen, I smeared onto the floor of the cement cell. Laure's eyes bore into mine as she holds the tray while Grey and I serve ourselves.

"Excuse me," I glance at her nametag, "Laure." My hands give the impression of inquiring about the ingredients to camouflage my real agenda. "Could you tell me if your brother is also working in the kitchen?" Laure stares at me as if I'm mad, but shakes her head. I skewer a dainty lump of liver onto my plate. "If I wanted to speak with him, where—"

"*Ève, ma chérie.*" The count leans across the table, a polite reprimand in his voice, "It is not at all acceptable for the servants to address one of their superiors directly. Of course, we must make allowances for the minister of uninfected." He grins to the table. "Our American cousins, from the other end of the pond, have a much more vulgar, democratic perspective but, in the New Order of Grey, it is essential that the uninfected respect and honor the benevolent protectors of their race." The guests twitter indulgently at my inappropriate behavior. "We mustn't allow them to take liberties."

"Many apologies, Your Excellency. I was inquiring about the ingredients. I have an allergy to, uh, garlic."

Her hands shaking maniacally, Martine leans between Margot and the count to fill his glass, just as he leans back in his seat. "Ah, I see. Very unfortunate."

Martine's hand collides with the count's shoulder, and the crimson cocktail splashes across his beige, silk sleeve.

The count jumps up angry as sin. "*Imbécile!*" His chair clatters over, and he backhands the girl across the cheek. She crumples to the floor, cowering and whimpering. Now we see the true colors of the count.

Beneath the table cloth, Grey's hand falls on my leg, restraining me. Damn, I'm predictable. He's playing his part and warning me to play mine. The count has to think we're sipping the poison Kool-Aid.

Most of the words that spew from His Excellency's lips, I've never heard before. Anger disfigures his well-chiseled features into the mask of a gorgon. My dad was this angry once when Cory took his BMW for a little romp and came home with a dent in the bumper. Only my dad didn't have a woman with a

Glock 17 strapped to her leg beneath her cocktail dress—and my dad loved Cory.

Beneath the cracked façade, the count's vengeful disdain for this sub-race he's created seeps out. In the time it takes him to lean over Margot and pull the gun from her thigh, the instincts to protect my little sister flare into an irrational compulsion to save this girl I hardly know. I just can't stop myself. I can't let him shoot her in cold blood. All the logic and reason behind my little charade melt to dust before the life and death of an innocent. My chair skids against the marble tiles, and I sprint for the girl huddled on the floor. Greyson tries to stop me, but he's not fast enough—he never was. I've thrown my body over the top of Martine by the time the safety snaps off and the count whirls to shoot the brains out of the kid that soiled the emperor's new coat.

The whole table gasps at my interference. Margot jumps up to drag me off but finds out pretty quickly that I'm not the prim blonde I appear—even in strappy heels and a little black dress. A sharp elbow to her gut sends her crashing against the wall. From down at the end of the table, Gabriel and Chantal object loudly. Their chairs scrape across the floor. The hulk and his girlfriend charge past Greyson, who always has my weak side. He slides his chair back. They trip over the top of him and then jump up throwing punches. All hell breaks loose at the table. Plates and silverware clatter to the floor. Food splashes the walls and the marble. The uninfected all flee the skirmish.

At the crack of a gunshot fired into the ceiling, the whole place freezes. "That's enough!" The count tugs on the edge of his coat, straightens his suit and reigns in his features. "Please take your seats, Ministers of the New Order." Margot and Chantal pick themselves off the floor. Everyone returns to their seat but Grey and Gabriel.

The mask of humanity has slipped from Gabriel's face. Murder and hatred distorting his features, the monster within glares at Grey, who—cool as ever, focused, and crazy sure of himself—only blinks at the combat knife Gabriel rips from the inside pocket of his suit. Gabriel's a weight class bigger than Grey. He definitely joined up with the count for the sanctioned bullying and violence. Oh, shit. Grey's about to pay the bill for my impulse move—again.

My nerves shouldn't flutter, but they do. Grey hasn't had to take on many of his own kind. Fully armed ZV soldiers are one thing, trained fighter greys are a whole other breed. The smell of battle invades the room. The other diners lean forward in their seats, hoping for a show to tingle the virus in their veins, like a stiff shot of meth. They've clearly seen their weapon's chief in action.

Gabriel has no idea who he's up against and lunges. A slash at Grey's abdomen, the signature move of feral greys looking to score some organs off the uninfected, begins the challenge. Gabriel is a professional, but Grey has had over a year of experience fending off bashers, SNCHRs and FBI agents. He dodges back and sneers. "Is that all you got, big boy?"

Gabriel doesn't understand English, but he gets the tone. He's clearly surprised. The spectators all titter. Humiliated in front of his fans, anger drives Gabriel's next assault—a straight stab at the heart. Grey reads him like a super predictable comic strip. He jumps sideways, grabs his wrist, and, while I'm blinking, bends the guy over with the knife hand behind his back. A good jerk and the blade clatters to the floor.

The count begins to clap, slowly, methodically. The others at the table follow suit. "Well done, M. Greyson. We appreciate the demonstration and your loyalty, although dinner is hardly the time for such an exhibition." He glances pointedly at Gabriel. "There will be ample opportunity for such instructional exposition during training tomorrow morning."

Grey lets go and bows, picking up the knife. "Play nice." He shoves the hilt at Gabriel's chest and strolls to his chair. He doesn't see the big man's face, but I do. If Grey's not concerned, he should be. We'll be locking our door tonight. There's not just cold-blooded murder in Gabriel's eyes, there's sick, perverted torture oozing from them as he slinks back to his place at the bottom of the table. Chantal sneers her disdain for his loss, and he glares belligerently.

So now everyone is back in their seat except me. Pretty sure I'm about to get my eviction notice. My eyes glued to the count's face, I raise myself off Martine, careful to keep my body between him and her. The count is a loose cannon in a self-imposed straight jacket. If he undoes the laces, the demon explodes.

His eyes narrow, but he relinquishes the gun to Margot. She tucks it under her dress. At a nod from her, Rémy exits to restore order in the kitchen. The count clears his voice and then turns politely to me, his face strained with the effort of self-control. "We must all thank our new minister of the uninfected for zealously performing her duties. Of course, at the birth of our new order, we must strive to establish the rule of law. *Mlle Ministre,* what counsel would you offer the New Order concerning the regulation of the conduct of the uninfected?"

Reprieve. Could I possibly just thank the demon gods and say what he wants to hear? No! I'm too much of an altruistic fool! At least I'm a woman and grew up practicing self-deprecation. Might be the only thing that saves my hide. "Well, *M. le Comte,* I'm an American, with my 'vulgar, democratic' ways, so I want to say we should all be equal." After my little *tête à tête* with him, I'm pretty sure those views won't get me the favor I need to get Laure and David back to their family, alive and uninfected. But I can't forget the old French proverb, "*Qui ne dit rien, consent.*" If I say nothing, then I consent to this madness. "But I believe that the stability of the New Order will require proper education rather than violence. As they say, 'violence breeds violence.' The uninfected should be properly trained before receiving the *honor* of serving among their grey benefactors." Load of shit but better than the alternative. Martine, still huddled on the floor, vomits.

"I see. Yes. Education. My own view exactly. Very well said." The count turns to Greyson. "*Et toi, M. Greyson*?"

Grey nods. My stomach lurches. He's as unpredictable as the count.

"Me?"

"But, of course. We would like to know your opinion on the treatment of the uninfected." The count's English trips ever so slightly.

"Personally, I think you should shoot the kid's brains out. Make an example of her. She's scrawny and scared. Won't survive the revolution anyway, so put her out of her misery. You'd be doing her a favor."

The count doesn't need a translation. An eyebrow raised, his head cocks to one side as he savors the response. The corner of his lip curls up. My mouth hangs open. His Excellency turns to Margot. "Oh, I like this one."

Margot's lips purse.

The count turns to Kasim. "My friend, you were right again. This is why you are my prime minister."

Kasim nods and raises an eyebrow at me as soon as the count turns away.

The daggers in my eyes bounce off the cold steel in Greyson's.

"M. Greyson. I have need of a personal assistant. Would you be kind enough to accept this post?"

"Sure. Why the hell not? Let's get this party started." And, once again, Greyson is in the driver's seat—exactly where I told him to be.

The count smiles. "Rémy, please see to it that M. Greyson's affairs are transferred to the boudoir adjacent to my room. Margot, love, you wouldn't mind, would you, changing rooms with my new personal assistant?"

Margot blanches but nods. Clearly, she minds. Clearly, the count doesn't care.

Rémy nods and leaves. Greyson and I are no longer roommates. Was that the goal? My new bunkmate is the court executioner. When we walked into the dining room, I thought I was the one filling Greyson in and playing the count. My look ping-pongs between their faces, and I wonder if I'm the one being played.

Chapter 18

Rémy is nothing if not efficient. A carefully folded, fully equipped RAID suit appeared in a neatly folded stack at the end of the bed. I stow the standard issue knife under the pillow. Pretty sure Margot won't hesitate to slit my throat in the night—eliminate the competition. A place like this, with an absolute overlord handing out power and influence like candy, is bound to turn cutthroat.

The quiet rap on the door startles me. Can't be Greyson. After dinner, the count hustled him off to his private rooms for some 'strategizing' after dessert—that's what they called the brains brûlés.

Grabbing the knife, I crack the door. A girl can never be too cautious.

"Salut, Evelyn."

"Joëlle!"

The perky little brunette leans expectantly forward through the crack, and I have no choice but to let her in. My first thought—always my first thought—Greyson. She's here hoping to find him. She bounces into the room and looks around. Clearly, she's come to make friends. Good strategy—making friends with the target's best friend. God, I'm cynical.

"Since you are the new minister of the uninfected, and I am the chief medical officer for the uninfected, I thought we should get to know each other."

"Your English is great."

"A bit rusty, though. Nanny for some Americans in New York when I was in high school."

"You're a doctor?"

"Medical student. I was in the last year of my residency in pediatrics. Our chief medical officer was a surgeon. All he can do is try to screw back on what gets broken off. You know we don't heal, right?" She reaches a finger up to the scar near my ear. "Sorry."

I was hoping no one would notice. There's not enough of Nicolas's miracle cream to treat the whole compound. "Yeah, it's nature's required weakness in the super race. Pediatrics is a perfect choice for an uninfected medical officer, though. Most of the uninfected are children."

"Do you know why this is?" She strolls across the room to admire the view.

"The original Z-Virus only infected adolescent couples. My friend Dr. Vadlamani explained it to me. Something to do with the hormones. Kids aren't as susceptible, which is weird because, with any other virus, their immune systems aren't as developed, so they're more likely to get sick. But this virus plays with the immune system. It seems to avoid the chemical soup in kids. It kills off adults pretty quickly, but the adolescent virals last longer. They get the nasty craving for human organs. The physical and mental deterioration set in when they start serving themselves from the human buffet. I guess you know that already. Greys lose their superpowers if they give in to the urges. Happened to my friend Chase and my brother, Cory— but he wasn't grey, he was just a ZV."

"You lost your family?"

"All of it." If only she knew. I bring death wherever I go.

"*Moi, aussi*. My boyfriend Jules was a musician. He infected me."

"That's how it starts. Couples. The doctors thought it was an STD at first." I've changed my mind. Maybe Joëlle is here to get information, not laid. I'm happy to share. The more they know, the less dangerous they'll be.

"But Jules was not like me and you, you know. He was not strong, fast. He started to—"

"—fall apart? Deteriorate? The virus was eating him from the inside."

"Yes." She nods, and her gaze seems to drift somewhere far away. "It was at dinner, on the patio, the leaves were just beginning to fall, Jules attacked my family. He bit my parents before I could—stop him." She falls lightly into the chair by the desk.

What she means is that she had to kill him. "I'm so sorry." Little ties of empathy wind their way between us.

"It wasn't him. It was the virus. My parents died quickly. My brother, Fabien, he was uninfected."

"Any chance you were vegetarian?"

"Yes. How did you know? My brother and I were, but not my parents."

"That's what makes the greys. Vegetarians. Apparently, without meat, we don't have the right juices stewing in our guts. The virus mutates to compensate. So, is your brother here, at the mansion?"

She stands. I know that look. It's the cement mask I draw over my face when I think about my parents and Cory, Josh and Jeremy, and the blood smears on my kitchen floor. I can't walk in the mire and survive, so I pour stone into the muddy void. "I sent Fabien north to the clean zone—I haven't heard from him for a week. The count says alpha gangs and their *boche* armies have overrun Paris now."

"I'm so sorry." Not just for Joëlle. For all of us. Nicolas and the progress he's making on the cure are in Paris. We can only hope the "secure facility" General Samson sent him to is still secure. Greyson and I have got to get out of here and get to Paris.

She shrugs the way I do. "The count adopted me. He is trying to make us a new family."

The appeal of starting over, of having a place to belong brightens Joëlle's face. Maybe this grey family is the only place I belong, the only place where I wouldn't rain down destruction on the people I care about. Contagion seeps through her smile and nearly infects me. But Amber is my vaccine against this viral new order. It's not what I want for her. I want the cure. I need to find Nicolas. "So, the count knew eating human organs would trigger neural and physical decay? I wonder how."

"Yes. I don't know how. But to eat human meat is forbidden. The penalties are severe." Margot made that abundantly clear to Catherine in the basilica. "That is why this is the safest spot for the uninfected children."

"You hope." After tonight's display, I'm not convinced. "I've seen greys crack. It's not pretty."

"But this is why the count was very pleased when Kasim showed him the effects of marijuana on the urges. Smoking allows us to shelter the uninfected without risking their safety."

"I'll give you that. Kasim gave me some. I actually felt human for a few minutes. Downside, we got attacked by a *boche* horde. The marijuana curbed the urges, but also put a damper on my fighting instincts."

"Yes, all military are restricted in their marijuana consumption. They are also restricted in their contact with the uninfected. I am not military." She grins and whispers, "I have a large store of weed." She stands up, back to her normal bouncy self. "I am responsible for accompanying the missions to salvage any uninfected and then integrate them into our society."

This is exactly where I was hoping the conversation would turn. "So, the girl and the boy that were with me in the basilica, you saved them?"

"Actually, you saved them. The count was quite impressed with the way you fought for them. But yes, thanks to you, they are safely here with us now." Wouldn't exactly thank me for that. Can't see a scenario where the count's little social experiment ends in anything but carnage. Of course, I don't *say* that.

"I saw the girl, Laure, in the dining room. I was worried about her brother."

"Oh, he is fine. He is too old for inside service, but he has considerable experience that made him quite suited for the farm."

"We have a farm?"

"Of course! How silly you are. If we're not going to eat humans, we must raise animals and cultivate fields for the uninfected. Meat for us, grain for them."

What really makes me wonder is how the count knew all this about greys and alphas. How did he set up this new order so quickly? Something like this needs planning, time and research. The virus hasn't been in France all that long.

"What do you know about the count, Joëlle? Who was he?"

Her eyes dart about the room. Cameras and microphones. Outside, dusk has fallen. The light in here gives any passerby a perfect view of the two of us consorting. I stride over and close the curtains. Joëlle compresses her lips, and then her face lights up. "Come with me. I want to take you somewhere."

"Uh, thanks, but it's been a super long day, and we have training tomorrow. I really—"

"*Non, non.* I will not accept 'no'." She grabs the arm I'm holding behind my back to draw me into the corridor. The knife I'm concealing behind my back swings between us. Awkward silence.

"I, uh, habit."

She giggles and opens the dainty little handbag she's carrying. There's a cute little pistol in there. "It's only prudent." She lets go of my arm and saunters to the dresser. "Rémy is highly predictable." From the top drawer, she pulls a thigh holster and tosses it to me. "We are all dressed up. We should go out."

Once I've attached the knife, she drags me down the back staircase to the servants' entrance. We slip into the small parking area in front of the chateau. Next to a couple of Teslas hooked into chargers, a variety of three or four French sports and luxury models wait in a row. Joëlle reaches into the driver's seat of a sporty black Peugeot and, grinning, jangles some keys in front of my nose. At least my little girl's night out has supplied me with a valuable piece of info. They keep the keys in the car. Good to know in an emergency exit situation.

Joëlle really is adorable. I haven't had a girlfriend since the virus broke out and Greyson dumped Julie when they got infected. She wasn't grey. The SNCHRs hauled her away. Joëlle ducks into the driver's seat. Shrugging, I take the passenger side. I always did want to check out the nightlife on the *Côte d'Azur*. I just always imagined it would be a bit more animated.

Chapter 19

The streets are deserted except for abandoned cars. Joëlle zigzags in and around the debris. "We have to be careful. Eliminating the alphas has unfortunate consequences. Their *boches* wander free in hunting packs."

"You know you're not immune to the *boches*, right?"

"Yes. They're very dangerous. They move quickly." The tires rattle over gravel in the parking lot of a night club called The Philosopher.

"I'm aware. I'm from Salt Lake City, you know. Ground zero. And I was at my aunt's in Houston at the Knight compound where the first alpha was created. That's why I'm so astonished that the count knows as much as I do about the virus. It hasn't been here that long. Who is he? A scientist? A doctor?"

Joëlle arches her brows and pulls into the space right in front of the door. Funny how we keep following the lines when they don't mean anything anymore. I mean, who else is going to want to park here? Maybe it's just wishful thinking. Maybe old habits are like zombies, they just keep walking around mindlessly, even after they've lost all meaning. "That's why we came here. The count doesn't like us talking about his past. But I knew him—before the virus."

She hops out, and I follow, too intrigued to pass up the opportunity. I need to play my cards close, though. The count is the type who would plant someone bright and perky like Joëlle to make friends, earn my trust, and report back to him. It's a delicate little dance, getting the information I need without giving too much away.

"Jules and his band played here all the time. The count owns the nightclub." Her keys unlock the door.

The club is in pretty great shape, post-apocalyptically speaking. Mirrors line the walls along the dance floors; none are broken. Posters of France's great philosophers line the yellow stone walls—Descartes, Sartre, Camus, Voltaire, Montaigne—I recognize most of the names. There's an open library corner opposite the dance floor. The lights glitter off multi-colored bottles lining the wooden bar. The count has a taste for old-world luxury, and the furnishings show it. This wasn't a dive. It was high-end.

"His name is Yves Rostand. We—really, he and Jules— were classmates. I'm a couple years younger. He majored in philosophy at university and then opened this club. His parents have—had—money."

From behind the bar, she pulls out a couple glasses and a bottle and waves me over. "I'm not much of a drinker. I was too busy in high school getting straight 'A's. And then I caught the virus, so I never went to college." I pick a stool and sit.

"You'll like this. It's champagne. Yves let me bartend when I was home on holiday. He likes pretty women."

"So I noticed."

From the refrigerator, she extracts a small decanter. Crimson red drops disperse in strings through the champagne and dye it a deep rust. Grinning, she tips her glass to mine. The crystal clinks happily. "To pretty women and the men who like them. We're always in fashion—and they don't realize how smart we are."

Oh, I like her. I take a sip, not at all bitter like the wine last night. The drops of blood make me crave more. Apparently, champagne is dangerous because there's no alcohol taste. Perfect strategy for getting someone tipsy and plying out the information you want. "Mmm, this is really good." I tilt my glass to make it look like I'm drinking more than I actually am. "So, spill. What is it you know that the count—Yves—doesn't want you—or me—to know?"

She comes around the bar and sits on the stool next to mine. "I know about his cousin." My eyebrows arch before I raise the champagne flute to my lips. With a gentle touch of her fingers, she stops me. "Careful, it's stronger than it seems. There's never a good time to let your guard down."

Unexpected. "Is that why you brought me here? To tell me about him?"

"Yes, because I saw how you helped those two uninfected children. I am a doctor, Ève. I can't stand by and watch what is happening to them. But I can do nothing alone. You and the other American, I think you can help me."

Somehow, I knew this would come around to Greyson. I still can't quite shake the feeling I'm being manipulated. Maybe I'm just jaded. "Tell me how."

In the silence of her hesitation, a gentle groaning rolls through the windows on the night breeze. Joëlle glances back. "The animals have no masters now to keep them. Many are lost in the woods. We are rounding them up."

"Along with the uninfected orphans and greys."

"Yes, but the uninfected, they are not safe here."

"Glad someone else can see that." The alcohol hits my bloodstream hard. A flash of weightlessness ripples through my whole body.

"*Non*, you misunderstand. The danger does not come from the greys. The danger is from Yves's American cousin, Gavin. He is not like the rest of us."

"Wait! This Gavin, would his last name be Tanner?"

"Yes! How do you know this?"

"Gavin Tanner's girlfriend Charlene and I went to school together. His father was very influential and wealthy. When Charlene got sniffed out at school, and they showed up on Gavin's doorstep to haul him away, his father's lawyers got him released. They shipped him out of the country before the courts could overturn the rules. This must be where he landed." I push away my cocktail. "But that was over a year ago. I guess we know why the count knew so much about the virus in advance, and why it spread so quickly. How long has Yves been sick?"

"I cannot tell you this, because I only saw him at the club. It's very dim in here. But I do know that Jules and I became sick because of him. We didn't know why I got stronger but turned grey. Perhaps you are right. I was *végétarienne,* and Jules was not. He decayed slowly, and couldn't fight the urges to eat the uninfected. This is not the worst of it, though." Joëlle throws back the rest of her drink.

"You don't need to tell me. Let me guess. Gavin was grey, like you and Yves. But he was weak until Yves brought him some human meat and, *voilà*, he started getting better."

"Yes! He used to come here to read." She nods at the little corner. "But, then he just went—how do you say—crazy. Yves could not control him. He killed so many or turned them into *boches*. He controls them, you know. The ones he doesn't consume."

"God! So where is he, now?"

"He lives in the Château Régis, very close to here. Régis and Reynarde were both schools for children. Most of the uninfected are housed in Reynarde, across the forest from Buzine. It is better if they are not too far from the protection of the greys but not too close to be a temptation. They have guards."

"Overlords, you mean." The breeze outside kicks up, and I wonder if it's going to rain. The buildings creak in the deserted streets outside. The scent of the dead, a tinge of the sinister, catches my nose. I wonder how close we are to Gavin's home. My super-hearing picks up the crack of loose gravel under hooves from the parking lot. The animals are probably drawn to the light.

"I thought the count was eliminating the alphas. Why hasn't he stopped Gavin?"

"Gavin is family."

"That didn't seem to matter so much with Kasim and Eugène."

"There is also another. *L'Impressioniste.*" Her shoulders shiver. "You have heard of the artist?"

I'd rather not have that image of the lobby reignited in my brain. "Yeah, I witnessed his handiwork the day I met Kasim."

"He stays mostly in the city. The count claims he needs Gavin to hunt and confront the artist for us. He knows that his cousin must be destroyed or we won't survive. We all know it." Joëlle and I share the pain of watching loved ones die, but I've never had to kill someone myself. Nicolas shot Sam before he could kill me. "But, from things he's said, I suspect the count needs the fear of an alpha to maintain loyalty. He never plans to completely eliminate the threat."

"Otherwise, why would the helpless little uninfected need us? This is total feudal bullshit."

"No, it is worse. The girl from dinner. You remember her?"

"Martine? Of course, I do. The count was going to plaster her brains to the floor for staining his new jacket."

"Yes, but she did not come back in to serve the dessert. You noticed this?"

"I was hoping they sent her somewhere else, somewhere safer."

"They sent her somewhere else. But not somewhere safer. I saw them escort her out to a car. When the driver came back. He told me he had gone to Régis."

"Oh, my God!"

"Yes. Exactly. We have to do something, Ève. You and I and Greyson. The count—"

The door swings open behind us, ushering in a breeze and the low gurgling snarl of *boche*s. Both Joëlle and I twist around and let our eyes adjust to the ZV silhouetted in the doorframe. The virus has been harder on him than on me. But I still recognize Gavin.

He brought friends.

Chapter 20

"Well, damn me to hell. Evelyn Cross. Never thought I'd see you again, not in a million years."

Did I mention Gavin and I both won State in our track divisions when I was a sophomore? I ran the 400m, but he was a sprinter. The boy was fast—in more ways than one. Did I mention he made a pass at me at the awards dinner? Probably not. His girlfriend Charlene and my ex Bridger were best friends since fourth grade. Pretty sure I didn't mention it to anyone. Yeah, it was awkward in the Homecoming and Prom groups. Not nearly as awkward as now.

"Hey, Gavin. AP French. I was bound to turn up in France sometime."

"Hm. Always the smart one."

"Have to say I'm just as surprised to see you here. Thought they sent you off to relatives in Houston."

"Yeah, well, things got a little sketchy with my cousin Ashley. Too religious for my taste. No vision for the New Order. My dad got me a charter plane out of there months before the Knight's personal hell broke loose."

"I was there for *that* party. Visiting cousins in Houston. Actually, my friends and I were staying on the compound. Only place willing to put up the infected." The scent of grey seeping off Joëlle and me has wandered out the door. Gavin's *boche* entourage sniff the air, growling and prowling. These aren't old, broken down, damaged, virus-devoured zombies. They're fresh converts to the cause, still in top predatory form. "And the count?"

"Cousin—on my mother's side. Yves." He nods appreciatively. "Now, there's a man with vision."

Joëlle has turned her back to Gavin and dropped her head, hoping he won't recognize her, I assume. She's clearly petrified, shaking so violently that my virus-pumped ears can hear it. I do my best to monopolize his attention. "Your family was a bit more liberal than mine. What do they say? Family: people that will take you in when no one else will? Maybe, in this case, it's the people who won't turn you in when everyone else will." I casually sip my champagne. "My family didn't quite see it that way. I've been on the street for a while. You seem to be doing alright, though."

Stereotypically Utahan, Gavin is blond and blue-eyed, but his collared white shirt and French-cut jeans have Rémy written all over them—as if he's just a regular French dude out for a night at the club and not the death angel of the apocalypse. He always had that thick, wavy hair that he refused to cut, probably just to drive his missionary-trimmed dad crazy. Tonight, he wears it long instead of up in a man bun. It suits the new Franco-Gavin well. "I see they helped you out with the arm."

He flexes and stretches. "Stiff. Hitches a little. But Yves's surgeon buddy is pretty handy with metal bolts and hinges. You, on the other hand, you look flawless. Not a scratch on you. No surprise there. I must say, Ev, grey suits you."

The long, blonde hair, the rock-star face, the long legs, they don't fool Gavin. He knows exactly how smart I am. The flirty banter might fool Joëlle, but Gavin knows I'm weighing my options, calculating my chances. It's an easy assumption. I survived for a year on the streets of Salt Lake, and I'm still sentient after the Houston outbreak. I most definitely have survival skills. "Apocalypse make-over. Not my best look."

"Apocalypse, is that what you call it? The end of all things?"

"Isn't it?"

"More of a revolution, I'd say. The beginning of the New Order."

"Rule of the super race?"

"Exactly. You belong with us, you know. We always knew some of us were faster, stronger, smarter—meant to rule. The virus just made the differences more obvious. The 1% has new meaning. All that democratic, equality bullshit—"

One of the *boches* behind Gavin has honed in on the grey scent. Snarling he crouches and springs for the space between Gavin and the door. A despotic glare rips the intellectual smirk off Gavin's face. "*Poilu*! What the hell!" He collars his minion like a disobedient dog and tosses him out the door, screaming at the rest of his bodyguard corps. They jerk and cower, spinning circles and biting at the air.

Under cover of the scuffle and the disciplinary action, my hand finds Joëlle's, trembling spasmodically on the bar. In the infected zone, many fates are worse than dying, and most of them are standing judgment in the doorway. From the corner of my mouth, I hiss, "Is there a back way out?"

Without looking up from her drink, she nods.

"At the right moment, run for it. Don't look back."

"Take my gun. You only have a knife."

"I don't need more than a knife, and you're going to need the gun. I'm only going to distract—"

Gavin collects himself and wipes the insanity and spittle off his face. He's recruiting—or toying with me. The failed pass wasn't pretty. He was a privileged white male. He didn't do rejection well. It's a sure bet he prefers to serve up revenge as a cold dish, despite the charming smile he pastes on his face. "So, Evelyn, what brings you here tonight?"

I glance at Joëlle. I didn't know greys could blanch like that. Ten to one, she's seen Gavin in action. "I'm new. Just got off the boat this morning. Intense day. Needed to unwind a little—away from it all, you know."

"Yes, revolution can be exhausting."

"Just indulging in some girl talk. What brings you here?"

"The books. And Yves asked me to keep an eye on the place. Protect it from looters. He likes to keep his things nice—nostalgic streak for things of the Old Order. I was surprised to see Joëlle here. She knows the rules—and the risks." His voice almost growls the last part. From the looks of him, the virus is winning the battle within.

"My bad. I twisted her arm. She finally gave in and brought me here. Who wouldn't? Look at this place. I could sit in here and pretend the apocalypse never happened. Besides, I'm the new minister of foreign affairs and the uninfected. Joëlle's the child catcher. We had business to discuss." I tip my glass towards the library. "So, you're here for a little light reading? Don't let us bother you. We'll get out of your way."

"No. Stay. As a matter of fact, since Yves moved out, I've been Facebook blighted—hundreds of friends—" he motions to the four *boches* on the terrace behind him, "—and lonely as death."

"Hundreds?"

"Making more every day. Had a whole army of them before the revolution started. Sacrifices had to be made for the cause, though. Not a big deal. Making friends comes easy for me. But since the count moved out to Buzine to set up his New Order, the books are all I have left."

"Yves has been a good influence on you then. You never really had a reputation as the studious type."

"Things change. Some don't. I'd still give my right arm, maybe even my brains, to date you."

Oh, God! Zombie pick-up lines. "Tell you what. Why don't we let Joëlle here run home? I don't want to get her in trouble with the count. She can tell him I stayed to catch up. You and I, we could have a quiet little evening together, just the two of us."

"Maybe not so quiet. But for sure, I'm totally down for a little heart to heart—*tête à tête* should we say? My, uh, associates struggle with sinking their teeth into a meaty conversation." Gavin turns around and shouts at the growling pack behind him, "Stay!" and then slams the door on their faces. "I wouldn't want to keep Joëlle. Yves can be a tad testy." He rubs his chin. "Isn't there a curfew, Joëlle? You know that's for your own good, right? Nasty creatures roam the night."

She doesn't dare speak. She only nods contritely. The two of us wait, hands near our weapons. Gavin could take us both. He only needs to score a bite, and our brains are toast. We'd have to kill him, and he's been bulking up on the human organ diet. The alphas thrive when they embrace the urges; the greys deteriorate.

"I personally have no problem keeping this little infraction between the three of us. But," he glances behind at our Peugeot, "boys will be boys. Mine seem to have taken quite an interest in your car, Joëlle. And, well, rules are rules. The count is very particular about natural consequences and such. I wouldn't feel comfortable interfering with the policies of his sovereign government. By all means, though, run home. I suggest the back door."

Joëlle doesn't wait a hot second before bolting. She's got a gun. She can take on a few, mindless *boches*. The odds worry me, though. She's a fairly new grey and a med student. I don't think she has combat skills. It's a gamble. But staying here with Gavin gives her no odds at all. Mine aren't that great. I can't read him well enough. The viral delusions have obviously set in, but Yves has been pumping him full of philosophy.

"Well, Ev, that just leaves the two of us." He motions towards the sofas in the library corner. "Join me?"

Chapter 21

A carved bookshelf, a stone fireplace, and a couple of couches create a cozy little reading corner with a cushy carpet and a coffee table in the middle. The traditional French something-or-other sofas aren't built for comfort. But nothing about this is comfortable.

Carrying my drink with a napkin for a coaster—as if anyone gives a shit whether or not the cup leaves a ring on the wood—I make my way over to Gavin. He pats the cushion beside him. "Nice try." Cocking my head and smirking, I grab a seat on the empty couch kitty-corner.

My choice was tactical, as well as defensive. From the couch, I have a better view of the window looking out to the parking lot. Joëlle is out of the building, but she still has to slip through the parking lot without attracting a tail. It's about a quarter mile before she hits the main road and another quarter mile back to the chateau.

Gavin grins. Apparently, neither one of us is deluded about where this is going. His eyes lick my bare legs and breathe in the cleavage that my little black dinner dress doesn't do much to hide. "See you're keeping in shape."

"Apocalypse work-out. Vigilantes with baseball bats, SNCHRs, zombies: I kept in shape. Did you hear what happened to Charlene?"

He snorts, disgusted. "I told her to stay home. I knew the dogs would sniff her out. Bitch." He's an insensitive bastard, but I can't say I blame him. Charlene should have known better than to show up at school. She didn't even get to say good-bye to her family. The SNCHRs just hauled her off to the Institute and dissected her. Who knows? Things could have turned out a whole lot differently if the SNCHRs hadn't come looking for Gavin, and his father hadn't shipped him off to the Knight Compound. "Bridger?" he asks.

"The Institute."

"Sucks." Outside, beyond the windows and the patio chairs, Gavin's staff stops milling around the grey-scented Peugeot and perks up, noses pointed towards the road. They've caught Joëlle's scent—unfortunate turn of the breeze. "So, tell me how it went down in Houston. That must have been something, center stage for the Revolution of the New Order."

Growling, the half dozen prowlers tear out of the parking lot and into the road. Gavin turns to get a better view of the chase. "Hope she's fast."

"She's grey."

"It's intoxicating, isn't it? The power, the appetites? You were a league above us all before. Look at you, now. I bet you fly."

I shrug. "Fast enough to keep ahead of the competition. Still faster than you." I toss him a cheeky smirk.

"Fourth of July BBQ. Too much meat, too much beer. I was drunk."

"Nothing's changed. You're still drunk—on the virus…and too much meat." The look on his face is Nicolas's brother Sam all over again. The only difference is, I know there's a cure out there now. With Sam, it was just kill or be killed. Nicolas did what he had to or I wouldn't be here now. I'm not sure I can do the same with Gavin. But if he leaves here, I sentence the girl I protected last night at dinner to a living death or vicious mutilation. Can't live with that either. Then again, none of us are really living, are we? "Don't you miss it?"

"What?"

"Normal. You know, going to class, checking your texts, watching YouTube videos until you fall asleep, track meets, video games, Amazon, Friday night football. That really great Italian place in Salt Lake. Normal." Probably shouldn't have brought up food at the moment.

"I don't miss my dad taking my keys because I got a C in Calc. Don't miss winning State and getting reamed because I didn't beat my personal best. Don't miss being ruled by morons with money." He leans forward. Our eyes lock. "That's what the revolution is about. Putting the right people back in charge."

Gunshots pepper the silence between us. Not a good sign. It means Gavin's henchmen are close, and Joëlle has no other choice. Who knows how many other *boches* are in the woods? They'll head for the noise and pick up her scent.

"It's not a revolution, Gavin. It's mass murder. It's enslavement of the population."

He stands up, his eyes pressed tight. Anger seeps out around the edges. This is the insane part of the virus. The erratic, mindless fury at the slightest provocation. Maybe the cure can't even fix this. "It's the natural order taking over."

"It's a disease, and it's eating away at your sanity." That doesn't make him happy. Really nothing I could bring myself to say would. If the count has set himself up as some sort of aristocratic Hitler, then Gavin is his Himmler, and his *boches* are the SS—created for the sole purpose of protecting the count and murdering civilians.

"He's using you, you know." I stand as well. "He knows what you are—what the virus is doing to your brain. When you've served your purpose, he'll exterminate you without a look back. I watched his grey guard take down a whole alpha organization this afternoon."

Gavin laughs out loud. "Is that what you think? Geez, Ev, I thought we'd established that you were the smart one." He takes a step forward, and I move back. His path to the door is hampered by the coffee table. Mine is clear. "Yves has his little fantasy. Why shouldn't he rule the chosen few? It's a good way to eliminate the Old Order. It makes him happy. I do him a favor now and then, keep his hands clean. But," he plants his palms flat on the table, his face transforms, the insanity melting into utter lucidity, "make no mistake. I AM DEATH." Oh, God! He's seen the void inside and embraced it. "In the end, they all bow to ME and my army. Kings and emperors, peasants and paupers. All life leads to my doorstep. Death is the only god."

He rights himself deliberately and delicately wipes a drop of spit from the corner of his mouth before rolling up his sleeves.

Words abandon me. He's right. With me on his team, the world wouldn't stand a chance. The count knows this. That's why no greys are with Gavin.

"The way I see it, Ev," he picks my drink up off the table and takes a sip, "you have two options. You can join my army, or you can be my consort. Every alpha needs a grey at his side."

I hear the low rumble of his *boche* guard shuffling obediently back to his side before I smell them. Shit! Maybe I could have outrun Gavin, but now I've got a fistful of prime zombies to trip me up. There really is no choice, though—either way, I'm living with death.

Then my ear picks up something else. "Maybe I have a third," I say and bolt for the door.

Chapter 22

A half-moon lingering behind the trees surrounding the club casts splotches of shadows over the little Peugeot. No help there. Joëlle took the keys.

Despite the winter breeze fluttering the dead leaves, a film of sweat coats my forehead and my palms by the time I cross the parking lot and catch sight of the *boches* up the street.

I've only got a knife so I'm looking at hand to hand—more like hand to teeth. My sandals crunch the gravel and slip as I run. The door slammed shut behind me and hasn't swung open yet. Evidently, Gavin plans to let his foot soldiers take me on first and see how I fare before he exerts himself to come after me. Why would he risk damaging that handsome, rich boy face when his *boches* can do the messy work for him? So much the better. I always appreciate a good underestimating. I've taken on fully loaded zombie national guardsmen. Gavin's troops aren't even armed. This is child's play.

The pack is one short—only three left. Maybe Joëlle's bullet was well-placed, and the zombie is lying dead on the street. Or maybe the bullet went astray, and he's enjoying a moonlight roadkill picnic. *Poillu,* the aggressive one that tried to tackle us at the club, leads them. His name fits. He looks like he was probably a ballsy military guy with a good amount of hair on his chest before Gavin sunk his teeth into him. Catching my scent, the three *boches* charge up the street, snarling at the audacious, rival predator lurking about their territory.

I don't know my way around enough to risk turning tail and heading the other direction. Besides, Gavin's waiting for me that way. Facing the onslaught of the *boches*, the virus boils in my veins and twitches my muscles. Behind me, the door creaks open. Gavin has come out to watch the games.

Wishing I was better dressed for the occasion, I break into a sprint on a collision trajectory with the charge coming up the street. The speed revs up a dose of adrenaline.

Boches don't veer off the target, injury to themselves doesn't calculate into their drone strategies. The gap between us closes. Dropping my head and my shoulder, I plow right into *Poillu's* legs and roll, sending him tumbling over my back. Scrambling to my feet, I keep going. His two buddies, definitely not sensory equipped for a quick stop, stumble right over his wallowing mass. The clacking of my heels carries me down the asphalt.

The glass champagne flute Gavin and I were sharing shatters in the parking lot behind me. Within minutes, the fleet slap of leather on pavement announces I've got a tail, and not a shambling brain-dead one.

Gavin was right. He IS faster now, and I'm already at a disadvantage in my strappy little princess heels. Obviously, I don't look back; that would shave a few milliseconds off my lead. Runners develop this sixth sense for knowing when a competitor is gaining on them.

By the time I've reached the highway to Buzine, I can hear him breathing. If he's going for the kill, he's definitely going to catch me. One bite and I'm a foot soldier in his dead army. My only hope is that we both know he needs a grey to keep the count at bay once he no longer requires Gavin's service. Bargains might be made to buy me time.

Rounding the corner, I catch sight of my third option—the rumbling one that sent me sprinting out the door. Two headlights grow brighter, racing down the road and closing in fast.

Gavin lunges for me. His fingertips brush my shoulder, but he can't quite grasp my dress. He stumbles at the near miss, and I dig deep for more speed. My lungs burn. Even with the virus powering my legs, I'm practically out of fuel, and Gavin's back on my heels. The headlights cast weak beams into the darkness between us.

At a certain speed, balance becomes an issue. I can literally run myself into the ground. Now there's an idea.

The car materializes in the darkness. In mid-stride, I pull up and drop to the pavement. Tiny pebbles cut into my hands and knees. Right on my butt, in high gear, Gavin can't stop on the fly and trips over the top of my huddled mound. He crash-lands, face-planting into the asphalt. In a hot second, I'm on his back with my knife at the base of his neck.

Leaning down, I hiss in his ear, "The only reason I haven't already sliced your spinal cord and driven this blade up into your brain, asshole, is that I know there's a cure out there."

He snarls and writhes to shake me off. The chase has overwhelmed any humanity inside with predator instincts.

The car squeals to a stop, flooding us with headlights. In one fluid motion, the door swings open and Margot bounds out. Not sexy, petit Margot in her navel-cut, black dinner dress and stiletto heels, but Général Gagnon, Margot in full RAID gear, *sans* helmet.

"Back off, asshole," she yells, shoving the muzzle of her gun in my face.

"Hey, I wasn't the one doing the chasing."

"I don't give a shit. I'd just as soon drive a bullet into both your brains and be done with it." I stand, hands up, and give her plenty of space. "But, the count has other plans for you two." She nudges Gavin with her gun, and he hauls himself up, groaning as he goes. He's got a new asphalt burn on his cheek to match the peppering of holes in my knees and palms. "And we don't mess with the count's plans, do we, Gavin?"

"She broke curfew. I found her and Joëlle at the *Philosophe*." Gavin's French is pretty good. I wouldn't have guessed it would be his thing. "Hey, chill. Ev and I know each other. We were just catching up."

"Joëlle is being dealt with. This—" she waves her gun at the little scene she just broke up, "—is not how we operate in the New Order. Get your ass in the car, Minister. And, Gavin, leash your dogs and take them home."

"They're not dogs. They're soldiers." Gavin has a sulky side.

The two of us duck back into the little sports car and zoom a U-turn back to the chateau before Gavin's three *boches* are close enough to snap at our fumes.

Chapter 23

Margot races down *Traverse de la Buzine* in her Peugeot 907 like some kind of ex-Grand Prix driver. The straight abandoned road screams for 100km/h + speeds.

"*Merci.*" I get the impression Margot doesn't speak English.

She rattles on in French, and I have to guess at some of the slang terms she uses. My street French isn't that great. "Don't thank me. The count wanted you safe, and I make sure that the count gets what he wants. Besides, you looked like you could handle yourself." She glances me up and down in my torn, dusty, black cocktail dress and heels. "Surprising. People don't really surprise me much."

"I surprise a lot of people. You learn to handle yourself on the streets."

"Gavin is an evil bastard. Why didn't you kill him?"

"I wanted to. I wanted to kill him the way I wanted Greyson to kill the grey that tried to rape me in Houston. But he didn't. Greyson has this stupid-ass idea that we greys should all stick together—just because we're grey."

"And you're starting to agree?"

I shrug. "Some greys are more black than grey. Miguel, the grey from Houston, was one of those. He took his whole gang to my aunt's home, killed her and my uncle, orphaned their four kids, just to spite me."

"I'm sorry." I do believe she is. Margot has her own story. "So, maybe, when it comes down to driving the knife into someone's skull, you believe we greys should stick together?"

"It wasn't that. Gavin's a sadistic murderer. But—"

"No 'but.' He's a sadistic murderer. When Gavin first came, we didn't know the virus was contagious. I think Gavin knew. Only Yves and I were infected. Gavin made a pass at me, you know. Even though he knew I was with Yves."

"Of course, he did. He made a pass at me, even though he knew I was dating his girlfriend's best friend. And, believe me, he knew he was contagious, but only in certain circumstances. You and the count were dating?"

"I'd only met him a few weeks earlier." A rare, reminiscent smile alters her whole face. "He was beautiful and charming; his mind was illuminating. I could talk with him for hours and, my God, the sex—" Oh, she's got it bad—love, I mean, not the virus.

"That'll do it. I have a friend, a doctor at the ZV Institute. ZV stands for Zoser virus, not Zombie virus. Doctor Vadlamani explained all the technical terms to me, but in short, it's the hormone soup in the body during the falling in love process that incubates the virus. Not sex. They thought it was an STD at first. But I've never had sex, and I have the virus, so—"

That catches her attention—not in a good way. She's already jealous of the count's attention to me. "You and Greyson, you're not together?"

"Yeah, we're together." I say that like it's true, but it's just not in our stars. "Not like that. My boyfriend wasn't vegetarian, neither was Greyson's girlfriend. The two of us ended up together for the *Tour de l'Apocalypse*. We've been through it all. It's being a vegetarian that makes us grey. You knew that, right?"

"No, actually we didn't. We only discovered that giving in to the urges for human organs brings on the neural and physical deterioration we see in the infected who are not grey."

At the speed we're going, Margot pulls into the parking lot in half the time it took Joëlle to drive us to the club. We share a room now, so I follow her up to the porch. She stops at the steps. We don't need to use the back entrance. "So, then, you still haven't answered my question. Why didn't you kill Gavin when you had the chance?"

"Besides the fact that you were pointing that little automatic weapon in my face?" Do I tell her? Maybe if they know there's a cure out there, they'll stop this madness. Maybe they'll even help me find Nicolas. Margot's sincere, honest eyes pierce mine. She'd blow my brains out in a hot second, but she wouldn't play games about it. She's reasonable. I'm willing to gamble the count will listen to her. Taking a deep breath, I spill my guts. "That doctor friend of mine is a scientist. An expert on the virus. He's been in on the research since it first broke out." I have her attention. "He's close to a cure. He may already have it. That's why I couldn't kill Gavin. Because he's not a monster, not yet. He's sick, and there's a cure."

It's only a flash, but I see it. She wants normal back.

"Nicolas is working with a French scientist in Paris. On the boat over here, they combined Dr. Pêsqué's genetic research with Nicolas's research on the virus."

The moment is gone. A frown furrows her brows. "The count doesn't want a cure for the virus. He wants a cure for our diseased society. He wants to start over."

"But what about you, Margot? What do you want?"

She turns away and strides up the stairs. I hope I haven't tipped my hand and blown us out of the water. The only thing I can't think of is that I sent Gavin back to Martine when I had the chance to stop him. Margot's hand is on the door when I touch her arm. "Margot, that girl at dinner. Did they send her to Régis?"

She tilts her head and squints like she doesn't even remember the incident. "*Ah! oui,* the uninfected who stained Yves's new jacket."

"Yeah, did you send her away to Gavin?"

"Do you know her?"

"No. She's just a kid. Her nametag said Martine."

"Ah! you noted her name. The count was right to make you minister of the uninfected." She leaves out the foreign affairs part. She doesn't find it nearly as hilarious as everyone else. "Yves is always right."

Shit! I had the advantage and lost it. I have to do something to gain ground again. We both undress in the light from the wall of windows. The process for me and my little black dress is much quicker than for her with her RAID suit. A trickle of blood seeps from one of the wounds on my knee. From the nightstand drawer, I pull out the vial Grey gave me, spread a little on the punctures, and then smear what's left on my finger over the wound on my temple. It's already pink and fading.

Margot just sat down to pull off her boots. I stride to her side of the bed. "Grey gave you that black eye, right? You know it's a permanent purple splotch."

"There's more to the New Order than beauty."

"Not to the count there isn't. Here." A drop seeps out of the vial onto my finger.

Margot's head jerks back when I reach for her eye. Turning my head, I display the healing abrasion above my cheek. Her eyes squint. She reaches to touch it. "That's not possible. The virus doesn't allow us to heal."

I hold up the bottle. "Nicolas made this for me—well, it was for Grey, but he saved some for me." She lets me spread the gel around her eye. "Believe me. There's a cure."

Chapter 24

Grey isn't at training in the morning. I know he can take care of himself, but I'm still worried. The line from *The Godfather* haunts me. *Hold your friends close, and your enemies closer.* Greyson is as close as you can get to the count.

Joëlle is fall-all-over-yourself grateful for last night. I took the blame, telling Margot I forced her to show me around, and since I was the minister in charge, she really didn't have a choice—that, and I took Gavin's heat so she could escape. Apparently, the shot in the night was Margot picking off the *boche* close on Joëlle's tail. She dropped her off at the chateau before swinging around to haul me off Gavin's ass.

The marks on my face and Margot's are only vague pink blemishes fading away to nothing. Only Joëlle, the doctor, notices. In the bright morning sun, her finger traces the faint pink lines across my cheek and neck. "*Incroyable!* No one would believe it if they didn't see it with their own eyes."

Standing at attention, shoulder to shoulder with her while Gabriel and Chantel bark out training orders, I widen the crack of dissent in Joëlle's mind. "My doctor friend Nicolas is a research scientist. He created this solution."

"Where is he now? In America? Not dead, I hope."

"No, he's here. He's a grey now. His brother was like Gavin—a carrier of the alpha strain. Nicolas was looking for a cure for him. This solution was just the start."

Gabriel stops his shouting abruptly and stomps over to us. "Are we interrupting important diplomatic meetings here? Because we have a serious raid coming up."

Joëlle snaps to attention. "*Non, monsieur! Désolée.*"

He glares at me but doesn't get much more than a glare back. I outrank him—at least until the count finds out I'm sowing seeds of dissension and tosses my butt back into that basement cell or hands me over to Gavin.

No worries. This isn't an extended stay. As soon as I spot the chance, Grey and I will watch this place disappear in the dust of one of those SUVs they keep parked out front. If it weren't for Laure and David, I'd have left already. I can't just cut them loose. That would feel like abandoning my sister all over again—like I had a choice and left her because it was easier.

As soon as Gabriel's back up front, I hiss out of the side of my mouth. "He's close to a cure."

Joëlle's head snaps to my profile and back to the front. She's a doctor. She doesn't see the virus as a gift, it's a disease—and she has an uninfected brother gone dark in the clean zone.

The announcement from our tactical chief Chantal distracts me from explaining. "—the group of uninfected have created a stronghold in the outdoor amusement park Accrobranche located not far from here. Even though they are armed, their weapons are primitive. The reconnaissance team observed medieval style swords, axes, and bows." Gabriel can hardly keep from chuckling. A giggle ripples through the ranks.

Shit! I'm not laughing. This has to be Laure's family and their fellow cosplayers.

"They have one grey and one infected adult, but they keep them locked up. The grey is often given night sentry duty so we assume he abstains from the forbidden foods." That has to be Joseph. The D-day for our escape from the New Order just bumped forward. *Where the hell is Grey?*

While Chantal and Gabriel spell out the details of the raid and the training exercises, three of the older uninfected, dressed all in white, herd a handful of cows up the road towards an enclosure recently constructed just east of the chateau grounds. Before the lovely, raw barbeque aroma gurgles the juices in my stomach, the low bellowing distracts me from today's lessons. The cows moan and worry about the grey supervising the round-up. They can smell a predator and a whole lot more of them where they're headed.

"—the goal is to subdue and relocate these wild whites to safety—" We're making color distinctions again—only now grey is on top, and white means you're on the bottom of the food chain. The group includes kids with skin tones of all shades of black, white and brown. The only thing that matters now is the virus. "They don't know what's good for them, so they won't come easily. You know the rules. Kill the adults, shoot them, bite them, gut them—it's all the same. Death will reward their ignorance one way or the other. The children must NEVER be bitten. The penalties will be severe. There is no room in the New Order of Grey for the wasting of a child."

At least in the New Order, there's an iota of humanity. But would I want this life for my little sister? No. My brain hasn't started to decay yet. At least, the meat is reserved for the grey class. The uninfected are all vegetarians so they'll all become greys if they're bitten.

Gabriel strolls down the rows of trainees shouting. "Only adolescents too aggressive or rebellious to subdue manually should be bitten. As among the white children of the order at the age of 16 and above, nature will choose the fittest to survive. The others will die."

My hand shoots up. He looks almost amused. The backward American is about to spew more of her democratic drivel. "Excuse me. As minister of the uninfected, I wondered if you would permit me a moment to do some quick research?"

Chantal and Gabriel both roll their eyes, but I outrank them. The count is fastidious about class distinction, and Margot has just strolled onto the veranda. The count's deferring to my advice at dinner last night set a precedent they don't want to challenge while she's standing there.

Turning to face the group, I conduct a quick poll. "Would you just raise your hand if you were vegetarian before the outbreak of the virus?"

The greys all look at each other, one or two hands vault righteously into the air, a few raise tentative hands and then the rest, encouraged, raise theirs. I stare at Gabriel and Chantal, who, not knowing where this is going, raise theirs as well.

"That's what I thought. The grey mutation does not mean you were chosen by God or that nature selected you as an inherently superior specimen of humanity. You were just vegetarian." The number of faces that fall shouldn't surprise me, given the culture and philosophy of the count, but it does.

Margot's eyes narrow over pursed lips.

Indignant, Stéphane, my socially challenged tablemate, steps forward. "As minister of research and innovation, I must object. We have no scientific evidence or research. This demonstration is strictly anecdotal—"

"—but compelling." Our lanes merge on this point, and I'm not going to stay on my side of the line.

"Until there is conclusive evidence establishing causality—"

A scream from the eastern side of the building turns all of our heads. I'm the only one that runs. The leap down from the veranda could do some damage, but the inevitable is unrolling in the animal enclosure. The aromatic *mélange* of human and cow has overwhelmed the grey supervising his uninfected shepherds. He's throttled one of them and another has jumped on his back. It's David.

Chapter 25

In a full-body throttle, the rogue grey holds the only girl among the uninfected hostage. The uninfected don't think about using their teeth and claws—nursery school discouraged those instincts. David shouts and strangles the grey with one arm, pummeling him with the other fist. It takes me a second to recognize him without his medieval costume. My feet hit the dirt as the rabid grey rips a bite out of the girl's neck. If she's been vegetarian for long enough—two weeks isn't long enough—she can still be saved.

"*David, lâche! C'est moi.*" Shoving David off his back, I collar the grey before he can rip another bite out of the girl's abdomen—that's the breadbasket, full of sweet and tasty organs. Snarling and snapping, he resists. The predator instincts are in the driver's seat. The human has exited the vehicle. He's not ready for me, and I land a really nice shot to his jaw before he even knows who grabbed him. The dirt thuds beneath his unconscious head right before Joëlle scurries down the steps and around to the enclosure. Ripping her shirt off, she applies it to the uninfected girl's wound.

David is stunned and horrified. The uninfected are guppies in the shark tank, and the sharks aren't as tame as they pretend to be. Helping him up, I throw my arm around his shoulders and bolster his shaking knees. He's pretty tough, under the circumstances.

Gabriel shoves through the crowd. Blood dribbles down the chin of the grey gone feral. He moans in the dirt. Before I can blink, Gabriel stomps over to him, sums up the situation, and hauls his gun out of the holster. The morning air cracks and echoes the shot through the forest. Joëlle and I jump.

Our little pediatrician freaks. "Gabriel, what the hell?"

But that's only the beginning. The gunshot didn't finish off the culprit with a nice neat hole in the head, it tore a starting point in his belly. Gabriel drops to his knees and digs both hands into the wound. The flesh tears around his fingers. The grey hurls and groans. "Disgusting flesh-eater! How do you like it? That good for you, too?" Twisting and yanking, Gabriel's fist jerks out of the crimson hole dangling jagged, blood-drenched organs. Beneath the blood spurts blotching his face, his psychopathic grin chills my bones. His hatred oozes with a deep, latent desire. Shakespeare flashes into my brain, *Me thinks thou dost protest too much.* How was Gabriel a vegetarian? Disemboweling another human titillates his senses and leaves his fingers twitching with pleasure.

Margot pushes through the small gawking crowd. The tortuous slaughter disgusts her, and she fires off a quick, mercy bullet into the grey's head. "Get up, Gabriel. You have training exercises to lead. Enforcement is not your purview. This is your last warning."

"Wait! Are you just going to let him get away with that?" I shove David behind me to confront her.

"The grey knew the consequences. Zero tolerance. I don't sanction vigilante justice, but the end is the same."

"But that's cruel and unusual punishment—it's barbaric. Gabriel should be arrested or something. Don't you have rules of decency?"

Margot ignores me and eyes the girl struggling to breathe under Joëlle's blood-stained palms. The general turns the gun on her. Joëlle grabs her arm, but Margot swipes her away like a fly.

"No!" Before I can lunge to stop her, she's fired a bullet into the girl's head.

"She could have been saved! The wound wasn't that deep."

"She was not a vegetarian. She would not be grey. Wasn't that the point of your little demonstration? The simple virals— the ZVs—feed on human flesh. The risk to the other whites is too great. She could wipe out the whole population." The general turns to the group that has gathered to gawk. "In the New Order there is grey, there is white, there is red, and there is dead. There is no room for in-between." She holds up her gun to punctuate her words to the crowd and remind them of the consequences of letting their urges rule them. "We greys will eliminate the *boches* and the blood-smirched alphas that create them. We will protect and govern the white. This is the New Order. It's very simple." She motions with her gun. "Joëlle, see to it that the rations of marijuana for the guards are doubled and that the smoking is supervised and mandated. This can't happen again. What a waste."

The human part of me stands open-mouthed horrified. In Margot, there's a little of the cut and dried, black and white, military logic I saw in Général Samson, Ryan's dad. On the flip side, the virus tingles the purple blood in my veins and, God help me, I can see the cold logic in her actions. The girl would have certainly decayed slowly, feeding off the uninfected, infecting more of them, killing others. Is quick better? God! Have I become Greyson? I guess it was inevitable that I would adapt to my new world. That's what has kept me alive and Amber uninfected.

"Joëlle, get your people to clean this up." Margot shoves the crowd away with her gun. "We need everyone back to training." Obediently, still reeling from the brutality, Joëlle pulls out a phone and sends off a text.

The smell of the girl's blood lingers heavily on the crowd. My mouth waters and the urges rise. Margot shoves back the spectators in the front and glares the rest of them into submission. "Anyone else want a taste of the forbidden flesh?" The crowd files away, murmuring. The tone rumbles with various levels of discontent and awe. My arm around his shoulder, I whisper to David in the easiest English possible, "Laure is fine. She is in the kitchens. I'm going to get you out of this place and back to your family. Watch yourself and keep your head down."

Some of Joëlle's medical group arrive and take charge of David. They have Joëlle's look of compassion, and marijuana fumes hang heavy on them. Leaving the situation in their hands,

Joëlle walks back up the steps with me. "We have to do something, Evelyn. This is tyranny. We can't embrace it."

I nod. When we leave, I'm taking Joëlle with me, but I'm not sure I can walk away from this place and leave it standing.

Chapter 26

We break into teams for the training. Joëlle, Margot and Stéphane are on my team, pitted against Gabriel, Chantal, the Ivoirian from dinner whose name, I think, is Guy. A very sturdy, trim looking girl called Audrey with sleek black hair and a yellow tinge to her grey complexion rounds out their team. Okay, it's stereotypical, but my elementary Karate classes are not going to cut it against this girl with her small, muscular build perfect for martial arts. But who knows? Maybe I'm wrong. Maybe she likes ballet.

Margot turns to lead us off the veranda towards the trees to strategize. We're playing our training game in the woods because David and Laure's family and friends are camped out in a tree park with zip lines and other high branch attractions—well, that and the trees shade us from the UV rays. Before we're down the steps, Greyson strides up to my side with Kasim. "You weren't going to play without me, were you, baby?"

Margot grins, clearly pleased to see him. "Bruno, Fahrid," she picks some big ass, gargantuan guy from the crowd and another trimly muscular olive-skinned guy and motions them off with the other team to "even" us out. I'm sure I recognize Bruno's bulk from the basilica, but he had his faceguard down, and I didn't see it. After she evens up the other side, as if anyone could call this even, Margot breezes by with a wink at Grey.

How the hell does he do this? He just usurped her position as the count's right hand, and she's all smiles and eyelashes about it. I'm not complaining, I'm the one who gave him his marching orders. I just wish he weren't so damn thorough about them.

Stéphane stomps along the makeshift path grousing in his clipped Parisian French behind us. "How is this fair? We have no power or size on our team. We can't possibly win. Does no one here care about the laws of physics?" Stéphane is the engineer that keeps the place powered and running, but he's no soldier.

"They're casting us as the whites." Margot has very little patience for pessimism, or any other self-doubt for that matter. "Well, we'll play our parts well, won't we? They underestimate the population camped in the tree park because they did not bother to ask for the intel that the count sent Greyson to gather."

My eyebrows shoot up. Greyson shrugs and debriefs our underdog troop as we walk. "The uninfected belong to a medieval combat society. They don't have guns, but they're heavily armed—and they conduct strategic drills. They're living in the reception and cafeteria building, but they have fortified the boundaries and guard them." Joëlle and Margot understand English well enough, but I translate for Stéphane.

The trees here are sparse in places. Margot scans the terrain while she lays out her plan. "Our objective will be to teach our team a lesson. Even though we are at a heavy disadvantage in physical prowess, as are the whites, we can still withstand an assault from a physically superior force—perhaps even route their attack. We will not develop our attack strategy until that lesson is clear." She directs the next bit of information at me with a glance. "Remember, although it is quite simple to kill a white, it is much more difficult to take one alive. But the penalties for eating a white are much more severe than for killing one, so watch yourselves."

In her quick light step, Margot leads us 100 yards farther to a more heavily wooded area. Our boots crack the twigs and leave waffle marks in the damp dirt. Dropping behind Stéphane, who still grumbles under his breath, I match my step to Grey's. "I guess you were busy last night."

"You told me to make myself useful. I did. I met David and Laure's father. He's heading up that group of cosplay survivors. They're way deep into that shit. The dude has a full suit of armor."

"Did you tell them we've got David and Laure?"

"Yeah," he pulls up the sleeve of his black t-shirt, "and I got this for my trouble." An angry, purple gash winks at me. "I ran into their brother—the grey. He took me to their dad. Almost got my throat slit on the spot. But I told them what was coming for them and that we would figure out a way to get David and Laure added to the raiding party."

"Nice work."

"I aim to please." He nods towards Margot, *tête à tête* with Joëlle. "How's the new roommate?"

"Actually, she saved my butt last night. Joëlle dragged me off to the count's club, just up the street—girl's night out. You'll never believe who we ran into."

"Your French soldier boy?"

My cheeks go hot. "Cute. Is that where you want to go?" If I'm honest with myself, a nasty habit I need to break, I'd have to say, when I thought Grey was dead, I started having feelings for Ryan. They're like the virus. They're in there, and they won't die. Even though I know I'm monumentally bad for him, I wouldn't be sad to see him turn up. But I'm not going to admit that. "No. Much worse. Do you remember Gavin Tanner?"

"Rich kid from downtown. Dated Bridger's friend Charlene, right? Dude's a manwhore—the kind that makes bets on getting laid."

"Don't I know it."

"Figures."

"What is that supposed to mean? I'm just trying to tell you Gavin is here, and you're going all jealous boyfriend on me."

Margot stops where the trees are thickest. Birds twitter in branches, irritated with the invasion. "This is what we do. We take a page from the book of Genghis Khan—"

"Gavin showed up? How the hell did that happen?"

"—we send our three strongest to attack—"

"He's the count's cousin." I stop, touch his arm, and whisper. "He's an alpha, now."

"I'm not interrupting, am I, Ève? Greyson?"

"Sorry, just some translation."

She totally doesn't buy it. "If I know Gabriel and Chantal, they will send their strongest up the middle, and the others will flank us. They'll assume we're doing the same. We use the enemy's underestimation of the target and their delusions of superiority against them. Greyson, you'll hang back and guard the rear. Gabriel would love nothing more than to avenge his humiliation from dinner last night."

"Then we should give him the chance. With revenge on his mind, he won't be sticking to their plan," Greyson responds.

"That may be true, and it suits my strategy, but you should know there are 'allowances' for 'accidents' during training. The count understands that the virus can be unpredictable and must be handled with 'compassion and understanding.' You noticed that notch on Gabriel's arm?"

We nod. Who wouldn't notice? It looked intentional like a scalpel carved it.

"To use your baseball terms: strike one. Every grey is allowed three before the fourth infraction is punished with death. Gabriel still has two 'accidents' left with no accountability other than the marking." Not to be shallow or anything, but a permanent mark on my skin would have totally deterred me. Gabriel, however, is the type to want to flaunt the banner of his war crimes. "I know him. He'll kill you if he gets the chance."

"Then let's make damn sure he doesn't get the chance."

Chapter 27

Ribbons of light toast the pine and filter through their needled branches. Grass and saplings spatter the shadowed earth, sucking at patches of sun breaking through the maple and ash leaves. Birds twitter nervously as Greyson, Margot, and I creep on parallel trajectories through the forest back to the chateau.

Our attack on the compound of the *non infectés* will happen in two weeks—fifteen days to the Frenchies. Even though the dark would give us better cover and the distinct advantage of viral night vision, the uninfected will expect a night attack because, even though it's winter, sun sensitivity still deters virals during the day. In the morning, the uninfected will likely be more spread out, going about their daily survival routines and less on their guard against an assault. The trees and our RAID gear will offer all the cover we need from the damaging solar rays.

Mangled maple leaves, damp and decaying, carpet our steps in a slosh of brown. About fifty yards ahead of us, blatant branch crashing heralds the attack of Gabriel's team. Their smell penetrates the tree cover, and Chantal's voice cuts through the stillness, baiting us, the French version of "Come out, come out wherever you are. We won't hurt you, we just want to play." Cats calling to the mice. It's all fun and games until the claws and teeth come out. No sign of Audrey, Bruno, Fahrid or Guy. No worries, sort of. Margot predicted this is how it would look. Chantal would have sent them in two teams to flank us.

We've thrown all of our power into the frontal assault, Greyson straight up the middle and Margot soldiering along his side about ten yards away. At least we'll outnumber them until they call in their back-up. On my right, through the gaps in the low brush, Greyson signals with a couple fingers to his eyes that he can see the enemy. Beyond him, Margot crouches out of sight. She's the hidden asset they'll assume is guarding our weak side on the right not creeping up the middle. The rolling meadow on my left makes a surprise attack difficult from their end and an ambush a sound strategy. They'll have foreseen that and either sent reinforcements there or focused their flank assault on our weak side. Either way, they're walking right into Margot's trap—until they're not.

The scent of disaster wafts through the trees. "What is that delicious aroma, Gabriel?" Muffled objections from David, gagged, hands bound in front of him, punctuate Chantal's sing-song taunts. No one mentioned taking an uninfected hostage was in the playbook. Rushing to his side earlier this morning tipped my hand. God! It never ends. Everyone I try to help ends up in the thick of the shit. They knew I was attached to him and intercepted him from the medical assistants. Last night displayed my Achilles heel for all to see. Our team strategized around their weakness, but theirs strategized around ours.

The low bushes hide Margot's position from me, but Greyson bobs his palm down vehemently, warning me not to take the bait. My predator instincts are already up. All the rabid demons spinning in my blood dispense adrenaline on supersize and ratchet up my pulse. I can smell the fear dripping off David over the rancid sweat of the greys. Logic slips away in the current. Gritting my teeth, I drive my fingernails into my palms. I will not take the bait.

Gabriel shoves David a few steps closer into a small clearing. A splotchy view of both greys and their hostage focuses behind a screen of leaves. The kid trips on a hulking root and face-plants in the dirt and pine needles. A flash of sunlight ricochets off the silver blade of a knife in Gabriel's fist. Snorting derisively, he hauls David to his feet. Dead needles cling to his white tunic and brown splotches stain his scrub pants. Gabriel dangles David in front of us. Throwing elbows and thrashing, the kid looks like a cat toy bobbing on a stick. "Calm down, little guy! Wouldn't want you to hurt yourself." Lifting his knife above his head so we can all see it, Gabriel grins.

My muscles tense, wanting so bad to spring. Grey shakes his head. It's only a bluff. He's not really going to hurt David. Margot just shot a grey for sinking his teeth into a white. They have rules here. I have to hold my breath and clench my teeth to stay still.

David bends over and shoves an elbow into Gabriel's gut, which does nothing but raise his shackles. He grunts, hauls the kid around, and slashes the knife across the inside of his arm. Oh, my God! He really did it! A ribbon of red spills down to David's wrist. Howling, he curls around the wound, smearing blood across his tunic. "What a shame. They're so fragile, these whites." Gabriel feigns concern. "Wound looks pretty deep. This could all be over in a couple minutes, kid. All we need is for your friends to come out here where we can see them, and we'll send you off to the med team. They'll patch you right up. No harm done, just a little demonstration."

David, not the defiant soul that Laure is, glances out pleadingly into the woods.

Chantal licks her lips, savoring the salty blood tang that emanates across the trees and triggers the juices in my mouth. My stomach rumbles. God, I'm no better than they are. "Sweeter than wine. What would you say, Gabriel? A hint of rosemary and garlic? Ah, nectar of the gods." The two of them giggle.

"Waste of good blood." Apparently, the rules only forbid consuming uninfected flesh and blood, not spilling it. Gabriel would laugh as David bled to death. No question.

Why the hell am I even hesitating? Staying at the chateau serves one purpose only: getting Laure and David safely back to their family. Am I really going to explain to Laure that I let her brother bleed to death to win at hide and seek?

In our little game, we greys are all firing blanks, but that blood running down David's arm is real, and he needs real first aid. Margot and Grey can execute their well-laid strategy. As far as I'm concerned, the other team can humiliate the hell out of us, as long as I get David some bandages and stitches. Grey guesses my thoughts. Shaking his head, he motions for me to stay down. Sure, he's probably a better option to give himself up, he's slippery as cow guts, but his non-existent French has no bargaining capacity. It has to be me.

The blood has covered David's palms by the time I stand up, my gun targeting Gabriel. "Hey! Over here." Trees and brush still camouflage me. "Cut the boy loose and send him back. When he's out of range, I'll surrender."

"We need assurances." Gabriel grabs a fistful of David's shirt. "You move towards the clearing while he moves away." My eyes shift to Grey's position, but he's gone. "Where's your teammate?"

"I'm alone. They sent me up the center. Look, I don't give a shit about winning your game. It isn't my thing." With measured steps, I approach the clearing. "Untie him and let him go, or your team will finish the game without you. Standing there with your hand on his shirt makes you a stable target. You want a little demonstration? Here it is. I don't know a single, uninfected mom that wouldn't give herself up to a band of greys to free her son."

I'm a prize too tempting for him to push his bargain. The red laser dot on his forehead is pretty convincing too. He's not the type to take one for the team. Gabriel checks Chantal. She nods and creeps away to my right while he pulls his hand away from David's shirt. Waiting until I'm actually in view, he rips a knife through the ties on the kid's wrists and shoves him back towards the tree cover.

David runs, but he's still in sight and earshot, crashing through the brush when I break into the clearing. "We had a deal, *Ministre*." The tone robs the title of its respect.

"Yes, we did." I toss my gun in the dirt and present my wrists.

With a sneer, Gabriel whistles and moves to close the gap between us. He's not ten steps before Margot and Grey spring from the trees bordering our weak left side. Too busy gloating, Gabriel isn't ready for them, and Grey tackles him to the dirt before he can swing his gun around. Margot scoops mine up and slams it into my chest, dragging me around by the hand, back to the cover of the woods.

Gabriel's whistle summons a convergence of his teammates from our right side. No wonder Margot diverted Grey to the left. She couldn't have missed the musky *eau de gris* overpowering the pine and the lingering scent of David's blood. Their plan was to draw us out and flank us, just like she thought. We played right into it—until we didn't.

Grey grabs Gabriel's gun, and the three of us haul ass through the trees and brush. Leaves slap at my face, branches grab at my arms and legs. All six of their team are on our heels. Guy, the Ivoirian, is the tallest with the longest legs. Margot is small and built for combat rather than running. Grey and I ran track so we're a few strides ahead when Guy catches up to her. The two of them go tumbling into a tree. Skidding into a turn, I scramble back to help her break his loose hold. In the time it takes me to pull her out, the others have closed the gap, and Guy is back on his feet.

"I can see the trail! Move!" Grey breaks through the brush onto the meandering line of a cow path. Audrey's breath huffs in my ear. She's so close I can hear her heartbeat, but I know how to accelerate at the finish. My feet stamp across the path into the trees on the other side. Margot's stride and Audrey's hit the path at the same time. Grey skids to a halt in front of us and comes back our way to a chorus of grunts and moans. Joëlle and Stéphane have pulled tight a rope across the path. The other team strike the rope almost simultaneously. Arms and legs flail as they tumble and roll through the low saplings and grass on our side of the trail.

Karim drops from a tree above, right onto Gabriel's back. His dexterous fingers wind and catch the cord ties around Gabriel's wrists before the big man even comes to his senses. Chantal hit something in the fall, and she's out cold, so Grey runs to take on Bruno, the massive hulk, before he can stand. Stéphane and Joëlle go after the others.

Audrey's the only one that made it across the line on Margot's heels. In this situation, I'd actually be happy to admit I was wrong about my stereotypical first impression. But saying that Audrey's martial arts would shame my Karate class self-defense was an understatement.

Once Audrey has caught her, Margot holds her own, but with more ducking and dodging than punching and kicking. She takes a couple good hits before I cover the six strides back to her side. If Audrey were biting the *non infectés* to take them out, Margot would be toast. But that's not the count's little game. He wants his subjects. Audrey has to take prisoners to win.

With Margot down, Audrey punches my chest with her foot to fend off my charge and throws me back off balance. The dirt skids across my butt and hands, and she comes full-speed at me. Throwing up both feet, I manage to roll her over the top of me so that I'm straddling her core. She obviously didn't expect that. I don't look like I can handle a self-defense move. Anchoring her foot around mine, she jabs her knee into my side and flips me beneath her. Now she's between my legs and choking me. I need to anchor her arm and wrap my legs around her shoulders to pivot her back beneath me and set her elbow up for the break. It's a tough move, and I'm out of practice. If Margot hadn't jumped back into the fray, Audrey would have strangled me unconscious before I could execute it. I only weasel out because Margot grabs Audrey's feet and Grey pulls her off in a chokehold. It takes all three of us to get her wrists clasped in the cord ties.

Seriously, I need this girl on my team.

Chapter 28

"You're a cheat and a liar." Gabriel glares at the clippers I shove between his bound hands.

"You demanded surrender, and I surrendered. How is that cheating?" Snip. The plastic ties fall from his wrist. My toes flex to bring my nose up to his. The pores across his cheeks are thick, and there's a red tint to the grey ball on the end of his nose—he's a drinker. Funny how I can actually smell the anger soup dripping off him. Still buzzing in my blood, the virus compels me to go for the kill. "You're a cocky coward who takes children hostage. Don't think for a minute the *non infectés* at the compound will be playing by your charade of a code of conduct. You take one of their kids hostage like that, they will walk through hell to take you down. We have a saying in English, *All's fair in love and war.*"

Shoving me out of his face, he stalks off to the terrace for the strategy meetings. I'm not the only one he shoves away. The snickers and smirks of his grey minions infuriate him. Humiliation flickers across Chantal's permanent sneer when Gabriel slaps away her consoling hand. People notice.

Stéphane is downright giddy about our victory. It's no stretch to imagine he never wins this kind of stuff. Margot uses the humiliating defeat to drive home her message that we can't show up at the tree compound half-cocked and expect to round up the uninfected. They might be physically inferior, but they have strategy, and they're armed.

She strolls up and whispers in my ear while I'm cutting Audrey's ties. "Watch your back." She nods at the nearly visible furor fuming off Gabriel. "Don't let him catch you alone—at least not for a couple days. And stay out of his way during the raid."

Audrey, at least, holds no grudge. She inclines her head and extends a newly freed hand. "I am Audrey Tran. Pleased to meet you." A slight French/Asian hybrid lilts her English. The last in the field, we hustle back through the trees to the veranda. The human blood scent is gone. Smelling the predator on us, squirrels and birds freeze in the trees as we pass. We stroll towards the pointed chateau rooftops in the distance. "You handle yourself well."

"Nice of you to say so, but you'd have kicked our butts if you weren't outnumbered three to one."

"Gabriel is strong, like a rhinoceros, but he doesn't maneuver well." Audrey's nose crinkles when she shrugs. "I can teach you a few things if you like. You seem to have some experience."

"Oh, I'd more than like. I've been around, been a grey for months. You learn how to handle yourself on the streets against the self-righteous hooligans with bats hunting us down. Is that what you did, teach martial arts? Before?"

"No, father teach martial arts. I study chemistry at university in Toulouse, but help father as instructor. He insist all girls must fight well. Now he is right."

"Where are they now, your family?"

"Escape to Paris. Younger brother and mother. Father dead."

"I'm so sorry."

"We were lucky. Alpha came to dojo, in first outbreak. Father and I fight while brother protect mother and escape."

French words rifle from the veranda—"secure surrender," "don't provoke," "our mission to protect the weak from danger in the new world." Empty words to Gabriel and Chantal. Either one would enjoy a good mauling more than a collar.

"Could not save father."

"The older you are, the more likely you'll die from the virus."

"No not die from virus. Alpha and *boches* consume father. Thought I die, as well, but become stronger."

"Vegetarian, right?"

147

"Yes, whole family."

"At least, your mother and brother will be grey like you if something happens."

A frown hardens her fine features. "Is curse. Craving for flesh disgust me." She nods at the troops assembling above us. "Others smoke the weed to subdue, but also subdues fight. Better to practice thiên."

"Thiên?"

"Zen. Thiên is Vietnamese. My mother French. My father Vietnamese."

"Yeah, I'm with you there. A joint works wonders, makes you feel human again, but dulls your edge." Peace floats around Audrey. She's as badass as they come, but it's separate from her, like armor she pulls out of her mind and clasps on for the fight but folds back up into its velvet case when she's done. She's the master of the virus, not its slave. "Audrey, would you train me? In Thiên and martial arts?"

"With pleasure. Give me just a moment." She jogs up to whisper in Margot's ear. The musky, leathery scent of Grey gives away the footsteps padding up behind me. For a fleeting second of fantasy, I imagine him wrapping his arms around my waist from behind, soft breath on my neck, lips brushing the lobe of my ear. Nothing would make me happier than to melt away into his embrace, forget the fresh tang of the pine, the chortle of birds that has seeped back into the wood, now that the predators have gone, and the sizzle on my grey skin from the scraps of sunlight sifting through the trees.

"What the hell were you thinking back there, Ev!"

Reality bites. "I was thinking David could bleed to death in this little game we're playing."

In one stride, his nose is inches from mine, and he drops his voice to a hiss. "You have no idea what kind of bear you're poking. I've seen things—"

"Don't be a drama queen. It's not like I haven't seen—"

"No, you haven't!" His fist collars my bicep. I've never seen Grey look at me like this. Maybe it's the tinge of fear behind the anger that stifles my bravado. "Miguel and his gang, back in Texas, that was kiddie games. Gabriel—" Grey has no words, no flippant snark. In the silence between us, the dread that crushes his tongue strangles my heart.

Grey is a player. Life is his game. Every catastrophe is just a new level to conquer. But not this time. Whatever he saw, it got under his skin. For the first time since he waltzed back into my life, and we partnered up for this tango of the undead, I relinquish the lead. "Sorry." My fingers unlatch his. I'm not defending myself, just explaining. "You know I couldn't sit there hiding while David bled to death."

He's not open to excuses. "Yes, you could. We had it covered. There was a plan. We'd have gotten him out if you could have just managed to swallow all that self-righteous bullshit you keep in your cheek and trust someone besides yourself. We're treading in deep shit here, Ev. And now you're in that Nazi psycho's crosshairs."

"I'm sorry!" I really am. The more I try to play the hero, the worse it turns out for the poor slobs I'm trying to save. His eyes pinched, Grey turns away from me. Again. Is it worth it, everything else I fight for? Amber is safe. Why the hell do I keep letting my crusades raise the walls between me and the only other person who matters? "Grey, please. I'm sorry—don't walk away, not again—don't be angry."

"Angry?" He stops in his tracks, shaking his head. "You just don't get me, Ev, do you? You never did." Spinning on his heel, in one stride he's covered the ground between us with a look I'd have imagined on Sisyphus. His arms wrap me up, strong and solid, anchors that keep me from tipping in the typhoon waters of the apocalypse. His lips press hard against mine. His arms tighten until I can't breathe.

But I don't want to breathe. I want to fade away into this moment of us locked together. Lifetimes flash between us before he finally lifts his head to breathe.

"When the helicopter left and the Knight compound exploded, I thought I'd seen your face for the last time." His fingers brush my cheek like he's committing the contours to memory. "I might as well have been one of those living dead wandering around the rubble. Without you, life lost all meaning. You ripped my heart away. All I could do was kick myself for not sticking around, whether you wanted me or not."

"Of course, I wanted you." My fingers slide around his neck. "You know how I am. I just—"

"No. Listen. The French helicopter that took Cameron to drop him off with the rest of your cousins in Montana made a stop to gather what was left of the research from the compound. I fast talked my way onto it. Had to give up my shoes." He shrugs at the tilt of my brow. "What can I say? The dude was really into Nike. That's not important. What matters is that I spent weeks in the dark belly of that helicopter carrier, knowing you were with someone else, knowing I'd let you walk away from me, knowing I need you to survive—to want to survive. I jumped ship the night we pulled in, and God, I'm sorry to say it, but nothing could have made me happier than to see the waves spit you up into this hell hole with me. But I didn't expect what they're doing here. Now I wish you'd stayed on that island. I'm not angry, I'm worried."

My palm cuddles his cheek. "Don't worry about me, baby. Here, I have a chance to survive. If I'd stayed on that ship, Lieutenant Samson's dad, the general, would have had me shot the second Ryan turned his back. Do you blame him? It's a clean zone. They even shipped Nicolas off to Paris with Dr. Pêsqué to finish off their research on the cure. Seriously, Grey, what could possibly be so bad that we haven't seen it before? You were in that compound with me. You saw what Sam did. You saw what Miguel did at my aunt's house."

Grey shakes his head, eyes closed against the memory. This is Grey we're talking about—the kid who basically organized the ZV gang that loosed the original flesh raid outbreak in Eli and sparked the apocalypse. And he's scared. A deep breath stirs up the will he needs to spill his guts, "Gabriel and Chantal, they—"

Audrey skips up behind us, all smiles, and grabs my hand. "C'mon. We have official permission to focus on intensive combat training."

Torn between wanting to know what's eating Grey and needing allies like Audrey if we're going to survive the New World Order, I nod at him. "Mind if my friend tags along? You're one of the few around with decent English, and he doesn't speak French." I wink at him and whisper loudly to

Audrey, "I'd like to practice on someone bigger than I am. You're game, aren't you, Grey?" Of course, he's game. He's a player.

Chapter 29

I'm a tiger, growling, the scent of warm blood tingling my nose. Fading into black shadows above, giant leaves slap against my body as I lope through the jungle. My prey is just three bounds away. Snarling, I leap. My claws sink into the soft white underbelly of the plump white bird. No blood spurts when I pull them out and rip in with my teeth. My mouth fills with feathers. The beak thrashes against my shoulder.

"Evelyn! Evelyn, wake up!"

Roaring, I turn my fangs to the bird's squawking head and drive my nails into Margot's forearm.

She slaps me, hard enough to leave a mark, and then the world shifts, and I'm back in the chateau with my teeth in Margot's fist and my throat clogged with down feathers from my masticated pillow. I choke out an apology.

"You don't smoke enough, and you spend more time than anyone around the uninfected." She tosses me a bag of joints. "It's when you dream that the virus seizes control. Eventually, it will take you when you're wide awake." Her combat boots clomp on the wooden floor before the door swings open. "Audrey's waiting for you."

Deep down, I always feared this would happen. The virus is tenacious. If I refuse to let it in, it will find a crack somewhere in my subconscious and slither through. What if my pillow had been Amber? How much longer do I have before I lose the ability to choose? Not wanting to know the answer to that question, I smoke a joint while I'm suiting up and another during breakfast. I'd rather lose my edge in a fight than attack one of the uninfected kids on the grounds. I've been spending hours touring facilities and setting up security policies for the uninfected.

Audrey's a beast, minus the badass, "better than you" attitude. She channels her ego into being an instructor. When her students are as good as she is—well, "as good" would be stretching it, almost as good—she's happy. More than just basic defense moves, she teaches us how to go after the *boches* hand to hand—or hand to teeth—without getting bit.

The best thing, though, about working with Audrey on combat skills is the "get out of jail free" card that lets us skip Gabriel and Chantal's field training—well, not the best thing. The best thing is that Grey and I are a team again. God! I dream about that one moment alone on that first night before dinner. Sometimes I wake up, reaching for him. Margot obviously factored that in when she made the call to let us train with Audrey. Anything she can do to make sure Grey and I are an item suits her purposes. That and, apparently, Gabriel's not the type to let the past die.

The long day's workout keeps me pretty busy. They issue us a variety of weapons and show us how to use them. Not many differences from the training on the ship with Ryan's troops. Crazy, but training makes me miss Amber more.

Even though I'm exhausted, I make time every evening to do inspections. Nobody questions my motives, given my new title. Ostensibly, my job description includes monitoring quality of life issues for the *non infectés*. Actually, I'm scouting out Laure and David. I learned the hard way that asking about them would only put them at risk.

About a week into our stay, I step out the front door of the chateau and head to the servants' quarters. The long, rectangular building stretches back from the street and flanks the right side of the paved parking. The yellowed stone accents on the terracotta orange of the two-story outbuilding blend with the stone of the chateau. The building blocks the view of the modern glass movie-theater reception added to the old chateau during the renovations.

Across the street, a line of luxury sports cars and SUVs crowds the theater parking lot. The New Order gathers up more than just the animals left behind in the quarantine. In the paved drive, a couple small trucks and a van pick up three or four RAID clad greys and speed away into the twilight. Security teams patrol the bordering neighborhoods for stray zombies or raiders.

If the greys have eliminated most of the red alphas, their *boches* must be wandering around in mindless hunting packs trying to feed themselves. That scenario brings back memories of the Knight compound. Don't really want to go there again. It was terrifying, but mostly, it cost me Grey. I like to think it was the chaos of the apocalypse on the compound that robbed me of him, but I did that all by myself, ripped him out of my veins like a taped IV needle.

Marijuana fumes float like a halo around the servants' quarters. Note to self: research the effects of second-hand smoke on the adolescent *non infectés* housed here. Four greys sit and smoke at a table in the guardroom. The furnishings here are super Spartan—nothing like the luxury of the chateau.

One of the guards nods at me and offers me a joint. Standard protocol for greys who want to wander around in here. Just to be safe, I take a drag.

"*Merci. Je m'appelle Evelyn. Je suis le nouveau ministre des non infectés.*" This band doesn't strike me as the New Order's brightest and finest. When they hear who I am, they stumble up from their chairs, not sure how to acknowledge me. The count has managed to instill a certain fearful respect in his followers. If I hadn't seen Yves's unhinged side at dinner, I might have wondered how. A beanie-topped scrawny kid with an over-sized nose hastens to excuse their lethargy. He tells me the whites are all over at the house getting ready to serve dinner, or they haven't come in from the farms yet.

Normally, I'd brush away their anxiety and make friends, but I need to earn for myself a little of their subjugation and awed dread of the count. When we come for David and Laure, I don't want any opposition.

"What are your names?"

"Gilles, *Madame.*" The scrawny kid calls me Madame, and I have to cough out a stern giggle.

"And you?" I nod at the second guard. He's pretty soft and chubby and keeps his head down when he responds.

"César, *Madame la Ministre*."

"From now on, Gilles et César, two of you will be on duty outside the door 24/7." Pointing at the two men, I jerk a thumb towards the exit. The scrawny one scampers out, and the heavy one lumbers, effacing himself, behind. Only the girls are left. Squaring my shoulders, I demand a tour of the facility.

Past the guard room, lie the kitchen, lavatories and a commons. Just like Yves's club, the walls are lined with shelves of books and a stone fireplace.

"The count insists upon the education of the whites. He has committed himself to an educated populace. We supervise a minimum of three hours per day reading."

Unexpected—most tyrants play better to an uneducated populace. Then again, most despots don't have the power to convert dissenters into loyal supporters with a single bite. Changes the dynamic a bit.

"How many *non infectés* does the count have in his service?"

"Here, there are only 40. Well, 42 since a several nights ago when Général Margot brought us a brother and sister, and we had to scramble to find bed and clothes for them."

Ah. The information I came here for.

"We could use more supplies, you know." Cécile speaks her mind a little more confidently than Marie.

"I'll make a note of it and see to it. Did the two of them stay?"

"Yes, but a few days ago, the brother went to the hospital on the orders of the chief medical officer."

That has to be Joëlle. Twenty to 1 we're talking about David and his run-in with Gabriel.

"He hasn't come back, yet. They may send him to *la Reynarde*. Most of the supplies go to the *Chateau de la Reynarde*. The last time I served guard duty there, they had close to 100 whites. Those we keep here serve in *la Buzine*. But I've seen whites shipped away after something goes wrong up in the chateau—and not to *la Reynarde*." The two of them exchange ominous glances.

The stairs creak. The wood is warped and worn in the middle. Out here, much of the antiquity was preserved in the renovation. Upstairs, the smell of marijuana fades. Through the doorways, a couple dormitories remind me of World War II hospitals with rows of thin beds on both sides. At the bottom of each bed sits a chest for the possessions of the bed's occupant.

"This room is for the boys and the second for the girls." Cécile walks me past the boys' to stand in the doorway of the girls'.

"The count forbids mixing between the two," Marie informs me, her hand clasped around the cross at her throat. Pretty sure that's not a religious move. Obviously, the count knew that falling in love makes you more susceptible to the Z-Virus.

From the back of the room, muffled sobs wind their way to the door. Cécile and Marie must have dulled their senses enough with smoking to not notice, but to me, it's loud and clear. Pushing past them, I reach one of the closets and throw it open. Nothing but towels and stacks of white clothing items. The whining subsides abruptly. Someone is hiding. A sniff points me in the direction of one of the chests. The tiny culprit has gone silent, obviously afraid of discovery.

"*Mademoiselle la Ministre, M. le Comte nous a ordonné de—*" Cécile and Marie move to stop my prying. Not a good sign.

"*Chut!*" I hush them and listen intensely. In my mind, I see children terrified into silence by their captors and locked up in chests for midnight snacking. Silence reigns for seconds while my stomach turns despite the fact that the virus-controlled center of my brain sees the sharp, pragmatism of the plan. Quick humanity check. Thank God for marijuana.

A sniffle gives the prisoner away. At the foot of the bed near the end of the row, I throw open the chest and then startle back when a small boy screams—I mean bloody murder screams—at the sight of my grey face looming above him. I can't tell which of us is more scared. Of course, the sudden shock whips up the virus, and I can't stop myself from snarling and ripping him out of the box by the armpits.

"*Chut*! Calm down, buddy." Too late for that. I've already scared the shit out of him. I hug him close to keep him from bringing the entire New Order up here. Minister of the uninfected or no, I'm not sure it's an entirely good thing for the count to discover I've been poking about the grounds on my own. "*Du calme, ma puce*, I'm not here to hurt you.*"

The screaming winds down into convulsive crying. "I want my sister. They took her away. I want my sister! Where's my sister?" He melts into sobs.

Glancing back, I interrogate Cécile and Marie with my eyes. Marie shrugs. Pretty sure she doesn't know much about anything. But Cécile, she knows something.

"Look at me." I brush the top of his head the way I've always done to soothe Amber. "Look at me, buddy. I'm going to find your sister." Hoisting him up against my shoulder, I pat his back like a baby. If he's much older than Amber he's malnourished.

Turning to the two guards, I demand answers. "Who is this boy's sister? And why was he in that trunk?"

Cécile hastens to cover her butt. "That's the new girl's bunk. What was her name?" She turns to Marie who only shrugs. Stalking over to a list on the wall, she flips to the back page. "Laure, her name is Laure. We moved her from the cot in the attic to this bed when they dragged the other girl away."

Why would Laure be hiding this boy in her trunk? I know she's not his sister. "Who had this bunk before?"

Marie flips the list back a few pages. "Martine."

At the mention of the name, an image of the unfortunate girl who spilled on the count's dinner jacket flashes across my memory, and the little boy's head pops up. "I want Martine."

"Is she your sister?"

He nods and sticks his thumb in his mouth.

Marie lets the pages fall and then turns with her hands on her hips. "He's too young to be here. He can't work. His sister must have been hiding him in there before they took her away."

Laure would totally keep hiding the boy here if she found him. She saw what happened to his sister at dinner. "Where did they take Martine?"

"Usually, they go to *la Reynarde*." Cécile and Marie glance at each other, as if nothing about Martine's removal was usual. But they're not letting anything slip. They're worried about the consequences.

"Then, that's where we're going, little guy. C'mon." I hoist him onto my hip and head for the door, wondering who I'm going to talk into taking me to Reynarde. "What's your name, *môme*?"

"Gaspard," he whimpers and cuddles into my shoulder. He must have grown accustomed to the smell—like Amber.

Throwing the door open, I run smack into the count interrogating his guards.

Chapter 30

"*Ministre Cross*, I see you do not take your responsibilities lightly." The count speaks French, most likely for the guards' benefit. "You embrace more than the title and the prestige. I agree that the security around the servants' quarters must be more stringent. I applaud you." His eye falls on my little charge. "And who is this?" He tickles the boy's chin with his finger. Biology must be playing her tricks on me because the sight of a man, who is as to-die-for attractive as the count AND who knows his way around children, triggers some deeply rooted feminine mating instinct.

"I found him stuffed in a box upstairs. He's looking for his sister."

"And who might his sister be?" The count narrows his eyes at Cécile.

"The girl Martine. She's been hiding him, here, 'stead of sending him to *la Reynarde* with all the other *mômes*. A couple of soldiers came and took her away in the night. She's the one that—"

"Yes, yes. I know the story. Well, then, we must definitely locate the sister. Come with me, *Mademoiselle la Ministre*. You and I, we will rescue this innocent in distress." The title impresses the guards. A calculated move on my behalf. Almost makes me feel bad that I'm going to use the respect he bought me to defect from his society of the depraved—almost. His magnanimity unsettles me though, makes me think maybe I'm wrong about him and that he really does plan on looking out for the uninfected.

The count commandeers a couple joints and lights one up. Each guard bows a little as we turn away. He hands me the second joint, but I shake my head. At the moment I'm responsible for the safety of an uninfected four-year-old. My skills and senses need to be sharp. The virus almost doesn't react to the scent of small children as prey anymore kind of like when I stopped eating meat, and the cravings stopped because the thought of a dead animal offended my heart. The count acknowledges my self-control with an appreciative nod.

Only a few, very select cars line the parking lot directly across from the servants' quarters on this side of the street. The count strides in the direction of a silver Tesla but stops as a black SUV pulls around in front of the door to pick someone up, and the window comes down. It's Margot. The count leans in to talk with her. Gaspard whimpers on my shoulder. "Where's Martine?"

"We'll find her, *ma puce*, don't worry. That's where we're going now."

The count finishes his conversation and nods at Margot. The door to the chateau opens. Grey strolls down the stairs chatting with Joëlle, Stéphane trailing behind. Clearly, he's not really psyched about patrol duty. On the last step, Grey glances over the SUV just in time to see the count turn and grab my hand. His face freezes, eyebrows slanted and smile gone, but only for a flash before he covers with a grin and a quick remark to Joëlle. Her face lights up in a giggle. Makes me wish her English was a bit sketchier.

Like the gentleman he is, Yves opens the back door for me to deposit Gaspard. Bending over, I try prying the boy's arms from around my neck, but he's not having any of that and starts squealing again.

The count steps in and slides his hands under Gaspard's arms. The boy lets go, and Yves cuddles him close until the wailing stops. "That's better now, isn't it, my little man?" Yves leans back. "Martine watches out for you, doesn't she, because she's your big sister? But now, we don't know where she's gone. She needs you to be a little man and help us find her. Can you do that? For Martine?"

He nods sheepishly.

"Then let's buckle you into the car so you'll be safe. I know a place much more fun than here. I bet we'll find your sister there, too. Won't that be nice?"

The kid nods and pops a thumb in his mouth. Plopping into the leather seat, pliant and submissive, he stares cow-eyed at the small arsenal on the seat next to him. Yves ruffles his hair. "Good man!" He snaps the door shut. Shaking off astonishment, and maybe just a little admiration, I slide in the door he holds for me.

"That was pretty expert. Do you have kids?"

"Me?" He laughs. "Afraid not. Never met the right girl. But I was a kid once—and scared."

Surprising. I imagined the count as more of a spoiled, rich kid, a bully with old money in his veins. He doesn't wear a seatbelt, but I do. Stronger than mine, his sense of invincibility emanates power to harness the chaos around him. Can't lie to myself. It's attractive. I run my fingers through my hair and stare out the window. In the glass, I see images of Grey.

We take the same road that Joëlle and I took to Yves's club but keep going past the turn off until we hit a fairly major road that parallels the freeway. The D2. Probably a good idea to get my bearings for when Grey and I bow out of this play.

Oddly enough, the count drives like he's taking his first road test for a license—unlike Margot who raced like a maniac fresh from the Grand Prix with no respect whatsoever for the old rules. Yves stops at all the stop signs, knowing good and well no one is coming from the other direction, and he keeps the speedometer strictly at the posted limit. It's a tad disturbing how married he is to conventions as if the apocalypse weren't collapsing civilization around him.

"You know," I comment, "you could drive on the wrong side of the road. The rules don't matter anymore."

His smile really charms the hell out of me. I expect to see a little twinkle glitter in his eye like in a 50s movie. Reaching over the console, he pats my knee patronizingly. "The rules always matter, *ma chérie*. We enforce them vigorously for the inferior and make a façade of respecting them fastidiously. So that when we, the superior, break them with impunity, our true power becomes apparent. If there are no rules, there is no power." His hand stays on my knee. His long, sculpted fingers caress my thigh, fingers meant for playing the piano—or women.

A couple streets past the round-about, he nods towards a street on the left, "You'll want to avoid driving down that road. A herd of wild *boches* wanders the vicinity around the *Château de Régis.*"

Little sucking slurps whisper from the back seat in the silence while I wonder whether to keep my mouth shut or confront the count about Gavin. Of course, I've never been able to keep my mouth shut, so I finally just blurt what I think is a subtle, non-confrontational invitation to spill his guts. "I know him, you know. Your cousin Gavin?"

Yves doesn't blink or look at me. He just nods, signals—for whom, I haven't a clue—and takes a left. Sycamore trees cover the road in a canopy of winter-weary leaves. Their fatigue speaks to me. I want to slip from the dying tree, leave the chaos behind, stop just surviving, and be reborn to live again. "Yes, I understand you knew each other in school. Greyson, as well."

"So, Margot mentioned my little outing with Joëlle?"

"She did. But, actually, Gavin himself made a point of coming to see me about it." The roads narrow here, twisting and turning. "He's quite taken with you. Can't say I blame him."

The compliment drowns in my repulsion at the idea of me and Gavin, but I'm supposed to be a diplomat, so I try to be diplomatic. "We're old friends, but he's not my type."

Clearly entertained, the count grins. "I agree. Greys and reds, these races should not mix. Any manipulation of the viral genetics for the progress of the species must be supervised, scientific, and orderly." Shivers run from my gut to my shoulders. Just when I think the count might be human, he drops some fascist bullshit on me. "But tell me, Evelyn, what is your type?"

Grey. The response pings into my mind, and I have to stifle it. "Haven't really thought about it—what with the apocalypse and all."

"Really? From what I gathered from Kasim, you washed ashore from the helicopter carrier that docked at the *Chateau d'If* a few days ago. Kasim, he's quite handsome, isn't he?"

I feel like I've stumbled onto an internet dating site. I shrug, but he wants me to swipe left or right. "Yeah, he's handsome, but he—he's not really my type. I think he's still damaged, you know, from losing people he cared about."

"Yes. Pity. Very observant of you."

"Not really. Just things he said in passing."

"I see. When I spoke with him, what most piqued my interest was how an American girl, specifically an infected grey, from a small town in Utah, found herself entangled in a French military scientific expedition. A liaison with an officer, perhaps?"

So now I understand my quick promotion. He wants to know what kind of insider information I have about the ship and the military on *If*. That island must be a thorn in the side of his infected brain.

"I helped them out, and they gave me a ride out of the dead zone."

"Come now, in such close quarters, you must have made a friend or two on the trip over."

I don't mind lying, I've done worse. But spicing the lies with a little truth helps them go down easier. "Sorry. To be honest, I got on board with another infected friend who was the valuable one. I jumped ship before the general got the chance to blow my brains out."

"This valuable one, that was Greyson?"

"Actually, no. Greyson bought his ticket on with some Nikes. He was hiding out for the duration. My friend was a doctor who, the last time I saw him, was close to a cure—"

The count bursts out laughing. "A cure? You make it sound as if we have a disease. Evelyn, *ma biche*, the virus IS the cure."

Chapter 31

"Humanity was sick." The count pats my hand as if I'm as lost as Gaspard. "The earth found a cure for what ails her. We simply follow her prescription." The count turns and we emerge from the trees into a square gravel lot that separates the courtyard of a U-shaped building to our right from a chateau with matching corner turrets on our left. A rectangle servants' quarters flanks the chateau just like at Buzine.

Bundling Gaspard in my arms, I follow the count to the servants' quarters. At the entrance, a guard—stocky, simple square-jawed—falls all over himself when the count walks into the marijuana drenched guardroom. A half-smile curls one side of Yves's lip. He enjoys watching them cower and submit.

I put the guard at ease and get right to the point. "We're looking for a girl named Martine. I believe she was brought here a day or two ago. This is Gaspard."

Yves ruffles his hair and smiles that smile that wrings a shy response from even a terrified kid. No wonder the greys flock to him. "Martine is Gaspard's sister."

"Well, I'll have to check the rosters—" He hustles to a clipboard on the wall.

"No, don't bother. We need to take this boy to the school and settle him in. Call *la Directrice* and tell her we're coming." As we leave, the guard fumbles for a cell phone—network still up and running courtesy of Stéphane, I suppose.

"I wanted to give you a tour, anyway. I'm quite proud of our school." An innocence, like a residual film of clarity and sweetness from his childhood, rips through his smile and the grey in his eyes. Grabbing my hand, he leads me across the parking lot, past a couple of school buses, and a few more SUVs. He's practically a boy who has built a sandcastle, charming and sunny, disconnected from the decrepit philosophies that cloud his brain.

His enthusiasm coaxes a smile to my lips.

The two legs of the U-shaped building across the parking lot form a courtyard. A fountain bubbles in the center. A small garden and play area surround the fountain. Just exiting from one of the doors that leads to the grounds, an uninfected teenage boy, probably about 14 or 15 from the looks of his scruffy stubble, laughs and wrangles a troupe of about a dozen five to seven-year-olds holding hands in a meandering line behind him. Their sunny giggles chase away the cloud of the apocalypse looming outside their bubble. Once they see the count, the line breaks into the mass hysteria of a paparazzi stampede.

"M. le Comte, M. le Comte!"

Yves passes me Gaspard so that he can greet the oncoming wave. A tiny, little *môme* in the middle, black curls more voluminous than she is, but not quite as bouncy, can't quite keep up with the raucous skipping and trips on her shoe. "Denis, Denis!" she wails. The group leader rushes to scoop her up, brush the pebbles from her knees, kiss her cheeks and snuggle her close.

"That's her brother." The count leans over to whisper in my ear. "He's a charming boy and an excellent role model for the children. *La Directrice* speaks very highly of him."

The rush of small people encircles his legs. He scoops them up in his arms, one by one. Yves knows every name and kisses each on both cheeks before setting them down sturdily with a compliment about how strong and tall they've grown. Gaspard's face blossoms into smiles, and his tears fade to twinkles as he watches the festivities.

From a classroom inside, a young woman with a mousy brown A-line bob, voluptuous lips, and bright eyes bounces up to us. Her flat slip-ons pad softly on the gravel. She throws an arm around Yves before kissing him enthusiastically on both cheeks. She's not infected, and she wears no make-up or signs of PTSD. On her shirt, a menagerie of cuddly cartoon animals celebrates with balloons and confetti. "Yves! I'm so happy to see you. It's been far too long. The children miss your visits."

They kiss on both cheeks.

"I have missed you, too." He shakes his head. "So much to do in the New Order, Anne."

"*Non, non, chéri,* don't apologize. We are so grateful—" She catches sight of Gaspard and claps her hands. "You have brought us a new student! You are too good, too good to us, *cher Yves!*" Her eyes pop open, and a sly smile crosses her lips, "Oh, yes, I must not forget. *Monsieur le Comte.*" She courtesies theatrically. In the dip, the loose shirt she wears gapes open to reveal a large and angry scar running down her chest, as if she's had open-heart surgery.

"No! Absolutely not. I will always be Yves to you, *ma chérie.*"

She turns to the children. "Okay, *mes enfants,* follow Denis and go tend our lovely garden. There will be a yummy soup tonight if you work hard. Stay close!" The little ones link hands and skip away down a garden path, warbling like birds in a sanctuary.

"Evelyn, may I present Anne Duprès? She and I went to school together. Anne, Evelyn is American. Like you, she loves our little orphans. I've made her my *ministre des non infectés.* You can whisper the needs of your charming school into her ear and know they will be heard."

Anne's face lights up. "*Ah! Enchantée, mademoiselle. Vous me permettez?*" She wants to kiss me on both cheeks. Her smile ignites the sun. Of course, I lean in, smiling and relieved that this is the girl in charge of the uninfected. I almost wish I were an uninfected kid rescued by the New Order so that I could bask in her *joie de vivre* every day. Makes me think I might have misjudged the count.

"Anne and I have been best friends since *l'école maternelle.*" I remember that's kindergarten. "She became a CP1 teacher and married my best friend."

Her face falls into a small cloud. "I lost Lucien in the first flesh raids—a red came to our church." The tragedy replays in her eyes until she blinks it away and lays an arm on the count's sleeve. "I would have died if it weren't for Yves. And now, I have this lovely school and all these children to fill the hole in my heart."

Yves turns to introduce her to Gaspard, and I sneak a gaze at his profile. It's so different this Yves that Anne describes. Can anyone as evil as I imagine him inspire that kind of love? Anne is not the type to skip through life with a bully. What's going on here? In the reflection of the classroom window, I see myself, gun holster on my hip, hair pulled into a messy ponytail, knife in my combat boots, and images of Amber, assembling FAMAS rifles and playing Texas hold 'em with French Marines. I would have never imagined us like this. But we adapted. We had to become this to survive. Is that what happened to Yves? Did he become the count, conceive the New Order to survive? Am I that much different from him? Do I even have a right to question the choices he made to ensure the survival of the people he loves?

Gaspar is more than happy to crawl out of my arms into Anne's. For one thing, she smells better than I do, a little citrus with a touch of lavender—really compliments the sweet *coq au vin* flavor floating around her. "Come and see the children, Yves. They miss you."

The film of dominating superiority has melted from his face. He takes her outstretched hand as if they were still in kindergarten, and she wanted to show him her Lego tower. The two legs of the U serve as dormitories while the bottom wing houses the classrooms. "We've trained some of the older children to serve as instructors for the younger. Then, in the evenings, the smaller children have playtime, and the older children work on their studies. It's not ideal, but the virus doesn't seem to spare many adults."

"Anne is modest. This place is a child's paradise."

Yves doesn't have to tell me that. Through the windows, we watch teenage boys and girls play games and read with the smaller students. Squabbles over toys or crayons disappear with a whisper from the teacher. When we walk into a classroom, three six-year-olds run over to Yves and wave their drawings in front of him. "Look, *M. le Comte*, look!" They've drawn pictures of his RAID teams saving them from the monsters. My eyes sting a little with wishing Amber could be here, back in the world of the living. Between these walls, the apocalypse doesn't exist.

"I'm afraid we have to get back, *ma chère amie*. Thank you for the tour." Yves kisses her on both cheeks. "Hope has always been your gift to the world."

The gravel crackles beneath our combat boots as we walk back to the Tesla. "Is Anne ill?"

"Why do you ask?"

"I noticed the scar—" I run my finger down my chest. "She's the heart of this place. To lose her—"

"—would be an unthinkable tragedy. No, fortunately for us all, she's not ill." He's quiet for a while as if he'd rather not dredge up the story buried in the scar.

My fingers brush his arm. "It's okay. I've seen things I'd rather not relive in words."

In front of the car, his progress stops for a moment, and he turns back to look at the children playing in the yard before opening the door. "No, you should know. You're *ministre des non infectés*." I duck into the seat, and he closes the door. In the rearview mirror, I watch him hesitate and drop a hand on the trunk for support before breathing deeply. He straightens himself and reaches into his chest pocket for a jewel-studded case of joints. He lights it up and takes a couple drags before walking resolutely around to his side of the car. The door opens, and a marijuana haze ducks into the car with him.

"Gavin made friends with Lucien's sister—"

"Oh, God." I know how this ends. The horror of being a ZV is that you strike your family first. "They both had Celiac disease, right?"

"It's the first thing they had in common. How did you know this?"

"My friend Nicolas is a doctor—very close to the source of the outbreak. His brother Sam was infected and suffered from Celiac. He made the connection when we ended up at the Knight compound near the research center in Houston—"

"The Knight's. My cousin's paternal relatives."

"Yeah. Gavin's cousin Ashley was unstable, to say the least. A religious fanatic. She's the one that turned Gavin into an alpha trying to cure him. I think she was in love with him."

"Yes, my cousin can be quite charming. But in this case, it was he who lost his heart to Lilou. She was an artist."

A familiar chill grips my spine as the image of the Foreign Legion resort lobby flashes across my imagination. "Red cape? Dog Whistle?"

He nods, apparently mortified. "Her signature. Lilou was flamboyant and a dog lover. Gavin was smitten, but she did not return his feelings. In the throes of an episode—" the count stumbles on his excuse for Gavin's travesty, "—my cousin imagined if she became what he was, she would see him differently. He transformed her. *L'Impressioniste,* they call her."

"I've seen her work."

"Days before the outbreak and evacuation, they assumed she was a serial killer. She attacked the chapel of the Sacred Heart first. Her family was there, including Anne. You know, I loved Anne. But Lucien—he was a professional musician. The youngest violinist in the *Orchestre Philharmonique de Marseille.* I actually introduce her to him. He was my tutor. I took her to the flash mob in Vieux Port in 2016, lost her the moment she lay eyes on him."

He pushes the button. The displays ding, but it's hard to tell if the car is even on. Silence reigns as Yves regrets this moment that changed everything.

"I was not the only one who thought Lucien's wife a saint. Lilou wanted Anne for the subject of her first work of demented art. Of course, Lucien was willing to die for his wife. We all were. Lilou killed her own brother before massacring the entire congregation. In the chaos, Anne texted me." His head slumps over his arms on the steering wheel. Regret bites. "I should have been at the service." He looks to me for some sort of absolution.

I have nothing to give. I have my own sins to atone for. Will I regret leaving Amber?

"I couldn't bring myself to sit next to Anne in a church with the love of her life at her other side." He can't meet my eyes and say the next words. "I was in a bar down the street."

His jaw clenches. My hand finds his on the console. Is this the source of the count's madness? Poor Margot. Does she know his history with Anne? Does she know she only fills the void?

"When I arrived with Gavin, Lilou was sawing through Anne's chest cavity on the altar. She intended to create her impression of the Virgin of the Sacred Heart." The memory of the gore catches the words in his throat. Reaching his arm to the back of my seat, the count looks behind and backs noiselessly out of his parking space. "Gavin subdued Lilou while I rushed Anne to the hospital. I thought I'd lost her—again."

Grey Daze

Chapter 32

W e don't take the same road back. Instead we pass the school and head towards the woods between la Buzine and la Reynarde. The street is narrow, and trees block the setting sun. The last mosaics of light fade into the dusk.

"I was rather small and timid as a child." He reaches across the console to take my fingers in his. His flint blue eyes, tainted with grey, hold mine. He's letting me in, and he wants me to know it. "Anne, though small, is a fierce champion of the oppressed and weak. She protected me from—how do you say? euh, bullies—until I grew and became quite capable of protecting myself and her." The scent of marijuana has faded, and Yves lights up another joint.

Enlightening revelation. The image he conjured cracks the crust around my heart. I've always tried to see the person behind the grey. Even before the days of ZV, I used to try to see the child hidden inside the grown-ups around me. Obviously, I'm going to mourn the terrorized little boy huddling inside the count. I haven't lost my humanity. Perhaps in the world of the greys, that's my greatest weakness.

I squeeze his fingers. "Your school is a lighthouse of hope in this foggy world, Yves."

He tosses off the admiration for his contribution to sanity with a wave of his joint. "Anne is the flame that keeps it burning." Our eyes meet again. His modesty isn't false. He really does see the school as Anne's achievement. But she couldn't be doing what she does without him protecting her borders and rescuing uninfected orphans.

Damn! I have to give him credit. I hate that I can see past our differences, see past the rotting shell of racism and fascism, into the naked compassion where our hearts meet on common ground. "You gave the dying world a gift." Patting his hand, I remove mine.

The count is dangerous, not just because he has demented social ideas, but because the charm seeping off him can cause brain damage. He has the universal pheromone. It attracts any X chromosome, like O+, but for love. Classic cult leader. You don't grow up in Utah without knowing all about that—unless you're in one and seriously information deprived. Frankly, I'd risk succumbing to the chemistry if he never spoke, and Grey didn't already have a fist clenched around my heart. Reaching past the console, Yves pushes a stray hair behind my ear and then turns his eyes back to the dark road—just in time to slam on the brakes.

The tires squeal and swerve to miss a small herd of uninfected children racing across the street. They probably didn't even hear us coming.

"*Merde*! They're fleeing the school garden." Screeching to a stop, he jumps out of the car and opens the trunk. The gun he tosses me is a large automatic something or other that we practiced shooting in training. He straps another over his shoulder. "C'mon!"

We stride across the street, only to run into Denis breaking through the trees carrying one howling child and dragging another by the hand. "*M. le Comte*! Thank God. Help us! It's a herd, a whole herd of *boches*. They broke through the fence." His voice breaks, and tears invade his eyes. "Mia, I couldn't find her. And Lucille, she's still in there with some of the children, I couldn't—oh, God—I couldn't get them all out."

Kneeling, I hug the squealing child dangling from Denis's hand. Yves claps his hand on the boy's shoulder. "Go! You did well!"

"No! You don't understand. I don't know where my sister is. She was near the gate, harvesting potatoes with Saïd. I couldn't find her. I couldn't find Mia."

"We'll find her.

"But—"

"Go! Make sure the others are barricaded into the school and warn the *Directrice*. Go!"

"Let me come! I have to!"

"No! This is what greys are for. We'll find Mia. Go!"

Nodding, Denis runs across the street. I head for the trees before I realize Yves isn't following. Gun on the ground, he's back at the trunk of the car where he opens a first-aid box. After rolling up his sleeve, he selects a syringe.

"Meth." He pumps his fist. "Counters the relaxing properties of marijuana but doesn't diminish the hunger blocking. Gives me an edge in a fight." Inserting the needle into a vein, he presses the plunger. "For emergencies only. Joëlle adapted it for me." Tossing the empty syringe into the car, along with the key fob, he grabs his gun and jogs in front of me into the woods.

Ghostly screams and snarls echo through the trees and intensify as we get closer. The night is falling fast. The coat of dry autumn leaves and pine needles crackles beneath our feet. Fifty yards in, Yves howls like a wolf—the drugs must be taking effect. After that, keeping up with him challenges even me. The mystery of the two faces of the *Comte de Gris* has now been solved. One drug makes him the mild-mannered and rational count, protector of the children, philosopher. The other summons the homicidal fascist, leader of the New Order— maybe the fascist part is just Yves, the little boy who was bullied.

Abruptly, the tree line ends at a plowed and furrowed field, a farm large enough to support the vegetarian population in the school. At the far end of the garden, about fifty yards beyond a greenhouse, a gate onto a dirt path behind the field gapes open. A two-foot stone base supports the glass walls of the greenhouse. Fifty-some full-on zombies clamber around the windows, banging and growling. The green wooden planks of the door shiver against their tenacious head-butting. A group of half a dozen children and, I suppose, Lucille, cower at the center of the enclosure, totally exposed and visible through the glass. But *boches* don't see, they smell. The breeze whips the scent of uninfected like meringue over the open fields.

"Is there a back exit to the greenhouse?" We kneel in the hedge that surrounds the gardens.

"No. There's only the one we see. The glass won't keep the *boches* out for long." The count unhitches the gun from his shoulder. Our virus enhanced vision lets us see across the fields even in the dark. A few of the windows have already cracked. "We can't shoot at them from here. With all that glass, we risk injuring the kids."

"No worries, they'll abandon the greenhouse the moment they catch my scent. All I do is break for that gate, and the *boches* will follow like dogs on a rabbit." I point across the garden to the opening in the chain-link fence where a shambling *boche,* severely damaged and on his last leg—literally—has just dragged himself into the field. "In the ZV mind, neutralizing the territorial threat trumps dining. You clean up the stragglers, get the kids out, and close the gate. I'll ditch the *boches,* circle around, and lock it back up."

"Absolutely not. I'll run. You—"

"Look, this is not the time for gallantry. The kids have never seen me. For all they know, I'm here to join the feast. No, it has to be you. They'll follow you without question." He's dubious. "Trust me, it won't be my first time running decoy."

He doesn't like it, but we don't have time to argue, and he knows I'm right on both issues. "We put up that fence before we moved the children in. The gate is normally locked. Someone had to cut the lock, unchain the gate, and let the *boches* in."

"An alpha? Gavin?"

"Who knows. Probably. He wanted me to turn you over to him." The count flips off the safety on his handgun. The situation calls for more strategy and less firepower. "When he left Buzine empty-handed, he was mad."

"In more ways than one." Not sure the count's English is good enough to pick up the double entendre.

"There is another possibility." I've seen a full range of emotions on Yves's face, but this is the first time I've seen anything resembling fear. "Lilou."

A shiver ripples across my shoulders. Images of the horror I witnessed in the Foreign Legion resort resurface. "It wouldn't be the first time she's wandered this far from Marseille looking for—"

"—art supplies?" Of course, the thought of children ending up in hands of *l'Impressioniste* terrifies me—more than Gavin does. In the end, I know him. I know the kid he was is still in there somewhere. But, Lilou? I'm not sure there's anything human left. I toss the bulky automatic onto the ground next to the count's. "You'll need this more than I will. It'll slow me down." I pat the Glock at my hip. "This will work in a pinch."

The growls and pounding intensify with the sound of breaking glass. Childish screams punctuate the cacophony. "I'll lose them in the trees over there. I think I know these woods, or at least the other side of them. Audrey brought us out here during training."

"Once I'm sure the children are safe, I'll come back to the gate to make sure you get in."

Turning to face the playing field, my eyes narrow, and my shoulders stiffen. My lungs swell with a deep breath. "You ready?" A breeze pushes loose strands of hair into my face and carries my scent across the darkening shadows in the garden. Perfect—sort of.

Standing, Yves grabs my hand from behind. "Take care of yourself, Evelyn. The New Order needs you." He kisses me on both cheeks. The blond scruff across his chin and under his nose tickles, maybe a little deeper than skin level. What he doesn't know is that I'm no Jeanne d'Arc. I'm not feeling as sure of myself as I sound. The only sure thing about this plan is that I have to survive to pick up my little sister. When I jumped ship, it wasn't a farewell performance.

Sprinting, I head straight for the gate about one hundred yards to the left of the greenhouse. Halfway across the field, the snarling and growling die abruptly into an unholy gurgling, and the shattering of glass wanes to a sporadic tapping. The *boches* have caught my scent.

The moon illuminates a menagerie of mottled faces drawn towards my movement and smell. Fumes of decay reach me about the same time the first of them howls and breaks into a run. His viral-jacked senses target my smell and trigger his fight reflexes. His decrepit buddies trickle in behind him, and then the herd gushes into a river of running dead. The rush of growls and gurgles rises to a crescendo, but the cries of the children die.

My peripheral vision catches the silhouette of the count dashing, without the guns, towards the greenhouse. He can't afford to fire on the few *boche* stragglers. They're stuck in the windows trying to crawl through the jagged holes. He's going to have to take them on in hand to tooth combat. A gunshot might recall some of the crowd charging me.

The furrowed ground beneath my feet slows me down. God, please don't let me twist my ankle. I can't recover from that kind of damage. I recognize the *boche* leading the pack. Gavin's main stooge, *Poillu*. He's a fast, bloody-mouthed son of a bitch. The fact that one of Gavin's bodyguards is here makes me suspect he's lurking out there somewhere, directing this scene of *Hell's Opera*.

The *boches* charge on a trajectory to intercept my straight line from one side of the field to the other. Poillu's snarls stand out in a guttural solo above the chorus. He barrels towards me about ten strides ahead of the other frontrunners. We stand to reach the fence at the same time, that is until my toe catches on a small body lying in a furrow.

My hands fly out to catch my fall. The damp earth squelches under the impact of my palms and knees. The body is a boy. Half his face and neck are gone, but what the zombies are really after is the insides. His whole core gapes open, bloody and bony, devoured. He won't be turning. Brains are gone.

Scrambling to haul myself up, I pull the Glock from my holster. Poillu dives for me. His meaty fist throttles my boot leg over the boy's corpse and keeps me on my belly.

Thrashing, I rip my foot free, flip and jam my heel in his face. His head jerks back, but pain doesn't slow him down. While he fumbles viciously for my foot, his two henchmen narrow the gap to only a couple of body lengths. The entire herd will be on me in ten shambling strides. The virus pumps in my veins. I howl like the count on his meth and swing my gun arm around.

Yves can't shoot, but I can. The crack might even draw a few more of the scavengers still hanging about the greenhouse.

The shot hits Poillu in the throat, so it's not a kill, but it opens a vein and derails the flow of virus blood code to his brain long enough for me to crawl away.

The distance between me and the *boche* platoon gives me no time to turn and shoot. I have to get out that gate or the zombies overwhelm me and swarm back across the yard to the children before my last breath is gone. My arm outstretched behind, I fire blindly at Poillu's henchmen as I run. I want the herd to keep coming, but slower. The bullets hit with disgusting squelches. The thrum of their footsteps stumbles, and their bodies thud behind me.

The rest of the herd has to skirt the pile, giving me a couple seconds lead. The gate opens out, obviously. Zombies don't pull—too much coordination required for that. They push *en masse* until the fence gives. Like frogs, they only go forward. The chain hangs loose on the gate. The lock isn't cut. Whoever opened it had a key. Stretching my arms in front of me, I crash the metal links with an open palm and the gun in my fist. No time to look back and see how the count is fairing. Jamming my gun in the holster, I sprint down the road. Behind me, from the greenhouse, a chilling child scream pierces the growling and snarling hot on my heels. What kind of sick, morally bankrupt bastard targets children?

Chapter 33

Where the hell do I run?

My feet pound the pavement. That puff of marijuana is slowing me down, making me too human.

When we were training, Audrey showed us a map of the woods to my right. A small neighborhood and a pretty substantial forest separate Buzine from Reynarde and Régis. New Order guards patrol the neighborhood, but the frenzied mob careens down the road just strides behind me. I don't know how far I have to run to reach the houses. Even pumped on viral adrenaline, I'm already gasping for air.

I shortcut through the woods, hoping to lose a few *boches* in the tangle of trees. Fall leaves crunch beneath my feet. The sound and scent keep them on my trail like bloodhounds. A couple hundred yards in, through the guttural heaving breath of the *boches*, a cry pierces the darkness beneath the bare limbs and pines. Not the desperate squeal of doomed prey but of a terrified child.

Like I'm gonna leave one of Anne's kids out here alone. I veer towards the sound and break into a clearing littered with the ruins of a stone shack. The door and window are jagged holes of crumbling cement.

The scream streaming through the window trembles and cracks into a sob. Behind me, leaves rustle, and roots crack at an alarmingly close distance. Leaping, I dive through the window. Dirt and rotted leaves cover the cracked stone floor. The force of my landing jams a pebble into the soft folds of my palm, and the worn cement floor scrapes a red rash. My lungs pump double time. Before I even stop rolling, the stench of an alpha overwhelms the sweet, apple tart aroma of the uninfected girl hiding here. The virus prickles in my blood.

The leaders of the herd reach the high window. Like tentacles, their arms flail and shove in relentless forward motion as they stack up behind the wall. Teeth clack and snarl behind me. Scrambling to my feet, I rip my Glock from its holster and target the three threatening to push through the dilapidated stone.

"Help!"

I whip around to the stifled whimper coming from a small storage room behind the main wall. The two-room shelter is mostly bare. Cigarette butts and wine bottles clutter the floor in the corner of the second room. A rusty, old lantern, a weather-cracked table, and one three-legged chair sit under an unhinged shelf to my left.

Glancing back at the mob, I figure I've got a couple minutes before they tumble through the hole.

"*N'aie pas peur, ma puce. Le comte m'a envoyé t'aider.*" The count is a superhero at the school. His name is sure to buy me some credibility. "Come out, sweetheart."

"I want Denis." Scuffles and squeals erupt from behind an unhinged wooden door. "Let me go, let me go!"

The door creaks open. The little girl, mostly sticks and skin, kicks and squirms.

"Evelyn, this is a pleasant surprise—well, that's not quite true, is it? So glad you could make our little evening of night games." Gavin grins at me from behind Mia's dark curls.

Chapter 34

Swinging around, I plow a bullet through the forehead of a balding hulk of a *boche* who has shoved his way through the crowd stuck at the window. He slumps forward, and his bulk plugs the hole, buying me some time to negotiate.

Mia screams at the deafening bullet crack. With his hand, Gavin smothers her mouth and nose. "Loud little beast, isn't she? Good plan, though, Ev, diving through. They don't climb well." He nods at the window, detached, as if a dozen foul-mouthed, cannibal ex-humans aren't clawing and gnashing to get around the fat corpse and dine on Mia and me. The poor little girl rips at his hand, fighting for air. "It was the brains, I think, that kept you in my head, taunting me. How does that happen? Smart, but still athletic, drop-dead gorgeous—" He grins. "That means something new now, doesn't it?"

Zombie wordplay! God. He has no sense of timing. "Gavin, let Mia go. She's suffocating!"

"Better to send her off like this than to shove her out the door and send my dogs after her, don't you think?" He shakes his head, lamenting. "They're not the smartest pack. They have trouble learning commands. Chase, eat, hunt—they're good at those. Sit, stop, wait—they struggle."

He's terrifyingly practical and logical like the virus is using his brain to think but has replaced all his human instincts with viral instincts. Mia is turning blue.

"Gavin, she's practically a baby. Please, let her go. This is between you and me." Another *boche*, a skinny, blood-smeared blonde, missing one ear, has wriggled into the gap over the blob blocking the window.

"How about this, Ev? You put down your little gun there, and I'll send Mia over to you. "Then we can work this out, you know, ZV to ZV."

Mia's struggles wane, and her eyelids droop. Even though I don't stand a chance against an alpha in hand to hand, I toss my gun on the crumbling stone floor. Not too far away, just on top of leaves piled against an uneven stone. I'm not worried about Gavin picking my gun up and using it against me. His teeth are far more lethal.

Grinning and acknowledging my offering with a nod, Gavin simply lets go of his hold on the girl. Gasping, she falls limp to the floor. I swoop in and sweep her up in my arms, carrying her to the table, holding her close like the baby she is. As soon as she can breathe again, she whimpers.

The zombie, thrashing and snarling in the window, drooling blood and bits of flesh, terrifies her speechless. She's been around the count too much to understand the horror that the alpha who kidnapped her could inflict.

Holding her head close to my body and stroking her hair, I try diplomacy—mostly because it's my only option. "Could you do something about that?" I jerk my head at the struggle in the window.

Like a clueless dog owner, his eyebrows crease in confusion until he realizes the snarling and clawing that he's grown accustomed to bother us. "So sorry!" Stalking over to the window, he barks. "Stay!" The blonde snarls and grunts, struggling tenaciously. He slugs her in the face. "Stay, stupid *boche*!" Her head flops back with the impact, but this time, she obeys, twitching. "German tourists!" He sighs, a resigned tour guide. Leaning his head through the gap above hers, he yells at the rest of the pack, "Shut up and stay, you bitches!" The worst kind of abusive dog owner, still, he has some control over the horde. The snarling dies to a low moan, and the grasping shadows outside the window slow to nervous pacing.

"Much better. Now maybe we can talk." He steps over and strokes Mia's head as if she were one of his mangy pets.

If I didn't know that, under the diplomatic surface, lurks a narcissistic, rich boy, marinating in lunacy, I'd actually be taken in. But I'm not, so I pull her off the table and set her on the floor behind me.

"*Quel plaisir inattendu*!" French really isn't Gavin's style, but maybe he thinks I'll be less repulsed by him if he's speaking a beautiful language. I'm not. It works for the count, but I know Gavin too well. "I really only intended to punish Yves a bit, break a few of his toys."

"There's already a little boy dead in the field. You've made your point. These children are innocent. What more do you want? God, Gavin, at least your cousin makes an attempt to stay human."

I'm not playing nice, and I've triggered the virus in his blood. He slaps my cheek. The alpha blow literally throws me off my feet. My butt slams into the dirt floor. Mia squeals and rushes to my side. "Human? Why would anyone want to be human when they could be a god?" He abandons the French and bends, shoving his nose into my face. "You have no idea what Yves is planning and what he is, do you? You're blinded by his charm."

That may be so, but Gavin has no idea he's knocked me on top of the gun. His thin film of sanity has evaporated, and deluded madness has blinded him to everything but his wanting.

Baiting the virus to take him over might be the smart move—if it doesn't turn out to be the most dangerous. Gavin will sacrifice logic and reason for emotion and instinct. I might be able to manipulate that. Nudging the Glock into a pile of leaves at my feet, I pick myself off the dirty concrete. Mia whimpers beside me.

"Doesn't matter what he is. He's given a bunch of orphan children a life, sheltered them from the apocalypse." My palm shoves his chest. "You just punched a hole in their bubble and murdered a kid."

Behind us the zombie time-out has expired. Two boys maybe twins, scrawnier and pretty young, claw their way over the top of the Aryan. She's not pleased. Snarling and snapping, they fight for the limited real estate. Mia dives for cover behind the door.

Seizing my wrist, Gavin jerks it. "I only showed him how precarious his little kingdom is. He's forgotten who's at the top of the food chain now. Maybe you have, too."

The growling has found its way around the building to the front. Mia whines, petrified. Pointing at the window, I question Gavin's authority over his minions. "Damn it, Gavin! Can't you control your beasts! They're scaring her."

"They're not beasts! They're soldiers!" Screaming maniacally, he turns to the window and totally distracts himself beating the crud out of the faces stuffed in the window. I grab the gun, scooping up Mia as I bolt for the door.

One foot out of the shack, and we run smack into a bewildered retiree in a brown cardigan, plaid pants, and a beret. His whole demeanor warps when my scent hits him in the face. My only option is to fire on him. The crack of the shot halts Gavin's frenzy. His footsteps slap on the cement and then thud into the ground behind us, closing the gap. Then, inexplicably, he stops gaining.

Mia whimpers, bouncing in my arms. Tree branches bat our faces. A bare limb rips across my forehead. My heart thumps super doses of adrenaline, and I breathe like a locomotive. I'm actually afraid. Maybe more for Mia than myself.

Why hasn't Gavin caught us? He should be on me like mold on Brie.

A buzzing whine filters through the trees—a motorcycle engine. The tree line breaks and gives way to rooftops silhouetted in the moonlight at the end of the road. A spark of hope pushes me to shoot into the dark behind us. At the crack, Mia buries her head in my shoulder and cries. Gavin's pace doesn't even miss a beat. The bullet missed completely.

My boot hits the road, and I run up it towards the houses. The headlight from the motorcycle flashes me. The tires squeal. Gavin's footsteps hit the pavement at the moment the motorcycle passes me in a braking skid. I can't help myself. I turn to look. Gavin leaps at the oncoming bike. The two projectiles collide. The driver and the alpha fly in a death grip to the other shoulder while the bike tips and scrapes down the road.

Setting Mia on her feet, I shove her towards the neighborhood. The houses around Buzine lie just around the bend.

"Run, *ma puce*. Run to the houses!"

"No! I'm scared."

"We can't be scared. Go!" I push her tiny shoulders down the road until she's running.

The two bodies have stopped rolling by the time I turn back. The kid's helmet came off, probably not strapped. It's in the ditch on the other side.

Gavin snarls and hauls the dazed and limp boy to his feet.

In the shadows of the moonlight, I recognize Denis. Of course, he came for Mia. Did I really think he'd wait safely in the chateau while his little sister took her chances out here against the *boche* horde?

Chapter 35

Denis's head blocks any shot at Gavin's, and I'm too far away to do anything else but plead and shout. "Gavin, wait! Stop! He was just trying to save—"

Gavin rips into the boy's neck like a wolf.

"No!" Pain chokes me, doubles me over. "No!" I scream again. I don't have a choice. Straightening up and squaring my shoulders, I shoot.

The boy's neck flops back. At least, he won't have to do hard time as one of Gavin's monsters for the crime of wanting to protect his little sister. Gavin roars. He wanted his revenge—another foot soldier. "Damn you, Evelyn!" He steps towards me.

"I can hit you right between the eyes from here!"

I'm not lying, I can. But I can't possibly take out the entire invasion force he let loose on the garden. They've finally caught up with us, and the leader of the pack emerges onto the road only a yard behind Denis's body. My finger squeezes reflexively. The bullet cracks. The vivid moonlight illuminates the front-runner's pale skin and the little purplish hole that blooms on his head. Pivoting, I sprint down the road after Mia. If I remember right, this kind of handgun only has 19 rounds, and I've used up some of those.

I can't see her ahead of me because the path hairpins just before it reaches the road to Buzine. I'm not too far ahead of the zombies, and Gavin runs at the head of the pack. My viral senses smell him, hear the throaty huff of his breath. The path forks. On the left, near the road, boulders block vehicles from entering. Mia took the left fork and turned right towards the houses. Through a break in the trees, I can see her across the field, running as fast as she can, crying and yelling for help.

Veering onto the right fork, I dash through the brown grass and scrub oak. She's hardly made any more progress by the time my path intersects hers. She's not fast enough to outrun the pack. I'll have to carry her into the neighborhood and hope to hell we find some grey patrols there.

When I scoop her up from behind, she screams loud enough to crack the sky

"It's me. Evelyn."

Her arms strangle my neck. It's already hard to breathe. ZVs don't register the fatigue, but I feel my muscles losing power, and I'm carrying an energy snack in my arms. God! The monster inside me just won't die.

The wall separating the neighborhood from Gavinland is still under construction, but vine-smothered walls surround the houses we pass. Out from a *cul de sac* drive, steps a RAID clad grey, gun still holstered to his shoulder, no helmet, as if he hadn't heard any of the gunshots. Damn! Of all the greys on patrol, it's Stéphane we run into in our moment of need. He's brilliant with an electrical grid or a computer, but useless in a fight with an alpha's platoon. Holding Mia out, I shove her in his arms. "Go! Get her back to the chateau. Just run!"

"But, we're—"

The sight of the riot trailing me shuts his mouth. He hauls Mia and his nerdy ass to an SUV parked just up the street. Wanting to keep as many of them off his trail as possible, I race towards the back of the *cul de sac*. If the zombies follow me down here, so much the better. They'll bounce around, stymied between the garages out front and the walls that surround the homes until something—or someone—turns them around.

At the back of the street, to the side of a double garage that serves the two homes behind, I cut through a little gate. My first idea is to turn and latch it to buy myself some time. Greyson, Margot, and Joëlle left on patrol with Stéphane in that same SUV. That means they're in the neighborhood, armed and, hopefully, readier for a fight than Stéphane.

The house sits on the lot at an angle so, once I'm inside the gate, I can see past the front porch to the back yard and an enormous swimming pool. I get an idea and leave the gate open. The horde is close on my heels, but, oddly enough, and somewhat worrisome, Gavin is not.

Heading for the pool, I startle a Jack Russel terrier hiding under a chaise lounge on the patio. He barks and dances, but avoids me like the plague—appropriate cliché.

Once around the pool, I stand halfway down the length of it. It sprawls in a huge block, a moat between me and the zombies. Running full speed, they all sprint on a straight trajectory at the target—me. All but one. He gets distracted by the dog and veers from the crowd. Some of the *boches* trip over the raised cement terrace that separates the pool from the front yard, but eventually, one after the other, they race off the grass and into the pool, like lemmings over a cliff. After a couple minutes, at least two dozen *boches* thrash and splash in their wet prison.

I don't have time to ponder how long it will take for their skin to waterlog and peel off their bones or for the virus to figure out swimming. The distracted teen *boche,* all in blood-smattered white, like he might have been at Buzine for a while, follows the dog off the straight path to the pool. I have to shoot him as I pass on my way to the open gate. The shot is bound to bring stragglers from the street into the cul de sac.

The whole time I'm racing past the bushes and trees that camouflage the walls around the mansions, my mind butts up against a wall of its own. Can I shoot Gavin? He's not one of these brain-dead, virus resurrected soldiers that, if they were still alive, would want to put a proper end to their existence. Sure, he's deep down the path of insanity, but insanity isn't a capital offense. For all I know, Nicolas's cure would heal him and restore him to the human that he was—an egotistical prick, but human.

Am I becoming Greyson? If I don't shoot him, and he murders anyone else, that blood is on me. That's the sticking point—his blood on my conscience or the innocents he slaughters. There's no way I come out of this unstained. An old French proverb scrolls across my brain. *Qui ne fait rien, consent.* It means, *He who does nothing, consents.* I can't consent. All philosophical meanderings aside, to save Mia, I'd ram a bullet through Gavin's brain in a heartbeat.

A couple *boches*, who got stuck in the hedges trying to follow the direct path to my scent, turn and charge me from inside the tangle of vines. I can't risk getting bitten, so I shoot them. After all the training I've had, I'm a decent shot, but not perfect. I use up three bullets, instead of two, before they face-plant in the road.

Where the hell are the other patrol guards from that SUV? The smell of grey permeates the air, but I don't see anyone.

When I break into the street, the worst possible scenario grinds me to a halt. Stéphane sprawls lifeless in front of the SUV. A pool of his own purple blood spills from a rip in his throat. In front of him, Gavin whispers into Mia's ear. Head tilted to one side like she can't support the weight of what's in her brain, she stares blankly, straight ahead. She should be wailing, screaming, and kicking, but Gavin must have murdered Stéphane right in front of her. She's in shock. He doesn't notice.

Two large *boches* stand in front of him, casting nervous twitches at the body. The smell of grey blood triggers their fight instincts, but they can't quite get past the fresh croissants and strawberries aroma dripping off Mia. If she weren't in Gavin's arms, they'd be tying on bibs for ribs. The burly, bald guy in the muscle shirt looks like he was grey. The tint of his skin tells the tale. There's only one bite mark in his bulky shoulder. Gavin hand-picked him and turned him. The other guy's not in good shape. Jaw clacks as he twitches, like maybe it was broken. Intestines spill from the tatters of his shirt. Claws wander towards Mia and then jerk away in a tug-of-war between his feeding instincts and the viral programming that connects him to Gavin.

The bushes to the side of me crack. I crouch, ready to fend off the attack from any of them stuck at the wall buried in the hedge. A light winter breeze rustles the trees. Gavin finally acknowledges me. "You're a bright girl, Evelyn. You know how this goes. You put down the gun and walk this way, or I hand this tasty morsel over to my friend Maurice here." For a second, I listen for the faint slap of boots on pavement. The others had to have heard the shots. *Grey was with them for God's sake. Where are they?*

I don't really have a choice. Dead, I'm no use to anyone, but Gavin's in the market for a grey consort. He's just vain enough—and deluded enough—to believe he can win me over if he blackmails me into coming with him willingly. I don't trust him at all to keep Mia safe once I give up the gun—and I have to give up the gun. "No way. You put the little girl down. When she's in the SUV, then I'll drop it."

He shrugs. "I'd be happy to oblige, but look at her." He leans in like he's confiding a guilty secret, "I may have broken her. I don't think she would stand. Feels a bit limp. You'll have to come and get her."

He's right. She'll crumble like an empty dress to the ground, an irresistible spill for his dogs. "Then you come here and hand her to me."

"You're much too familiar with that gun for me to give you a close-range advantage."

"I'm not like you. I wouldn't risk hitting her."

With his free hand, he taps his lip. His insatiable lust has gotten the better of him. He could kill Mia, shield behind his stooges and take me down. But that's not what he wants. He wants me, not just virally subservient, but willingly. His narcissism reigns supreme. "Fair enough." Hitching Mia up so that she shields all his vitals, he steps past his goons. "I'll bring your little pet to you, and we'll trade. Girl for gun. Sound fair?"

I nod.

He covers half of the ground between us. "You see, Ev. You've misjudged me. I'm the same guy you knew in high school, just the super-hero version. I love a baby as much as you do."

In his mouth, those words have a double meaning. The picture I get isn't the one he was going for and doesn't really cinch his case. "We'd be 'goals.' Everyone would want to be us."

"Listen, Gavin, we're not super-humans. We haven't evolved, we've devolved. There's a cure and sooner or later, when the virus has run its course, the humans will take back the planet. Be human with us. Lock yourself up somewhere and wait out the infection."

He's ten paces away. The full moon reflects off his pale face. The shadow of the tree above our heads bleeds into darkness. "Drop the gun."

Instead, I stretch my arm to him, the gun dangling towards the ground. I still don't trust that he'll save Mia. "I'm putting her in the car. You keep your distance until I slam the door."

"That wasn't our deal."

"It's the new deal. You know as well I do, I can't trust you."

"You just can't wrap your head around it, can you?" He steps closer. "You'll see, I'll convince you. You and me, we can rule this world." As I reach for Mia, he closes his hand around the gun. She slumps into my arms, and we step, a connected mass, towards the SUV.

Two shots crack from the hedges. Gavin's two *boches* topple over. Margot and Joëlle emerge from the leafy tangle.

Gavin glares and snarls, ripping the gun from my fist, "Bitch!"

My hands wrap protectively around Mia's head, and I swivel to take the attack. In my peripheral vision, a black-clad figure drops out of the tree, right onto Gavin's head. The two forms tumble to the ground, and the gun clatters away. Gavin, enraged, snaps for the kill as they roll, but the RAID suit of the patrolman repels him. The grey slams Gavin's head with the side of his gun and scrambles to his feet. Gavin vaults up and springs for him, teeth bared. "The bitch is mine!"

"Gavin, stop!" Margot orders.

The patrolman targets Gavin's face.

"Greyson, don't shoot! Damn it!" Margot is right on top of us, a gun in each hand, ready to shoot anyone who moves.

Greyson throws up his visor. A small bead of sweat traces a path from the corner of his eye to his lips, trailing a path through the pair of matching moles on the side of his jaw, stars in a grey sky. He can't resist a last shove. "This 'bitch' doesn't belong to anyone. She owns us all." He reaches for Mia, and I let him take her. He's got the suit and the gun. Without a look back at Gavin, we head for the SUV. Joëlle rushes up and takes charge of the little girl.

"Go home, Gavin. The credit the count extends to you because you are his cousin has a limit." With the muzzle of her gun, Margot shoves him down the path towards Régis.

Chapter 36

Above the trees, tranquility falls on the chateau in shades of purple descending into pink and yellow. If my grey skin weren't immune to the chill of the evening breeze, my new red dress and stiletto heels, compliments of Rémy and his staff—who must be ghosts because I've never once even seen them—would be woefully inadequate. Dusk soothes the buzzing of the virus in my blood. In these scarce, serene moments, my mind wanders to Greyson. I can't help but wonder what it would be like to be with him outside of the apocalypse, beyond the terror and gore, somewhere on that taffy horizon. Is love always love, or does it only burn against raging waves and storms? What happens when the sea calms? Does it drift into oblivion or sail farther and faster into deeper waters? I'd like to find out.

The chateau door opens, and the scent of burning crayons reaches me before Kasim steps onto the veranda.

"Oh, sorry! Didn't expect to find anyone here." He strolls my direction and leans in to press his cheek against mine, first one side and then the other.

"It's not exactly private property. Actually, I'm happy for the company. I've spent my fair share of time alone." After we moved in, Kasim showed up for one day of training and then disappeared. "Haven't seen you for a while."

"I've been away. The count needed some reconnaissance. You don't mind if I share in your moment of tranquility? After training, I need some space before I face the dining room."

"It's all yours. I won't trespass on your solitude."

"No, it's fine. Stay. We haven't exactly had a quiet chat since we met. It's all been quite tense." He takes a puff of the joint and hands it to me.

Why not? Could be foolish, though. Dinner isn't always the civilized affaire the count would like it to be. Probably wiser not to be too subdued. Then again, it is rough with all those delectable *non infectés* lingering around the dining table. Boils the viral juices. Training with Audrey only excites them even more.

Looking at the horizon every night before dinner settles the little demons. Banking on the rest of the greys towing the line behind the new weed rations, I inhale the smoke that soothes the grey gods so they don't consume the disciples in their wrath. The drugs do nothing to quell the missing. Just beyond the horizon lies the beach and beyond the beach the island where a little six-year-old keeps at least one solid piece of my heart safe. I want more than anything to have her back with me, but I have to fight the urge to take a car, drive to the coast, steal a boat from the port, and go get her. I can't let myself. My hands grip the guard rail. I can't let my need to keep Amber safe rob her of true safety.

"The urges hit me hardest at night." Kasim's French has a rich, roasted flavor. "With all the *non infectés* serving, I need a little—*calme*." A quiet *tête à tête* with him before dinner is an *hors d'oeuvre* in itself.

I've been wanting to get a taste for him. I need to see where his politics lean so I know if I can count on his help with Laure and David. I'd like to take him with us to find Nicolas. Could be tricky. He's obviously valuable because the count keeps him close. Now that I've seen the other side of the count, I understand the ambivalence Kasim must feel. But, I also see the rift that the count is too egotistical to notice. Ordering the death of someone's half-brother doesn't usually translate to love and loyalty.

Kasim takes another drag as if the last one dissolved one worry, and now he's moving on to the next. "Are you settling in well?"

"Oh, yeah. Everything here is perfect. Rémy is a god. It's like a utopian novel—" A couple of *non infectés,* supervised by a grey, drive a pig into the yard below the balcony. Each white-clad kid also carries a basket with a couple chickens in it, "—at least for the greys."

Unlike the Nazis, the greys don't need guns to guarantee the submission of the prisoners. They're faster, so running is pointless. And then, one bite is either a death sentence or infection. I wonder if some of the *non infectés* have reached a point where they think the smart ticket would be to become a grey, or if the infection, and the uncertainty of its pathology, still scares the shit out of them. They're all vegetarian, so if they do get bit, they'll become greys. If the count doesn't manage to propagate the race the natural way, this might be his plan B. Whatever else it is, the plan is balanced. The *non infectés* eat the produce, and the greys eat the meat.

In a scuffle of pecking and clucking, one of the *non infectés* drops his basket. The chicken inside scuttles away. The grey slaps the kid up the side of his head. Kasim exhales, sending a gentle smoke column into the cool, evening air. "Not so sure the *non infectés* find the arrangement as appealing."

Our eyes meet, and my look says everything: that I'm surprised to hear the New Order's prime minister express an opinion so incongruent with the count's, and that I'm not surprised to hear Kasim feels that way. What's in a person's heart shows on the face, doesn't matter the color—grey, white, or red.

Kasim only notes my surprise. "What? I was a brown man, a Muslim in Marseille. I know what it's like to be on the wrong end of racism."

"So, you're not anxious to turn the tables and oppress your oppressors?" Obviously, I'm thinking of Miguel in Houston. Don't get me wrong, though. The animal in me senses the vast differences between him and Kasim like a dog who knows instinctively if a master will kick or not. I just want to hear Kasim say he's not the count's man.

"The count thinks I would love nothing more than to dominate my past oppressors. But there are two kinds of people in the world. You've read *Animal Farm, non*?"

"Yeah, required reading in high school."

"Well then, you know the wheel turned. The farmer went to the bottom, and the pigs rose to the top. But in the end, the swine slept in the farmer's bed. Some just want to turn the cycle and others want to obliterate the wheel." Kasim offers me another puff, and I decline.

"And which type are you?"

He raises an eyebrow. We both know where he stands. Instead of answering, he inhales the dissonance of actually voicing that statement and continuing to live here. Now I know he doesn't just see grey, he sees both sides of it. He points the joint at the guard and turns his head to look me in the eye, telling me that what he's saying is more than what he's saying. "They don't smoke enough here. Before the count made smoking mandatory, there were *incidents* in the servants' quarters. Despite what I said when you first arrived, I've noticed your level of control is extraordinary. Why is that?"

Shrugging, I lean over the balustrade and let my gaze wander beyond the trees to where I know the Mediterranean Sea meets the coastline. The reason floats over there on a little island called *If.* But can I trust Kasim with that information? Risky. "Because I have to. I have a sister. She's not infected. I survive, I control the urges, to keep her that way."

"So, you don't think they'd all be better off like us?"

Kasim doesn't have a readable face. What's he doing? Spying or gauging my political leanings? Tough to tell. The three travelers pass by, headed for the kitchen entry below the chateau. The sun dips, and the breeze laments its passing.

"I'm sorry about Eugène."

Kasim shrugs, but the tightening around his eyes gives him away. The loss hurts, the way it would hurt me to lose Amber. Doesn't matter that the virus turned Eugène into a fiend. He could have been locked up to wait for the cure. I'm pretty sure that knowing Nicolas and his cure are out there eats at Kasim's gut. "The reds have to be eliminated for the New Order to thrive."

"All the reds except for Gavin, the count's cousin. That doesn't seem quite fair."

He looks away, so I can't see his reaction.

"This isn't a utopia, Kasim. It's a reversion to feudalism—lords and serfs. It can only end in brutality and oppression. My offer still stands, you know. Go north with me. Help me find Nicolas."

"You're not staying? I thought the luxury accommodations and the VIP treatment had persuaded you. The count thinks so, too."

Did I just wander into dangerous territory? If I'm reading Kasim wrong, Greyson and my most favored status with the count is toast, and our chance to free Laure and David dwindles to charcoaled crumbs. I haven't forgotten the cells in the basement. If we don't play our cards right, we could find ourselves back where we started, or worse.

My hesitation doesn't escape Kasim's notice. The clink of crystal on silver, high heels on marble, and laughter on whispers spill out the open doors from the great hall behind us. The others congregate to share an aperitif before dinner. Others. I don't see these people as *us*. These greys are *them*. The cloud of designer cologne-camouflaged decay mingles with a fresh, tantalizing hint of *non infecté*. Kasim drops a casual hand onto mine as we both stare out to the horizon.

Call me impulsive—I've been called worse—but I trust Kasim. My instincts, which are above average, count him as *us*. He belongs with Greyson and me. He deserves a chance at a cure. As genteel as Buzine's façade might be, it hasn't blinded him to the ugly realities beneath.

"So, reconnaissance? I thought that was Greyson's 'mission'."

He grins at the mock gravity of surrounding the last word with quotes. Not all of us can take the count seriously. "Greyson did scout the tree park, yes. But this is different. There's another, uh—"

"—another group of *non infectés*? Is the count going after them, too?"

He glances back, and then down at the patio below us, taking a drag. The look he gives me resembles the looks I've been giving him. He's debating whether to trust me or not—or maybe that's wishful thinking.

I encourage him. "You know where I stand, right? You watched Grey and me in action. I've seen enough here to know we don't belong here, and neither do you."

He won't look at me. "You haven't seen nearly enough. Be careful who you say this to. The count won't abide disloyalty. The consequences are severe."

Smiling, as if we're enjoying a little pre-dinner flirtation, I take his arm and walk him to the far corner of the veranda. My sharp heels click against the marble. The candy splashed sunset melts to grey. "Tell me, Kasim. What do you know?"

A deep breath of the night air pumps his courage. "Have you ever stopped to wonder what I was doing in the legionnaire vacation resort the day you washed up? Did you think it was just coincidence?"

"I gathered you were hunting *l'Impressioniste.*

"I only ran into the artist on accident. The count sent me. I was reconnoitering his next target—the *Chateau d'If.*"

Oh, God!

Chapter 37

The night before the scheduled raid on the tree park, Grey and I head back to the chateau with Audrey to dress for dinner. Given a slight tactical advantage, either of us can now take down the other two. Every other night, either he or I have been playing our part in this stage production of the New Order. I haven't been able to corner him with the intel I got from Kasim. I figure I have time. The count's military are tied up planning the raid on Laure's camp. But Grey and I need to figure out how we can take advantage of that maneuver to hit the road. We have to find Nicolas so we can get cured and get back to Amber.

The feral cry in the distance, muffled between the branches and the crunching of dried leaves beneath our combat boots, catches my radar ears but not Grey's and Audrey's. They're too busy calling me out for contriving a tactical advantage that might have included a little unfairly distracting public display of affection.

In single file—Audrey, Grey, then me—we trudge, beat, along the narrow, single-lane path. "Like I told Gabriel, *All's fair in love and war.*" I pause, tilting my head towards the whine.

"Is this love or war?" Greyson doesn't even bother to turn around.

The noise doesn't repeat itself, and I hustle to catch up. Most likely an animal. Breaks my heart. Most of the pets lost their owners when the virus went viral. Pets don't know the streets well enough to forage and scavenge for themselves. And even if they do, the *boches* are only too happy to supplement their diet with a little canine or feline delicacy when human is scarce.

"Love IS war." I tangle my fingers in Greys. Training with him and Audrey makes me feel normal again, like high school—where our school colors are grey, and we're the mascots. Makes me miss Amber more. Not that I don't worry about her every day. Is she safe? Is she mad at me? Has she forgotten me? Does she have someone to tell her the princess story and rub her toes at night until she falls asleep? Who holds her close when she wakes up in a cold sweat grasping a knife in her fist? No, this missing is different. This missing involves ghostly visions of us playing hide and seek in the trees and her laugh echoing in the twitter of a bird I can't see.

The high-pitched whine pricks at my ear again. "What's over there, Audrey?"

She glances behind us and to the right, into the trees. "The border with the reds."

"You mean Gavin and his *boches*?"

She nods, eyebrows bent. "It's best to avoid that area, even before curfew. Gavin doesn't have as much control over his minions as he claims to—and there are rumors."

"What kind of rumors?"

She shrugs and frowns, her eyes tight. The look is familiar. She doesn't want to tell me, but really thinks I should know. Probably doesn't even want to know herself. Staring into the living eyes of buried truths stirs up all sorts of angst. "Gabriel— " Her eyes dart through the trees. The forest might have ears so her words shift direction. "Sometimes whites disappear, but only the girls."

My shoulders haven't shivered like this for a while. Not much freaks me out anymore.

"And there's another alpha. I'm not sure you've heard of— "

"—*l'Impressioniste?* "

She nods and glances over her shoulder, like just saying the name might conjure the devil. "She wears a red cape. It might just be a myth."

"Believe me. She's not a myth. I've seen her work. You see a red cape, you run."

Eau de grey creeps up the trail in front of us, ahead of branches snapping and muffled footsteps. A runner in fatigues rounds the bend. "Audrey, the count would like to see you in his chamber before dinner."

With a quick wave of apology, she hustles to follow the messenger.

When they're out of sight, Grey stops. His eyes bore into mine. The performance is over. Charming, playful Greyson has left the building. "What the hell are we doing here, Ev?"

"What do you mean?"

"I mean, why haven't you and I blown this place, already? Is it the count? You've bought into his New World Order bullshit? That doesn't seem your style."

"What? No, of course not!"

For as long as I've known Grey—well, Grey as a grey—he's been convinced the virus set us vegetarians apart, branded us the super race. His influence brings me back from the edge and convinces me—almost—I might not be the monster I think I am. It's no coincidence he and the count hit it off. A supremacist can spot another one coming. But he's not buying it this time. I wonder why not? Is it me? It always has been me—everything he does. If he pulls me back from the edge, I keep him from going there. Balance of the opposites.

"So, what's keeping us here? He's seduced you with his French boy charm, the way he has every other woman in this place?"

"What are you talking about? You actually think I'd hook up with a Nazi just because he has a pretty face and a nice house? I'm not the one who's been scarce. I've been looking all over for you."

"Except when you're off on your little evening dates with the count."

"I'm playing my part, just like you, making sure the school has security." I don't have to tell him that Gavin's a real threat. He was there. Honestly, his insinuations offend me. "Yves is charming and French, and the school is actually, surprisingly, philanthropic. He genuinely cares about the kids. They barely know there's an apocalypse going on outside the gates." My enthusiasm alarms me. It has a completely different effect on

Greyson. "But underneath it all, the count's a fascist racist and a chauvinist." I have to keep reminding myself of that every time we visit the school and he gushes gratitude for helping him close the breach and save Mia.

"Then what? Why aren't we gone? You want to live the aristocratic life? You like the warm bed, the hot shower, the social life, the servants? You have no idea what's under the floorboards of this luxury all-inclusive. Believe me, baby, you don't want to wander into the cellar. We gotta get the hell out of here while we still can. The count smokes enough dope to believe the appeal is too sexy to pass up. We could be long gone before they even know we were thinking about it."

"But—"

"But what? Don't buy into the fishbowl. You and I, we could get Amber, make our way north, and survive."

Amber's name on Grey's lips pings through the dark sludge I've stuffed between my feelings for her and the pragmatic reality of choosing to leave her at the chateau with Ryan and the French military. "I had to leave her, Grey. Ryan's dad was going to execute me. No question about it." I'm not sure if I'm defending myself to Grey or to me. "If I'm dead, she has no one. On that island, she's got a whole platoon looking out for her."

"But none of them would die for her, Ev, would they? That's just you and me. We're family. They're soldiers."

And there it is, right there. Greyson is my family. He's risked everything for us, over and over again. We save each other. It's the only constant in the apocalypse. How did I get so distracted from that?

I'd like to think that the virus triggered my survival instincts so that I rationalized abandoning my little sister, but deep down, I suspect I was just weak. My lips tighten and quiver. Tears sting my eyes. Somehow, I managed to let Laure and David camouflage the guilt and the gaping hole left behind when I hit the ocean and the protective ties that bind me to Amber shredded. My head sinks into my hand, and I scratch at my eyebrow. "I don't know what I was thinking. I woke up. I had to act."

Grey steps up and wraps his arms around me. "I'm not accusing you. I'd have done the same thing. Dragging a six-year-old into this shit, when she was somewhere safe, that would be reckless." A cheeky grin turns up the corner of his lips. "I'm the reckless one." He hugs me. "Hell, I jumped ship, just like you did, to figure out the lay of the land before going back for the people I love. But we know what's here now. It's time to get back to what's number one and end the reconnaissance."

"You're right. I know it, I just—" I shake off the guilt. Guilt only slows me down, keeps me from making the critical choices. "Look, I've been trying to get you alone for a reason."

"I'm not the one putting up resistance to alone time." He drops his hands onto my hips and pulls me close enough for our noses to touch. I've been daydreaming about getting him alone for so long that I'm distracted by the velvet of his lips. The touch, the soft brush of his tongue, they empty my brain.

Throwing my head back, I breathe deeply the pine spiked air so I can think again. He starts to speak. I stop him with a finger to his lips. Poor move, it makes me want to kiss them again. "Wait! I have to tell you this. It's important. I couldn't say anything with Audrey around. I'm not positive she'd be on board with us. I'm guessing, but I can't gamble because it's worse than you know. The other night I had a little chat with Kasim. Do you trust him?"

"He's decent. I think he's only putting on an act for the count. He was pissed about Eugène. The count promised to lock him up, not kill him."

"I feel the same. Kasim told me the count sent him to the legionnaire resort the day we washed up. Every night you've been gone, he's been out too, on reconnaissance—putting together supplies and a tactical plan. The count is planning a raid on the *Chateau d'If*."

"Damn!" He grabs my hand and turns down the path like we're going home to pack right now. "We have to warn them. They need to know what's coming for them."

"Absolutely!"

"But?"

"But we can't, not yet. I want nothing more than to cut through the woods, grab a car, and make our way out to the island. But how would you and me showing up now, infected like we are, be any different from when I left? We'd end up just as dead. They'll shoot us on sight."

"Then we'll figure out a way to sneak you in to see Ryan."

In the back of mind, it's not just the dance with death that waits for us on that ship, I'm also having trouble just walking away from Laure and David. And then there's Joëlle. I mean, we're friends, and she's on Gabriel's radar now because she's a pediatrician and took the side of those uninfected kids with me the first day of training. I can't just abandon her, not when there's a cure out there. Nicolas is up north with Dr. Pêsqué. All we have to do is get there. "What about Laure and David? I promised them I'd help. You told their family we'd bring them. Are we those people? We make promises, but when it doesn't suit us anymore we walk away?"

"That's why you don't make promises—not in the apocalypse."

"Geez Grey, if there was nothing we could do, that would be one thing. If it was a choice between them and Amber, that would be another. But it's not. Look, there might be a plan that works for all of us." Is it insane that I keep trying to help, to make a difference, and every time I do, disaster and carnage swarm in my wake? Maybe it's only my ego, my insatiable urge to prove I'm still human that won't let me walk away until the damage is done. Why can't I see like Grey? Ignore the periphery and focus on the front and center?

From between his arms, I raise my hands to the sides of his face. "Please, Grey, just one more time? Convince Audrey to suggest we bring Laure and David along on the raid. If you or I bring it up, it's a death sentence for them. You saw what happened to David because I defended him. Gabriel can't know we want them along or that they mean anything to us."

I've seen this look in his amber eyes before, hard, like solid gold. He's about to be super practical, and I'm not going to like it. "That's the thing, isn't it, Ev? They *don't* mean anything to me. They're just a couple of kids you ran into out here, and now you feel responsible for them. But really, they're just two of probably thousands that got separated from their families in the quarantine. Let their family fight it out. In the middle of the fray, they'd shoot us with all the other greys. If it were up to me, you and I would pack up our RAID toys and get the hell out of these woods, now."

"Please! Just listen to me—"

"Don't, Ev. For once, *you* listen to *me*. It's dangerous enough for just the two of us to defect. With a couple of uninfected kids weighing us down, it's a public execution waiting to happen. It's not worth the risk of leaving Amber on her own for the duration of the nightmare."

He's right. I know he's right. The wind whips up the feral whine from deep in the trees. My neck shivers because we're closer, and it sounds more human. Dropping my hands from Grey's cheeks, stepping out of his embrace, breaks my heart. That's the one place I want to be. We should be on a college campus somewhere in the states, getting coffee and studying the science of climate change. Then again, maybe the Z-virus is the earth's own home remedy for what ails her.

"Okay."

He's not convinced "Okay, but—?"

"No *but*. Just okay. You're right. Amber is all that matters."

"So, we're leaving? Tonight?" Not sure I've ever seen Grey so happy or so surprised. It's not going to last.

"Yes. And we're taking David and Laure with us—"

"No way—"

"Exactly! There's no way we're going to get into the *Chateau d'If* without a couple uninfected kids to get us there. We need them if we want a shot at getting Amber out."

"Damn!" In about two brain flashes, he's come to the same conclusion. "Fine! Tonight after dinner, we round them up and get the hell out of here."

The whine from the woods crescendos, but now it seems more like a scream.

"What the hell is that?" Grey peers into the trees.

"I don't know. At first, I thought it must be some kind of animal, but now I'm not so sure." My feet move instinctively towards the cry.

He grabs my arm but matches his stride to mine. "If we're both late for dinner, the count won't like it. There's a reason he separated us."

"I know, I know. But, to be fair, it's not just me. He's got some warped ideas about spawning the super race." Rolling my eyes, I shake my head. "The virus is too stingy to waste resources to maintain us beyond essential first aid. Our skin doesn't even heal. What makes him think we can reproduce?"

The trees thicken and the trail dwindles. The moon struggles in a half-circle attempt to break through the branches. Grey stops short, about half a second after I do. The smell sparks our virus-soaked neurons.

"*Boches*. Whatever's out there, it's on its own now."

"It's human, Grey. Probably one of the kids from Buzine wandered off—or ran away—and got trapped. C'mon."

"God! It never ends with you."

"That's my line."

The virus surges, but I fight it. The only time it's safe to let the demon have its head is when we're fighting *boches*. Maybe Nicolas isn't the only one looking for a cure. Maybe Nature, herself, created Grey and the other's like us to rid the world of the alphas and zombies. So, what happens to the predators when the prey is all gone?

Chapter 38

A hundred yards in, the moon can't penetrate the gnarled branches of the canopy. The crying leads us to a dark, dilapidated farmhouse somewhere between Reynard and Buzine. The walls are stone. Metal bars patch the holes where they've crumbled. Of the outer buildings, only partial walls and foundation footings survive. Between the weathered cracks of the boarded-up windows, light seeps into the darkness around. We're not the only creatures in the woods to have followed the whimpering screams. The scent of *boche* flies heavy on the breeze. We have the slight tactical advantage of being downwind. Who knows for how long?

"It's coming from there." Moving single file through the trees, sparser now but still overgrown, Grey and I approach the structure. We won't be surprised. The stench and trampling of the *boches* will reach us before they do. At the back of my mind, though, I wonder if Gavin is with them.

We slide along the back wall. Faint light seeps from bars at the base near the center. The crying and moaning leak out with it. The sweet tang of uninfected hovers under the sourness of grey.

In the woods, a scuttle erupts. The zombies are hunting. Growls, snarling, the frantic whipping of branches, and the ripping of leaves, followed by blood-curdling yelps, and then silence under the faint metallic tinge of blood on the wind. The look I exchange with Grey screams, "We have to hurry."

Approaching on tiptoe, to slide under grey radar, we reach the crack in the base. Sparse gravel digging into my knees, I peer into the lantern-lit room. My line of sight takes in only an automatic rifle lying on the bare floorboards and the base of a cot. The source of the pathetic whining and screaming lies huddled in a fetal position next to the cot, her back to the window, her gaze locked under the rickety bed. Only a thin, white, cotton slip shelters her from the cold, much too little— at least for a *non infecté* as slight as this girl. My heart cringes 'cause her violent shivering isn't from the cold.

Behind her, a black RAID t-shirt crumples to the side of combat boots. "Get off the floor and stop whining, whore. Do you think this is pleasant for me? We all do what the count orders, don't we? You think I'd be here if I had a choice?" The voice is Gabriel's.

Oh, God! The count is desperate to find a way to pass on the grey traits. The impact of this horrifying scene of exploitation shatters into a thousand jagged shards the glass bubble I imagined around the count's compassion for the children of his school. Suddenly, my insides go cold.

"Consider yourself lucky. After your little performance at dinner the other night, you should have been shipped off to Régis. Would you be happier there, *hein*? Dinner with reds? Is that what you want?"

The girl stops whimpering and gasps. She turns her horrified face to plead. "No! Please. I'll be good. Please don't send me there." My breath catches and my back stiffens. It's Martine, the little serving girl we haven't seen since she spilled blood wine on the count's silk jacket.

"If you don't want a one-way ticket to Gavin's dinner party, get your ass off the floor and on the cot. I haven't got all night." A zipper grinds, and Gabriel's black pants crumple around his bootstraps. My stomach turns. Glancing back, hopeless, Martine trembles so violently that she can't quite navigate the metal edges of the cot. She stumbles. A smear of blood stains the back of her slip beneath the bony curve of her butt. This isn't the first time.

"For God's sake!" Gabriel's burly hand shoves her up onto the mattress from beneath. For two seconds, his profile descends into view. Calculating cruelty and malice writhe in a permanent struggle on his face, but this is the first time the lines of calloused depravity have wormed across it. "*Putain,* there's no flesh on you. Are you even old enough?"

Quivering, she pleads, anything to avoid the nightmarish carnage at Régis. "I'm fourteen."

My eyes close. Grinding my teeth, I dig my nails into the flesh of my palm. My heart folds in on itself. How could I have let the count's charm fool me? Only a Nazi pig could conceive this cesspool of human experimentation. Yves plays the genteel, benevolent ruler, hiding behind his fine linens and crystal, behind his philosophical posturing, and all the while, he's training Gabriel, his human pit bull, to rape children in order to satisfy his insane scientific curiosity. I can't take it anymore.

Blind steps carry me to the corner of the back wall, away from the gut-wrenching scene in the window. Grey grabs my wrist. He knows what this is doing to me. The horror of it gnaws at my insides, but what can we do? Gabriel is fully armed. If we stand up for Martine, he'll either mow us down or use her against us the way he did David. She'll be in more danger than she is now. I'm not doing that again. It's bad enough that we have to walk away and leave her or piss away any chance we have of saving Laure and David and getting the hell out of here. I'm not going to be the reason she gets fed to the *boches* or turned into one. She can still survive this. No one is coming out of it unscarred. The best anyone can hope for is alive.

The sun has gone down, leaving us in the charcoal grey of early evening. A gust of wind thickens the smell of decaying flesh blowing from the direction of Régis.

Peeking around the corner, I can see a gravel driveway beyond the side yard. A dirt road winds past the shack in the direction of Buzine. Grey nods at the woods behind us. "The *boches* are gonna come crashing through those trees any minute. We gotta go. We can't take on a herd."

He wraps his arms around me and kisses my forehead, a bandage and balm for my body of pain. I want to cry.

"You know we can't help her, right? It's too risky. We can't save everyone, Ev. There's too many of them."

"I know. It just hurts."

He's right. Of course, he's right. We're just a couple of kids from the states. We don't even belong here. Taking on Laure and David is more than I signed on for when I jumped ship. Since saving them gets me closer to Amber, I have to keep my eye on that.

Why can't I be more like Grey, fix my eye on the goal and ignore everything else? How many times can I let him suck up the consequences because I can't get my shit together and fight the impulse to save someone? Do they ever survive? No. Everyone around me dies, no matter what I do—everyone but Amber.

Martine can't survive outside of the New Order. That's the blunt truth that I have to look in the face. She doesn't stand a chance. She just doesn't. What's the point of letting the nightmare go on? What's the point of risking Grey's life, Laure and David's freedom, Amber's safety on another hopeless cause? I've got to woman up and do the right thing—even if it feels all wrong.

Turning out of his embrace, I square my shoulders and risk another glimpse around the corner. "There's no sign of a guard." Why would there be? What chance does scrawny little Martine have out here if, by some miracle, she escapes?

The question sparks another possibility and loosens the knots in my guts.

"Grey, can you distract Gabriel long enough for me to get inside?"

"C'mon, Ev, be reasonable. It's risky. Even if you do get Martine out, we'll never make it back to the chateau with her alive." He glances back at the woods. The low gurgling and wheezing of *boches* rides the evening breeze.

"What if we're *not* trying to get her back to the chateau? What if I just need enough time to get in there and bite her?"

Grey looks at me like half my brains are spilling out my ear. "You want to infect that girl—intentionally? Has the count's insanity infected your brain?"

"Now you're all ethical? You said it yourself at dinner. She'll never survive the apocalypse. You were being honest, and I'm facing up to the truth. Why does she have to end up a slab of mutilated meat or the worst kind of slave? The uninfected are vegetarian. She stands a chance of becoming a grey. She'll have a shot at defending herself." I wrap my fingers around his wrist and squeeze. "She has a little brother over at the school that she's trying to protect."

That clinches the argument. We both know Amber has only survived this long because she's had a couple of greys in her camp. Shaking his head, Grey lets me drag him into the madness. My guts twist as we tiptoe along the side of the house towards the gravel drive. It's the right thing to do, but I know only too well the horror of becoming the monster. I just hope Martine has what it takes to fight the urges and make peace with the demons inside. It sucks, but it's the only chance she has.

At the front corner, my feet grind to a stop, and Grey plows into me. He grabs my waist and the wall to steady his sudden halt. Headlights pierce the darkness of the woods surrounding the farmhouse. We flatten ourselves against the stone. A silver Renault sedan rolls up and stops a few yards behind the black SUV that's already parked in front of the door. The back-passenger door flies open, and Bruno, the big grey from Gabriel's training team, drags a petit brunette out if the car.

My gasp carries on the night air, and Bruno glances around, eyes narrowed. The girl, gagged, hands and feet bound with plastic ties, struggles and screams—a muffled siren. Her legs flail in the air. Throttled in Bruno's massive arm, she's too small to touch the ground. It's Joëlle.

Chapter 39

It's all over now. Sneaking out. Grabbing Amber. Freeing Laure and David. The whole plan crumbles to ashes in the blast of Joëlle's muffled scream. And then there's the look on Grey's face. He's willing to risk a fight now—100% on board. She's part of our pod—an *us*, not a *them*. It nearly breaks my heart that he's so fond of her. But who wouldn't be? She's cute, fun and friendly. I used to be like that. The virus, the need to survive, they've turned me into a bitch, and I know it. Now isn't the time for petty jealousy or self-pity. This place is more horrifying than an extreme haunted house, the kind where the monsters are allowed to torture the idiot tourists who pay for the pleasure.

Grey slides in front of me. Hard to tell if he's shielding me with his body or putting me—and all our baggage—behind him.

A screaming groan from inside the stone shack interrupts Joëlle's strangled cries. My shoulders shiver as an image of Martine and Gabriel flashes across my imagination. Gabriel's harsh cursing garbles into a smear of guttural mush through the stone walls.

"I know you want to get to Martine, Ev. It's too late for that. It's shit, but it's happening." He pulls the knife out of his holster. "No guns. Shots will bring the damn *boches* running. If I go after the big guy, can you take the driver? We can't take these two SOBs on and Gabriel, too. Get Joëlle a weapon. She's small, but I've seen her handle herself."

Of course, he has. Late-night patrols while I was out with the count, lapping up his altruistic drivel at the school. Now we see the nasty, shit-covered underbelly of his philanthropy. "I think it'll take both of us to bring Bruno down. Let's hope the driver stays put."

"The air out here reeks of *boche*. If we're lucky, he'll think we're a couple strays out for a picnic in the woods and let the big boy fend for himself. C'mon."

Joëlle isn't making it easy for him, but Bruno is halfway to the SUV before Grey and I sprint for them. Our footsteps crunch the gravel. Bruno turns around just in time for Grey to drive a blade into his meaty shoulder. Rather than go down, he drops Joëlle. Growling and cursing, he swings at Grey's jaw. Grey's only advantage is that he's much faster. Ducking, he charges, driving his shoulder into the guy's gut. Grunting, Bruno doubles over, but wraps an arm around the back of Grey's neck and hauls him off his feet. While Joëlle squirms and wriggles on the ground, I jab my knife into the hulking bicep strangling Grey.

Roaring, Bruno jerks his free elbow up and clips my chin. The force rattles my brain. I stumble back onto my butt without my knife, but Greyson slips out of the chokehold. Bruno plucks the blade as if it were nothing more than an annoying thorn, from his arm. The guy is a monstrosity, and now he's waving a knife. Before he can strike, Grey lands a sharp, cracking punch to his jaw. His head barely even jerks.

The driver jumps out of the car. Bruno charges Grey. Hauling my ass out of the dirt, I jump on his back. Both hands around the monolith's wrist, Grey wrestles for control of the knife while I choke the air from Bruno's throat.

On the ground, Joëlle's hands and ankles are bound, but when the scrawny driver runs around the front of the car, she throws her legs out and trips him up. Grunting, he thuds to the ground.

With me on Bruno's back, strangling him, Greyson manages to shake the knife from his fist. It flies wide. Joëlle screams. The knife has clipped her thigh.

His hands freed up, Bruno slugs Grey squarely in the gut. He gasps and stumbles backward. The brute grasps my arm, leans forward, and flips me over his head. My back crunches flat against the gravel, knocking me senseless and ripping the air from my lungs. In the daze, the stars, freed from the dulling power of the city's electrical grid, wink happily from their distant black sea.

Warbled stomping and yelling filter through the crumbling walls of the farmhouse. Groans, trampling shuffles, and growls creep from the trees behind us. The stench of *boche* works like smelling salts. Reviving, I stumble to my feet, trying to gain my bearings. Bruno jabs again at Grey's face. The impact throws him to the ground next to Joëlle. My brain is too scattered to react when the big boy comes after me. His meaty palms crush my neck, and my mind hasn't reassembled the gears enough to fight back.

A resounding crack makes me jump. Bruno's eyes tip to mine. The pressure on my throat falls limp. His face goes slack, losing all expression as he tilts forward. Scrambling, I can't get out of the way in time, and the momentum traps me beneath the falling wave of his bulk. Air abandons me for the second time as we smash into the gravel. Joëlle has scrambled over and holds the driver's gun in her bound hands. Shit! She had no choice, but now the *boches* are coming for us.

To the side, a sickly light bleeds from the open door of the farmhouse. Gabriel, fly still gaping open, steps onto the porch, his Glock in his fist. "What the hell—?" His grey eyes make out our faces in the dark, and anger turns to sick pleasure. "Glad you invited friends to our little date here, Joëlle."

"You're a sick pig son of a bitch." Joëlle raises the gun to shoot again. She's pulled the knife from her leg and cut the cords around her ankles and wrists, but she can't stand and her hand trembles with the shock and pain of the wound that the virus hasn't yet shut down. Bruno's dead mass pins my gun leg. While I struggle to shove him off and help Joëlle, the driver comes to his senses. He wrestles Joëlle for the gun, but she can't stand, and he rips it from her hands. Grey rises to his feet, caught between Gabriel targeting my head and the driver aiming at his.

Strolling to my side, Gabriel grins. My glance pivots between Grey and Joëlle. "You know, *Mademoiselle la Ministre*, my first impulse was to put a bullet in your brain, swat the little mosquito that keeps buzzing in my ear and biting me.

But that was too easy—a quick, painless exit." It takes everything I have to heave Bruno's dead bulk off my leg. "And then it occurred to me that everyone would be so much happier if I just delivered you to the alpha. I'm sick of the count and his polite, aristocratic pretenses. We are—"

When he hears Gabriel's plan, a flicker of his eye tells me what Grey is going to do, and I know the part I have to play. Audrey trained us well. The driver is much scrawnier and doesn't stand a chance against Grey. The second my boy makes a play for his gun, I take advantage of the distraction and sweep Gabriel's legs.

In the scuffle, two shots crack through the shadows as Gabriel crashes down to my level. "Shit! No!" Joëlle yells. A herd of about ten snarling *boches* break into the clearing on the other side of the farmhouse.

Gabriel and I wrestle, scrambling for control of the gun, but he's way too big for me. My fingers barely reach the metal handle. Gabriel lunges over the top of me and snatches it away. The last thing I see, before he drives the butt down on my temple and the darkness invades my brain, is Grey, stumbling towards us, bloody hand clasping his chest.

Chapter 40

Rattling and bumping. Cold leather beneath my cheek. My eyes focus sluggishly on the back of the driver's seat. The sensation of forward motion nauseates me. Oh, God, my head! A sharp stab of pain radiates across my skull in a persistent, pounding throb. I'm going to puke. My eyes squeeze shut. Drool dribbles from the corner of my mouth. I try to swipe it away, but my hands won't follow commands from my brain. Behind my back, a plastic tie binds my wrists.

Churning bile convulses my gut. Heaving forward, I wretch onto the rubber floor mat. Purple green sludge sticks in the hair escaped from my ponytail. Chunks linger on my tongue. I can't wipe the murky strands from my chin.

"*Merde! Salope!*"

The blur of Gabriel's face flashes around to the upper limits of my vision. And now I remember. He hit me in the head. I struggle against the ties around my wrists and ankles. "Where are we?" Air grates across my dry throat, and the French stumbles off my tongue. "Where—are you," it hurts to find the words, "taking me?"

And then the last scene that hit my eyes before the butt of Gabriel's gun hit my head crashes across my memory— Greyson, falling, next to Joëlle and the silver sedan. A hole in his chest. The scene chokes me. I can't breathe. Tears invade my eyes. "Where is he! Where's Greyson?"

"The count didn't much trust him. He won't mind—there were *boches*." He turns again, leering at me through a vengeance-soaked smirk. "Yves might be a little angry about losing *you*, though. He wasn't finished with you yet, and the count likes his whores!" He turns back to navigate a curve. "The maniac cousin will be happy to take the blame. His blood is hot for you. When he's had his fill of screwing," he chuckles, "he'll make you one of his dogs—or maybe his dinner."

He's taking me to Gavin.

Shadow-smeared treetops flash through the windows. Tires crunch across a gravel drive. We slow to a stop. The night obscures the large grey stones looming above the car. Weak light shines from only one of the windows glimmering dully in the moonlight. Gabriel slams his door. His footsteps crunch, and the door opens behind my head. The stench of *boche* permeates the breeze. The virus boils my flight or fight reflexes, but both my feet and hands are bound, and the chemicals just pool in my blood and pound in my head.

Struggling against the massive biceps that slip beneath my armpits and drag me onto the gravel only intensifies the throbbing in my head and stirs up another wave of nausea. Gabriel drags me, choking, across the drive, but not to the front door. I struggle but don't dare scream. Deep in the heart of zombiedom, there's no doubt any *boches* wandering the yard have sniffed us out already. I can't afford to turn their curiosity into a fixed target.

"You know," my writhing makes Gabriel grunt and jerk me tighter into his grip, "I always thought Régis was a better chateau for the New Order—bigger, with dungeons. That's what the count needs to keep those disgusting little whites in line—a few whips and chains." The grey walls rise up to turrets, like the towers in the Sleeping Beauty castle—when it was blighted and covered in thorny vines. "Perfect for his little breeding project, too."

We turn the corner and run into a locked, wrought iron fence separating the front gardens from the back. Gabriel drops me. My head crunches against gravel. The throbbing reverberates, and my gut clenches in a dry heave. My thinking goes fuzzy. "But the count prefers his aristocratic charade and his little theater in the basement. Gavin, though," he stops to catch his breath, "spoiled rich kid. He likes his decadent luxury. The count thought he could make better use of a dungeon for his little hobbies. Can't say I disagree."

A patrol of Gavin's *boches* rounds the corner of the chateau. The second our movement and smell crash into their hot-wired nervous system, they break into a sprint. Gabriel shoots the lock and unlatches the gate. *Damn! What an idiot!* He grabs my wrists and hauls me after him, shoving it closed before my feet are through. The metal clangs against my ankles, leaving a gap wide enough for a bloody-mouthed head.

These guard dogs are fast. They ram into the fence and claw through the bars. Gabriel rips out a knife and stabs the first in the eye, shoving him out of the opening. The *boche* falls back and the one behind him tumbles to the ground. He finds my boot and latches on, dragging my leg back through the gap. Kicking and yelling, I crack his nose with the heel. His head jerks back, but he doesn't let go and dives back in for a mouthful of leather.

"Oh, no you don't." Gabriel can't reach him and hold on to me too. Dropping the knife, he pulls out his Glock and risks another shot. The zombie topples over. Gabriel pulls my foot through the fence and slams it shut on a small herd that emerges from the trees flanking the chateau's front grounds. "You're not getting off that easy," he spits at me. "You're going to wish I'd let that *boche* wolf you down before Gavin is through with you." He chuckles and retrieves his knife. "I've seen the alpha king at work. He'll rip you apart slowly. He's an artist." Stuffing the blade back in the holster, he grabs me under the armpits and drags me across the pebbles to the back of the chateau.

He doesn't even realize what an imbecile he is until the back garden starts spewing *boches*. At this point, I'm not sure I should struggle. He's right, maybe it is better to die now, spare myself Gavin's psychotic wrath.

But Amber—

Gabriel heads for a big wooden door in the back wall of the chateau. We won't make it there before the herd converges on us. He takes aim at the front-runners, but there's no way he's got enough bullets to shoot all of them. He drops me and turns to the door. There's a latch, but no lock. By the time he's got it undone, another half a dozen are on us. The snarling and growling could wake the dead. He shoots the first few, but another plows into him, knocking the gun from his hand. His back against the door, he fends off the teeth with his arm and gropes for his knife. One of the incoming trips over my feet and writhes around to attack. I've got nothing, no weapons and no hands. Even if I wanted to just give up and die, I couldn't. The virus won't allow it. Hollering, I pull my feet back and jab them into its face.

Just as Gabriel drives his knife through the *boche's* eye, another hits him.

The one on the ground flings himself back on me.

The hinges of the door squeal, and I'm pretty sure Gabriel isn't going to risk his own neck—literally—to drag me in there with him. About a dozen more are only yards away.

"Stop!" The command rips from the doorway. The *boches* don't respond to the words, it's the tone. The growling and snarling die into low guttural rasping.

The stinking, living corpse on top of me hesitates. I've seen dogs dance around, their eyes shifting between their master and the instinct driving them. This is no different—no guarantee the master will win out.

"Get the hell out of here! All of you." Gavin steps into the moonlight.

Chapter 41

Gavin flings his arms at his troops. "Go! Go on!" He shoves the one on Gabriel off. It backs into me and tumbles backward, landing on my chest and knocking the other off me.

The air is tense with the jitters of indecision. One of the newer zombies breaks the vacillating ranks, snarling. Gavin strides over and stabs it in the head—not to set an example, the others don't care. He's killing the pack attack instinct before it can infect the mob.

With his foot, he shoves his dog off my chest. The others move backward, slowly, confused by the crosscurrent of instinct attacking their nerves: obey the alpha, attack the rival predator.

"Get inside!" Gavin jerks his head at Gabriel. Grabbing me beneath the arm, he drags me into the dungeon. "Get! Go!" Gavin yells and slams the doors on our smell.

My cheek grates across cold stone. This is the main chamber and leads to a hallway of doors, some wood and some with metal bars. Cells?

"What the hell are you doing out here after curfew?" Gavin doesn't need a gun to menace a grey, not even a knife-packing one as lethal as Gabriel. The big guy knows he would lose in a fight even against a scrawny alpha like Gavin—all it takes is one bite.

Fear twitches Gabriel's white lips. "I brought you a gift." He nods at me. "Thought you might be willing to bend the rules to get your hands on this one. The count wouldn't like it if he knew."

"We have rules for a reason." Gavin steps right into Gabriel's face. The soldier's knife fist twitches, and Gavin snatches it in his iron grip. "Here at Régis, the justice system is not quite so polite as at Buzine—different management." Gavin snaps Gabriel's wrist, and the knife flies from his hand.

I hate Gabriel with a deep and driving passion. He doesn't deserve to live. Half of me wants Gavin to rip him to pieces while he's still breathing. But I'm not the judge. I can't be the judge because I'd have to condemn myself—over and over again. Does that make Gavin the judge? Has this sorry, grey world made him god?

Gavin turns his face to me, and Gabriel can't stifle a half-relieved, half-amused grin.

"You're right, Gabriel." The chill in Gavin's voice belies the logical reason. "Evelyn upset me, betrayed our national loyalty. All I wanted was a little company from a fellow American." Shoving Gabriel away, he strides over and kicks me in the gut. Air abandons me.

Turning on Gabriel, Gavin points to the stairway at the end of the hall. "Get your sorry ass out of my chateau. If the count finds out about this, you'll—"

"He won't find out." Gabriel turns but changes his mind. Vindictive bastard that he is, encouraged by Gavin's violence, he can't resist. "You'll get yours now, whore." With the full force of his combat boot, he kicks me in the head, and I pass out again.

***

When reality is a nightmare, it's hard to know when I'm sleeping and whether or not I should wake up. Abandon the comfort of dark nothingness only to embrace the terror of the light? Why? In delirium, I watch zombies tear Greyson apart. I can't get to him because my feet are frozen. I have to will myself to run because all I want to do is stay and let the *boches* strip my heart from my chest so I don't have to feel the crush of it breaking anymore.

Screaming in a cold sweat, I wake to darkness—icy, broken stone beneath my cheek, my hands and ankles bound in plastic ties.

My eyes struggle open against the weight of their lids. Saliva and blood drip across my lips and onto the stones beneath my head. The world rocks and spins. My stomach boils with bile. The smell is rank—even to a ZV. Exhaustion drives my face back onto the rock.

Boots on the stone next to me. A hand brushes the hair from my face. "You're safe now. You're gonna be fine."

"Dad?" No. He's dead. This is the dream. My mind dives back into the blackness hoping to swim into the day again.

***

My eyes flicker, but won't open. I'm starving—for human flesh. Am I one of *them* now? I force the lids open a crack. A barrage of light, pink and shimmering gold, attacks my lenses. The lids flutter shut again. Do *boches* see color? Somehow, I assumed their world was black and grey—or maybe they see infrared. Who knows? Am I in heaven, then? Maybe I escaped the worst, and this is just plain dead. But would I be hungry? And would I go to heaven? Doubtful.

My lungs suck up breath. Definitely not dead. My head throbs. Oh, yeah, Gabriel kicked me. My hand, sluggish like it's moving through wet cement, explores the lump above my ear. Crusted blood.

Blood. I can see it all again now, on Grey's chest, on the ground. *Oh, God! Grey!*

Weightlessness consumes my head. Overwhelmed with nausea, gasping for air, I sob, holding my stomach.

When no more tears will come, and the numbness of grief starts to set in, the room focuses around me. Pink floral curtains, four-poster bed. Gold-framed mirrors and embossed ivory desk and vanity. Empire furniture, pink velvet cushions, ivory wood brushed in gold. Clouds and tree boughs with pink blossoms in a blue sky float across the ceiling. Where the hell am I? The doorknob twists, and I'm about to find out.

A black combat boot breaches the sill. In my head, I pray for Grey to follow the black, but I know that's a fool's daydream. He's gone—again. *What happens to a heart that's already broken? Does rigor mortis chill and still the pulsing, bleeding pieces?*

I was right. It's not Grey. My hands grip the sheets—pink satin. Gavin steps into the room.

My whole body shakes. I shouldn't be surprised. Gabriel wanted his revenge. Raped and locked up or a living dead carnivore, either one is a much messier way to get rid of me than a simple bullet to the brain—and both get him his revenge. What does surprise me is the smell of marijuana that sweeps into the room in Gavin's wake. Weed makes us human, and I'm pretty sure Gavin's humanity is nothing more than a shriveled worm inside his demon soul. He settles into one of the pink chairs near the window, takes a drag off the butt of a joint on a golden, jewel-encrusted clip, holds it, and blows. The stream of smoke snakes towards me but evaporates before it reaches the bed.

In the ray of light that floods the chair, the self-assured half-smile, as if he has a secret he's keeping from the world, and the careless slouch remind me of the Gavin I knew in high school.

Sitting up, I steel myself against the new wave of nausea. "Where's Grey? Gabriel shot—" speaking chokes me, "—him." If Grey's gone, what do I care what happens to me? I might as well be the undead. I feel undead inside.

But, Amber—

A week ago, at the club, Gavin would have gloated at the demise of the competition. Surprisingly enough, his face clouds over. "Sorry. Couldn't say. You were out cold, so I went back to the farmhouse with my dogs." He means his zombies. "If there were bodies outside, they were gone."

He doesn't need to tell me that can be good OR bad. Most likely bad. Joëlle had a stab wound in her leg, and Grey was shot in the chest. If the remnants of their mangled corpses weren't there, the odds are good they got up and shambled away with the herd.

Greyson a *boche*? I can't even imagine it. The world, the universe, my heart—everything stops. Can anything go on without him? Of all the people in the world, he was meant to survive the apocalypse. And why didn't he? Because of me. Because everyone I care about, sooner or later, dies—or worse.

Chapter 42

The void of Greyson gone collapses my world. Inside, I'm a fish on a hook, flopping on the deck of a ship. The story isn't supposed to end this way. I can't breathe. My fists grip the blanket. My teeth clench, and my eyes squint against the sting.

Gavin walks across the room to put a supportive hand on my back. I flinch. He backs off and takes a drag. "Chill, Evelyn. I'm not who you think I am."

"Gavin has a twin?"

"Sort of. I haven't been spending much time with my buddy, here." He waves the joint at me. "My flesh-eating alter-ego suits the count's purposes better than his doped-up cousin, so I don't get rations. I have to wait 'til they're smuggled in or scavenge the magic weed myself. When I run out, the beast runs wild." Is this an act? I know Gavin. He can be charming when he wants to be. "Look, you have every right to hate me. I hate me. I was a rich dick. What can I say? The virus didn't do me any favors."

"Not sure I'd use the past tense. I watched you kill Mia's brother and then take her hostage. You're a sick son of a bitch." With Grey gone, maybe Gavin thinks the field is clear, and he's putting on his best behavior. His long hair is pulled back into a man bun to enhance the façade of self-control. I do my best to crack the mask. He doesn't take the bait. He walks back to the chair. "You were always a snake, even without the virus. Just ask Charlene."

He doesn't crack. Instead, he stares out the window. "I'm not arguing." Sitting, he drops his elbows on his knees and stares at the patterns in the marble floor. "Getting sick changes you. You see yourself through different lenses." I'm expecting the heart-wrenching, poor little rich boy story. But he doesn't resort to clichés. "I thought I was going to die until I cracked and gave in to the urges. I killed people to save myself." His voice cracks. He stops and takes a drag. "Hyped up on flesh, the virus goes to your head, literally. I mean, you saw me. The disease plays on the shit we all keep locked up inside. Yves, he's bright, and he has aristocratic blood. Look what it made out of him. When they evacuated the south, he saw his chance. While he was turning into a royal despot, the virus preyed on my entitled-brat instincts. High on that kind of thinking can only make me a monster—Yves's perfect weapon."

"So, what? You want me to feel bad for you? You're a murderer." My sharp tongue is the worst part of me. The virus makes it more lethal.

"I am." He drops the used butt of his joint in the dainty, gold-brushed wastebasket near the desk. "At least, I was until I met Kasim." From his pocket, he pulls a gold cigarette case. The sunrays glitter the diamonds on the lid. Taking out a hand-rolled joint, he lights it with a gold lighter and walks it over to me. This could be a ploy to bring down my defenses, but the hunger is snarling out of control, and I grab it like a junkie in the middle of rehab. "He's like you, you know. The virus can't find much of violence, or a nice little power complex to work with, so you two fight the urges, maintain your humanity."

"Mostly." After holding in a lungful, I hand the joint back. "Nature usually isn't like that. What you fight you strengthen—unless you kill it." The fumes invade my blood, and calm trickles through my body. I only know what being human feels like because I've lived as a predator for so long, blood buzzing with violence, brain teeming with hunting instincts.

"Depends on how you fight it. Kasim smuggles this in for me. It's dangerous crossing the count, but Kasim's not like the rest of them, and his half-brother was like me. Sympathetic, I guess."

Marijuana doesn't just kill my flesh hunger, it manhandles the nausea and headache. Pushing against the tapestry headboard, I struggle to sit up. Gavin strides over to help, but I shove him away. Sure, this masquerade strikes me as pretense with a hidden agenda, and I trust Gavin as much as I do a zombie crouching in a corner, but mostly, the thought of Greyson falling over the driver, the gun drooping from one hand, keeps rewinding in my imagination. The frenzied thinking of the virus left the canvas clean for my heart to paint the picture there, over and over and over. Human anger and crushing sorrow boil together in my veins. This can't be how it ends! "Let's drop the bullshit, Gavin. What's your game here?"

"Oh, this is no game. It's dangerous as hell. But the count made a critical error when he ordered the kill on Eugène. He lost his best man, and I gained one on the inside. Kasim and I are together now, and we need you on our side. I've been trying to get you over here since the night I met you at the club."

"Oh, you are thick if you think I'm interested in hanging around here as your grey whore."

He sneers. "No! Don't get me wrong. I had a hard-on for you in high school, but you're not really my type. That night at the club, I actually came for Joëlle. Cute, smart. Always nice to have a doctor on the team. But you sabotaged any chance I had there. I was out of weed. I shouldn't have come. I always think I can control it on my own, but no way. The virus always wins. That time, I let it. Yves can't guess why I want you with me, or he'll kill us all. You, me, Kasim, and Joëlle."

A tinge of guilt pricks me. For a second, I get off my high, black horse and stare at the pink, silk sheets. "Joëlle was at the farmhouse. Grey and I heard screaming. We went to check it out and found Gabriel there. He—" I can't even finish what I saw and shift out of the image burned on my brain. "We were going to help a girl they had locked up in there, but Bruno drove up with a delivery. Joëlle—she was tied and gagged."

Not even two joints can contain the anger that invades Gavin's eyes. I never would have guessed it. Evidently, he was hoping to drown his Lilou sorrows in a bottle of Joëlle. He grabs the delicate vase from the stand next to the chair and heaves it at the wall. Delicate pink shards crash and shatter on the marble floor. Bending over, Gavin breathes deeply to calm himself, stands at the window, and takes a drag. It's a full minute before he's collected enough to turn around and face me.

"I'm sorry. She had a knife wound in her leg. A herd of your *boches* showed up. I was unconscious. Gabriel just left them."

His jaw grinds. I feel his pain. And, I have to say, I'm impressed with his control. After another deep drag, he's finally ready to speak. "Kasim and I need you on our side."

"Let's be honest. I like Kasim. He seems like a good guy. He saved my butt when I washed up on the beach. But I don't trust you, Gavin. At least the count makes a pretense at civility. And he has a damn good school for orphans."

"Pretense. Good word. That's what it is, though. You know that, right? You saw what was going on at the farmhouse."

"Just because the count is evil at the core, doesn't make you a saint."

"No, but at least we share a common interest."

"Oh, yeah? What would that be?"

"You came off that boat docked at *If*. You must have friends there."

I scoff. "I came off that boat because my friend's father is the general, and he was determined to make my brains a stain on the deck floor."

"But you have contacts?"

"Yeah." I don't say a word about Amber. I don't want Gavin to know she even exists. She's not going to be the Achilles heel he exploits to manipulate me. I saw what he did with Mia.

He nods. Like the plan I can't see might work. Walking back to the bed, he offers me another drag. I take it. "The count has changed his plans. A platoon of soldiers landed on the beach last night. Yves isn't going after the white camp at the tree park anymore, he's going to attack the military on *If* instead."

"Shit!" I inhale and hold the fumes until they quell the riot in my blood.

"Yes, 'shit'! But, Kasim wants to use the war to bring down the New Order, give control back to the uninfected. You're the only one that can convince the soldiers we're on the same side. We need you with us, Evelyn, or they'll massacre us all."

"Shit!" And here I am, the grey in the middle of the war again.

Chapter 43

Gasping and reaching for Grey, I wake to a blur of pink and gold drenched in sunshine. A few brain impulses later, and I remember what this place is and why I need to get out of here. *Amber!* I was gambling on having more time.

Now, Kasim's plan is the only one that makes sense. Like the predators that we are, the greys have fulfilled nature's purpose. The New Order has taken down most of the alphas and thinned the herd of *boches* they created. But the greys can't be allowed to dominate the landscape. General Samson's troops are the only possible solution. The uninfected got us here in the first place, so I'm not sure they're necessarily the best option, but for Amber, they're better than the greys. The school for orphans would only last as long as the food supply, and then it would become a meat processing plant. Yves would beg to differ, but he's insane and doesn't even know it.

What worries me is maybe I am too. I must be crazy to take Gavin at his word, but Kasim trusts him, and I trust Kasim. And then, what do I care anymore which team I'm on? *Greyson is gone.* Every time I close my eyes I watch him fall again, and then I see the *boches*. I squeeze my eyes shut, but the pain wrings out tears that dribble down my face and stain the pink sheets. Greyson was right. We should have left, survived—let them all fight it out between them. If we'd left when Greyson wanted to—

God! Everyone I touch dies. Martine—I don't even know what happened to her. For all I know, Gabriel just abandoned her to the herd to save himself. There's no chance she escaped. My mind can't erase the images I glimpsed through the hole in the farmhouse walls. Insidious ideas crawl across the stage. Maybe some living is worse than dying.

I can't let myself think like that. There's always after. There's always healing. Martine might still be alive, maybe she could have escaped, joined the tree people, if I hadn't insisted Greyson and I go charging in after her. Greyson might still be— my shoulders convulse under the weight of the sobs.

Someone knocks. Taking a deep breath, I collect myself. What matters now is Amber. There is only Amber. I have to focus. Whatever it takes—Amber. I only need to exist long enough to make sure she has a future, a future free of monsters—inside and outside. *But does that even exist?* Yes! As long as Amber exists, somewhere that future exists. When Amber is safe, I can embrace this emptiness inside, let it swallow me. I throw off the blankets and drop my legs to the floor. The headache isn't gone, but it's bearable. The virus doesn't take sick leave. What I really need is a drag off the joint I can smell from the smoke seeping beneath the door.

"Evelyn?" The doorknob turns, and Kasim steps into the room. He's carrying an elaborate silver plate of cow delicacies. "Gavin's peace offering."

My knees wobble as I stand to meet him. He takes one look at my face, sets the tray down and strides over to wrap me in his arms. "I heard about Greyson. I'm so sorry!"

I can't take the sympathy. The sobs start again, and I muffle them in his shoulder until Gavin walks in. Turning away, I wipe my tears and free the virus to stampede through the gorge of pain, beating it down, feeding on it, transforming it into a beast who feels no remorse, no scruples, just the need to feed. When I turn back, my face feels rigid as steel.

"I'm starving." I don't even try to feign any sort of civility as I pounce on the plate and shovel in the tasty morsels with both fists. We greys will never be anything more than tigers dressed in white linen and cocktail dresses. Yves's social experiment is nothing more than a circus. "What do you need me to do?" The mashed giblets in my mouth spew out with the words. There's enough here to keep the virus satisfied for a day or two.

"Are you sure you're up to it?" Kasim hands me the joint he's smoking, and I don't refuse it.

Gavin, oblivious to anything beyond what he needs, is all business. "We need you to take the ferry out to the island and get the military to send a team to Marseille. You're the only one they might listen to. The count knew that. That's why he was giving you the VIP treatment. If we leak his plans to the military, they can ambush his attack team at the port."

"Why would the general risk bringing troops ashore? The *Château d'If* is a perfect fortress."

Gavin's eyes narrow. He's not used to lowly greys questioning his logic—if that's what we can call it. "Because, he's a general, and his job is to take back Marseille, not cower behind the walls. All he needs is a tip that he has a man on the inside, and he'll seize the opportunity."

I'm not so sure, but then again, what do I know about military strategy? Kasim looks like he's down with the plan. Shrugging, I sigh. "I'm willing, but I don't know anything about boats. I swam here, and I grew up in a landlocked state."

"I have a sailboat—well, my step-father does—did. It's still in the port. My parents were shopping during the first wave. Anyone in the downtown area—" He can't get the words out. When the New Order killed his half-brother, I felt bad for him. But I don't think I understood, until just now, how much it hurt him to lose the last member of his family. To look at Gavin, still alive because of a simple chance of birth, must turn his guts, especially since he knows there's a cure. "I can get you out to the island on the ferry. It was still in the port the last time I did reconnaissance, but it's up to you to figure out how to contact your people."

"That'll be a trick." I can't stop myself from scheming how to get Laure and David out of the New Order. I've learned nothing. "If I had a couple uninfected decoys, I could probably get them to contact the people I know. The general would just as soon use me as target practice as let me speak to his son."

Kasim's eyebrows raise. From the look on Gavin's face, like he just won the lottery, I guess that neither of them suspected how well connected I was.

"I'll take care of it." Gavin's enthusiasm makes me uneasy. Then again, he's smart. He has to have read the writing on the wall. At some point or another, his usefulness will expire, and the count will want him gone.

Gavin isn't the type to be the hired sword. He wants the crown. I don't quite buy his marijuana-induced philanthropy. Deep down, he's got a god complex that will power through the fumes. He doesn't understand that he won't be able to unite the greys the way the count has. So much the better. A bunch of free agents might be easier to round up and hold for a cure than a united, resistant front. Under the circumstances, maybe Gavin and I can use each other, and both get what we want.

Once Laure and David are clear, Amber and I are gone. Kasim just said he has a boat—that's interesting. Once we've disbanded the New Order, I think Kasim would leave with us, help us find Nicolas.

"There's a brother and sister that know me." I glance at Kasim and he nods.

"David and Laure." He's already on board—no pun intended. "Better let me handle that, Gavin. Margot's team brought them in with Greyson and Evelyn. The count is already suspicious that Grey, Joëlle and Evelyn all disappeared together, on the same night." He nods at me. "Gabriel fed him a story about you running into some stray *boches*, but I'm not sure he bought it," he turns back to Gavin, "not after your little tantrum the other night. If you show up asking about those two kids as well—well, he wasn't happy your dogs were running loose in his backyard. And he was pretty angry about Evelyn. Better for everyone if you keep your distance from Buzine for a bit."

Gavin sneers, and Kasim hands him the end of his joint. The virus is seeping through the veneer of his calm. "I'll be back in a couple hours with David and Laure."

Chapter 44

Laure jumps out of the black SUV before it even stops and nearly topples me over in a full-throttle hug. Life for her the past weeks must have felt like sleeping in a room where a viper slithers about freely. She shouldn't be so happy to see me. Everyone I touch ends up mangled and bloody. David gets out a little more coolly. "They said you were dead." His eyes wander up the front of the Sleeping Beauty chateau. "But you were just sleeping, I guess." The two of them have, at least, been outfitted with RAID suits instead of chain mail. David, still a bit wary, offers me his hand. "Thanks." He glances at the spot where Gabriel cut him. "I wouldn't have made it through their little game."

"I'm sorry about that. If I hadn't barged in to rescue that girl—"

"I'd be dead too—and you'd be a monster."

"I'm not so sure that I'm not."

The driver's side door slaps shut. Hustling around the car, I give Kasim the hug that Laure gave me. He's the one taking all the chances to finally get my two protégés out of the New Order.

A joint fumes in his fingers. Must be hard for him driving around in a closed vehicle with a couple of uninfected who reek of rosemary and garlic prime rib. "We have about three hours. I convinced the count that these two would be perfect decoys for luring the military out of their stronghold onto the mainland." He offers me a drag.

"No, thanks. I need to be on my toes."

231

"The message that David and Laure will actually relay to your contact on the island is the plan for a squad to be waiting for the count's team when they arrive for the ambush."

Sounds like a plan, ambush the ambushers, then again—*the best laid plans of mice and men…*

"Won't the count be suspicious when you don't come back with David and Laure?"

"Not at all. I told him the façade of subterfuge had to be complete. In order to gain the military's trust, I would have to either deliver these two back to their families or leave them on the island. My intent is for the two of them to get word to their family and, hopefully, they'll provide the reinforcements for our counter-ambush. David tells me his father has radio communication with *If*."

Gavin emerges onto the front steps of the chateau. Kasim turns to greet him and claps his shoulder. "I was sorry to hear about Joëlle."

Gavin's face stiffens, his lips crimp. "We don't know for sure what happened to them. No bodies." I wish I could dwell in denial the way Gavin does. But Greyson already came back from the dead once. In my experience, fate is a tight-fisted bitch. She's not going to let him off twice. "Let's go."

Kasim shakes his head. "We talked about this, Gavin. We decided you shouldn't come with us."

My hand on Gavin's shoulder, I back Kasim up. "It's not a good idea. The general was going to shoot me because I was a grey. There's no way he's even going to talk to us if we have an alpha tagging along."

A single strand of wavy blond has escaped his ponytail. He tucks it behind his ear, maintaining a dignified calm in the face of opposition. "Then I'll wait onshore. If something goes wrong, you two may be happy I hung around. Reds have some influence over the *boches,* even if they didn't make them. Joëlle thinks it's a scent thing." I notice Gavin's not smoking. He's in business mode—makes him a powerful ally, but an unpredictable and dangerous one. It's hard to know who's driving the machine at any given moment, Gavin or the virus. Laure and David exchange glances. Neither one of them wants to risk getting into an enclosed space with a rabid alpha not on drugs.

"Okay. You're right. But maybe you should drive your own car. It'll give us a separate means of escape if things go wrong."

"Car? Cars are for Boomers." I hadn't noticed it before—of course not, it was dark, and a psychopathic grey was dragging me—but there's a motorcycle on the opposite side of the front porch. He digs a fob from his pocket. He never planned on going with us. "Besides, what could go wrong?"

"Oh, I don't know, we're a couple of greys and an alpha, humanity's biggest threat at the moment, waltzing up to their military base asking if they want to come out and play."

Laure and David climb in the back of the SUV. Kasim slides into the driver's seat, and I take shotgun. Gavin waits until we've pulled out and then revs up behind us.

It's only a 20-minute drive. Kasim and I share one of a fistful of joints he deposits in the cupholder while David and Laure doze off. They're kind of adorable. Laure curls up on her brother's shoulder. His head flops over onto hers. My arms ache for Amber. The thought of finally hugging her to me again numbs the pain of Greyson...*oh God, here it comes again...he's gone.* "Poor kids. They must be exhausted. I don't know how they could ever sleep at night knowing the famished lions were roaming the house."

"I know the feeling—the sense of a target on your back. It's intolerable. This is why the New Order cannot stand. I was the oppressed; I won't be the oppressor."

It would be ignorant for me to say I get where Kasim's coming from. I'm white in a white man's world. But I am a woman, and I know what it's like to be judged on what I look like. I've learned to use that to my advantage, but it's a shame we can't see past these colored costumes we wear. "I wonder if things will be the same, you know, if my friend Nicolas really has the cure and humanity bounces back?"

David snores and startles. Kasim scoffs. "You have more faith in humanity than I do if you believe that. Humanity will always spiral into its worst state. Want will always drive the pyramid. The insatiable will eventually turn and feed on those beneath them in their rise to the top. You don't consume a larger chunk of the resource pie without devouring the masses on your way up."

"Then what's it all for? Why even bother to bring it back?"

"That's Yves's whole point, isn't it? It's all absurd. Democracy, communism, socialism, monarchy, tyranny. It always ends the same, the demented few feed off the rest."

We're traveling through the smaller towns. We won't hit the large hordes until we get to the once densely populated port city. The terracotta roofs peek out from behind vine and shrub-covered walls. The French in the rural areas, hidden behind their hedges, stood a better chance of surviving the initial zombie raids. Americans are too vain. Only the really wealthy surround their estates with walls and fences. The rest like to show off their front yards. Makes them easy walk-in targets for bands of greys. I wonder how many of these people locked themselves in for the duration. They'll have to come out for food, eventually—the French don't stockpile. Not many of them keep the massive basement stores that Utahan's horde.

"You're right." It pains me a bit to say it. It feels like giving in. But for me, the darkness holds a point of light, the lodestar that drives me. Amber is my hope. "Not everything is absurd. The people we love, the experiences we have, that's the point." And I've lost so many of those...*he's gone*. My eyes sting, and I gaze out at the small hotel we pass and the people trapped on the roof—Christmas on the *Côte d'Azur* gone horribly awry. They think the *boches* are their worst nightmare. From a distance, they can't see that we're a couple of greys and an alpha. They wave and cry for help as we go by.

"Well, if that's true, then I haven't much to live for anymore. All the people I loved are gone." Kasim merges onto an expressway, but it's there again, that silent void that rumbles through his skin and shakes my heart. "I guess I'll have to cling to the experiences."

"Sadly, those are not the same without the ones you love." My hand covers his on the console. He smiles, a sad appreciation of the human gesture. "You could be part of our patchwork family." He squeezes my fingers and puts both hands back on the wheel. "I always wanted to visit France, ever since I took my first French class in 7th grade. But now that I'm here—"

"It's not what you imagined?" His half-grin is more than half charming.

"I imagined the French Revolution like this. *The Marseillaise* is a bloody song, isn't it? The whole affair was a brutal mess." Abandoned cars and devoured carcasses block the lanes of traffic on the expressway. I imagine the poor souls driving frantically, trying to save their infected loved ones. In the end, their love devours them—the way my love devoured Greyson...*oh, God, he's gone*.

Chunks of the Mediterranean Sea appear on the horizon wedged between the cityscape profiles. We exit the expressway. "I'm going to have to circumvent and come in from the north. The direct route is impassable—I've tried. It will take a bit longer, but the streets are less congested."

Like us, the *boches* generally avoid exposure to the sunlight, so, although we start seeing more of them, they cower under cover. A smattering of simple ZV teens, eyes still living, dodge between buildings, feral and scared. Not many wander around. In the states, I would expect to see more. But the alphas and *boches* that developed so quickly here have swallowed up the teens that usually survive, feed on their friends and family, deteriorate slowly like Bridger.

Seems like a lifetime since I thought of my ex. There's so much of my life that has nothing more than the quality of smoke in my imagination. Dreams and aspirations—the virus has ground them to pulp in its teeth. "What is it you always wanted to do, Kasim—you know, before?"

He snorts out a laugh. "Not sure that's an option now. It's at least a two-man job, and it involves a lot of sun."

We pass the modern port and the cruise ship docks. Did the virus wander aboard? What did that look like? A handful of *boches* roam the deck. It's totally possible people are still hiding out, trapped inside. My own drama is only a minor scene in a much bigger play. Makes me feel smaller than I already do.

Sprinkled among the modern structures are ruins. Kasim motions towards the white limestone cliffs and islands that dot the water all along the coast. "The Nazis occupied this port.

You can still see the bunkers there." Gun holes glare from strongholds forged into the rock. "Marseille has seen her fair share of invaders. The Nazis were only the last in a long parade. With the help of *Notre Dame de la Garde*," he nods up to the basilica where the New Order murdered Eugène. The virgin guards the port from the top of its spire, "the city always managed to keep what was hers."

Laure startles awake with a cry, and David jerks to attention. Reaching my hand back, I pat her knee, but she's still in her nightmare world and gasps, jerking away from my grey hand. I pull it back and use my words to drag her into this reality that's probably not much of an improvement. "We're almost there, Laure."

David reorients himself and wraps his arm around her shoulder. She snuggles up and breathes more slowly. A gentle aroma of oven-fresh croissant wafts off them to the front seat. I snatch the joint from Kasim's fingers and take a long drag.

Several domes rise up from a dusty rose and white striped Romanesque Byzantine cathedral sitting right on the coast. "Wait! What is that?" It looks just like *Notre Dame de la Garde*, all except for the beachfront property.

"A church."

"Obviously. But it can't be *Notre Dame de la Garde*. That was on a hill, remember, where we found Eugène—" God, that was insensitive. Of course, he remembers.

"This is the cathedral, the wealth of the church in Marseille. *Notre Dame de la Garde* is the patron saint of sailors."

Cerulean water glistens behind the towers. Beyond the jut of land that blocks our view to the east, I know the island of *If* floats on the waves. I should have left when Greyson wanted me to—

Smoke lingers, hazing the space between us. "Eugène and I, we were going to sail the world." Kasim turns into a broad avenue. Several blocks away, it spills into an open square in front of the old port. Rows of masts and rocking hulls prick the electric blue of the harbor at the end of the street. On the horizon beyond, the crooked teeth of civilization spring from the land that juts around the opposite side of the water and forms a small gate leading to the sea.

As we near the port, the avenue still appears quite broad, but the street itself is narrow. Sentinels of waist-high metal poles stationed along a raised cement border block vehicles from passing over into the broad pedestrian passageways on either side, each wide enough to allow for motorcycle and bike parking. Six-story apartment buildings and hotels line the street. Near the end of the avenue, I spot a Metro entrance just in front of a *tabac*.

"*La Canebière*?" I orient myself with the words on the blue plaques that identify the streets. Just a precaution. Never know when I'll end up on my own.

He salutes me with a tip of the joint. "Cannabis. The whole place used to be hemp fields. Marseille was the world's largest trader of hemp baskets and ropes from the Middle Ages on until they found better materials." The tops of masts rise up, and we crawl more cautiously towards the sun-spackled blue water. "But, everything changes."

"It doesn't have to. You could still sail the world."

"Sailing the boat takes at least two. Eugène and I were going to cross the Atlantic together. It's a nice boat. Sailboat. 40-footer. Solar panels. Electric engine. Completely off the grid. I suppose I could sail away, maybe find an island with a small population, ride out the apocalypse. But then I'd be bringing the infection with me."

"Not if we find Nicolas. Not if he has the cure."

"Even if he does, society won't just pop back online as if there were no service interruption. It'll be ugly."

"Then you could sail away during the reboot."

A couple blocks before the port, we pass a pedestrian square with a Carousel. *Boches* huddle thick beneath the shelter of its elegantly carved dome. A block closer to the mouth of the avenue, opposite the office of Tourism and the Metro station, we can see into the square of Vieux Port. Hordes of *boches* shelter beneath the boardwalks in front of the shops that surround the docks. Just to our left, we glimpse a shaded pavilion. Kasim stops. *"Merde!"*

Chapter 45

Kasim and I stare open-mouthed into the seething mass of *boches* sardined beneath the metal awning that stands between us and the ferry dock. Driving into them would be suicide. The car would smash through dozens and then stall out on severed limbs against the sheer wall of bodies pressing into it. We'd be trapped.

"I was afraid of this. This area was one of the most populated in the city. They had the fish market there," he points to the right of the covered pavilion, "every morning." Toppled tables and rotting fish corpses strewn across the pavement mark the last market. On that morning, the fish were off the hook, and the fishermen were the catch of the day. The shade nets all the *boches* into the pavilion. "I liked to grab a fresh catch for the evening. I was living on the boat." He points beyond us, through the horde of bloody-mouthed roamers. "The blue one there on the right, the last row." A magnificent sailboat all wood with a navy blue hull floats majestically in the harbor.

"You weren't roughing it."

He grins. "The market district is adjacent over there. There's a mall."

"Dense population, hence the zombie-topia."

He points across the square, just past the shaded pavilion. "The ferry for the islands of *If* and *Frioul* is still in the dock. That's our ride."

Gavin's motorcycle whines up behind us. The mass of swarming human sharks ahead doesn't seem to bother him. Leaving the bike running, he strolls up to my side. I hit the button to lower the window. The stench of human death and decay mingles with rotting fish and overwhelms the salty ocean breeze that waltzes into the car.

"What's the hold up here? You afraid of a few mongrels running wild in the street?"

"These are not your dogs, Gavin." I remind him.

"No worries, princess. Never met a dog I couldn't master." He's such a narcissist. He can't possibly know what happens when an alpha gets bitten by his own. Then again, maybe he does know. He didn't talk about Lilou. It wouldn't do his reputation with me much good for him to tell me he intentionally infected the girl he was in love with because he thought that was a great way to hook up with her. For all I know, he's been keeping tabs on *l'Impressioniste*. Gavin isn't one to let the woman he wants just slip away because she says "no." If he's been working with Joëlle, maybe he knows more about his mutation of the virus than even Nicolas.

Our combined aroma of predator and prey has seeped into the square. A few dozen rabid heads in the port pavilion and the fish market snap to the smell, instincts clashing in twitching grimaces on their faces.

"Follow me. I told you I'd be useful." With the remote, Gavin shuts his bike off and stalks towards the stuttering mob of dead. Arms out, palms forward, head dipped, he commands them back. "Go! Get the hell out my way, you mangy curs." He passes the Metro stop.

The living dead now clog the entrance into the portside market square. They're no longer passively milling about. The *mélange* of scents has stirred them into a twitching frenzy. They hesitate, jerking erratically, at contradictory signals to their brain—an alpha from another pack, a couple of competing grey predators just beyond, and the juicy whiff of fresh, uninfected prey. It's an overload.

One hand on the door handle, I'm poised to jump out the minute it looks like Gavin's in over his head. Forgetting to breathe, I watch the circus.

A good number of the market residents are—were—Middle Eastern. At the front of the crowd, a tall *boche,* with an olive hue to his morbid pallor and a tattered black and cream scarf dangling from his bloodied neck, snarls at Gavin. His snorts attract a stocky sidekick and a couple of females, one in a hijab, and the other a mousy blond tourist in sunglasses and comfortable ballet flats covered in rusty bloodstains from a gaping wound in her calf. Our outsider alpha is going to have to assert his dominance the old-fashioned way—with a fight.

Shoving the door open, I throw my leg out before Kasim grabs my arm. "No. You'll only stir them up." He holds up the butt end of the joint. "Neither one of us is in fighting form."

He's right. Doesn't matter. "He can't take on the four of them alone."

"You don't know that. Give him a minute. I've seen an alpha at work."

So have I. There's an excellent chance Gavin can handle this on his own, but there's a small chance he'll need help. Still tense, I set my butt back into my seat, but leave the door open.

David's not at all down with our choices. "What the hell! Shut the door! Back up! Turn around. We don't have a chance against that mob!"

"We can't just leave him." I put my foot out again, and Kasim grabs my arm.

I shake him off and slam the door closed behind me. "Kasim, get these two to *If* and, for God's sake, open the trunk!" The New Order vehicles all come standard with a garden variety of guns. Leaning through the front window, I brief Laure in the back seat. "Find Lieutenant Ryan Samson— or Clément, 6'4", *costaud*, buzz cut. Can't miss him. Might have a little blonde *môme* hanging about, around six, wearing a tight ponytail. You got that?"

"Ryan Samson, Clément." Laure nods, still staring wide-eyed at the menacing mob.

"The trunk, Kasim!" I thump the roof with my fist.

"You're insane!" He finally pops it open.

"Insane in an insane world is sane." Grabbing a handgun that won't slow me down, I toss an automatic affair to Kasim through my open passenger window as I run by.

The tall *boche* is in no hurry. The woman in the hijab is much more enthusiastic—or just hungrier. She outstrips the others and hurtles, snarling, smack into Gavin's fist. The impact knocks her flat on her back, but she's up in a blink. Gavin grabs her by the collar, lifts her off her feet, and hurls her into a row of motorcycles parked on the broad sidewalk. Her body topples the first onto the next, and the motorcycles domino in a clatter of metal and shattering glass.

Kasim nods at me, but I'm not convinced. The subliminal waves of violence infect the brainwaves of the others. The lulled little monsters dozing in my veins begin to wake. The loiterers at the mouth of the square turn and respond in a frenzied run towards our car. The woman heaves herself off the pavement and launches at Gavin about the same time the other two musketeers reach for him. Gavin slams his fist into her snapping jaws. The crack of the bones echoes through the street. Tipping her on her side, he lifts her crosswise to his chest and vaults her entire body at her oncoming cohorts.

Running across the street, I fire my gun and lure the attention of the *boches* away from the car. "Get the hell out of here!" Pale heads whip around, and suddenly, I'm in the crosshairs of their hijacked sensory neural net. "Now! Get the kids to *If*. Go!"

"I'm not leaving you here with Gavin."

"Go!"

Despite Gavin's furious barking, the stream of *boches* has now circumvented his mound of fallen semi-dead. Some vacillate like psychotic schizophrenics fighting the opposing voices in their head, others push past, their viral instincts locked onto a rival predator.

Shooting into the oncoming torrent, I retreat back down the road to the *tabac* on the corner of a narrow cross street. Temporary wire fencing surrounds a backhoe doing construction on a section of the side road. I vault the barrier.

Laure screams. A couple of *boches* have broken through to the car on the other side of the avenue. Oh, God! I left the window open! They swarm and plug the hole. Kasim has no choice, he guns the SUV into reverse and squeals back, past the small street where I'm barricading myself in. A clamoring crowd presses on the fence lining the main avenue.

Down the side street, low metal barriers form a lane of entrance through the construction zone onto the business sidewalks. They're not secured in cement blocks, so I grab the front section and swing it towards the opening to close off the gap. The grate of the feet against the cement attracts a handful of *boches*. There's still an opening of at least two feet wide when the stragglers round the corner of the fence. Their heads dart from side to side, trying to pick up my trail.

An elegant, older gentleman, with a large nose and the bloom of a bite mark across the abdomen of his white linen shirt, locks onto me and bolts to the opening. Kicking and grunting, I fight him off while shoving the gate closed but struggle to avoid the clacking teeth and push forward at the same time. His grasping claw seizes a pocket on my vest. A finger gets stuck in the loop. The gate slams on his forearm as another half-dozen *boches* hit the barrier. The three parallel bars are only chest high. One of the newcomers, shoved from behind, tumbles headfirst into the pen.

Struggling to get through, the old gentleman leverages his arm against the fence. I'm forced to waste bullets on him and the clown flailing on the ground inside.

"C'mon, Evelyn, run through the front! You can make it!" Kasim hollers from farther down the avenue, just in front of the carousel square.

That boat has sailed. The crowds, attracted by the gunshots will be stacking up behind the *boches* piled against the fencing They'll block the front entrance by the time I run through the store. I'm fast, but I won't be able to run through the pack.

The chainlink is flimsy with squares broad enough for arms and snapping jaws to reach through. I'm not wasting bullets on the pack; my supply is too low. It won't be long before the barrier gives way. Only cement blocks secure it to the ground. "Just go, Kasim, now, while the *boches* are distracted! Go!"

The second stream has reached the car again. Kasim has to shoot a couple climbing through the open window before he shakes his head and revs the car back down the street. Mutilated bodies dangle from the passenger side. The SUV swerves into the next crossroad and shoots away in the direction of the pavilion.

And now it's just Gavin and I, standing our ground against the swarm of *boches,* hopefully long enough to give Kasim time to deliver his messengers to the ferry.

Chapter 46

Outside the construction barricade, Gavin holds a small group captive with his alpha powers, but they're jittery. He's not the supreme overlord he thinks he is—typical. The fence in front of me bends with the weight of the masses crowding against it. The wires press bloody blocks into the pale dead flesh of the *boches* pasted to them.

The *tabac* has two entrances: one inside the barrier and the other behind the stairs to the Metro on the avenue. I couldn't have run towards the car from the avenue door, but the Metro station is the opposite direction, only steps away. A low rock wall on the far side guards pedestrians from falling into the escalators from the sidewalk. *Boches* don't do stairs well. They'd have to climb four to the entrance platform to follow me. Vieux Port has to be a huge central station. There's bound to be another exit somewhere down there. I could disappear and come up on another street where the *boches* haven't been worked into a hunting frenzy. Although, who knows what kind of zombie shit show is going down in those tunnels?

But if I escape through the Metro, I leave Gavin to fend for himself. The possibility is tempting. Really tempting. He's an alpha. He can probably hold his ground and break away. Probably. He's also a dick who knew what he was getting into when he insisted on tagging along. He's murdered enough people to deserve whatever end he gets.

The pompous idiot is completely unarmed. While I hesitate, he rips the arm off one of his tentative minions and beats the closest to him with it. I've seen lots of emotions on Gavin's face, but never this one. He's not accustomed to fear and doesn't know what to do with it. Maybe I'm wrong. Maybe there is still an ounce of humanity left in the beast.

The press of *boches* against the mobile barrier shoves it open enough for two of them to clog the gap. Only a few seconds, and they'll be on me. The fence on the avenue side leans in precariously. Another few dozen, and it will fall.

Behind me sits the backhoe. Impossible to grow up in Eli, Utah without having experimented with driving farm equipment. The backhoe has tank tracks instead of wheels, built to plow over obstacles—maybe not, specifically, these obstacles, but I'm not picky. The driver's mostly devoured carcass sprawls over the tracks, one arm still reaching for the windows of the cab. His fingers hold the key in a death grip.

In the two seconds it takes me to make up my mind and race for the backhoe, an ambitious *boche* shoves the two competitors for the gap through the fence. I snatch the key. The front-runner plows over the other two and snatches my foot. The leak has sprung. A whole swarm of them crawl over the backhoe. The *boche* attached to my ankle hauls himself up to bite range. His teeth sink in as my bullet shatters his skull. Pulling my leg through, I slam the door shut. The fence in front of me gives way, and the hordes pour in, pounding on the glass, snarling. Now I'm a zombie apocalypse meme.

My eyes squeeze tight. I'm scared to look at my ankle, but I can't afford not to. Not knowing puts everyone I love at risk— even more than just knowing me does. I don't actually feel a wound, but that could just be the virus blocking my pain receptors. God, in ten minutes I could be one of Gavin's minions. Breathing deep, I block out the snarling and the scrape of nails on glass, look down, and open my eyes. Thank God for combat boots. The teeth marks in the leather are deep, but the thick socks beneath are intact—no blood. My head bangs back against the vinyl seat, and I breathe again.

Time to go.

The machine lurches a little while I play with the controls, but eventually, I figure out the basics. *Boches* clutter the windshield, so I have to drive peeking through the gaps in the bodies. The engine roars and the tracks turn, crunching bones and squishing guts beneath their flat treads. The cab bumps and jumbles over the top of the fallen fence. The waist-high posts that block the sidewalk stand in my way.

I maneuver into the street not far from Gavin. If he can make it into the shovel, I'll let him hitch a ride to the ferry. He sees me coming, and he's way ahead of me. When I'm close enough, he vaults from the center of his doubting congregation into the shovel and begins shouting hellfire and damnation at the *boches* clinging to the cab. Turning left, I pass the Burger King on the corner between the fish market square and *la Canebière*. We're on easy street now. I can see the SUV parked in front of the ferry entrance. Shots from the dock confirm that the ferry isn't clean. Kasim, a gun in each hand, escorts Laure and David towards the boat. I don't want to aggravate the pest problem. We need to lose the crowd trailing behind us before we join them.

Gavin's preaching works on most of the vermin clinging to the backhoe. The banging and scraping against the glass stops. The snarling recedes into an insecure rasping as we pick up speed. Nothing can stop us now.

And then, the shrill tones of a dog whistle rip my eardrums.

All of the *boches* snap to attention. Gavin and I lock eyes. We both know what this is. Another couple quick trills, and all of the *boches* descend from where they are and lie facedown on the pavement. The throng of them streaming in from *la Canebière* follow suit until the ground is covered with undead playing dead. An eerie shiver shakes my shoulders. Gavin and I hone in on the origin of the sound and turn in unison towards the red-caped figure controlling the zombies from a balcony of the hotel above the Brasserie next to Burger King. By the time we fix on her location, Lilou has targeted Gavin with a rather large handgun.

"Run!" I shout. I know what comes next. I've already seen one of *l'impressioniste's* art shows. No one, no matter what they've done, deserves to end up in her studio.

Gavin leaps from the shovel. In mid-air, his neck snaps sideways—no crack of a gunshot. That was a tranquilizer dart. I hit the brakes. Gavin holds his neck and yells as he pulls out the dart. I know from experience, he's only got a couple minutes before he gets faint and dizzy. Lilou has disappeared from the balcony, no doubt to come gather her art supplies. If Gavin can just make it into the cab with me, I can drag him unconscious onto the ferry and keep him from becoming human clay.

Gavin staggers towards me. I throw the door open. The virus is revved up and charging through my blood. "Get in! Hurry!"

Without the calming effect of Lilou's training, the *boches* in the street stir. One grabs Gavin's foot. He stumbles, shouting obscenities at the undead. The alpha scent confuses them. It's his only saving grace.

My scent, on the other hand, riles up any *boche* near the open door of the cab. Not even the heavy fish overtones lurking in the air can hide my stench. The *boches* don't just stir, they rise up and bolt for the kill. I drop the first couple with the precious few bullets I have. Their bodies create bridges up the backhoe. "C'mon Gavin!" He's back on his feet, but now he has to fight through the rabid throng. He teeters in the jostling. The rearview mirror throws me a glimpse of the mob rushing up from behind.

I don't have a choice. I have to leave without him. He created Lilou. Now his monster has come back to return the favor. There's nothing I can do.

From the corner in front of us, Lilou emerges, red cape flowing in the salty, sea breeze. She toots on her magic pipe, and the *boches* all fall into submission. The tranquilizer gun hangs in her hand. Shit! I have a clear shot to Gavin, now. Before, I didn't have a choice. There was no way I could get to him. Now, if I drive away without him, it's a conscious choice I made to abandon him. I should. I totally should. At the very least, I should shoot him in the head so he doesn't have to live the rest of his pathetic existence in Lilou's hell.

He's worth a bullet and close enough that it won't take more than one. But, God help me, tranquilized, he looks so young and vulnerable. It would be like shooting my little brother for the crime of catching the virus. If the little egomaniac hadn't risked himself for Laure and David, this would be so much easier. My finger won't squeeze. I can't do it. I can't leave behind a man down, and I can't pull the trigger. There's only once choice left.

Jumping out the cab door onto submissive bodies, I bolt for Gavin. The air gun pops, and a dart lodges into the vest of my RAID suit. It doesn't penetrate the skin. Wrapping my arms beneath his shoulders, I haul Gavin back towards the Brasserie. If we can get behind closed doors, I might stand a chance against *l'Impressioniste* until the tranquilizer in Gavin's neck wears off enough for us to escape back the way we came. His bike is still out there.

It's not a bad plan. At least I think so until I have to drop him to open the door. The red cape flutters into the open patio between the café tables and chairs. Grabbing a limp hand, I heave Gavin through the opening. A dart sinks into the skin of my neck. I still have enough time to drag him in and lock the door. Futile, I know. It's glass. The world dims and spins as I drag furniture in front of it. A muted smudge of red invades the glazed glass before the darkness sets in.

Chapter 47

A soul. I think I have one. It's floating. I left my body somewhere. I was hoping, if I died, I'd find Grey again. But I don't see him. I don't see anyone. Not my parents, not Josh and Jeremy, not Cory, not even Bridger—I'm alone, floating without a body.

The darkness lightens, and I think I'm standing in front of God. A fuzzy haze of pink-tinged white surrounds us. This god doesn't sit regally on a throne. This is a tortured god, crowned in thorns, his body splayed on stone, the lower half covered in a light blanket. He looks exhausted and defeated in his humanity, a mirror of my own fatigue. His head rests on the shoulder of a woman. Mom? No, not mom. Mom is dead.

Nausea grips my stomach, and I realize I'm not dead. A wave of bile rushes up from my gut, and I vomit myself into reality. Wiping the spit from my cheek with bound hands, I slide away from the pile of green sludge. Plastic ties bind my feet as well.

Squeezing my eyes shut, I try to refocus and orient myself into the present while the past rushes back into my consciousness. The pink and white marble blocks of a church alcove create the illusion of a pink haze. Cold stone grates against my cheek. In front of me looms a sculpture of Saint Veronica cradling the head of the fallen Christ on her knees. Behind them, light sifts in colored prisms through the Roman arch window.

Moaning from behind attracts my attention. Rolling over is tricky and stirs the nausea in my gut. Pausing, I clench my teeth.

My head flops over. In the blur between columns, on a wooden platform, Gavin, stripped, his lower half draped in a thin blanket, lies sideways as if he's fallen in mid-step and tried to raise his torso up on his arms to stand again. Uncanny how the trim, muscular lines of his arms and chest mirror the dimensions of the statue behind me. Even his long fingers, graceful with prominent bones, match the hands that support the fallen Christ.

To reflect the art, his upper leg extends along a wooden base constructed to mimic the shape of the sculpture's base and plastered with dirt and stones for realism. The knee of his lower leg juts from the cloth just next to his hand. The moaning doesn't lament his nauseated emergence from the tranquilizer, he's bleeding purple tainted blood from the thorns of the barbed-wire crown he wears. But even worse, to maintain the crawling pose and still prop his torso up to mirror the art, the artist has driven a nail through his right hand to the lower knee and another through his left forearm to the base. The suffering on the Christ's face doesn't need sculpting onto Gavin's. The virus can't dull pain like that.

My stomach lurches again, and tears sting my eyes for him. No one knows where we are. Neither one of us will die. We'll struggle against the nails for as long as Marseille is quarantined. What will that be? Months, years, decades?

Quiet steps, like slippers, pad down the stone aisle. Black leggings and a cami show off a well-sculpted petit form. A tool apron encumbers the trim waist. This is *l'Impressioniste* in her atelier.

She's a work of art herself. I can see why Gavin was attracted. She's his type.

"Lilou—" he moans. Nothing else will come out, but it doesn't have to. The plea oozes from the name.

Adorable, clear French echoes in the vastness of the cathedral. "Don't worry, Gavin, *mon chèri*, the pose will be so much easier to sustain once I have wedged your friend beneath your shoulder. She will comfort you, just as St. Véronique comforted our Lord." Her hand caresses Gavin's hair above the bloody crown. From her arm dangles a large thin blanket. "I only wish your hair were a bit longer. Everything about you so resembles the Christ of this sculpture, but the hair. Perhaps I will find something."

My gut rocks again, and my whole body convulses and rolls into a pile of clothes—the uniform and protective gear that Gavin was wearing before Lilou started sculpting.

"*Oh, la, la!* Your little friend is waking. I'll have to hurry before she becomes difficult to pose." Pose? "It was so kind of you to bring her to me."

"Lilou—" Gavin moans again.

"I know. I know. You didn't want your portrait done. We had an arrangement—you deliver her to me for my rendition of the *Vierge Marie*, and in return, I do a portrait of Yves for you. But, you see, don't you, Gavin?" She leans in to lightly kiss his cheek, cajoling, like a small child asking for a puppy. "She is the perfect model for this piece!" She points at the sculpture of St. Veronica offering comfort to the fallen Christ. "When I saw the two of you slumped together, I knew, I just knew I would never find two others so suited for my *chef-d'oeuvre*. I have loved this sculpture since I was only a little girl."

The French words jumble together. Gavin set me up in exchange for Lilou capturing the count—his own cousin? The impact of the revelation jerks the acid in my stomach. My chest heaves, and another mess of green spews from my mouth and dribbles down my chin. Of course, he set me up. What does this mean for the rest of the plan? At least I know he wasn't plotting against us with Yves. The count is one of his targets. Gavin is a rat masquerading as a human. Of all the people on the planet, only he deserves this torture.

"Lilou—" sweat illuminates his face. The mask of pain gives me no pleasure, but he's an egomaniac, backstabbing player. I can't pity him.

Lilou steps towards me and leans down to lift my head and torso. The sudden shift in orientation destroys my equilibrium. The world rocks, spins, and rolls all at the same time. I can barely keep my eyes open, much less struggle. My muscles have turned to cotton. The volcano in my gut erupts again, and the vomit splatters the front of Lilou's cami. Undeterred, she pats my head, and hugs it to her chest, smearing the sticky sludge over my cheek. "*Ma puce*," she sympathizes, "art is a cruel mistress. She will have her sacrifices."

Wrapping the blanket she carries around my shoulders, she molds it into a hood and shawl. "Hmm." She wipes the grime from my face with a cloth. "This will not do. I thought, perhaps the blanket would hide this bulky uniform. But see how it bulges beneath the cloth? It will ruin the effect." She grabs a handful of my hair, long since escaped from its ponytail and pouring from the hood. She clucks her tongue. "*Non, non, non.* A true saint of the sacred cloth would not have all this hair beneath her veil. *Non.*" Wagging her finger, she leans down to look me in the eyes and coaxes me with a smile. "You see?" She changes over to halting English. "No hair on statue. No worries. I have scissors. We will fix, *non*?"

I think she's going to cut my hair. Compared to all the other horrors going on in this little workshop of terror, that shouldn't bother me, I know. But those pathways in my brain run deep. Suddenly, I'm back in the Institute facing the razor that will shave my head just like they shaved Greyson's...*he's gone*...so the doctors could dissect our brains. All my flight and fight instincts kick in, and the virus staunches every sensation but blind rage.

Lilou hums *À la Claire Fontaine* as her little slippers pad away.

As much as I would love to use the privacy to beat Gavin with my words, I need to focus on getting the hell out of here before this church becomes my own personal hell for the duration of the apocalypse.

Chapter 48

"Ev'lyn—" Gavin's eyes plead because he can't get the words out. I'm done with him. He can choke on this wine he's pressed. He's murdered hundreds, maybe thousands, he had a choice. "I'm sor—"

"Don't." I don't want to hear his lies. They'll just screw the knife deeper. This place brings all my morals to the surface, and Gavin offends them all. They riot with the virus scurrying around trying to animate my limbs. My bloodstream is a crusade, religion and war all jumbled up together, each one churning the other into nonsense.

Who knows how long I've been out, but the marijuana has completely evaporated from my system. The virus chomps through the tranquilizer. My fingers twitch. Lilou left me a pretty good amount of wiggle room—why wouldn't she? I was out cold, probably on horse tranquilizers. She didn't even bother to strip all the weapons out of my RAID suit. A Glauca G-1, my little sister's PTSD therapist, still bulges from the pocket in the side of my pants. Along with a custom blade, the knife features a plastic handcuff cutter. *Ma puce.* Lilou called me "my little flea." Like everyone else, she's underestimated me. I won't make the same mistake on her behalf. She might be small and dainty, but I've seen how brutally lethal she can be.

My muscles tingle and lumber back online. Concentrating enough for a sweat to break out on my forehead, I shimmy my arms around to fumble for the knife. My fingers are barely coordinated enough to grab the handle. My muscles have turned to rubber bands. The blade clangs against the stone floor twice.

"Ev'lyn—"

"I'm done with you, Gavin." Words struggle to unwrap themselves from my chapped lips. My hands fumble blindly for the tie cutter feature before the sound that bothered Gavin enough to bother speaking reaches my ears. Muffled gunshots outside.

I'm not even sure where we are, but the size and space of the place make me think we're still only a few blocks from the port, inside the Marseille Cathedral. Pausing to listen, I hone in on the sounds of a gunfight. Maybe Kasim got to the *Chateau d'If*. Maybe Ryan came through and counter ambushed the team from the New Order. I wonder if Laure's family brought reinforcements. I can only hope. I don't want to be on a side anymore. I want to find a place apart. Just me and Amber—and Grey...*but he's gone*. Either way, if I don't get out of here, no one will know where Gavin and I are, and I'll be pinned like a butterfly to this display board, possibly for years—with Gavin. Oh God! Sartre was right: *l'enfer, c'est les autres*.

The knife stumbles in my hands as I try to manipulate the cutting feature between my wrists to cut the ties. Even with my hands free, it won't be easy defending myself against an alpha, and especially not with the bauble head that's replaced my brain.

"Ev—e—" Gavin is losing consciousness.

The tool locks up against the ties, and I force it down, cutting through the thick plastic like a sharp knife in cold butter. The effort winds me. Dragging my wrists around, I try to rub the chafing away and then heave myself forward to cut the tie around my ankles. The soft footfall behind me alerts me that the strain of my endeavor blocked out Lilou's approach. My head turns just in time for my eyes to make out the blur of a mallet before it bangs against the side of my skull.

Chapter 49

Pink and white stones swirl and sway to the rhythmic snip and clip of scissors. Beneath my cheek, long crunchy strands stick in the saliva that trickles out my open mouth. A tug on a thick strand pulls my head back. Snip, snip, and a string lands across my nose, trailing another into my eye. It tickles, stings, and itches all at once. My hand lobs across the floor, aiming to brush my eye. My palm sweeps up a handful of hair.

My eyes cringe against the dim rose-colored light streaming from the blinding stained glass. Lilou stands above my head wielding long metal shears against a 16" strand of blond. A one-second delay stands between the moment I realize the hair is mine and the chomp of the twin blades. Half of the clump tumbles into my open mouth. The floor around me is covered in blond clippings.

I thought losing my hair would horrify me. I feel nothing. Maybe it's the drugs or the nausea. Maybe I feel freed. I don't have to worry about damage anymore. It's already done. Or maybe I'm concussed and not interpreting the world in the same language I used to. One thing is for sure, my love of art is dead—or at least living dead. I'll never be able to look at a Rodin again and not imagine a semi-living human suffocating inside the stone.

My head lolls, thumping and thrumming, as Lilou drags me under the arms backward towards the wooden platform. A deep groan rumbles up from my throat. A sticky, wet trickle stains my ear below the throbbing. My face slides past my RAID suit, lying in a heap, cut to pieces. Only my cami and briefs protect small parts of my skin from the cold scrape of stone. Plastic ties still secure my ankles. She had to cut the pants off.

The double benches, the flower patterns in the window, the stone rectangles, everything expands, shifts, swirls, and then realigns into single images. My heart, virus-fueled, double pumps. The beast doesn't believe in surrender. That would be handy if my muscles weren't on strings controlled by a drunk puppeteer in my brain. Maybe I'd actually resist instead of just growling like a trapped animal.

Lilou lurches me back. My shoulder jerks past my clothes. My hand stumbles over the pile and hits solid metal. The knife.

Vague gunshots, closer than before, reverberate in dull, subdued plugs and collide with my ears. Lilou pauses. "This will not do." Halting, she frowns at the big doors past the rows of benches.

My fingers fumble along the blade to the hilt.

"They're getting closer." She drags me a little farther.

My fist tightens around the handle. Do I stand a chance? No. Not one in a million. But I might as well do as much damage as I can. She won't die, but at least I can cripple her so she can't work.

"Not to worry. I've stationed my dogs outside. Such good pets. The guardian instincts come naturally—" she heaves against my lump weight "—it was the 'stay' command that I found tricky to train into them."

An explosion rattles the doors. Lilou stops to cast a worried glance over her shoulder. Up to this point, the locals haven't been willing to destroy their city to eradicate the *boches*—although it wouldn't be the first time they'd had to resort to it.

We've reached the base of the wooden platform. Gavin is out cold, his head flopping over his shoulder. "You see, he needs you to support his head and brush the drops of blood from his face." She navigates the step up, pulling my shoulders with her to drag me into position.

A little dose of vengeance feeds the virus as my back slides against the stones and dirt. My arm twitches with adrenaline. Grunting and heaving, I swing it over my shoulder, driving the blade into the pale, soft flesh of her arm. No, it's not the same as when a regular uninfected gets stabbed, but it's not nice either.

Lilou screeches, equal parts of fury and pain, and I rip the knife free. She cradles the injured arm, moaning and screaming as if she hasn't done the same thing to dozens of greys, ZVs and uninfected.

Released, I lean up to the ties around my ankles. The motion ripples a wave of dizziness from my gut to my throat. My head spins. Lilou throws her other elbow around my neck. She growls and hisses at me, purple blood from her wound sliding down her arm and dripping onto the stones and my shoulder. With the virus amping up her strength, she wrenches me easily up onto the platform. "Little whore. You don't deserve the honor of *St. Véronique*. You are a devil."

I'm already struggling to control my muscles, and now I'm gasping for breath. Words barely grate from my throat. "Then we'll be neighbors in hell." The knife, awkward in my fist, lunges blindly behind me, plunging through air before slicing through skin. Lilou screams again, drops my shoulders and throttles my arm, neutralizing the knife. Three good shakes, and it clatters across the stones. She bares her teeth in a vicious snarl. My whole frame shivers. I'm going to finish the apocalypse as one of her pets. Bitten and obedient.

Not quite. While I struggle to free my arm, Lilou reaches for the nail gun lying on the platform. Scratching and clawing, I resist, but I'm only half here, and this alpha is in full maniac mode. I'm not going to end this story brain-dead and gorging on human flesh, I'm going to finish the apocalypse here, displayed on the platform, teeth gnashing and groaning until someone finds me and shoots my brains out.

"Did you think I would let you die? The death of Our Lord, the nails in his palms and feet, is too good for you. You will live to repent of your wickedness." She jams the nail gun against my palm, pinching it to the platform. The nail gun thumps. The metal penetrates my hand, piercing the skin and tendons, shattering bone. My scream resonates through the hall, an orchestrated crescendo punctuated with the staccato of a gunshot.

Against my writhing, she pulls me up onto my knees and shoves my shoulder up underneath Gavin's lolling head. The syncopated beat of his strained breathing grates in my ear. With a nail in my palm, I repent my condemnation of him. I was wrong. No one, not even the traitorous demon whose head is resting on my shoulder deserves this. The constant, throbbing pain will drive us mad before the virus finally gives up on outside nourishment and consumes us from the inside.

Striding around to the front, she compares her work critically to the model before us. "Your look is not right. Gavin has played his part magnificently. One truly feels pity for the suffering etched into his features. But you, you must display some sympathy for Your Lord." Her fingers grasp my face, tilting it around and down to behold Gavin's. It's not the virus, just hate that clamps my teeth onto her delicate finger. Lilou squeals and slaps at my face with her free palm. The unholy union of acidic alpha blood and the tangy salt of humanity burst into my mouth before the bone cracks. The pain shooting up the nerves of my arm saps my will and tenacity before I can sever the appendage. She wrestles the finger out of my jaws and slaps me hard. "*Putain!*" My head bangs against the top of Gavin's. Lilou's finger hangs awkwardly.

Wincing and crying, she grabs my free hand and stuffs a fold of the blanket into it. Dragging it across my body, she poses the fingers to dab at the beads of sweat and purple blood on Gavin's forehead.

My hand flops back when she turns to grab the nail gun. She's going to drive a nail through my finger into Gavin's eye. If he's lucky, the spike will kill him. Working with only one hand, she fumbles the gun while trying to repose my fingers against Gavin's cheek with her broken hand.

It occurs to me to use what strength I have to plead, but she's so angry that I don't bother to waste breath on her.

The cold steel tip of the gun wobbles into position at my finger. The door at the back of the cathedral bursts open. Gunshots from outside echo through the vaulted hall.

The nail gun thumps again. Shooting pain sears my finger. Gavin groans deeply. I don't have the strength to scream. Tears fill my eyes, and I sob. The virus is no match for this kind of torture. If I'm lucky, the wounds will kill me sooner than the virus will put me out of my misery and consume me slowly from the inside. I welcome the blackness seeping around the edges of my vision.

Chapter 50

A beam of light streaks across the center of the building, penetrating the darkness and silhouetting a single figure in an aura of blinding light. A gunshot cracks and echoes in the empty stone hall.

Above me, Lilou's face freezes, hangs in wide-eyed confusion, and then tips forward onto my shoulder, exposing a bloody purple hole in the back of her skull.

***

Tugging on the nail that bolts my hand to the platform revives me. My vision bends, muddled, halfway between hallucination and the pain throbbing viciously in my palm and the finger that has already been separated from Gavin's eye. The tip still oozes purple-tainted goo. The nail wrenches free from the wood, and human fingers gently slide it through blood and tendon. Relief. The bright sunlight from the window projects an aura around the silhouette standing over me. "Grey? Greyson?" *No, he's gone.* Maybe this is God. I've done my penance. Game over.

Footsteps approach, boots slapping against stone. The voices bloat and bend in slow motion. "That one's an alpha. Shoot him."

A gunshot echoes through the pink corridors. In the blur of my vision, I see Gavin's head jerk and fall. "No!" I'm not sure the word actually makes it out of my mouth. My lips are lead. Everyone. Everyone I help dies. It has to stop. My breath stutters and hiccups. How is it that I still care? Gavin was an alpha. A ruthless killer—worse. And yet, in the end, deep down, he was just a kid who wanted love and didn't know how to get it or hang onto it once he had it. How am I any different? Didn't he do his penance as well? Maybe being shot is his reward.

The silhouette leans over, gathers me under the arms and heaves me onto his shoulder. All the blood shifts, and my head lolls forward into black.

Chapter 51

"E—ve—lyn!" The sounds hit my ear muffled and slow. They jumble together and don't make sense. Hands grip my shoulders and rock me back and forth until the world focuses around me.

No. I'm done. Finished. Game over. The world is bright. Is this heaven? There's been a mistake. Monsters like me go to hell.

My ears come back online. Screaming and growling float in the air like smog. Gunshots rattle through the cacophony of a battle in the distance.

"Evelyn." The sounds coalesce into my name. "Can you hear me? I know the wound is bad, but the virus should shut down the pain reactions. We need you to run." The center of my hand throbs deep, and a sharp bolt of pain skitters up my arm. The virus has staunched the pain of the less severe wound in the finger of my other hand.

My lids flutter against the daylight. Dark hair, smoldering eyes, square jaw. "Ryan? Ryan." My arms fly around his neck. "Thank you! Oh, God! Thank you. Thank you for Amber. For Amber—where's Amber?"

"She's fine. She's on her way to the boat."

"You left her?" I struggle to sit. "It's not safe—"

"*I* left her?" He hasn't let that go but decides this isn't the time to hash it out. "Don't worry. She's in better hands than mine."

"Clément? Okay, yeah, he's—" The grey sky spins above me. I must have been in the cathedral for hours. The sun, obscured behind a wall of smoky grey, hangs low in the west.

Ryan drops his palm on my back and nudges me forward. For the first time, I notice the bandages. Raising both hands, I croak out another thanks.

"The bandages are mine, but I can't take credit for getting you out of the nightmare in that cathedral. My job—" he nods at the handful of soldiers around us, "—our job is to get you from here to the boat." He points across several terraces that drop about one hundred feet to the level of the port. Directly across the bay, the Virgin Mary rises up on the spires of *Notre Dame de la Garde* to protect her city. Below us, in the wide streets in front of the port and the pedestrian walkways surrounding it, *boches*, soldiers, and medieval warriors in chain mail exchange blows with axes, swords, guns, teeth and claws. An explosion kicks up dust and smoke in the direction of the ferry.

"Laure and David made it to warn you?"

"Laure made it."

God, it never stops. Is it me or am I just taking the blame for still breathing and thinking when others are not? Sometimes I think, deep down, I left Amber with Ryan because I was afraid she'd die, just like everyone else I try to protect.

"Sorry. It's a war. People die. We save who we can—the people who mean something to us." Ryan's dad is wearing off on him—not enough, apparently, to convince him to let me be one of the casualties. His meaning is clear, and my heart breaks a little for him. I didn't intend to mean something to him, but I didn't stop it from happening either.

I put my hand on his arm. "Thank you." His eyes tell me everything his words don't.

"Do you see those two buildings?" His finger directs my eyes past a bronze statue of a boy training bear cubs and down to the water level to two long, narrow buildings with terracotta rooftops that front the docks. The outer walls of a Romanesque church, but not the cathedral, cover our backside. Very few windows break up the older, yellow walls. We crouch against a rounded turret. "The boat at the end there, that's where we're going." He points out the large, navy blue and wood sailboat that Kasim showed me before.

"Through that?" My nod takes in the mob melee on the horseshoe streets that outline the port. A major expressway separates the levels of terrace below us from the two waterfront buildings. In front of them, in the port itself, a battle rages between RAID-suited greys and medieval warriors allied with modern soldiers. Everywhere, ragged *boches* attack both sides indiscriminately.

The terraces themselves are only mildly contaminated. The brain-dead don't appreciate stairs. Several struggle to crawl up them, and others lie cracked and broken on the down side or caught in the rusty, white metal side rails. Only the poor souls that were infected on the terrace still wander there, trapped.

"That's why we need you to run. The roads are blocked. We couldn't get the armored vehicles up to the cathedral. At the bottom of the steps to that terrace, there's a bath boutique on the street level. We have transport there. We can plow through to the boat in the port. But we have to get to the vehicles on foot." Ryan pulls off his military jacket and hands it to me. "Sorry, your clothes were—"

"Yeah, I know. She cut them off."

For the first time, I glance down and remember that Lilou cut off my hair, too. It's the last thing I care about, should care about, but my hand reaches up subconsciously at the thought, and my fingers assess the jagged damage. Without commenting, I grab Ryan's jacket and throw it on. It falls to just the top of my thighs. My legs are completely exposed, I'm barefoot, but at least my arms and chest have some cover from stray teeth.

The virus has neutralized most of the tranquilizer effect, so I get to my feet without toppling over. My gut is empty, and these guys smell like backyard barbeque on the fourth of July. "You wouldn't happen to have a spare gun?"

I only recognize one or two of the squad guys. The others are General Samson's men. They blink at my grey skin and then exchange "not likely" glances at my request. Most of them probably wonder what the hell they're doing risking their lives for a grey who would gladly hunt them down and carve them up like a five-point deer in season.

Ryan reaches back. One of the guys I recognize from the voyage—Didier, I think—hands him my combat knife. "We recovered this." Ryan looks mortified that he can't offer me more, but he can't risk mutiny. In the port, people who look like me are the enemy. My bandaged right hand has a throbbing hole in it, and the fingers can barely close around the hilt. Left hand, then.

Behind me, combat boots slap the pavement. Clément jogs up. "We're all set. The package is on its way to the boat." He stares down his platoon—most of them over a head shorter than he is, and not one with the bulk to object with any weight to what he does. Pulling a gun from his holster, he hands it over. "Glad you made it, Ev. Amber missed you. I'm running out of Skittles."

"If I ever get home, I'll ship you some from the States." Stuffing the gun for safe-keeping into the cargo pocket of Ryan's coat, I throw my arms around Clément and get one of his signature bear hugs while I look past his bulk and the huddle of soldiers for some sight of Amber. "Where is she?"

"Gummy Bear is secure. Delivery on the boat in t minus five."

What the hell does he mean by that? Turning I grab Ryan's sleeve. "I thought Clément was delivering Amber. You can't just leave her with a babysitter in the middle of the apocalypse."

"I didn't. She's—"

Clément interrupts. "Lieutenant, the cosplayers are nearly all loaded onto the ferry. Any stragglers are retreating there with armed support. Most of the grey assault team has been eliminated. Operation CAFARD is set for t minus 30 minutes. We have to be clear of the port by then. We need to go. Now, sir."

"Let's move!" Ryan signals his men across the street and onto the statue pavilion. The stairs drop onto the lower terrace to the left of the statue. All of the terraces are guarded by white iron railing so the zombies aren't just stumbling in.

I trot behind and catch up with Clément. "Wait!"

"Don't worry about Amber. She was Lieutenant Ryan's first priority. Your man insisted on taking charge of her."

My man? Kasim? That could be okay. He knows how important Amber is to me, and he lost his own little brother. Kasim will do what it takes to make sure she gets out of this port alive—pretty sure. I'd have felt better if Clément had stayed with her. She doesn't know Kasim. Now, all I want is the same thing Ryan's team wants—me on the boat with Amber.

"We have to get you to your boat and evac with that ferry before the bombs start dropping."

"Wait! Bombs?"

Chapter 52

Ryan is my own personal bodyguard for the odyssey to the boat. "General Samson ordered an airstrike on Marseille and some of the other more populated cities."

"What good will that do? The enemy is already dead."

"Trapped under rubble and blown to pieces, they'll be easier to eliminate on the ground. Intel suggests that the known alphas have been eliminated. They won't be creating more armies of dead. The military is going to eliminate the residual *boches* and infected."

"You mean your dad is purging them. He can't do that. Nicolas and Dr. Pêsqué may have a cure. They were close before they left. They could save the infected teens."

"Collateral damage. They do have a cure, but we have to clear the quarantine zone. Risks are too high for trying to round up the infected and getting close enough to administer the serum. We wouldn't just sacrifice our men, we'd be increasing the number of the enemy."

The zombie exponent. The reason the uninfected can't win. Every loss for our side is a gain for theirs. "Yeah, and we all know your dad isn't one to take risks."

"Not his call. This comes from Paris Command." Three troops, Clément at their head and Didier flanking, run guard at the front and fire on the handful of zombies on the first terrace, clearing the path for the rest of us running down the stairs. Didier is small but lethal—like Amber. If I remember right, he's the one that taught her to assemble her rifle faster than some of the privates. The shots attract a congregation of *boches* from the street so the rear soldiers stop at the bottom step and take them out before the stairs trip them up. They'll still shamble up and feed after a tumble, but not with a bullet in the head. We don't want to get surrounded.

"Did I hear right? Did Clément say the whole of the grey assault team was wiped out?"

He puts an arm out to stop me from descending the stairs to the next terrace until the scouts have cleared it. "Yes. They brought a much larger team than your informant suggested. He thought someone tipped them off that we'd be coming and that we'd have back-up from the cosplayers."

It's not a stretch to figure out the snitch was Gavin working both sides. If he wanted Lilou to sculpt Yves, he probably informed the count about our counter-ambush of the grey ambush team.

"Look, I don't know about the master plan, but they can't bomb this entire area!"

"Go!" Grabbing my hand, Ryan bolts down the next set of stairs to the terrace below. This roof is the last one before the stairs dump us into the battleground in the avenue. Amber and my passage out of this warzone are floating only a five-minute walk—and lifetimes—away. I need to focus, but all I can think about are the hundred or so innocent, uninfected children in Anne's New Order school. They don't know what's coming for them, and the "intel" could very well indicate they're a New Order controlled compound—a target on their roof.

Ryan and I hunker at the bottom of the stairs while Clément, Didier, and two other troops pick off the *boches* that run towards them. They're thicker here. The entrance to an apartment building flanks the east end of the terrace. The living dead inhabitants that wandered out were caught between stairs. The gunfire attracted the attention of the horde in the avenue below. The stairs down are now a carpet of snarling, crawling monsters.

A mob overwhelms the scouts and pulls them to the ground. Clément shoots one off the soldier closest to him. But the zombies don't care about bullets. They just keep swarming the poor kid. The only thing for it, in these close quarters, is for Clément to bat them away with the butt of his gun.

"Wait here," Ryan yells and moves in to pick them off once there's some space between the downed soldier and the ravenous mass. The two soldiers behind us are busy mopping up the stragglers that rolled down the stairs above and are now shambling their way to our rear. Didier doesn't pack quite as strong a punch. The scout he's trying to untangle gets mauled and mangled, and the tide moves in on him. He backs away shooting, but one of them, a crawler, slips through the legs of the mob and grabs the ankle of his boot. He falls back, spraying bullets into the air.

No way I'm just going to stand here and let the *boches* devour him. I should be thinking about Amber, about getting to that boat, no matter what the cost, but in the moment, the only thought in my head is to keep Didier alive. I'm not going to let him die for me. I charge in, Beretta in my bandaged hand and knife in the left, to give the marine a chance to get back on his feet. My legs are vulnerable, so while Didier shoots at heads from his back, I drop to my knees and drive the knife into the skull of the zombie attached to his boot.

Of course, I'm the perfect decoy, and one whiff of me shifts the agenda of most of the snarling dead to the rival predator on the ground. Bad for me, but good for the rest of the platoon. When the zombies jerk my direction, Ryan, Clément, and Didier fire a concerted shower of bullets long enough for me to wriggle out, shooting holes through the eyes of the *boches* that latch onto me.

Ryan grabs my arm and hauls me back between Clément and Didier's cover. "Are you insane? We came here to get you out alive!" The horde is overwhelming. The gunfire attracted more. The stairs down are now a carpet of snarling, monsters crawling over the top of each other, creating a semi-human ramp. The only way out is the way we came, and that won't get us any closer to the boat. "Back up the stairs! Now!"

Following the rearguard back up, we tiptoe through actual dead bodies. Near the top, there's a bottleneck that we have to plow through, and I donate a few of my lowly handgun bullets to the cause to clear the blockage. Pulling the trigger with my injured right hand is easier than gripping a knife.

Blood smattered all over his face, Clément joins us, dragging the soldier he pulled out of the mob, interrogating him as they hobble along, "Are you bitten?"

The soldier doesn't respond. "Are you bitten, soldier?" Ryan demands.

"*Non. Non.* I think I broke my ankle." Ryan doesn't take his word. He rifles through his uniform. The coat has some nasty ripping going on, but no holes or bloody punctures. The boot is still intact.

Clément points down the broad red sidewalk running past the upstairs of the apartment building and its twin. "C'mon. I saw these buildings from the boulevard on my way up." With the injured soldier hanging off his shoulder, he leads us past the first building. On the street above, we're about even with the fourth floor of the apartment buildings below. Between the two, a narrow street dead-ends into a steeply sloped stone wall. Iron railing blocks access at both the top and the bottom, but both sides have a gate.

Tiny cars line the edges of the sidewalks that flank the impasse below us. Twin buildings face each other lengthwise across the impasse doubling as drive and parking lot. The upper walks appear clear of *boches*, but that's deceiving. In broad daylight, they've all found cover for their UV sensitive skin in the leaves. They'll abandon it as soon as they pick up a scent and their hunting instincts engage.

At the end of the street, a bath boutique occupies the lower commercial space of the building underneath the terrace we just abandoned. The window displays curve around the corner to the main entrance on the street that intersects the impasse.

The rearguard firing on our pursuers has brought more *boches* into the relatively deserted street above. With a nod, Didier hands me the machine gun he pulled off the kid that went down and takes up a spot at our front to pick off the newcomers from the other side of the avenue. The virus has started shutting down the pain receptors around my hand. I can clench my fist well enough now to strap the gun over my shoulder.

"We don't have many other options." Ryan shoots the padlock off the chain, and we all pile in. Didier, the last one, wraps the chain around the posts. The *boches* cling to the railing, stretching arms, feet, and bloody jaws through the bars. The wall is too steep for anything but sliding down the sloping concrete on our butts to the street level below.

The small, dead-end street looks empty, but I know, only too well, these predators hide. "Head for the walkway in front of the building. Single file, back's to the wall. No guns." He nods at the mess of zombies wandering the intersection of the street and the impasse. The sea breeze blows in our favor, or they'd be on our scent already. Rust marks smatter the iron railing, and the gate creeks something fierce when it opens—a siren announcing the lambs have arrived for the slaughter.

Chapter 53

Our platoon advances single file down the front sidewalk that runs the length of the apartment building. We're better off behind the barrier of cars parked along the impasse with the building at our backs. A *boche* claws and snarls at the window of his apartment as we pass. "Listen, Ryan, let me go on my own. I can make it from here." He's at my shoulder.

"I'm not letting you go."

"Let me go. Everyone around me dies. It's inevitable. Let me go."

The hedge of bushes lining the front of the building across the street from us crackles. Ryan trains his sights on the source of the sound. Not sure if the *boches* can manage to blaze a trail through the branches of the seven-foot oleanders. They're trying, that's for sure. The leaves shake and the hedge snarls. "I promised Amber." The look he gives me oozes with disappointment that I left her behind.

"You know your dad was going to shoot me, right? I'd have been dead within the hour." He doesn't respond. "What? Was I supposed to drag her here with me to the infected zone? At least, on my own, I had a chance to come back for her."

Across the *cul de sac*, behind the line of cars, a zombie in a short, pink skirt half emerges from the hedge. Purple-tainted scratches streak her arms, legs, and face. Not wanting to attract the attention of the hordes in the avenue, Ryan cuts between a yellow Fiat and a silver Peugeot to head her off before she becomes a threat. He strides across the street, through a gap in the cars, and meets her as she pulls her last leg out of a laurel bush. He drives his knife through her eye. She face-plants onto the narrow red sidewalk between the cars and the hedge.

When he returns to our ranks, my fingers touch his shoulder. "I appreciate you coming for me. I really do, but I'm not the one you should be wasting your time on."

"I'm not wasting my time."

"Yes, you are." A couple *boches* squirm out from underneath a red Renault van as we pass. Before they can stand, Didier lunges forward and punctures holes in the backs of their heads. Behind them, another zombie, a little guy—can't be more than five—struggles to crawl past the blockage. He won't be a problem for a while.

"I would have worked something out, Ev. You could have had a little faith in me."

"I'm sorry. The situation was urgent. I can take care of myself."

"That was apparent back there in the cathedral." The irony bites.

"Look, what I'm trying to tell you is so much more important. You know about the New Order, right?"

"The grey compound up in the 11ᵗʰ *Arrondissement*? Yeah. That's where the ambush team came from. It's not a problem. The airstrike is going to purge the whole of Marseille."

"But that is a problem!"

"Lieutenant!" Didier leads the line. Clément brings up the rear, supporting his wounded comrade. "They've locked on to our scent." The zombies in the street are no longer shambling and wandering aimlessly or standing comatose in the shade of the buildings that line the avenue. They twitch, noses in the air, honing in on their prey.

I grab Ryan's arm before he can respond. "There's a school for uninfected children in the *Chateau de la Reynarde*. I've been there. There are at least 100 kids there. They can't bomb that site."

"It's too late now. There's nothing I can do. The planes from the north are already in the air." He hasn't become his dad, yet. I can see on his face that the dilemma is twisting his guts.

"You *can* do something. You can leave me here now and take your men to evacuate them. The chateau is close to the outer edge of the city. They have buses. The New Order leaves the keys in the cars."

"It's at least a 20-minute drive to that *quartier*."

"Speed."

"*Merde*!" He has to convince himself, talk out the details. "Satellite data shows the infected tend to migrate to lower elevations, towards the sea, when not controlled by an alpha. They'll hit the ports first to eliminate the greatest threat. We probably have at least 30 minutes before they start hitting the countryside, especially the forested areas."

Our troops reach the hedge that lines the slope between the apartment building's front walk and the street. We tread more cautiously behind the row of oleanders. A few feet in, arms stretch suddenly from the branches and suck up the lead soldier. Half of him disappears into the bush, and his screams flood the sidewalk. Another couple of zombies, caught in the branches, snarl and tear their way through.

"Pierre!" Didier enlists the stocky kid next to him, and they attack with knives. Didier's *boche* slumps over, facedown into the sidewalk, Pierre's hangs suspended on the leaves and branches. Clément drops his charge against the building and plows through the screaming soldier's writhing limbs to drive his knife through the head of the *boche* gnawing at him. The zombie's arms go slack, and Clément pulls the soldier out of the branches. Half his face is hamburger. He's sobbing and screaming hysterically, tears gushing from his one good eye. Somberly, Clément pulls the gun from the kid's holster and hands it to him. He shouts, "*Putain*!" and blows his brains out.

My whole body cringes. Would that marine still be alive if they hadn't come for me? I didn't want this. I didn't ask for this. I'm not worth the sacrifice.

Ahead of us, the hedge curves, and the front walkway dead-ends. We halt at the railed stairs that lead down to the red sidewalk.

"Through the bushes or down the stairs?" Didier asks. Either way, we take our chances. The bushes are a more direct route to the end of the building, but we won't see the *boches* coming if we try to descend the slope to the bath boutique on the street level where the military vehicles are parked. We're much more exposed if we take the stairs down to the street and run the rest of the way down the impasse to the corner of the avenue, but we'll see what's coming for us.

"Stairs," Ryan barks. "We may have to make some noise. Break for the bath store and the vehicles. Evelyn, you're with me."

"Sorry, Ryan." My foot is on the top stair before he can turn and grab my coat sleeve. The platoon of *boches* that have invaded the street will be much more interested in me than a quick soldier snack. If I distract them, the pack will follow my scent while Ryan and his boys make a safe getaway to their vehicles and Annie's school. I take the stairs three at a time. "Too many people have died in my wake. I'm not letting you die for me."

"Evelyn! Don't do this!"

"Go! Save those kids!"

The second my foot hits the red sidewalk, the *boches* are on me like bees on barbeque. I was counting on that. The marines need to turn right at the bottom of the steps and head down the sloping sidewalk of the impasse to the intersection with the street below. Fifty yards farther down, that street dumps into the main avenue where the *boches* wander in bulk in front of the soap store. I sprint for the stairway directly across the impasse. The steps lead down to a café terrace that sits on the lower avenue, just up the street from the bath boutique. If I can stay ahead of them, I can suck the zombie crew away from the soap store and down the steep stairs where a bunch of them will crash and tumble behind me. This is where my grey speed needs to kick in. God, why couldn't these be slow zombies?

The snarling behind me and the slap of combat boots on pavement fading away down the impasse tells me my plan is working—for the moment.

Chapter 54

Knife clenched in my left fist, I race across the *cul de sac*. A stream of *boches,* like groupies spotting a rock star, chase me. The tide attracts the attention of other zombies in the street, and they flow away from the bath boutique into the swarm. I shouldn't have glanced back. Even with the virus supercharging the adrenaline in my veins, either I've slowed down a bit, or the leader of the charge is a runner. Hard to tell. He's wearing a tie and professional slacks, but he's yards ahead of the pack.

The moment my bare foot hits the top stair, the runner's arm skewers the space between Ryan's jacket and the strap of the automatic that Didier handed me. My whole body jerks. We stumble down a couple steps as I lose my balance. To keep from falling, my free hand whips around and grasps at the nearest hold—the *boche's* tie, pulling me face to face with a guy that looks hardly decomposed at all. The only mark on him is the bite on his greying neck. He looks chosen, intentionally bitten and well-preserved.

The knife flies in my left hand. My aim is a little jerky, and the blade glances low and skewers the *boche's* neck. The blow only forces his jaws back for a second while I wrestle to slip the gun strap from my shoulder. He snarls and snaps at my throat. The strap entangles the two of us. I writhe in a desperate dance with an unwanted lover. Metal meets my hand. My finger finds the trigger, the shots shake his bones and muscles, but he just keeps coming. A handful of his buddies have caught up to us. Even if I finally get him off me, I won't be able to fight off the pack.

If I can just get my foot going on the stairs, start the downhill ride, even tumbling, I stand a better chance. My foot slides behind me. A grey hand grabs the sleeve of Ryan's coat and jerks my arm into the attached mouth. The pressure of jaws clamping constricts the thick fabric. Pulling away from the bloody-lipped groping of the runner, I shove back and propel us towards the fall. Another *boche* dives for my bare legs, where I'm most vulnerable, and lassos my ankle.

I'm finished. A football field away from Amber, from my ticket to the open sea and a little tranquility, and I'm caught like a moth in a web of claws and teeth.

A single shot cracks from the terrace café below. The runner's head flops back as we plunge down the stairs in an unholy embrace. My arm flies out to break the fall and slams into the concrete on the first bounce. A bone snaps and pain rips up to my shoulder as the gravity flips me. The three *boches* ricochet off the cement into the iron railing. My knee crashes into the next step before I roll and hit the terrace flat on my back.

The pack has reached the stairs and rushes blindly into the void, tumbling over each other to create a human ramp down the slope. My head spins until my vision rests on an outstretched hand. At the moment, I don't care whose it is. Three snarling bodies are rolling towards me. Grasping at the lifeline with my bandaged palm, I let it vault me to my feet. The second our skin touches, a vibrant streak of life ripples through me. The broken and bruised bones shoot pain through my arm and my knee, but a warm sense of familiarity overwhelms it.

"C'mon, baby, you're late. We gotta run."

Chapter 55

The fall rattled my brain. I must be hallucinating. Is fate not the stingy bitch I imagined her? Or is Greyson simply more of a god than I gave him credit for? No one ever said the gods weren't ruthless. Only the new gods love unconditionally and mercifully. The old gods survived on violence—love and hate in equal measure. If he's not an immortal child of the gods, how else could Grey be standing here in front of me?

"Can you swim? Kasim's already weighed anchor and pushed away from the dock. They won't wait long. We can't risk Amber." And now it's all clear, the silhouette that saved me in the cathedral, "my man" that took charge of getting Amber to the boat—Greyson.

"Greyson?" My elbow and knee throb. Sharp bolts of pain shoot down my arm and across my shoulder. An unnatural bulge throbs at the side of my knee. I've dislocated something, something more than my heart. All the shattered pieces expand in my chest. This can't be real. But, God, I love him, and I want it to be. "How did you—? You're not dead?"

The *boches* that fell down the stairs with me struggle to their feet, only to be bowled over by the falling tide behind them.

Grey pulls me to my feet. A wince contorts my face when my weight hits the deformed knee. His arm wraps around my waist, and I shift my weight to the other leg. His lips brush my ear, murmuring a confession. "I was dead, when I woke up on the ground, shot, with twenty *boches* coming for me. You were gone…I didn't save you." His voice cracks. "If Joëlle hadn't been on the ground next to me, I'd have let the damn herd drag me down to zombie hell with them. Dead just means 'without

277

you'." He throws his free arm around my shoulders, and our lips collide, linking us like welded chains, hard and unbreakable, both of us devouring the aliveness of the other. "Definitely alive now." The grin is vintage Grey. I'm not dreaming.

Crowd surfing over writhing corpses, one of the *boches* has reached the bottom stair. Grey steals one more kiss, like throwing back a shot of whiskey, and pulls me, hobbling, across the terrace. My knee gives out halfway across, sprawling me out like a rag doll.

A handful of *boches* have crawled to the terrace. They're lumbering, cracked and broken, to their feet. Our scent fixed in their noses awakens the indomitable instinct to eliminate rival predators. "Grey, I love you. I've always loved you, baby— even when I hated you. But you have to go. Amber needs you— maybe more than me."

"Like hell, she does." He swoops beneath my good shoulder, lifts me, like I'm weightless, and matches his steps to mine. The *boches* crash through flimsy metal café tables and chairs. "She needs us both."

In mid-stride, my bandaged hand pulls the gun from Ryan's coat pocket. Our speed won't get the job done for us. When my bare foot and Grey's combat boot hit the asphalt of the avenue in perfect sync, the *boches* up the street catch our scent and turn from devouring and attacking the cosplayers and marines to pursue their more urgent instincts. By the time we're across the street, the virus has begun shutting down the pain receptors in my brain. My arm and leg feel disconnected— puppet limbs with snapped strings—but at least, they don't throb.

We head for the ancient back door of the building that separates us from the boat. Grey can't kick it in because then we won't be able to shut them out. "Shoot the lock!" He pivots, spattering bullets into the rabid crowd pursuing us.

That job is harder than he makes it sound. My left hand hangs useless beneath my broken arm, and the nail that Lilou drove into my palm has severed some of the nerves in my right. Seconds tick by before my fingers manage to squeeze the trigger. The *boches* have descended *en masse*. Grey can't keep them at bay anymore. "Now!" He yells as the trigger clicks in my hand. At close range, the lock clanks and shatters with one shot.

I fumble the door open, but Grey and I are besieged with grasping fingers and teeth. He shoves me through the opening. His gun pelts the oncoming tide, but they trip over the fallen and keep coming. With my one good arm, I drag Grey through the crack in the doorway and try to shove it closed again by leaning on it. Arms and hands prop it open. Jaws and teeth snap through it. Several hands grip his gun, trying to pull him through the door. Shooting doesn't matter because he can't target the brains. The gap between widens against my weight. Grey groans under the pressure of pulling free and finally sacrifices his gun. The *boches* fall back briefly when he lets go, but too many arms and legs prop the door open.

I should have made him leave me on the terrace. At least then, Amber would have someone to watch out for her. If nothing else, we distracted the *boches* from the last of Laure's people and the marines long enough for them to make it out before the bombs fall. The roar and hum of engines outside tell me they're retreating.

The horde surges again. The gap widens. A whole *boche,* minus one leg still tangled in the masses, grapples in hand to hand combat with Grey. Still leaning on the door, I work my gun around to fire on him, but I can't get a head shot. The two of them tumble to the floor, and more *boches* clog the opening. I can't hold them back.

Engines rumble in the avenue behind us, and suddenly a shower of bullets besieges the mob pressing into the building. As the bodies fall, two camo-painted armored vehicles appear on the avenue behind us. With less pressure on the door, I manage to train my Beretta on the head of the *boche* pushing in and, gripping the door for balance, shove him with my good knee out of the gap. Even the virus can't dampen the pain that rips through my leg when I transfer too much weight to it. In the middle of my agonized scream, I glimpse a sharpshooter on the roof of the front truck. Dark hair, no coat. This is the second time Ryan's pried me from the clutches of the rabid mob.

The door slams shut under my weight.

Body slams from three or four *boches* shake the timbers. The indoor bolt, rusting and stiff, slides reluctantly. It won't hold long. Sweating from the exertion, I lean towards the zombie on top of Grey and blow his brains out at close range before crumbling to the floor.

Grey shoves off the corpse. Breathing hard, he hauls himself up and reaches me a hand. "Sorry, Ev, there's no time."

"I can't. My leg—"

"Don't have a choice. Nicky boy is on the boat. We get you there, he'll fix you up."

Just hearing Nicolas's name makes me want to hobble, but the leg doesn't respond. "Does he have it—the cure?" The wrenching pain of weight on my knee wrings a groan from my gut, and my legs collapse beneath me.

"Ask him yourself." He reaches down and helps me pull out of the jacket. "Just outside the front door is the port. When we hit the water, this will weigh you down." He tosses it to the ground. "There are about twenty yards between us and the water. The *boches* don't swim—yet."

It's like ballet, the way he reaches down and sweeps me into his arms.

At the end of the building, he kicks open the front door that spills us into the alley between the twin structures. A wrought iron fence blocks the *boches* from the avenue we just left, but on the narrow street between the buildings and the sea, the battle still rages. We have to pass the distance of two rows of cars and a narrow street to get to the water's edge.

"This is not our fight, Ev. We're going straight for the water."

"Don't worry, I'm not gonna run off."

I might be faster than Grey, but he's stronger. I'll give him that. My dead weight weighing him down, he sprints the distance. We've only passed the first row of parked cars when the mob picks up our scent. We're like a magnet, pulling all the zombies away from the skirmish to chase us down. Even if we don't stop and jump into the fray, our diversion frees up the cosplayers and marines in the street to retreat to the ferry for evacuation.

A couple of curly, black-haired teens with a Mediterranean tint to their grey skin outstrip the rest of the mob. Greyson slides slightly left, aiming for the waterway between the docks. We weave between two cars. One of the *boches* follows us into the space. We reach the cement border that outlines the water. The boat floats in the open port about a hundred yards away. The swim from the *Chateau d'If* to the coast was no problem, but when I started this zombie tour, I had no injuries. I'm not even sure I can swim now. The kid behind us dives and latches onto Greyson's foot. We vault through thin air and hit the water flying.

Rachel DeFriez

Chapter 56

The world floats, rocking gently on a coastal breeze. Sunlight streams through the port windows that surround my berth. My consciousness swims slowly to the surface, riding the wave of a deep breath. The days of startling awake are gone. The wide-open blue erases the nightmare on land like it doesn't even exist.

Amber purrs and cuddles closer beneath my arm. There was no pouting or churlish recrimination. Ryan and Clément told her I'd gone ashore to find more gummies. Clément educated her on the mysterious delights of *Haribo* and then delivered a stash to the boat before coming to escort me to my exit strategy.

I don't know what happened to Ryan and Clément. I don't know if they saved the school children or even if they survived. Marseille burned for a couple of days, though. The fires lit up the horizon behind us as we sailed through the Mediterranean towards the straits of Gibraltar and the Atlantic. Kasim says the sailing there can be a bit rough, and the tides are tricky. But he's good. This isn't his first voyage. Apparently, he was using his reconnaissance missions to stock the boat. That's what he was doing in the kitchen of the Foreign Legion resort on the day I washed up there.

My stomach rumbles and growls like only the virus can. Slipping quietly from our bunk to go in search of food, I stop to gaze at my sister and brush away from her forehead the few little hairs that have escaped her neurotically tight ponytail. The grey tint of my hand clashes with the pearly white paleness of her skin. Apparently, the marine boys were sunblock Nazis, outfitting her with as many bottles of *lotion solaire* as weapons. She stirs. "Evy, don't go. Stay!"

Instead of grasped in her fist while she sleeps, her Glauca G-1 sits on the nightstand now. I know it disturbed her, my leaving—deep down on some emotional level. It's a charade we play that I went for candy. We don't talk about it. We left it behind to drown in the waves of the sea. Would her mental state be more stable if I had stayed and let General Samson plaster my brains to the wall of his ship and feed me to the fish? I'm not a licensed therapist, and we're in the middle of the apocalypse. No one is coming out of it mentally stable. All we can hope for is alive—alive and sentient—with the possibility for healing.

Leaning over, I kiss her cheek. "I'm going to get us some breakfast, kidlet. You sleep."

"Can I have peaches?" she murmurs, closing her eyes and turning away from the sun in the windows. "The *Haribo* ones, not the ones in the can."

"We'll see when you wake up—maybe I'll sneak one in with your cereal."

Smiling, she nods off again.

Out of habit, my fingers brush my hair back when I stand, but there's nothing there. It still surprises me. The closet mirror reminds me again that it's gone. At least it's not the chopped mess it was. Joëlle is not just handy with a scalpel, she's got a knack with scissors as well. It took a while to get used to it, but she trimmed it into a pixie cut like hers—well, hers before Nicolas shot her up with the cure, and she started growing her hair out just because she could. The salty sea air gives my locks a bit of natural curl I didn't know was there. It's growing on me—well, not growing, that's figurative.

My knee still hitches a tad, but Nicolas's magic potion has let the tendons and the bones actually heal.

In the galley, I meet the miracle man in the flesh—olive flesh, void of grey. The two of us are the early risers on the ship—well, other than Grey, who captains the night shift. Hunger drives me; research drives Nicolas. "I thought you'd be up soon." He hands me a joint, and I take a couple drags to curb the urges while I rummage through the spectrum of delights Kasim stocked in his freezer.

The number of greys on the ship has drastically reduced, so our supply of cow guts and marijuana is much more abundant. Although, I'm pretty sure Kasim still dips into the weed from time to time, just for recreational purposes. The vegetarians are rationing the real food. I find a nice liver to munch on. "Kasim says we'll have to risk a stop at Sao Miguel in the Atlantic to resupply before we cross into the deep blue desert."

"Can't say I'm sorry." The first few days at sea, pale green tinged Nicky's natural tint, but it's back now. He doesn't like the water, but he likes Joëlle. She's neck-deep in his research. The cure attacks the virus and heals simple ZVs and greys, but they still haven't found a vaccine. That's the holy grail. I grab a hoodie before heading for the deck. The sun at sea brutalizes my grey skin. "You know, you wouldn't need that if you'd just let me give you the cure. Dr. Pêsqué was very generous with the number of vials he gave me to get by until I can set up a lab in the States."

Draping my arms around his neck, I kiss his cheek. "Have I thanked you lately, Nic, for giving me back my knee, my shoulder, my hand? For hope?"

"Only a thousand times." He hugs me close.

"Let me make it one more." My lips brush both his cheeks, French style. Joëlle's given him a taste for it. "You know, in the Institute, I would have jumped at the chance to lose the grey. But now, I don't know." I step out of his embrace. "I think maybe nature needs a little grey to finish what she started. When we get to the States, my predator tendencies might just prove useful. Amber's alive and *un*infected because Grey and I *are*. I'm not willing to give up that edge before I know she doesn't need it anymore—or the marijuana runs out." Grinning, I pull up the hood and tip the joint at him before heading up the stairs to the deck.

A nice little breeze has kicked up. Greyson stands at the front reefing the sails. He's pulled on a hoodie against the sunrise behind us. The pale-yellow rays flood him with light against the azure canvas of crystalline seas that rise up to meet the startling sapphire of the sky.

Stealthily, I pad up and throw my arms around him. "You suck as a lookout. I snuck right up behind you." The few radio communications we get from other sailing survivors report pirates off the coast of Africa.

He ties off a couple ropes and turns to slide his arms around my waist. "That's because I knew it was you. I picked up your scent the moment you rolled out of bed, and I overheard your little conversation with Nicky boy." I offer him the joint, but he takes my lips instead. Grey's kisses are always hungry. Sometimes, I wonder if a bit of my soul slips out on the tide with them. If it does, some of his flows into the void. Our ebbs and flows have molded us into new people, smoothed the edges of the jagged rocks that divided us.

My head slips snugly into the hollow of his shoulder. My body melts in a meditation of sea, sky, and flesh. These sunrise moments are ours. We're supposed to be sailing off into the sunset, but instead, the sunrise has our backs as we sail into the blue daze.

"Greyson, babe, what's that?"

He squints to follow the line of my finger to the tiny white dot at the horizon, a bit to our port. "Sails."

We both look at each other, knowing there are only two options—other survivors…or pirates.

FIN

Rachel DeFriez

Acknowledgements

Many thanks to Curt and Josh for reading the raw words. Sorry I killed you off in the first book, Josh. Thanks to Libby, Anna, Pat, Norm and John, who graciously collaborate in my obsession. Thanks to all my readers. Without them, these words would drift away, unanchored, into the blue haze.

WALKING GREY series

Edgy romance and raw suspense. Zombies for the insatiably romantic.

The Walking Grey series chronicles the desperate story of Evelyn Cross and Greyson Childs in a dystopian world infected with the Zoser Virus. Infected, the virus has made them look like ZVs and crave human flesh like ZVs, but instead of slowly consuming their organs and brain, it has transformed them into super predators, fighting both sides of a looming conflict to protect Evelyn's uninfected little sister Amber.

GREY MATTERS
Book 1
They bash our heads and chain us up because we're different. Well, maybe knowing we would happily throw on a bib, rip out their guts, and devour them like hotdogs on a stick, without the stick--or the bib for that matter--probably has something to do with it. No one really wants to hang out with a girl whose idea of a Slurpee is grey matter and blood splashed in the snow, hold the straw.

Evelyn Cross has everything: shampoo commercial hair, a letterman jacket, a tiara, a 3.98 GPA, and now the Z-Virus that is infecting teenage couples in the small town of Eli. The virus has made her look like a ZV and crave human flesh like a ZV, but instead of slowly consuming her organs and brain, it has transformed her into a super predator, fighting both sides of a looming conflict. And she's not the only one of her kind—here's also Greyson Childs, the vicious pack-hunting player that dumped her best friend when they all got infected.

Rachel DeFriez

GREY KNIGHTS

Book 2
Angels or Demons? The grey is fading.

The Z-Virus has mutated and the infection looms large on the Texas horizon. As the rushing tide of the apocalypse smears the lines between Heaven and hell, Evelyn and Greyson escape the fire of one quarantine zone, only to find themselves fugitives in the inferno of another.

GREY DAZE

Book 3

ALSO BY THIS AUTHOR

I AM KRONOS

It's not every day you get a friend request from a dead girl.
I Am Kronos is a thrilling blend of gaming, sci-fi, and supernatural romance.

Keven Meyers, gamer and classic underachiever on the fringe of cool, gets a friend request from Sierra Sands, recently deceased and haunting his video games. Sierra is stuck in the Nexus, the center where all the universes and realities collide. She desperately needs Keven's help to stop Silas, another lost soul using his diabolical understanding of the world between the worlds to prey on gamers.

When Silas attacks Keven in his video game, Sierra drags Keven's soul through the game and into the safety of the Nexus where he becomes painfully aware that he is inextricably connected, across universes and realities, to this dead girl. But with the infinite possibilities of multiple realities come options—options like his best friend Lexy Granger.
Only the strength of the ties that bind Keven, Sierra, and Lexy, on multiple levels, in and out of existences, are strong enough to overthrow Silas.

Rachel DeFriez brings us a spine-tingling supernatural thriller that delves into the metaphysical world of the multi-verse.

ABOUT THE AUTHOR

Rachel DeFriez is the author of the chilling zombie romance series WALKING GREY: GREY MATTERS, GREY KNIGHTS, and GREY DAZE. She is also the author of the supernatural sci-fi thriller I AM KRONOS.

Coming Soon:
RAVENS AND LAVENDER in Romance
7 SECONDS in YA

Her books have won multiple prizes in the 2018 and 2019 League of Utah Writing Contests.

Due to her husband's nomadic nature, Rachel has taught French and Creative Writing in a variety of states including: Texas, Massachusetts, and Utah. She is particularly surprised to find herself writing YA horror since she's afraid of the dark. Visit her at www.racheldefriez.com.